# THE TOLL HOUSE

# THE TOLL HOUSE

## Patricia Wendorf

Thorndike Press • Chivers Press
Thorndike, Maine USA    Bath, England

This Large Print edition is published by Thorndike Press, USA and by Chivers Press, England.

Published in 1998 in the U.S. by arrangement with A.M. Heath & Co., Ltd.

Published in 1998 in the U.K. by arrangement with Hodder & Stoughton Ltd.

U.S. Hardcover   0-7862-1554-2   (Basic Series Edition)
U.K. Hardcover   0-7540-1184-4   (Windsor Large Print)
U.K. Softcover   0-7540-2131-9   (Paragon Large Print)

The text of this Large Print edition is unabridged.
Other aspects of the book may vary from the original edition.

Set in 16 pt. Plantin by Rick Gundberg.

Printed in the United States on permanent paper.

**British Library Cataloguing in Publication Data available**

**Library of Congress Cataloging in Publication Data**

Wendorf, Patricia.
    The toll house / Patricia Wendorf.
        p.   cm.
    ISBN 0-7862-1554-2 (lg. print : hc : alk. paper)
    1. Large type books.  I. Title.
PR6073.E49T65   1998
823´.914—dc21                                    98-25653

For Jane and John

# Glossary of Gypsy Words

| | |
|---|---|
| racklis | girls |
| chals | lads/boys |
| diklo | coloured neckerchief |
| tatchi Romanes | genuine Romanies |
| chavvies | children |
| gorgio | non-gypsy |
| mullo | ghost/spirit |
| diddecoi | dirty gypsy — insulting term used by non-gypsies |
| atchintan | camping ground |
| rawnies | ladies |
| gavvers | police |
| sar shin | How are you? |

Source: *Romano Lavo-Lil — A Book of the Gypsy* by George Borrow

# Nina

The estate agent was young.

Young enough to be my grandson.

He sat behind a desk of pale-grey wood which held a stack of wire trays, a computer screen, and an oblong of black plastic on which was printed the word MANAGER in bright gold letters.

I settled into an upholstered chair in the waiting area of the office, and watched with interest the changing expressions on the young man's face as he dealt with the couple who sat before him. His satisfied smile confirmed that they were committed house buyers. Annoyingly, a slight deafness prevented me from overhearing their conversation. When it came to dealing with estate agents in the nineteen nineties, I would have welcomed the sketchiest of pointers.

The walk into the city in the unseasonal heat of the May afternoon had tired me; my head began to droop, I surveyed the scene through half-closed eyelids. The electric fans, placed strategically around the office, simply moved the heavy air from one level to another. Now if I was painting all this, I thought, what medium would I use?

It could be a most effective study. Silvery walls, blue carpet, the dove-greys and darker grays of wood and metal furnishings. And right bang in the middle of the symphony, the single acidic green of the computer screen. But even as the thoughts drifted through my mind, my gaze already returned to the main focus of interest. It was the young man who made my fingers itch to wield the pencil and fix his image in my sketchpad.

Although the day was hot, a dark-blue tie was knotted at the neck of his light-blue shirt. Beneath the desk I could see the knife-edged creases in his navy-blue trousers, and the gleaming black leather of his shoes. His only concession to the heat wave was the shirt cuffs, unfastened and rolled back a discreet few inches to reveal a gold watch on his left wrist, and the fine reddish hairs glinting on his forearms. A lock of the same fiery shade of hair fell disarmingly across his forehead. He pushed it back at intervals, and I suspected he might practise the gesture before his bathroom mirror.

Could he possibly be as young as he looked?

I began, as was my habit when meeting interesting strangers, to invent a life for him.

Perhaps he still lived at home with a devoted mother. Some woman had ironed that immaculate shirt, put the sharp crease in his trousers, and the shine on his shoes.

On the other hand, the boyishness could be a clever business ploy, purposely cultivated to disarm difficult clients. One would, I thought, tend to trust that open smile, those blue eyes.

He probably had a nagging wife and four unruly children! I at once awarded him an executive-type house, a mock-Tudor horror on an exclusive estate, with a three-car garage, a pony in a paddock, a dog of some impeccable breed, a kitten and a tortoise. His wife would be an animal-rights protester who believed that children should have pets. He would play golf with his father-in-law on a Sunday morning. He would have a crippling mortgage and a serious bank loan, both of which would cost him sleepless nights.

Well, serve him right! He had no business living beyond his means. But didn't most young people in this profligate age? So with all that responsibility how did he maintain his air of morning freshness, that eagerness to please; that TV-commercial brand of glitz and polish? A wife and children would have long since dimmed his glamour.

No, of course he wasn't married!

I closed my eyes, wiped clean the image of the family man and replaced it with a smart mews cottage which had a white painted front door and scarlet geraniums in window boxes. There would have to be a live-in partner. They would give exclusive little dinner parties, fly out for a weekend in Paris or Hong Kong. I began, enthusiastically, to sketch in a silver Ferrari, state-of-the-art matching luggage. Martinis at sunset on a palmy oasis. The girl would be pale and blonde, a perfect foil to his burnished image.

He would of course require a private income with which to support this glamorous lifestyle. Well, that posed no problem. His father was obviously the managing director of this nationwide chain of estate agents. The young man was learning the business from the bottom upwards. He — he was beckoning to me, and smiling a forgiving smile. The chairs which stood before his desk had been vacated without my notice. I felt foolish, awkward; I should never close my eyes in public places. As I walked towards him his smile broadened to a grin.

He said, 'How may I help you?' and I knew he thought I had nodded off while waiting. I sat down, taking my time, placing my handbag beside the chair, arranging the pleats of my skirt so that they lay evenly across my knees. The wall behind the desk was tiled with mirrors, which gave back a reassuring image of my neat appearance. I sat straighter in the chair, approving my choice of the navy-blue silk suit and the new short style of my silver hair.

I said, in a tone sharper than I had intended, 'I wish to place my house on the market.'

'Certainly,' he said. He pulled a scratch-pad towards him and prepared to write. He looked expectantly towards me. 'And the name and address?'

'Franklin. Nina Franklin. Infirmary Avenue. Number eighty-four.'

His effort to retain the smile was brave.

'Let's see now, isn't that the street which leads down to the city hospital and which — ?'

He paused, and I continued, with wry satisfaction, to add the words he could not bring himself to utter.

'And which stands directly underneath the

11

west wall of the city gaol.'

He leaned towards me, his elbows on the desk, his fingers steepled. He had the air of a man about to do his best with impossible material. 'Ah. Yes. Well — a substantial property in that case. Terraced? On three floors, with cellars and attics? Late Victorian?'

I nodded and he began to study me with the close attention I had recently awarded him. He began to pick his way among the usual, essential estate-agent type questions.

'Not a modern property, obviously.' His tone was deprecating. 'How long have you lived there?' His smile flashed briefly. 'All your life, perhaps?'

'All my *married* life,' I corrected. I too leaned slightly forwards. 'And if you're implying that I might lack indoor plumbing and central heating, let me set your mind at rest. I did away with the thunder-box at the bottom of the garden some time in nineteen forty-eight. Gas central heating was installed in the nineteen seventies.' I ended on a note of triumph. 'I am fully modernised, the property is freehold and I have no mortgage.'

The manager made notes. 'Well, that's good,' he murmured. 'Yes, very good.' He pushed his left hand through the fiery locks.

'There is of course the rather unfortunate matter of location. So close to the prison. Not everybody's cup of tea. The recent riots and escapes haven't helped the sale of adjacent properties, as you will appreciate. But, we shall do our best for you, you may be sure.'

I sat very straight in my chair. 'I'm not a fool,' I snapped. 'I don't expect to have a queue of purchasers forming daily at my front door. I brought up a family in that house, and for the past seven years I have lived alone there. Having one of Her Majesty's top-security gaols as a neighbour has never caused *me* a moment's unease.' Not a totally true statement, but I had been goaded!

The boyish look fell away, his gaze was frank now and curious, almost admiring. 'You will have installed your own burglar alarms and security system I imagine?'

'Oh, yes.' I smiled. 'I am well provided for in that department. I sleep with a Kitchen Devil knife under my pillow, and a coal hammer on the bedside table. I have a dog, but he's very old and incurably friendly, and I don't know how much help he would be if the worst should happen. Fortunately, our courage has never yet been put to the test.'

The silence in the office was broken only by the whirring of the fans. I watched, amused, as the glossy young man went through his repertoire of puzzled gestures. He rubbed his chin, tweaked his ear, tapped the scratchpad with his pencil. He made an obvious effort to regain control of the situation. He squared his shoulders and spoke in a brisk tone.

'Well now! I had better send someone out to Infirmary Avenue to view your house, give you a valuation, take the necessary measurements and details. How would eleven tomorrow morning suit you?'

The decision to sell had been made subconsciously many months ago. In my usual over-optimistic fashion, I had not envisaged the brutal practicalities of moving, but had cherished in a corner of my mind the misty image of a small white bungalow somewhere in the country, a village green, trees and hedges, wide skies.

The recent bitter winter, lived in large, high-ceilinged rooms, had shown up the inadequacy of the central heating system, the need for better insulation. Or perhaps advancing age had played a part in my need to wear extra cardigans, a camisole and bedsocks. I had spent a miserable six months

14

plugging draughts I had never previously noticed, averting my gaze from minor repair jobs, already too long deferred. Through the snow and freezing temperatures of January and February I had read my way through the best of the biographies and crime fiction in my public library, had actually been obliged to fight boredom by watching day-time television. I had started to slip down into the dangerously irreversible depression of a really old person.

*And I was not old.* I would admit to edging towards the upper reaches of late middle age.

Well, very late middle age.

But not elderly.

Elderly was meals-on-wheels and walking frames, and Tuesdays and Thursdays spent knitting in the Day Centre.

In the April of that year I walked the city pavements, sat in parks and cafés and thought about my situation. I did not discuss my problems with my daughter or granddaughter. Widowhood had taught me the wisdom of making my own decisions and, just occasionally, my own mistakes.

A house, once offered for sale, is no longer the exclusive possession of its owner. Already, in my mind, I had loosened the first of the links that had held me there in the long years of my marriage, and through the empty years since Jack had died. In the light of early morning, yesterday's visit to the estate agent now seemed like a betrayal of both the house and Jack. I remembered the young man's deprecating tone, his patronising smile, and began to see my home as he would see it, old-fashioned, cluttered, too many ornaments and pictures. And nothing, not Venetian blinds nor lacy curtains, could conceal the adjacent high prison walls topped with searchlights and alarm devices. Over the years I had grown used to the whine of ambulance sirens as they raced to the hospital emergency bay which was visible from my rear windows; I hardly noticed the passage past my front door of paddy wagons and windowless police vans. Forty years ago the ambulances had driven fast but silently down Infirmary Avenue; the prison walls had been topped merely with rolled barbed wire and broken bottle glass set in cement. In those days the six grey crenellated towers of the facade had possessed the unthreatening appearance of a child's toy fort, the kind that came at Christmas, complete with moat and drawbridge and a box of red-painted lead soldiers.

I washed and dried the breakfast dishes, fed Roscoe and filled his bowl with water. The slap of letters landing on the tiled floor of the hall brought the single warning bark that he was capable of lately. I wondered how he would view the move away from Infirmary Avenue. Roscoe was a townie, accustomed all his life to dusty city trees and lampposts.

I was standing close beside the front door when the knocker sounded. Its clatter alarmed me; most people used the doorbell. My family when visiting came in by way of the garden entrance, tapping at the kitchen door, calling my name. The time was nine twenty, the estate agent not due until eleven. I peered through the spyhole and looked directly into the face of a very young woman, a pale and anxious-looking girl, who must therefore be harmless.

It took some moments to release the chain, turn the deadbolt, take the keys from the hall table and unlock the mortice, the Chubb and the Yale. The girl, who was heavily pregnant, now leaned against the porch wall, her face contorted in an agonised expression.

I said, 'Oh — oh my dear! Are you — you're not in labour, are you?'

The girls voice was shrill. 'Just as well I'm

not, missus! I could have give birth to twins before you got that door open.' She nodded towards the prison wall. 'Not as I can blame you for being all locked in, living right next door to them perverts.' A violent spasm twisted her features. 'It's me bladder,' she confided in a quieter tone. 'Well nigh bursting I am. Could I use your convenience, missus?'

It was a request that I would not normally have granted to a stranger; but my granddaughter, also pregnant with her first child, was experiencing similar frequency problems. With hardly a blip of hesitation I held wide the front door and invited danger into my quiet life. 'Come in,' I said. 'The downstairs loo is on your left.'

The cistern flushed, the cloakroom door opened and closed. I called from the kitchen, 'Are you feeling better?'

The girl appeared in the doorway, she leaned against the lintel. 'I could murder a cup of tea. Hot and strong and with plenty of sugar. A couple of biscuits would go nicely with it.' She slumped dramatically and heavily against the wood as if about to fall. I pulled out a chair and helped her towards it.

'Sit there,' I said. 'I'll put the kettle on.

You really shouldn't be out in your condition.'

'I've got my living to earn, missus.' She sighed. 'Babies! Who needs 'em? I've told my Kingdom, he can tie a knot in it after this one. First and last this'll be. He says condoms is against his religion. Then change your religion I tells him.'

I filled the kettle, pressed the switch, and set mugs and sugar bowl on the table. Embarrassed by her conversation, I kept my fingers busy and my gaze averted from her. I had noticed when sitting in my doctor's surgery and at the dentist's, that advancing pregnancy often had the effect of loosening some young women's inhibitions. Otherwise private and reticent girls had confided to me, a total stranger, their most intimate personal symptoms and sexual problems. But perhaps such open discussion was commonplace these days? I was secretly shocked by the contents of some of the popular and expensive women's magazines seen on newsagents' racks. 'Do you have a right to experience multiple orgasms?' was the kind of question posed in scarlet lettering on the front cover of this month's *Michelle*.

I placed a mug of tea and a plateful of chocolate digestives before my unexpected guest, hoping that food and drink would divert the gypsy girl from further embarrassing revelations.

Gypsy? Now where had that thought come from?

There was nothing in the least traveller-like about her. In her speech and behaviour and in her clean and tidy appearance she was in no way like those pathetic New Age youngsters who sat on city pavements with their flea-ridden dogs and begging bowls, their mud-caked boots and clothing, their nose-rings and Rasta locks. I was shocked every time a cultured, well-mannered voice emerged from one of those grimy faces to beg me for a handout. I sipped my tea and studied the pregnant girl. Well, this one was no university dropout, no absconding little rich girl. Cheeky she certainly was, self-confident and bold. Look at her now, wolfing down the chocolate digestives as if they were to be her last meal for the whole day; drinking the tea in thirsty gulps and reaching out a hand towards the teapot and milk jug. And yet, there was something about her, some quality that intrigued, and yes, that *fascinated!*

She wore the style of clothing currently favoured by my granddaughter, a simple full-length maternity dress of blue and white checked cotton, and heelless sandals. The differences between the two girls in the wearing of the garment were minimal yet significant. Perhaps it was the scrap of emerald silk knotted at this one's throat, the matching emerald ribbon in her hair; the insolent lift of her head, the way she accepted a favour as if it was her right? And then there was the gruff, staccato manner of her speech, the wariness that lay beneath the bravado. Wariness? Yes, of course, that was the key to the girl's behaviour. I knew very little about travelling people; I had picked up scraps of information from magazine articles about their characters and way of life. Sometimes on a Sunday there would be a full-page newspaper article, with illustrations, showing an old-fashioned gypsy wagon and horses, bronzed and smiling men and women, cheerful tow-headed children and fat babies. But the pictures had a posed and artificial quality which had vaguely disturbed me. What about winter, I had thought. What about mud and rain, and making a precarious living from door-to-door hawking and scrap metal dealing? The newspaper journalists always made the point that this was a dying breed of people, that there was no hope for their survival and no place any more for their customs and beliefs. 'An anachronism' was always the reporter's final judgement on them.

I studied the anachronism seated at my kitchen table; and I noticed for the first time the zipped plastic bag pushed almost out of sight beneath the girl's chair. The sales pitch would begin as soon as the gypsy had eaten and drunk her fill. And wasn't that situation in itself unusual? I had gathered from reading about them, that these were a peculiarly choosy and suspicious people when it came to physical contact with the non-gypsy population. How rare was it, I wondered, for a young and pregnant Romany to sit beneath a house roof, to eat and drink and have a conversation with a woman who was not of her own kind? A woman who was one of 'them'. As if the girl had read my thoughts, she said, 'I'll have to go now. Me ma and sisters'll be looking for me. They won't like it that I came into your house.'

I moved swiftly to refill the plate with biscuits and to recharge the teapot. 'You're still looking pale,' I said. 'A few more minutes will put you right. You don't want to faint out on the street, do you?' I smiled. 'And you'll need the lavatory again, won't you, after drinking so much tea.'

The answering grin was uncertain and defensive and confirmed that the girl, for all her bluster and bravado, was actually nervous and deeply anxious to be gone. The indecision in her face was comical. She glanced downwards at the zipped bag. To miss the chance of a good sale would be folly, especially when it could be made to a woman who was so obviously a soft touch. She had the hunted look of one who was caught but tempted by a potentially risky situation. She lifted up the bag and began to unzip it.

'No,' I said firmly. 'I don't want your clothes-pegs, or whatever else it is you have to sell.' I stood up and walked towards the kitchen dresser, picked up charcoal sticks and sketchpad and returned to the table.

'If you allow me to draw you, I'll give you five pounds.'

The girl looked surprised. 'You a proper artist then, missus?'

'I like to draw and paint. I've won a few competition prizes.'

'Big money?'

'No, not big money.'

The girl looked scornful. 'No sense in doing it then, is there?'

'I paint and draw because I love to do it. I would really like to sketch you. Just your head and shoulders.'

The laughter was spontaneous, and almost consenting. 'You'd need a big sheet of paper, missus, to get all of me on it, way I look now.'

'You'll sit for me, then?'

There was a silence. 'Money up front? On the table? A tenner for me trouble?'

I fetched my purse and laid a five-pound note beside the girl's plate. 'Just sit quietly as you are. It won't take more than a few minutes. Five pounds now and another five when I've finished.'

It was a pretty little kitten-face, sharply triangular with a pointy chin, rosebud mouth, small nose and wide appealing eyes. The skin was pale underneath a light tan. The straight black hair, caught high in the green ribbon, fell to the girl's waist from a centre parting. Her bone structure was curiously catlike, her whole aspect so completely feline that I would not have been surprised to see tiny paws instead of hands and fact. Because of her condition the girl would be an impatient sitter. Already she fidgeted, changing the position of her head and body, tapping her sandal on the tiled floor.

I worked swiftly. I paused at intervals, the charcoal poised, while I tried to match up the lines on the paper with the delicate planes of the sitter's features. It was the girl's face that was emerging and yet it was not her. Each time I reapplied the charcoal the result was not quite what I intended. It was someone else who looked back at me from the sketchpad. I began to feel uneasy.

Something was wrong.

Something was very wrong. I felt faint and slightly nauseated. The charcoal stick broke in my fingers and rolled slowly down the table. A cold dread settled in the pit of my stomach. I said, 'I don't think I can draw you after all.'

The girl's hand snaked out and grabbed the banknote; she pushed it into the pocket of her dress.

'A deal's a deal!' she snapped. 'It's not my fault if you can't draw me. P'raps you're not much of an artist after all, eh, missus?' But then the gypsy showed an honesty I had not expected of her. 'Look,' she said, 'I'd as soon earn the other note off you, proper. Give it another go, eh? You needn't pay the other five sovs if you don't want to.'

I ripped the sheet from the pad and laid it to one side. I picked up the charcoal and focused all my concentration on the drawing. But some power beyond my control still locked onto my fingers, leading them once again to create a face that was human and yet feline, and not quite that of the girl who sat at my kitchen table.

The kitchen had grown unusually cold. The girl rubbed the skin of her bare forearms. She shivered. 'It's like a rotten fridge in here,' she muttered.

I struggled for normality. I threw down the charcoal and switched on the percolator. 'I need a coffee,' I said, 'and you can have the other five pounds. But I won't offer you another drink or you'll have further bladder problems.'

The girl rose awkwardly and began to move around the table. I turned, percolator in my hand, in time to witness the horror in her face. Supported by her hands she leaned across the sketches. 'What 'n Lord's name have you done to me, missus?' she whispered. 'Oh my God, whatever have you done?' She pulled herself upright and pointed. 'That's never me you drawed there! That's my dear mother's great-granny. You've melted my bones into her bones. You've made one person of us. I don't want to look like her. She was a poor unlucky woman. Oh, missus, you have brought ill-luck down on me!'

'Rubbish,' I said. 'How could I possibly know what your mother's great-grandmother looked like? How could *you* know it? I don't imagine she had her photo taken a hundred and sixty years ago.'

'No photo. Better'n that. There's an oil painting of her, done by a famous gentleman. Hangs on a wall in a museum in London.'

The girl began to beat her fists upon the table. She started to scream and sob. 'What for did you have to make me look like her? See there — even the clothes is all wrong, and the hair done up in curls atop her head, and them dangly earrings — that's not my style, and you can see it's not, so why have you put it down on paper?'

'I don't know,' I said quietly. 'Something seemed to take me over. It's never happened before. I can't explain it. I'm sorry I've upset you. I didn't mean to.'

The girl grew calm, resigned. She rubbed the tears from her face, picked up her bag and moved towards the door.

'It's me own fault,' she said dully, 'me mammy said never to go inside a house, only to knock and stay on the doorstep.' She sighed. 'I never should have let you 'tice me in.'

I opened the front door. 'I didn't entice you in, you know! You asked to use the loo, now didn't you?'

The girl still hiccoughed from her recent sobbing. I pushed the second five-pound note into her hand. 'Will you be all right now? Do you want a taxi?' I felt responsible for her distressed state.

'It's okay. Me family will still be "calling" somewhere hereabouts.' She looked back to where I stood on the doorstep. There was venom in her face and voice. 'Anything happens to my baby though, it'll be all your rotten fault. I'll remember you, missus, I'll remember how you upset me. And I reckon you'll remember Sorsha! You ain't seen the last of me, oh no! And I'll tell you something else. You won't be living in this house much longer. You'll be going to a bungalow next to a field what's got a coloured pony in it. You'll think that place is going to be your heart's delight, but mark my words there's danger for you in that new home. You'll meet a gentleman friend, but beware of him, for he'll give you a present that is bound to upset you, and there's a woman who will do you mischief.'

She turned away, and spoke across her shoulders. 'There now!' she said. 'I've told you your future and it never cost you a brass farthing. I must be going soft in the head.'

The girl walked away down the hot bright street, her black hair swinging on her shoulders, her small ungainly body swaying, her head held high. Waves of hostility and threat still emanated back to where I stood rooted on the doorstep. A sudden weariness overcame me so that I could scarcely find strength enough to close the door and cross the hall into the kitchen. I sat at the table and drank the cooling coffee.

'Sorsha!' A strange wild name. My hand went out to the abandoned sketches and I found myself reluctant to touch them; but if I intended to keep them they would need to be spray-fixed. I rose on an impulse and collected the spray can from a cupboard. When the charcoal drawings were safely preserved I held the sheets of paper by their utmost corners and slipped them into a brand-new folder. I placed the folder carefully into an empty drawer. The confused thoughts in my mind were all of evil and the dangers of contamination; I washed my hands at the kitchen sink, and began to clear the table of assorted mugs and empty plates. It was only when the china rattled in my grasp that I noticed the trembling of my fingers.

His lapel badge told me that his name was Ashley Martindale. I expressed surprise that the glossy young manager had come in person to do my valuation; I had expected that a less important employee would do the donkey work of measuring and calculating.

'I like to get out of the office,' he confided, 'especially in this hot weather.' He looked up at the rose-brick facade and long sash windows. 'And I must admit to a certain curiosity about your house. I've never actually viewed a property in Infirmary Avenue.'

'You seemed to know all about it when I told you my address.'

He smiled kindly at me. 'It's my job to know what type of house is in a given locality.' He moved from the doorstep and into the hall. His gaze took in the interior oaken doors and brass fittings, the graceful curve of the staircase, the black and white tiled floor. 'Hm,' he said, 'rather nice — if you like this sort of thing. But it's all a question of taste, you know. The market is pretty depressed at the moment, most of our recent sales have been to first-time buyers, and this house is deceptively large for your average young couple.'

'I'm prepared to leave the carpets and curtains, and certain items of furniture if necessary.' My daughter and granddaughter, who were knowledgeable about that kind of thing, had told me how when selling properties of their own these concessions were vital bargaining points in a time of recession and falling values.

Ashley Martindale nodded and strode to the staircase. 'We'll begin at the top I think, and move downwards?' It was not really a question, he was halfway up the stairs before I could formulate an answer. He worked quickly, and without further comment. I found myself willing him to like the house, to make some appreciative remark as we moved from room to room, but even his normally expressive features remained blank and unimpressed. I began to point out the good points he appeared to miss; the replacement mahogany windows, made in the original sash style to comply with conservation rulings; the recently decorated bathroom. I led him finally into the kitchen which was my especial pride; each oaken unit and rolled-edge worktop had been fitted expertly by my son-in-law to my specifications. I really expected some complimentary remark from Ashley Martindale at this point, but he said nothing. He sat down in the carved pine chair vacated lately by the gypsy, Sorsha, and opened his briefcase. He slapped a batch of printed forms onto the table.

'So now,' he said, 'we come to the valuation of your property.' He paused. 'I have to advise you, Mrs Franklin, that if you wish to sell within a reasonable time you will need to accept a realistic asking price.'

'I would like to be out of here before winter. I don't relish moving in rain and snow.'

'Exactly so.'

I waited, confident that he would name the sum which was already in my mind. He hesitated for some moments, looked around the kitchen, and then mentioned a figure that was seven thousand pounds less than the one I had expected.

'No,' I said. 'I can't possibly let it go for that low price.'

Without the ever-present smile Ashley looked much older. 'I must warn you, Mrs Franklin, that if you put your house up for sale at such an inflated figure, you will not even get one single viewer, never mind a buyer!'

'But we won't know that until we try.'

He sighed. 'We shall just be wasting time,' he said, 'and with today's depressed housing market we simply can't afford to do that.'

I said, 'Give me a few days. I'm not sure if I want to sell at your price. I need to think about this.'

I phoned Imogen that evening. I could hear the faint hurt in her voice when I con-fessed the action I had taken without prior consultation. I told her about the low valuation, the estate agent's lack of enthusiasm. 'I would have come over, mother,' she said. 'I could have been present when the valuation was made — if I had only known about it.'

'I didn't want to trouble you,' I told her. We both knew that this statement was blatantly untrue. There had been times when I had not hesitated to involve her and Niall in my problems when it suited me to do so.

'I'd just like to know what Niall thinks about this ridiculously low figure I've been quoted. I've spent a lot of money on the house. I don't intend to make a gift of it to someone!'

'Don't upset yourself,' said Imogen. 'We'll come over at the weekend and talk about it. If we'd known what you had in mind we could have prepared you for a shock or two.'

I knew then that Imogen and Niall would be on the side of Ashley Martindale.

I would go, without benefit of family, to the estate agent's office first thing in the morning, and put my house on the market. At the price *I* considered fair and sufficient.

# Sorsha

Kingdom was parked at the end of the long street. She could just make out his dark head and the yellow colour of his tee-shirt as he sat, hunched across the steering wheel, waiting for her. He had the look of a man who had grown angry with the heat of the van and the long delay. Sorsha slowed her pace deliberately to annoy him further. The woman in the house had said that Sorsha should not be out 'calling' in her condition. She could feel the woman's gaze like a weight across her shoulders; knowing she was watched, she tilted her head at a defiant angle. Everybody in the whole world thought they knew now what was best for Sorsha. Even the child she carried had taken possession of her body and slowed her thinking, making her fearful and cautious where she had once been reckless and unafraid.

Only desperate need had made her knock at that door and beg admittance. The woman had been kind to her. Sorsha had enjoyed the tea and biscuits. It had felt like being in a café where she was the sole customer and could eat as much as she fancied, knowing there would be no bill to pay. She had noted every item in the woman's lav and kitchen. What the woman called the downstairs loo had a dark green carpet on the floor and a pale green lavatory and wash basin. The curtains had frills and a pattern of red poppies. The lav paper and the light shade were also pale green. She had lingered there for as long as she dared, fingering the solid block of pine-perfumed stuff on the windowsill, and washing her already clean hands.

The sight of the kitchen had lowered her spirits. Brown floortiles, brown cupboards, brown chairs and table. Even brown mugs and plates, and a brown electric toaster and kettle. Come to think of it, the biscuits had been brown as well! It was a colour which reminded her of winter mud and flooded brooks, and fallen leaves. No wonder she had come over all depressed and mopey. She glanced sideways and upwards at the prison wall, and shivered. Better dead, she thought, than to be locked up in that place.

She wondered how the woman, who had seemed a nice enough body for a *gorgio,* could bear to face that wicked wall every day of her life.

Sorsha smiled, remembering the woman's shocked face when told that she would soon be moving from that house. She had added the bit about the field and the pony just for the devil of it! As for the bungalow, well that was a guess; most elderly people, she had noticed when 'calling', preferred to live in the single-storey home. The move itself had been easy to foretell. The table in the hall had been stacked with estate agents' advertisements for little cottage places in the country. People, thought Sorsha, should never take for granted that gypsies cannot read or write.

The words of warning, the mention of danger from a woman and a gentleman friend had come, as such predictions always came, into her head from out of nowhere. She would look at a stranger's face, and feel the fear in her own heart, and she would know that some awful future lay in wait for that person. And that was the nature of gypsy fortune-telling. Among all the flummery and window dressing, there would always be one single shocking forecast that was bound to come to pass.

As she approached, Kingdom unfolded his long thin body from the driver's seat and leaned his arms across the van's roof. She slowed her ambling progress to a mere crawl and put a hand against her side, indicating some unspecified but agonising pain. Sorsha saw his concerned face and smiled inside herself. It worked every time, this wordless plea for sympathy and understanding, she could tell he had been anxious about her by the high note of his voice. 'Where the hell have you been?' demanded Kingdom. 'Your ma and the rest of them have took the bus back to the *tan*.' He nodded towards the Infirmary buildings. 'We thought for sure that something sudden had happened and you was already took in there.'

It had came as no surprise to Kingdom or the rest of the family, that Sorsha, slight of build and tiny, would require a hospital confinement if she and the child were to survive.

'Not yet. Not ever, if I has my say!' She smiled sweetly at him. She knew how desperately he longed for the child's birth, and for this present threat to his manliness and independence posed by her condition to be removed. She herself would not mind too much if the baby carried well past its proper time. Let him stay guilty and worried for as long as possible; and then, just to make everything perfect because he, of course, wanted a son, it would be a girl!

The interior of the van was hot and stuffy, the heat from the leather seats scorched through the thin cotton of her dress. She felt nauseated and said so.

'You'll be all right when we get moving,' said Kingdom. 'It'll be cooler outside the city. Anyway — where were you all that long time? I drove around the streets but I couldn't see you.'

'I was took with a funny turn. I had to rest awhile. A woman give me a drink of water. I had to sit for a long time on her doorstep.'

'So you never sold nothing?'

She reached into the pocket of her dress, pulled out the two five-pound notes and rustled them between her fingers.

His eyes opened wide. 'How did you — ?'

'I told her fortune,' she said swiftly. 'She asked me to.'

'It must have been a damned good *dukker!*'

'Oh, it was,' she said. 'That woman won't soon forget Sorsha.'

Kingdom held out his left hand palm upwards.

'Oh no,' she said, 'not a single penny. I

38

earned it. I keeps it!'

'My mother —' he began.

'Your mother 'ud let your father walk all over her, if it would make him happy. You'd better get used to the new idea right now. What Sorsha works for — Sorsha keeps! You want money for beer and fags, then you gets off your lazy backside and earns it. I need this cash for baby clothes and what else. 'Tis *your* baby too, Kingdom!'

He drove in silence through the city outskirts and into open country. She watched him from under lowered eyelids. He was so beautiful, so absolutely living gorgeous that she could eat him with a bent spoon and no salt and pepper. But he would need careful watching; she sensed that Kingdom could be pushed just so far and no further. Once the child was born and life was back to normal, she would need her King, loving and considerate, for he had spoiled her entirely for any other husband.

The air was cooler in the country. She slid lower in her seat and closed her eyes. Whenever King was close she could think of nothing else but him. Even her aunts, who were old married women in their mid-forties, gazed hungrily at Kingdom and fluttered their eyelashes at him. Her oldest aunt, Dru, had declared that Kingdom was the very living image of the dead pop star Elvis Presley. There were people who believed that this Elvis had never really died, but lived on in some other fella's body. When Drusilla's tale reached King's ears, the fanciful aspect of it grabbed his very soul. He begged Sorsha to read aloud to him an article on Elvis which was printed in the *News of the World.* King carried that story, folded in his wallet, until the paper fell to pieces. He studied the pictures of Elvis which were pasted in Drusilla's scrapbook, he showed them to Sorsha and she laughed him to shame for a dreamer and a fool. But Kingdom bought a second-hand guitar, a pair of tight flared trousers and a frilled shirt. Dressed in the old-fashioned outfit, his likeness to the dead man was mindblowing. The sight of King, a lock of straight black hair falling over one eye, the top lip curled into a snarl, had left a cold place deep inside of Sorsha that would not go away. A part of her believed in ghosts and wandering spirits. In the small hours of the morning when she could not sleep, she wondered who the coming child would favour in its looks. The newspaper article had said that Elvis Presley was part Chippewa Indian and part American gypsy. When the woman in the house had tried to put Sorsha's likeness onto paper

it had been the face of Great-great-grandmother Estralita that had come from the
*gorgio's* hand. There was a significance in
these two links with dead faces which she
did not dare to dwell on. From one generation to another anything could happen! But
to put her fears into words would make
them real and certain to come true. She
could have confided in King, but he was a
part of the horror which gripped her. Elvis
Presley had been a bad man who died a sad
death. Great-great-grandmother Estralita,
so it was whispered, had given birth to a
son while she was locked up in prison, and
that child was stolen from her.

Sorsha shivered and held tightly to the
edges of her seat.

Kingdom slowed and turned towards her.
His tone was anxious.

'You're not starting, are you?'

'No,' she said. 'I told you, not for ages
yet.' If she had her way, and in spite of the
discomfort, she would keep the child safe
inside her for ever. She had not wanted a
baby, but now all her feelings of resentment
towards it were changing into protectiveness
and love.

King patted her knee in the way he might
have comforted a frightened lurcher. 'You'll
be okay. Ma says every woman gets nervous

when it's her first time.'

Sorsha did not answer. She did not care to hear what King's mother thought or said. In any case he was probably lying. No woman in the world could utter so many words of silly rubbish as those put down by Kingdom to his mother. She closed her eyes and thought about the *gorgio* woman. Now there was a smart lady. Or was she? Kingdom pulled sharply at the wheel and Sorsha clung to the edges of her seat as the van bumped down the rutted track that led to the Hollow which was their own place in a hard world.

In nineteen seventy-nine, Kingdom's Uncle Manju had bought the field cheaply from a nearly-bankrupt farmer. It was not so much a field as a bit of low-lying grassland, marshy and wet even in the hottest summer, and boglike in winter. The charm of the place had been its isolation; hedged all about with alder and willow, and blackberry bushes, reached only by way of a narrow dirt track, it had, for at least a hundred years, been a peaceful if soggy winter home for Manju and his extensive family. But times were changing and ownership would give them security, or so they had hoped.

The shock had come six years ago. The

strangers had walked down to the field towards evening when the scrap and tarmacing lorries had returned, and the men sat around their fires, eating supper. The visitors had been recognised by their suits and briefcases as being official, dangerous and *gorgio*.

'Government bastards,' Sorsha's father had muttered. He scraped what remained of the stew on his plate into the fire, for he would never allow a *gorgio* to see him eating. Sorsha, aged ten, had regretted the wasted food. With so many older working brothers who were of course served first from the stewpot, she was always hungry long before the irregular mealtimes. As the men drew close she edged away towards her mother and the safety of the trailer. But her uncle called her back to come and stand beside him.

'If there's paperwork,' he whispered, 'I shall need you, girl.'

Of her father and mother, her aunts and uncles and eight brothers, Sorsha was the only good scholar in the family; the gypsy who could read and write with ease.

They had come at first with nervous smiles and polite good-evenings, those men of business. But their respect had been all for the growling dogs. They were not government officials but a speculative builder and his solicitor. The fields adjacent to Manju's *atchintan* had already, they said, been purchased by them. They were not proposing to actually build on Manju's field, but wished to acquire it all the same.

'How much?' asked Manju.

A sum was mentioned which was exactly half the amount her uncle had paid ten years ago.

Manju had laughed and told them to clear off, or he would set the dogs on them. The solicitor had changed his high-handed manner to one of exasperation. 'So how much would you be prepared to sell for?' he enquired.

'What makes you gentlemen think that I would want to sell?'

The solicitor, his shiny shoes deep in mud up to their laces, said, 'Surely you would all be better off in a more healthy venue?'

'Nothing wrong with our health!'

'But it's so damp here. It's bad for these children, especially in winter.'

Manju stirred the fire with the toe of his boot, so that blue smoke wreathed the stranger's heads. The builder spoke for the first time. 'Ah, come on, man! One field is as good another to your sort. We'll double our offer, but that's as much as you're likely to get.'

Manju said, 'If you don't want to build on my bit o' land, then what for do you want it?'

The two men, coughing through the smoke, looked at one another. It was the solicitor who spoke. 'My client proposes to build a small estate of executive-type houses. Expensive, exclusive houses — you understand me?' He waved a hand towards the blackberry bushes. 'Their windows will overlook your — your camping ground.'

'Oh, now I understands you right enough.' Manju laughed. 'And you want us out of here before we spoil the view and put your posh buyers off? Well, tough luck, mister! Get back in your car and sod off, because I ain't selling. Not an inch, not a blade of grass, and there's nothing you can do about it.'

'We shall see about that.' The builder's face was red and angry.

'Oh no you won't,' said Manju. ' 'Tis my land. I got the deed to prove it.'

The solicitor's voice was soft but threatening. 'From where I am standing,' he said, 'I can already see that you are contravening several bye-laws. You may not be conversant with the law, but I can assure you that a magistrate can have you evicted from this field even though you own it. Perhaps you should give more thought to our proposals. These children, for example, they look pretty neglected. They could be taken into care, you know!'

Manju was most dangerous when his voice was soft. 'These *chavvies* want for nothing, ail nothing,' he whispered. 'They may not be as clean and tidy as your kids but that bit of dirt washes off 'em. You touch our children, mister, you bring them social people down here, and you will be a dead man before that day is out!'

The solicitor took two steps backwards. 'Your threats don't frighten me,' he shouted.

'Oh, I ain't threatening you, mister. Oh no, well I would never need to do that, would I?' Manju stepped right up to the stranger and spoke into his face. 'In case you didn't recognise it, that was a gypsy's curse, my fine gentleman, and you better believe in it. I've wished many a bad man dead, so you won't be the first one to drop in his tracks because of Manju's power.'

Manju turned and strolled back towards his trailer. The solicitor and the builder walked back to their car, never to return. Manju heard the car door slam, watched the rear lights wink away towards the village. A great shout of laughter went up from his assembled family.

'Oh you should have been a film actor, yes you should!' cried his sister Drusilla. 'Whatever bad thing happens to them two from now on, they'll surely put it down to your old gypsy-curse!'

# Nina

My failure to sketch the gypsy girl had upset me more than I was willing to admit. I was not a superstitious woman; her fortune-telling antics had not really impressed me, and yet — I believed her when she said we had not seen the last of one another. Although I could not easily imagine in what circumstances we would ever meet again.

I visited Ashley Martindale in his blue and grey office. I agreed to put my house on the market at a figure which was three thousand pounds below my estimate of its value, and two thousand pounds above his.

He was not pleased. He pointed out that he had been making property evaluations for the past sixteen years, and knew what he was doing! Once again I was sidetracked briefly into fantasising about his private life. If his looks were an indication of his age then he must have been an estate agent at the age of five years. Or maybe he was also fantasising? Perhaps it was his sister's doll's house he had valued sixteen years ago?

I came back into the conversation with a sense of having missed some vital aspect of the negotiations.

'And so the FOR SALE board will be put up tomorrow morning, Mrs Franklin, and as soon as the paperwork is completed I will submit it to you for your approval. We shall still be way above a realistic price, and I doubt very much if we shall attract any interest. But you are the client, Mrs Franklin, and we are here to carry out your wishes. I am going to pass you over now to Poppy, our sales negotiator.'

Poppy was the sort of forthright, cards-on-the-table, let's-knuckle-down-to-business girl with whom I knew I could get along. She had a fluff of golden curls, big blue eyes and a reassuring manner of speech which suggested that this business of house-buying and selling, and precise valuations, was a tremendous joke, only a game, and not for one moment to be taken seriously.

If I had a son I would want him to be just like Niall. My son-in-law was the kind of man who tended to be overlooked by most people, until, that is, those same people had problems in their lives. His looks were unremarkable; stocky build, medium height, nice grey eyes and brown hair. But in times of trouble and uncertainty Niall was a rock in a wild sea. I could never have wished for a more suitable husband for my temperamental and emotional daughter.

Imogen came first into the house that evening, while Niall parked the car.

'Mother!' she cried; she only calls me 'mother' when she plans to dominate me; 'the FOR SALE board is already on the house!'

'Yes dear,' I said. 'I had noticed it was there. It's a necessary evil when one wants to sell a property.'

'But I thought you loved this house? It's been your home for more than forty years!' Her sweet face crumpled into tears. 'And after all, Mother, it is the place where *I* was born!'

I wondered briefly and unkindly if the promise of an historic pale-blue plaque placed above the front door and with her name and birthdate on it would help to pacify her. Sometimes, my daughter, who is impulsive and warmhearted, can also be extremely irritating.

I said, in the steady voice I had learned to use in Imogen's childhood, 'I gave it a lot of thought before I decided to move. The house is too big, too draughty, and expensive to maintain. I can no longer cope with it all.'

'But you've never complained, Mother!'

'And I'm not complaining now. I'm taking action. I do not intend to spend another winter here in the city.'

'But where will you go?'

'I shall move out into the country. A bungalow perhaps, in a village. Not too far from the city of course, and since I no longer drive, I shall need to be on a reliable bus route.'

'You've worked it all out, haven't you?'

I spoke gently, not wishing to hurt her, but still needing to make my decision absolutely clear. 'I shall be very grateful for your company when I go to view properties. I'm sure your opinion will be invaluable.'

Her face brightened, she smiled. 'Oh yes! Yes, that would be great fun.' She began to tick off the names of 'suitable' villages on the fingers of her left hand. When Niall came into the room Imogen told him of my plans as if the proposed move had been all her own idea. 'I shall be busy in the next few weeks,' she said, 'looking for a bungalow for Mother. I'm to help her choose a new home. Isn't that exciting, darling?'

Niall's gaze met mine above my daughter's head; we smiled uneasily at one another. We both knew that any property thought suitable by Imogen would be too upmarket, too expensive, and not at all my style. But I had travelled that particular road with Imogen many times and learned a trick or two on the journey. And Niall and I both loved her.

I smiled fondly at my daughter, knowing how deep was her need to feel wanted and important. 'It might even be fun,' I said, 'to take Francesca with us on our house-hunting expeditions. After all, once the baby is born, she and Mitch will also need a larger place, something with a garden; and three heads are always better than one.'

'That's an excellent idea,' said Niall. If he spoke with an excess of enthusiasm it was because he knew that Francesca was more skilled at curbing her mother's wilder fancies than he or I could ever be.

I made a mental apology to Francesca for daring to involve her in this convoluted family scheming. If the house sold well — if it even sold at all — I would buy the cot, the pram, and anything else required by my coming great-grandchild.

The unseasonal heat of May gave way to

a cool and rainy June. Roscoe and I took our customary twice-daily stroll around familiar streets; often we ambled through the tree-lined walk which contained the museum, the Roman Catholic cathedral, and several attractive little cafés which were patronised mainly by students. We were well known by the Italian owner of one particular café, a large cappuccino and a bowl of water would be brought soon after our arrival. If trade was slow Anna, the proprietress, would sit for ten minutes at my table, and we would exchange news about our lives. The students petted Roscoe and surreptitiously fed him bits of bacon and cheese although I begged them not to. The walks, the café visits, the familiar shops, were a part of my life, a means of holding loneliness at bay. Each time I returned to Infirmary Avenue now, and saw the green and white FOR SALE board nailed above my front door, I was gripped by a pang of uncertainty and fear.

Was Imogen correct in her judgement that I was about to make a foolish move? What would I do in a village? In the country? Among strangers? And did I automatically reject all advice given by my daughter, simply because it was she who was giving it to me?

Meanwhile, I waited for the phone call which would alert me to impending viewers; it came sooner than predicted by Ashley Martindale. The prospective buyers were two young women, I was told by an excited Poppy; girls who were already enchanted by the photograph and printed description of the house. I was to learn in the ensuing months that Poppy regarded every viewer as an almost-certain buyer. But on this first occasion her enthusiasm was infectious. The viewers had made an appointment for seven thirty that evening, which gave me three hours in which to go through every room obsessively tidying, vacuuming and dusting.

They came in a small black car which they parked, laughing and illegally, beneath the prison wall. I observed them from my bedroom window. Both girls wore black; enveloping garments that reached to wrists and ankles, but in very different styles. The tall girl was elegant and thin, probably, I thought, anorexic. Her companion was short and plump. The tall girl wore high-heeled sandals and carried a handbag, her hair was combed neatly into a French pleat. The friend wore a pair of Dr Marten's boots which contrasted oddly with the floating chiffon of her dress. Her hair was done in Rasta locks, with strings of coloured beads hanging onto ears and forehead.

The tall girl smiled winningly at me. Her plump friend glowered. As advised by Imogen and Francesca, I at first conducted them from room to room, pointing out what I considered to be the most attractive features, and then I invited them to re-explore the house alone and at their leisure.

I waited in the kitchen while high heels clicked and Dr Marten's clumped from room to room. When they reappeared the tall girl was smiling and excited.

'It's quite delightful,' she said, 'I love everything about it, especially the beamed ceilings. I do so admire your taste. I wouldn't want to change a thing.' She paused. 'Will you be leaving any of the furnishings?'

I said, 'Quite possibly. Almost certainly, in fact. I plan to buy a much smaller place.'

'I assume that anything you leave will be included in the selling price?' The plump girl spoke sharply; her acquisitive gaze was already putting a price on the kitchen furniture and fittings, assessing the value of the washing machine and the fridge-freezer.

I said, 'All carpets and curtains are certainly included. As for any other items, well, we would need to discuss the matter.' I could hear the faltering note in my voice, and knew that Miss Rasta Locks would take full advantage of my indecision if permitted.

She struck at once. 'You need to be prepared to make concessions these days,' she informed me, 'if you really want to sell. We've looked at twenty properties similar to this one. Not much to choose between them really. Of course, if we find a place that is already furnished — at no extra cost — then that would be a big factor in its favour.'

I said, 'Isn't this a rather large house for just the two of you?'

The tall girl smiled patronisingly. 'Oh, we shan't be on our own here. We have several friends who are anxious to move in with us.'

A commune, I thought. Oh my God, they belong to one of these crackpot religions! They will sit on cushions and recite mantras, and burn candles and joss sticks. They will sleep on mattresses, seventeen to a bedroom! No wonder they had not remarked on the undesirable proximity of the Infirmary and prison! All I had ever read or heard about the Moonies and The Children of God began to flash through my mind. I remembered tales of Aleister Crowley and his satanic practices, witches' sabbaths, free love and black magic.

I imagined my dear old house becoming notorious and written about in the Sunday papers. I moved briskly towards the hall, shepherding the girls before me. I released the Yale and held the front door open. Out in the porch, the thin girl said, 'We'll be in touch quite soon.'

The booted one took her last chance to disconcert me. 'What,' she asked nastily, 'is the state of your floorboards? Any rising damp, dry rot or woodworm?"

It was my turn now to be condescending. 'This house,' I told her, 'is early Victorian and built to last. There *are no floorboards*, neither upstairs nor down. All the floors are solid — hence the supporting beamed ceilings. Does that answer your questions?'

Her mouth fell open but no words emerged. She turned and walked away followed by her friend.

I watched the small black car speed away towards the city. My only regret was that they had not received a parking ticket. No offer was ever made by my first viewers, a fact which must have given Ashley Martindale a certain satisfaction.

I keep a photograph of Jack on my bedside table. I placed it there on the day after his funeral. Sometimes, when I have important news for Jack, I talk to his photo. I also tell him about the amusing things that happen to me; and the events and people who make me angry. Well, I always told him those things, didn't I! Why should I change the habit of a lifetime? Anna at the café understands my need to confide in a photo. She believes in an afterlife and is, like me, dismissively and apologetically superstitious. Together, over coffee, we study our horoscopes in the *Daily Mirror* and are appropriately downcast or elated at the predictions, while assuring one another that the whole thing is rubbish.

I told Jack about Sorsha; and about the two black-clad young women who had expected to buy my house for tuppence ha'penny, with the furniture thrown in.

'It's all going wrong,' I wailed, 'and I thought it would be simple. I thought one merely put up the FOR SALE board, and somebody nice came in and looked around, and said, "Yes". It's a different world now,' I told the photo. 'You wouldn't recognise it any more. I don't know what to do, Jack. I'm no good at this bargaining game, all this wheeling and dealing.'

I had long since ceased to reproach Jack for leaving me to grow old alone. The solution to that particular hardship, I had learned, was never to actually grow old, alone or otherwise. Think young! I told myself. I sat on the edge of the bed and held the photo in both hands; it had been taken when Jack was in his twenties, and even in black and white it was easy to see that his hair was blond and his skin fair. I traced the high cheekbones and firm jaw, the long-lipped smiling mouth, the calm gaze.

Imogen has my looks. Whenever we are seen together, even total strangers remark on the likeness. As with identical twins, and but for the difference in age, we were, from her early childhood, doomed to be judged as a unit, as having similar tastes and enthusiasms. 'Two peas in a pod' people gushed, when in fact nothing could be further from the truth. I replaced the photo on the bedside table.

In the morning I would telephone Francesca; perhaps we could have lunch together. Talking to Fran helped me sort out my feelings. She had a dry, delicious sense of humour, a turn of speech which dispelled any tendency towards depressed and gloomy thoughts.

I had driven a car in the days before the wearing of seat belts had been made compulsory. Fran waited, as did Niall and Imogen when I was their passenger, for me to obey the law and fasten the beastly strap. I fumbled, failing as I always did to immediately find the connecting metal slot. I muttered an obscene word. Fran turned towards me and smiled. She knew I would never have used that expletive when in her mother's presence.

'Bet that made you feel better!'

'Yes,' I said. 'There's nothing quite like a very rude word for relieving tension.'

I studied her while she negotiated the city traffic. The morning was warm and sunny. I had suggested a riverside restaurant on the outskirts of the city. In the two weeks since I had seen her, Fran's appearance had changed. Her pallor alarmed me. I began to doubt the wisdom of this outing, and it was too late now to turn back. But it would be cool beside the river, and the restaurant provided garden loungers. I would see to it that Fran relaxed today. We would talk about the expected baby, and allied pleasant subjects.

We ate salad and drank mineral water. Fran's appetite was poor. We moved from the restaurant to the garden loungers.

'How much longer?' I asked.

'The hospital says three weeks.' I waited for further information but Fran was unusually silent. I made my offer of pram and cot and whatever else was necessary, but it seemed that I was too late. Imogen had long since ordered a pram, and Niall a cot; Mitch's parents were to provide the essential car-seat and several other items.

Fran said, reluctantly, 'I suppose we shall need a high chair.'

'But not for ages yet!'

'The time will soon pass.'

Again I heard the uncertainty in her voice. I tried to visualise my great-grandchild beating on the tray of a high chair with a plastic spoon, squeezing mashed potatoes between fat fingers, but the image would not come. Fran sensed my disappointment about the pram. I sensed her anxiety. I said, 'All I can see at the moment is a tiny bundle in a white shawl.'

'I can't even imagine that much,' she admitted. 'It's no more than indigestion and sleepless nights at this point.'

I thought I understood her reluctance to anticipate the future. My mind had a tendency to run in similar channels.

'Tell me about your house sale,' she said abruptly.

So I told her about Ashley Martindale, and the black-clad girls who had made derogatory remarks and not a single offer.

'You may find that you have to bring your price down,' Fran said gently.

'No,' I said. 'At least — not yet.'

'Of course,' said Fran, 'it will all depend on what you intend to pay for the new place. How much do you have in mind?'

'I don't know. I haven't thought that far ahead. I've just concentrated on the selling aspect of things.'

'And what happens if you sell quickly, and have no house to move into?'

'I'll book into a hotel for a few weeks.'

'And what about your furniture?'

I gazed helplessly at her. We began to laugh. She said, 'You're as scared as I am when it comes to making plans. But Gran, you must have some idea of what you want?'

'I've picked up a few advertisements in the estate agent's office,' I confessed. 'Village properties mostly, small with little gardens.'

'And?'

'Nothing takes my fancy.'

Fran's voice was hesitant. She said, 'Mum has a few ideas. She's found quite a number of suitable villages and bungalows. If you ring her, she will take you out to view them.'

I looked at Fran and saw the knowledge in her eyes that we two were unwilling participants in Imogen's game of manipulation. Messages and requests made to me through Fran were always guaranteed to be acted upon promptly.

'Yes,' I said, 'I'll call her this evening.'

Fran said, 'You don't have to buy any bungalow or house that you don't really love.'

I smiled. 'Your mother means well, I know. But she's always so damned sure that she knows what's good for other people, especially her aged parent!'

'You just have to be firm with her, Grandma. You should have seen the impractical pram she tried to talk me into having! It was pale blue with an all-over daisy pattern. I convinced her in the end that navy blue was a more sensible colour for a pram that would be constantly heaved in and out of a hatchback.'

Oh yes, I thought. Well, it's easy for you, my darling girl! You are twenty-five years old, and you have all the self-confidence and chutzpah of your generation. I am no longer sure of my place in the scheme of things, or if I even have a place.

I said, 'I shall know what I want just as soon as I see it.'

Fran asked me about her own babyhood and childhood. The anecdotes I chose to remember were amusing; she began to smile, to laugh. When she dropped me off in Infirmary Avenue, my granddaughter had a little colour in her cheeks, her eyes were brighter. I wanted to tell her not to worry, that everything was going to be wonderful, that she would sail through the coming birth and have a beautiful baby.

But to utter such platitudes would be to underline the very doubts in both our minds; and so I kissed her and said, as I always did, 'Ring you in a few days!'

I watched the car out of sight. I looked across to the red-brick and plate-glass of the new maternity wing of the Infirmary. Three weeks, Fran had said. It was then that I remembered standing on this same spot and watching Sorsha, who was also to give birth in a few weeks. I had been tempted to relate to Fran the story of Sorsha and her visit.

The gypsy girl's unusual attitudes to life and men and childbirth would have made amusing telling. Then I remembered just in time the sketches of Sorsha which had changed into someone else's likeness even as I drew them. I recalled Sorsha's horror when she saw those drawings, and the threats and predictions that had followed.

I went into the house, closed and drew

the many locks and bolts on the doors, and sat down by the telephone and punched out my daughter's number.

The heat wave returned. The temperature rose swiftly, in exact proportion, it seemed to me, to my anxiety level.

Imogen telephoned or visited daily. Sometimes both.

The house took on a jumble-sale appearance. Estate agents' handouts were to be found on every flat surface, even in the bathroom. I began to worry about the accumulated junk of forty years' occupation of the same house. I could not recall the last time I had visited attic or cellar. I put those particular areas firmly from my mind, while making a mental note never to mention the subject to Imogen or Niall. In an effort to ease the eventual transition from spacious house to tiny bungalow, I began to turn out cupboards and wardrobes, and to stuff most of their contents into dustbin bags for delivery to Oxfam. Fran assured me that nineteen fifties' fashions, in clothing and bric-a-brac, were in great demand in charity shops, and would be welcomed by them.

Roscoe and I began to take our morning walk even earlier than usual. I discovered that the café did crack-of-dawn breakfasts and so by seven o'clock every morning he and I were seated in the cool interior sharing bacon sandwiches or egg on toast, and I talked to Anna about my problems, while drinking milky cappuccino. Those quiet couple of hours were the best part of the day for Roscoe and for me, a time in which I could bolster my determination to go through with the house-sale and the subsequent move. Also, while in the café I was safe from telephone contact with Imogen and Niall, and Ashley and Poppy.

Only Anna and Roscoe knew the true reasons for the self-imposed upheaval in my life. The first, and possibly least significant of these, was the fact that Francesca and Mitchell had recently sold their flat and moved from my part of the city to a village which lay to the north of the county. It was the announcement in January of Fran's pregnancy that had initially shaken me loose from my inertia, and turned my thoughts towards the future.

A great-grandchild!

A fabulous and unexpected gift, but one which would now be out of easy reach and more miles away than I could easily travel. For several weeks I was content to delight in the thought of the coming baby. Fran and I went shopping. We bought first-size garments in shades of white and lemon and pale green. I commissioned a friend, an expert knitter, to make a large woollen shawl in an all-over pattern of scallop shells. I browsed in baby-wear shops, noting the current infant fashions. And then, very tentatively, while denying that this was a feasible plan, I began to toy with the idea of moving out of the city, to a place which would be close to Fran, but not too close. I had no intention of planting myself on my granddaughter's doorstep, but I bought a map of the county, pinpointed the area in which Fran and Mitch now lived, and circled in blue ballpoint surrounding villages and hamlets.

But there remained my strange and distressing inability since Jack's death to take any action, make any plan which I felt would not meet with his complete approval. I had lately begun to impose even little restrictions on myself which in my more rational moments I knew would have actually upset him.

But even those rational moments had become infrequent in the dark months of the recent winter. My conversations with Jack's photograph had become pointless and depressing; I went on at great length, listing the shortcomings of the house, never telling him the whole truth.

In the end, it had been the prediction by Sorsha, the gypsy girl, that I would soon be moving from Infirmary Avenue that had finally pushed me to give a definite instruction to the estate agent. Sorsha had sounded so definite, so convinced, that there was nothing left for me to do but believe her. And this was a development so unexpected, so bizarre and senseless that I would never admit it to a living soul.

Imogen, once embarked upon a project, is impossible to deflect or halt. Bungalow-viewing now became a daily feature of our lives. I had invited her cooperation and my daughter cooperated; but to an extent and with a passion which made me feel guilty, since in my heart I already knew that I would settle only for a certain type of property in a specific location.

After my repeated rejection of bungalows in cul-de-sacs, on retirement estates, detached and semis, brick-built or stucco-rendered, even Imogen's enthusiasm flagged. Yet I still felt obliged to keep my promise that she should be involved. But with each new and artfully presented photograph and house description I found it more difficult to dissemble. The day came when I sat in my daughter's car, opened the county map and spread it before her across the steering wheel. I placed my fingertip on the circle that marked my granddaughter's present home.

'There!' I said. 'Well, no — not exactly there perhaps, but in that vicinity. That's where I really want to be.'

A waiting silence fell between us. I risked a sideways glance and saw my daughter's trembling lips. I willed her not to cry. Jack had always dealt with Imogen's tears. His voice spoke now inside my head, accusing me of not knowing how to be a mother to her.

She said at last, 'You'll be quite a distance from Niall and me.'

I forced a jolly note into my voice. 'Not at all!' I said. 'In fact, if Fran and Mitch and I are living closer to each other, you will save a fortune on petrol and on time. When visiting in future you can take in the lot of us on the same day.'

Imogen folded the map and handed it to me. Her trembling lips had thinned into a bitter line. I had an impulse to comfort her, to touch her hand, to attempt some sort of explanation, but could not seem to find the courage. The words I actually spoke took me by surprise. 'You miss your father, don't you?'

She carefully did not look at me. 'Yes, Mother. I miss him. Sometimes I think I miss him more than you do.'

She is usually a cautious driver, but we drove north that morning at a speed which had me crouching in my seat and grateful for the seatbelt. I could have asked her to slow down, but to do so would have been demeaning. I tried to make amends by buying her a good pub lunch, but she was not to be mollified by food. Back in the car she said tartly, 'So now what? We are in the area you asked for. Where do we begin?'

I opened my bag and pulled out several house agents' handouts, ones that were of my own choosing.

'I see that you came here well prepared,' said my daughter.

'Just a few odd addresses. One or two possible bungalows. But not,' I said firmly, 'in Francesca's village.'

'Quite!' said Imogen.

We found bungalow number one without any trouble. It stood on the verge of a busy main road. Container lorries roared past it, spraying dust and exhaust fumes over the red-brick and bilious yellow of its paintwork. I consulted the house agent's flattering photo. Who says the camera cannot lie?

Imogen slowed and would have stopped, but I said, 'Just keep driving, dear. Better luck next time.'

I would not have believed there could be so many dilapidated properties on offer. We viewed sagging roofs, blistered paintwork, rotting windows and jungle-type gardens. Where, I wondered, was the small white structure I had dreamed of through the previous winter?

We drove fast and in silence past Francesca's house and on through to open countryside. As we came into the outskirts of a neighbouring village I began to recognise certain landmarks. A conical hill, a windmill, a small lake; farms which had been worked for many generations by the same families.

I said, 'Slow down a bit. I think I know this place.' It was when we came into the centre of the village that I knew exactly where I was. My daughter parked beside the triangular green. She climbed from the car and I followed her on shaky legs. We stood for a moment in the shade of a tall copper-beech tree. Fifty years had passed since I last stood there.

I said, 'I remember this tree when it was a sapling.'

Imogen thought that I was joking. It was the kind of ageist joke I often made against myself and was guaranteed to annoy her. She turned back, all set to reprimand me for my foolishness, and then she saw my face.

'Oh, my God,' she whispered. 'Oh, Mama, what is it?!'

It was my turn now for the trembling lips. Her use of the babyhood word, as always, dissolved my almost permanent state of irritation with her. I knew how I must look. I had felt the blood drain from my face into my sensible sandals, had felt my features distort into the kind of rictus seldom seen upon the living.

'You look as if you'd seen a ghost,' she whispered.

And so I have, I thought. But don't expect me to tell you about it. I dredged up the kind of brave little smile that I would have found obnoxious if seen on any other person. 'It's just the heat,' I muttered. 'I should never have eaten roast beef and Yorkshire pudding at lunchtime.'

Imogen still looked contrite. 'It's my fault,' she said. 'I was driving too fast. I know you feel poorly when travelling at anything over thirty miles an hour.'

My head came up, my shoulders straightened. 'Nonsense!' I said, 'and of course it's not your fault. Even you can't hold yourself responsible for the heatwave, dear.' I looked desperately for a diversion and saw a Walls' sign outside a shop.

'An ice-cream is what we need.' I began to walk, allowing her to take my arm, and was unexpectedly grateful for her support. I had come very close to collapsing beneath that copper beech, and not for the reasons I had given to my daughter.

The Asian shopkeeper spoke with a broad Dorset accent. He called me m'dear, smiled to show perfect teeth, kindly unwrapped my ice-cream and put the wrapper into his bin.

I came close to hitting Imogen when she asked him for a chair. 'My mother is feeling the heat,' she explained confidentially. 'Became a little faint when she left the car. If she could just sit down for a moment — ?'

At once he was all concern. A chair was brought, a glass of water. If he'd had a banyan leaf to hand he would have fanned me with it. It was well known that the Asian community took great care of their aged relations. He'd clearly had plenty of practice!

To be perfectly truthful I was rather glad to sit down. The shop was cool and shady. Mr Patel and Imogen, united by my elderly frailty, struck up a *sotto voce* conversation which, since her face was turned towards the grocer, I strained to hear.

'We are looking for a suitable property for my mother,' she told him, 'something quiet but nice. You know what I mean.'

He knew exactly what she meant. The village front gardens, he said, were bristling with estate agents' boards. Some houses had been on the market for over two years. The state of the economy was ruining his little business. When it came to a general election, he and his family would know precisely where to put their crosses on the voting papers.

While talking to Mr Patel my daughter underwent an amazing metamorphosis. I watched amazed as she licked her Strawberry Split and leaned nonchalantly sideways upon the counter. She began to tell this total stranger the most private financial details of Niall's business ventures. Although her face now turned towards me, it was easy to see that my presence was forgotten as the two of them became immersed in talk that was way above my head. Cash flow and liquidity and negative equity were what Fran would term their buzz words. In five minutes' conversation they had demolished and reformed the income tax and VAT systems, voted in a labour government and abolished the Monarchy and the House of Lords. Imogen was, I began to realise, knowledgeable and articulate in areas which meant nothing to me. I viewed her now with the deep respect I always award to people who know more than I do. Given the chance, she would make a most radical politician. I also began to understand that all was not well with Niall's business. Knowing that I was a little hard of hearing, Imogen spoke softly to Mr Patel. What she did not know, and I did not intend to tell her, was that I had, in the past year, become very proficient at reading lips.

This village was no different from all the others we had zipped through. The house agents' blurbs failed in every case to tell the full story. I wondered how accurate were the advertised details of my own property, and decided that any discrepancies would have to be Ashley Martindale's and the other party's worry.

We were about to give up, call it a day, and start the homeward drive when Imogen spied a positive bristling of House for Sale signs. She slowed and then halted beside an imposing board which informed us that we were about to enter HOMESTEADERS' VAL-

LEY. The sign also said that we were on the approach to a private road which led only to RANCHERS' CLOSE, FARMERS' CRESCENT AND PIONEER WAY.

For the first time that day I could feel a smile spread across my face. The laughter began to well up until I shook and spluttered.

'Oh,' I shrieked, 'this is absolutely priceless! It's bloody *Oklahoma!* without Howard Keel.' I regretted immediately the use of the b-word.

Imogen did not smile. 'It looks rather nice,' she said primly, and then more thoughtfully, 'a private road, mother. Now isn't that a promising feature?'

I said, 'Oh, come on! Homesteaders' Valley in the English West Country? It'll be one of those twee little enclaves where the wearing of chaps and ten-gallon hats is obligatory. There'll be rustling of apples from neighbours' back gardens and mini round-ups of stray cats and dogs in the autumn. There'll be hoe-downs and clambakes instead of barbecues and picnics.'

But Imogen was already turning into the private road, where the parking of non-residents' cars was Strictly Forbidden. We drove slowly past the forest of FOR SALE signs.

I said in a knowledgeable tone, 'A lot of negative equity about in this place.' I was not altogether certain what the phrase meant, but it earned me a respectful glance from my daughter.

We paused in Ranchers' Close. The houses, as Imogen pointed out, were large, detached, and of red-brick and half-timbered stucco elevations. She was beginning to sound like an estate agent's handout. 'Probably,' she went on, 'built about six years ago to a pretty high standard of perfection.'

I gazed at the elaborately landscaped gardens, the ruched-brocade curtains, the fake-farmhouse doors and gaudy stained-glass windows; the Volvos and sports cars slewed carelessly on gravelled drives. 'Yes,' I agreed, 'a very high standard indeed. Just the kind of cosy little shacks that would be bound to appeal to ranchers and farmers.'

Imogen drove on through Farmers' Crescent and out again, down Pioneer Way. She said, regretfully, 'No bungalows, not a single one. Well, isn't that disappointing.'

I maintained a diplomatic silence. I hardly needed to point out that the whole set-up had clearly been built for the yuppies of the nineteen eighties. Bungalows suitable for older widowed ladies had never been part of the grand design. We had reached the exit road of Homesteaders' Valley. I sank low in my seat, overcome by weariness and boredom when Imogen slowed and said, 'What's that funny little old house doing in amongst all these grand ones?'

The funny little old house stood some distance apart from the triangular design of the new estate. Its faded FOR SALE sign leaned at an acute angle and was almost concealed by the fuchsia bushes. We approached it down the steep and winding lane which led to Witches' Hollow. I remembered the fuchsia bushes.

Imogen pulled in and parked on the strip of baked earth which had always been a quagmire in winter. She opened my door and waited for me to climb out, but I could feel the return of weakness in my legs, even though seated.

'Oh,' I said brightly, 'it's so pretty, I'll just sit here for a moment and enjoy it!'

For once in her life she did not question my action. Niall's primary business was the renovation, and resale at a handsome profit, of shabby old cottages and houses. She walked away intent upon investigation.

I leaned back in my seat. I did not need to investigate the Toll House. My memories of it reached back over sixty years and more. It worried me that I had not recognised its location but I had been disorientated by the shoddy opulence of Homesteaders' Valley, and no wonder! I realised that the ground on which thirty houses now stood had once been soggy marshland, impossible to farm and difficult to graze or mow. Ladysmocks had grown there; and in springtime a mass of saffron crocus. A windmill had turned where Ranchers' Close met Farmers' Crescent.

I climbed from the car and stood for a moment, studying the cottage. The picket fence had been renewed, but nothing else of the golden stone structure had been altered. The tiny leaded-paned mullioned windows, the three tall crooked chimneys, the iron-strapped black oaken door were just as I remembered. The steeply pitched roof could do with attention; weeds grew between the flagstones of the garden path and around the doorstep. The roses, unpruned for many seasons, had reverted to their wild state, but delphiniums, hollyhocks and lupins, self-seeded over decades, remained as profuse as they had ever been. I pushed open the gate and walked up the familiar path. I used my handkerchief to wipe away the grime from the diamond-shaped window panes. The rooms were tinier than I remembered, dark with oaken panelling, and the smoke of three hundred years of open fires.

I was still peering in when Imogen rejoined me.

Her face was as bright as if she had just found the Koh-i-Noor diamond down a crack in the flagstones. 'A perfect gem!' she cried. 'I must get Niall out here as soon as possible.'

'Yes,' I said, 'that would also seem to be the next move on *my* agenda!'

She looked at me, uncertain if this was yet another of mother's tasteless jokes.

I took a pen and diary from my handbag. I leaned against the broad stone windowsill and peering at the sloping board I made a note of the estate agent's name and telephone number. Imogen stared as if I had grown an extra head.

'I have found my new home, dear!' I told her. 'We need to look no further. Niall can do whatever is needed in the way of repairs. I should be ready to move in here by the autumn.'

'But,' she said weakly, 'you haven't sold your own house yet. And in case you hadn't noticed, mother, this isn't a bungalow, it's a dark and poky little cottage.'

'A few minutes ago,' I reminded her, 'you

were calling it a perfect gem. Anyway — my mind is quite made up. My house is sure to be sold very shortly, and as for this not being a bungalow, well it really isn't that important. I don't always believe everything that gypsies tell me!'

As we drove away I noticed a recent addition to the Toll House as I had known it. An eight-foot-high wooden fence, its attempt at privacy reinforced by a dense line of conifers, now stood between the houses in Homesteaders' Valley and the boglike bottom known as Witches' Hollow.

The drive home was made at the sedate pace of a royal cortège. Perversely, and silently, I willed Imogen to put her foot down, but she was in the mood to dawdle. The sun was no longer directly overhead and scorching; a pleasant breeze came up, there were dark clouds banked on the horizon. We came to a café which had parasols fixed over garden tables. Imogen insisted on buying tea for both of us. The menu listed speciality teas. I ordered Lapsang Suchong.

My daughter raised her eyebrows. 'I didn't know you liked anything more exotic than Typhoo?'

She does not often catch me on the wrong foot. There was no reason why I should be embarrassed by the idle question. But I was.

I said, 'Well — I never actually *buy* it.' I hesitated. 'I sometimes drink it in restaurants and cafés, if it's on the menu.'

'But why not drink Lapsang more often if you really like it?'

'Oh.' I tried to sound dismissive. 'You know how your father liked his tea — hot, and made strong enough to stand the spoon up in it. The very name Lapsang Suchong would have had him laughing. As for the smoky flavour of it — !'

Imogen said, with an insight that alarmed me, 'Mum. He's not here any more.' Her voice was gentle. 'Stop behaving as if Dad is looking over your shoulder. He wouldn't have wanted you to do that.'

I clenched my fists beneath the table; if I'd had an answer for her I could not have voiced it.

We drank our tea to the sounds of an approaching storm.

It was one of those nights when I knew that I would not sleep. The storm had moved slowly from the north of the county; it broke above the city late in the evening. Roscoe, in his basket, whined and looked to me for reassurance. I patted his head and told him not to worry.

I reflected that Roscoe, in Jack's lifetime, would never have feared the approaching storm. Imogen had said that I should stop behaving as though Jack was looking over my shoulder. That he would not have wanted me to do that. I knew that she was right. What I could not explain, what she would never comprehend, was the emotional and practical dependence of the women of my generation upon their husbands; a dependence which death could not seem to change. I was eighteen years old when Jack and I married. Within two years I had become a mother and a housewife. Jack and Imogen became my whole life, my reason for living. I never looked for company or interests beyond my home and family.

Fifty years on, and it was hard to change the habits of a lifetime. I should have said to Imogen, 'If you haven't walked in my shoes, how can you tell me where to go?'

I sat beside the open bedroom window and watched the lightning fork above the crenellations of the prison walls. I thought about the men, locked in their cells. From a high-security gaol there is seldom hope of a release. Since Jack's death, the house I had cherished in his lifetime had become my prison, and Jack could no longer make my decisions for me.

The rain came suddenly, cooling the air.

I remembered the recent day, the odd exchanges between Imogen and me, the way we had hovered on the very brink of a closer understanding, and then retreated. I came finally to the matter which stood foremost in my mind. The Toll House; the dilapidated cottage which in my childhood imaginings had been a habitation of fairies and hobgoblins. I recalled the elderly woman who had lived there; the thin silver bun of coiled hair atop her head, a starched snow-white apron reaching down to the tops of her black boots. Butterflies and birds had flocked into that garden. The old lady could be seen in the fields in the very early mornings, collecting grasses and wild flowers. The area now known as Homesteaders' Valley had been soggy marshland then, its lower reaches impossible to drain. The land had obviously been bought cheaply by some speculative builder. Those luxury houses would be attractive only while still relatively new. A few more years and the gravelled drives would sink and become uneven; mould would spot the coloured stucco, and disfigure the expensive hand-coloured wallpaper and paintwork. The clothes in the wardrobes would feel damp to the touch. The manufacturers of humidifiers were probably already doing a roaring trade among the Homesteaders.

Damp, like depression, is insidious and destructive, and almost impossible to eradicate, even though its source is known.

The storm rolled away towards morning. I slept for an hour, and to my surprise, awoke rejuvenated. I showered, dressed, clipped on Roscoe's lead and with my hair still wet I walked down to the café and ordered the full breakfast.

Anna said, 'You're looking happy! What happened? You won the Lotteria, Nina?'

I told her about the Toll House, its convenient proximity to Fran and Mitch, and the expected baby.

'All I need to do now,' I said, 'is to sell my house at a good price.'

Imogen phoned me later that morning. I was told that I must not make a move regarding the little old house until Niall had talked to me about it. They would come over that evening and we would thrash the whole thing out. She was phoning from her office and needed to be brief, for which blessing I was thankful!

I laid down the handset and reached for the telephone directory. I needed the address of the estate agent who was handling the sale of the Toll House. If I wished to be informed and in control of matters, I would need to visit his office straight away.

The overnight storm had washed the streets clean and cooled the air. The office I sought was conveniently close to Infirmary Avenue. It turned out to be dim and shabby, little more than a hole in the wall, and open only in the afternoons. I must have passed it a thousand times without noticing through the dusty window-glass the faded, curling advertisements for inexpensive houses and commercial properties. An old-fashioned bell, suspended above the door, 'pinged' as I went in.

He sat at a small oaken desk which stood to the rear of a scarred wooden counter. Antique bills of sale for farm implements and land, hung in heavy frames on every foot of wall space. Brown linoleum covered the floor; a bentwood chair provided the only seating. The telephone was the candle-stick type seen in old black-and-white films.

His age, and the fact that I had inter-rupted his siesta, dispelled my nervousness and made me smile. I also dozed after lunch, given half a chance. He smiled back. He said, 'What can I do for you, madam?' His appearance, his clipped speech reminded me vaguely of General Bernard Montgomery. Perhaps it was the military-style moustache, the short-back-and-sides cut of his grey hair, the erectness of his bearing, when fully awake? He was, I thought, a man who had once been addressed as 'sir' by a lot of people.

I said, 'The Toll House, out towards Ashkeepers. It's been on your books for a long time.'

'Most of our properties,' he said, 'have been on the books for a long time.' There was no note of regret in his voice, no hint that his inability to do fast business might categorise him as a failure.

'I would like some details,' I told him, 'especially the price.' I realised as I spoke that I could never have approached Ashley Martindale in so uninhibited and business-like a manner. Perhaps Imogen was right, perhaps I was ageist in my outlook. It was true that since Jack had died I could feel comfortable only with people of my own generation. Except, of course, for Fran. But my relationship with her was special, and like no other I had ever known.

'Ah,' he said, 'the price. Why now, that is of course negotiable.'

'It would have to be,' I said. 'I was over there yesterday with my daughter. A lot of work will need to be done to make the place habitable.'

'It is a listed building,' he demurred. I could see that the historical aspect of the Toll House was all he could truthfully offer me in its favour. I could also see that he was a man of honour.

'Listed surely means,' I said, 'that a buyer will be limited when it comes to making improvements and alterations.'

'Quite so. But I would say you are a lady of some discernment. I could hardly imagine you wanting to put in white plastic windows and front door, or applying pink paint to the stone walls.'

He paused, then said uncertainly, 'I could run you over there if you like? You could have a look around, see how you feel about it. That's if you're really interested, of course.'

'Oh, I am really interested. I'd be grateful if you could show me around. It's so difficult to make a proper judgement from the outside.'

I could see by his expression that he did not think me foolish or annoyingly indecisive.

He said, 'How about tomorrow morning, then? About half-past ten?'

'Fine,' I said. 'I'll meet you outside the Italian café in College Walk.' He looked surprised; he had clearly expected to collect me from my own front door. But I had no intention of giving out my home address to a total stranger. I am not a trusting person. Especially where money and business is concerned.

I had neglected to ask his name. The signboard had said J. and B. Properties Ltd. He arrived in College Walk the next morning, ten minutes late and apologetic. I sat at a pavement table which was shaded by the café's dark green awning. Heads turned as the vintage sports car rolled up to the kerb and halted. At first I gazed disinterestedly at the gleaming maroon paintwork and sparkling chrome. It was not until he left the car and walked towards me that I recognised him as the man who had promised to collect me. If I had thought at all about his means of transport I would have placed him in a battered Ford.

Today he was dressed to match his vehicle, cavalry twill trousers, old school tie, and a well-cut blazer in a shade of deep maroon. I rose to meet him feeling thoroughly inadequate in my cotton frock and sandals. His military air was even more pronounced this morning.

He had been delayed, he said, by his inability to at first find the keys which would open up the Toll House doors. It had been so long since anyone had wished to view the property. Fortunately, his partner kept a spare set at home in his private safe.

He drove as smoothly and efficiently as Jack had driven, without the jerky stops and starts and the furious histrionics I have noticed in younger male drivers. The car was a dream, it floated, almost flew. I seldom enjoy motor travel, but in this car I loved it; I expressed interest in its make and age, and he talked happily about it. We were out of the city and heading north when I said, belatedly. 'I'm afraid I don't know exactly who you are.'

'Barnacle,' he said. 'George Barnacle, known as Monty to my friends.'

Stifling the urge to laugh brought tears to my eyes. I controlled my features with enormous effort. His likeness to Field Marshal Lord Montgomery of Alamein was so extraordinary that it did not surprise me that his friends called him Monty.

But Barnacle?

Was there such a surname or had he invented it?

'And you?' he asked. 'May I know your name?'

'Nina. Nina Franklin.' I settled into my seat, feeling unusually relaxed. I studied his profile, clothed him in khaki battledress, placed an angled black beret on his head, a swagger-stick in his hand. A widower, I decided, army officer, retired and living alone in a service flat; this car and its care would be his single hobby and passion. A sad and childless man for whom I should feel sorry.

I told myself to get a grip, to stop the fantasising. I remembered Sorsha and the sketches which turned out to be of her and at the same time someone else. This habit of mine, of imposing dual personalities and alternative lifestyles on perfect strangers, was becoming obsessive and could actually be dangerous. But even as these doubts floated through my mind, I was despatching poor Mr Barnacle back to nineteen forty-two, banishing him into the Libyan campaign in which he would pursue the German Field Marshal Rommel all the way to Tripoli and back. I then compensated him by elevating him to the peerage, and dubbing him Lord Montgomery of Alamein who, on his death, was to be given a state funeral.

We came to the village by the direct route; minus the detours made with Imogen it was closer to the city than I had imagined. I was braced this time against the shock of the village green, the copper beech tree. We drove into the main street and out again to

Homesteaders' Valley. Mr Barnacle parked briefly in Ranchers' Close. He said, 'You mentioned that you had recently looked at the Toll House.'

'Yes. I came out here with Imogen, my daughter. We were looking for a suitable bungalow.' I waved a hand at the executive homes. 'Instead we found this musical-comedy set-up.'

His lips twitched, his head tipped back and he roared with laughter. 'My thoughts exactly,' he spluttered. 'We had this estate on our books when it was first planned. I could hardly keep a straight face when people began to come into the office and ask for details. Of course they were all young folk, the upwardly mobile mob, described at that time as yuppies and reared on American soap operas and spaghetti Westerns. I often noticed that they seemed to find a kind of glamour in the street names. Just to live in a place called Homesteaders' Valley seemed romantic to them.'

I felt more than ever relaxed in his company knowing that we shared the same quirky sense of humour.

He studied the houses within our view. 'Looking shabby already,' he said. 'Well, that doesn't surprise me. Sharp operator, that builder, but he had no luck at all from the day he sank the first footings. Everything went wrong that could go wrong with this particular project, and he'd always been such a successful man.'

Mr Barnacle switched on the ignition and we floated downhill in to Brickyard Lane. He helped me from the car, his hand beneath my elbow. I should have been wearing a long frock and a floppy hat swathed in chiffon as did Dinah Sheridan in the film *Genevieve*. I was, I thought, fated always to be wearing the wrong outfit in any significant situation. I opened the picket gate and stood among the fuchsias. I knew that I had reached a turning-point, that a decision made now would determine the course of what was left to me of life and living. But I knew too that when it came to making that decision, I would be as certain as I had been fifty years ago, when Jack and I had married.

He invited me to call him either 'George' or 'Monty', for which dispensation I was very grateful. I could not trust myself to remain po-faced when addressing him as 'Mr Barnacle'; as for using the nickname 'Monty', the risk of further fantasising on it was too great. We were standing before the door of the Toll House and about to enter.

' "George",' I said, 'will do very nicely. I am Nina.'

We had arrived at this stage of exchanging first names in the space of one fairly short car journey. Imogen would not have approved of such familiarity in her mother. Fran would be delighted and amused when I told her about it.

The door creaked open on stiff hinges. There was a powerful smell of damp and mice and old dust. From the tiny hallway three doors led off into two small living rooms and what appeared to be a single-storey room used as a makeshift kitchen. A staircase rose abruptly, its final treads invisible in the dim light of the upper regions. Festoons of cobwebs hung in every corner. I longed to rush about throwing open windows and doors, letting in the sunlight and the perfumed air from the rambling garden. I asked George if he knew how long the Toll House had stood empty. He wasn't sure. It was vacant when the building of Homesteaders' Valley had begun. From the state of the furnishings and fixtures it had been unoccupied for several years.

I began to study in detail those furnishings and fixtures. I was reminded strongly of my grandmother's house, and that of my Aunt Hannah. Here was the same endearing mixture of staid Victoriana and gaudy nineteen-thirties Woolworth's Art Deco. Most of the soft furnishings were stained and mildewed beyond repair. A man who offered house-clearance services advertised regularly in the city newspaper. I caught myself making mental lists of what I would keep or dispose of; the thought never crossed my mind that I would not soon be living in this house, I was able to say to George, when only half-way up the stairs, 'I've seen enough. I'll buy it!'

To my surprise, he showed no enthusiasm at my swift decision. The house had, on his own admission, been on the books for several years. He and his partner must long ago have given up all hope of selling. I had, mistakenly, been seeing myself as a client heaven-sent to these clearly unsuccessful house agents. As we moved through the rooms he began seriously to dissuade me from purchase, pointing out defects I had already noticed and dismissed as trivial.

'Nothing that my son-in-law can't fix,' I assured him.

We were standing at the window of the rear bedroom when George Barnacle pointed out the line of tall conifers and the high wooden fence which bordered the vegetable garden.

He said, 'There is something rather un-usual down there that your son-in-law *can't* fix. On the other side of that demarcation line, down in the Hollow, is a family of travellers. They live there on and off, ac-cording to the season. They own the land, which means that they think they can regu-larly flout the law. They are definitely not the sort of neighbours for a lady who is living on her own.'

I smiled at his intensity. 'There have al-ways been gypsies camped in Witches' Hol-low,' I told him. 'They were there when I was a small child; and that is long enough ago! Put yourself in their place! If you and your family had lived in the same spot for three hundred years and more, I think you too would feel you had a prior right to be there. As far as those travellers are con-cerned,' I said, 'it will be the Ranchers' Close mob, the Homesteader yuppies, who are the interlopers.'

He said, 'Well, at least bring your son-in-law out here. If you won't be advised by me, then perhaps you will listen to what he has to say.' He paused. 'I don't want to sell you a property in which you are at risk of being unhappy, if not actually frightened.'

I smiled. 'Mr Barnacle — I have lived for most of my life beneath the walls of the high-security prison in Infirmary Avenue. You may rest assured that I do not frighten easily! As for my son-in-law — I will listen to what he has to say, and then I will do precisely what I intended to do in the first place.'

We drove back to the city in almost total silence. At my request he returned me to the café in College Walk. I released the seat belt and picked up my handbag. I took a sideways glance at his stony profile. I said, 'Look — it's good of you to be so concerned about my welfare. If it will ease your conscience I'll take Niall to view the house tomorrow.'

I could hear the note of pleading in my voice, and almost laughed aloud at the bizarre situation in which I was begging to be allowed to buy a house which had stood empty and rejected for twenty years or more. 'But I must warn you,' I continued, 'I intend to make a firm offer for it no matter what my family says.'

I had the car door open and one foot on the pavement when I added, 'Oh, by the way — who is the owner of the Toll House?'

'I am,' said George Barnacle. 'The Toll House belongs to me.'

Poppy phoned late that afternoon. It

seemed that as she was about to close the office, two separate clients had shown interest in my house. Appointments were made for them to view at seven and eight o'clock respectively. Once again I tidied, polished, vacuumed, while Roscoe hid beneath the kitchen table. At seven precisely I opened the door to a small family; parents and a boy who told me he was eight years old. They were pleasant people. They admired, without prompting, the best features of the house. The child, who was very well behaved, lingered beside, but did not touch, Jack's chess set which stood on a low table in the sitting room, and my doll's house in the window bay. When they had visited each room twice, we came together finally in the kitchen.

The house, although very nice, they said regretfully, was rather too large for their requirements. I asked, timidly, if the proximity of the gaol had affected their decision.

The unlikely answer was that they had hardly noticed the high prison walls, the searchlights and alarm systems. It was as they stood in the porch and about to depart that the offer came.

'That is a very fine antique desk which stands in your dining room,' said the father of the family. Unsuspicious and gratified I agreed and said it was a family heirloom, inherited by my late husband from his grandfather. We began to discuss the history of the desk; I was asked if my husband had inherited any other items. I said there was the chess set and a little walnut table, and still I did not suspect the motive behind the questions.

The child stood quietly between his parents; he was, I thought, abnormally good for an eight-year-old; he was in fact better trained than Roscoe, who would by this time have been pulling at his lead and anxious to be gone.

The proposal came almost as an afterthought, tossed across the departing man's shoulder. 'Oh — by the way — if you should ever want to sell that desk and any other old items, I would be interested in doing business with you. After all, if you are moving to a small place you'll need to dispose of quite a bit of furniture, won't you? I could save you the bother of advertising.' He pressed a small white card into my hand. 'My name and phone number, and thanks for allowing us to look round.'

I closed the door and went into the kitchen. I switched on the kettle and reflected that people were not always what they appeared to be. The experience had made me nervous. There was no time to summon Imogen and Niall before the arrival of my second set of viewers. I envisaged my elderly, vulnerable self and Victorian house on the visiting list of every unscrupulous antique dealer in the city and district.

I made a strong coffee and positioned myself in a window which would give me a good view of the street and the approach to my front door. Any doubt in my mind as to the genuineness of clients mark two, and they would ring the bell in vain!

I saw them coming from quite a distance, walking slowly and holding hands along the pavement which lay beneath the prison wall. They were young, very young. I knew at once that these were my prospective buyers; they had that air of scarcely suppressed excitement shown by children who are embarked on a great adventure. I remembered Jack and me, fifty years ago, walking that same pavement, looking up at the house for the first time, and knowing we had found our home. I opened the door before the young man's finger had lifted from the bell-push.

It was the girl who introduced them. 'Lindsey,' she smiled, holding out her hand, 'and this is my partner, Darren.'

'Nina,' I said, clasping hands in turn. If

informality was their approach then I could be equally informal.

Once again I began the Grand Tour, commencing this time with the ground-floor rooms and patio. Lindsey loved the patio and kitchen. Darren favoured the beamed ceilings and mahogany window-frames. We were halfway up the stairs when Darren halted. 'I've seen enough,' he said. 'We'll buy it!'

'Oh no,' I said. 'You can't decide that quickly. You must look at all of it.' I left them to explore the bedrooms and the attic. I waited for them in the dining room; they came back smiling. Lindsey said, 'We love it. We'll see the estate agent first thing tomorrow morning.'

The speed of their decision amazed me. I supposed there had been a time when Jack and I had been similarly impulsive. 'But I want you to be sure,' I said. 'Why don't you go round again. Be absolutely certain.'

'We are,' said Darren.

# Sorsha

Sorsha's little world was ruled by omens, superstition and taboos. Stories of vampires, werewolves, and the power of the evil eye were as familiar to her as the plots of soap-operas viewed nightly on the television. She believed in the existence of fairies, brownies and pixies with the same unquestioning ease as she accepted the reality of her parents and brothers, and of Kingdom, her colourful husband.

Of one thing she was absolutely certain, that evil and ill-fortune ruled the world of travelling people; that goodness was a *gorgio* invention, and that pregnancy and childbirth were desperate times for the child and its mother. There were rituals and rites by which such dangers might be overcome. Certain hospitals were considered to be 'lucky' should a woman be so unfortunate as to require the services of the medical profession. Certain churches were known to be possessed of a powerful magic regarding the Christian baptism of an infant. A journey of many miles would have to be undertaken should the baby be born at some distance from the 'lucky' church.

Sometimes fortune and misfortune came in equal portions to a family. It could be said that Sorsha's ill-luck was in having a mysterious internal condition which might harm her child. Her 'saving' would be in the nearness of a hospital well-known for its 'good-luck' reputation. Not a single traveller infant had ever been known to die in that place.

The van swung into the approach road which led up to Accident and Emergency and the main entrance doors of the Royal Infirmary. On their first visit she had read aloud to King the words on the painted boards which gave directions to various hospital departments. He had shown no sign that he had heard her, he pretended to believe that reading and writing were of no importance; and when he learned from the book that told all about Elvis Presley that the singer had also rarely attended school, Kingdom's beliefs had been confirmed. She had pointed out to him that if she herself had not been a scholar, and able to read aloud the Presley book, then King would never have known such details about his idol. But the argument had left him bewildered. Sorsha had concluded, from his lack of grasp, that Kingdom was past saving. She took a sly and secret pleasure from the knowledge. One-upmanship was important to the women in a culture which, for centuries, had encouraged the males to behave as if they owned the world.

Kingdom halted just long enough for Perla and her to climb from the van and walk through the clever doors which, when approached, opened by themselves. He would not go inside with them. He would not even emerge from the driver's seat to set his foot on Infirmary ground.

'So what about afterwards?' she had demanded. 'What happens when it's born? Do you want to stand out in the street, and have me come to a window and jiggle the *chavvie* up and down for you to look at?'

'Afterwards is different,' he had muttered. She knew exactly what he meant, what his problem was, and the knowledge struck her silent. Kingdom would set foot in the Infirmary only if the baby lived.

For Perla's sake, once inside the hospital walls, Sorsha showed a confidence she did not feel. They walked through the carpeted bit that was called reception, past the dispensary which gave out medicines and pills, past the flower shop and the booth which sold chocolate and newspapers. They turned into the corridor marked with a sign which said MR ROBINSON. CLINIC. They sat on the very end of a long row of chairs. Sorsha pulled from the pocket of her dress a grubby battered card which listed previous appointments. It felt, she thought, as though she had been attending this place for years instead of months. Kingdom's mother had wanted to come with her. Since the early days of pregnancy when Sorsha almost lost the baby, her mother-in-law had tried to take over her life and Kingdom's and the fate of the unborn child. Sorsha had listened attentively to Mr Robinson's explanations and instructions. She read the leaflets he gave her about not smoking, and vitamins and proper diet. For a long time now her head had been distracted by the conflicting *gorgio* doctor's advice, and the ancient beliefs of her own people which taught that an infant, from the moment of conception, is threatened by evil forces, by all the demons of the world. No matter how many iron pills she swallowed, no matter how many oranges she ate, these *gorgio* tricks could not save her baby from the powers of evil if the Devil meant to take her. She had half-inclined towards King's belief that if she had not learned to read she would never have had the knowledge to worry about the possible dangers described in the *Your First Baby* book and the hospital leaflets.

In the end she had compromised, but secretly. She let it be known that smoking made her feel nauseous, that strong tea gave her indigestion. She swallowed the pills and ate the fruit in the evenings when King was in the pub. Magic was still magic, no matter what the source.

The heat and stuffy atmosphere of indoors made her head swim. When her name was finally called she rose and swayed, and Perla caught her arm and made to go with her into the doctor's room. But she pushed King's sister away, not wishing her to see, and later tell King and his mother about the needle which drained blood from her arm, and the other indignities forced on the private places of her body.

Things went much as usual in the little room that smelled of hospital and sickness. She said yes, she was taking her pills and resting. Yes, she had long ago told her husband he must sleep alone and on the spare bunk. Sorsha smiled when she remembered King's reception of the *gorgio* doctor's instruction. 'What the hell does he take me for!' King had shouted. 'I don't need any hospital quack to tell me that. Does he think I'm an animal or something?'

When her clothing had been made decent, and the blood taken from her arm, the doctor smiled. 'So far — so good,' he told her, 'but you still need to be careful. No strenuous activity. No sudden shocks. Another week and I hope to be handing you a beautiful little daughter. You've made all arrangements to get here, I trust? If there's any problem, ring the ambulance service.'

'Another week?'

'Maybe less,' he said. 'In fact, as I've said before, I would like you to come into hospital at once.'

'I'll need to think about that,' she said. But she wouldn't think about it, not for a second.

Sorsha walked slowly back to where Perla was waiting for her. 'Any day now' could mean tomorrow, could mean this evening, or even worse, this very minute. Terror made her mind blank, she looked at the two women seated next to Perla and did not at first recognise either of them. When recognition came she felt her legs give way, her stomach turn.

Perla stood up and pushed Sorsha down

onto the vacant chair. 'You's is looking awful sick,' she whispered. 'Bide and rest a minute and I'll fetch a drink of water.'

Sorsha sat, her head bent low to fight the faintness. She drank the water Perla brought her. 'I'se all right now,' she whispered, 'let's go from here. Kingdom'll be waiting on us.'

Ten paces from the row of chairs she turned and looked deliberately back at the two women. She had not been mistaken, it was the artist woman from the house beside the prison wall. The young one sitting with her could be a granddaughter. Whoever she was, the cheeky mare was wearing the exact same maternity dress as Sorsha, bought at the Next shop in the city, and very expensive too! From the look of her, the girl was also due to give birth 'any day now'.

Meeting the artist woman must be seen as a bad omen. Although they had not spoken, each had recognised the other. It had to signify something! It could not be coincidence that the woman's close kin should be here in this place on the same day as Sorsha, wearing the same dress, seeing the same doctor, and also near her time.

Sorsha tried hard to forget about what had happened between herself and the *gorgio* woman. Their separate lives should never have touched — but they had touched.

There should never have been any link between them — but the link was there. The woman should not have been allowed to put Sorsha's likeness down on paper; something bad had happened in that dark brown kitchen. The woman, through her drawing, had called up the *mullo* of Sorsha's great-great-grandmother, who was said to have had her firstborn son stolen from her. That such a ghost should make itself known to Sorsha by means of a drawing, and at this dangerous time, was open to interpretation. It could be said that this spirit had appeared for the purpose of protection and out of love. On the other hand, not all *mullos* were well-disposed towards the living; the appearance of this one in the *gorgio* woman's sketch could also be taken as a warning of coming troubles. If only Sorsha could talk about it all, but such relief was denied her. She should never have gone into the *gorgio* house in the first place.

Questions, put casually, about this great-great-grandmother had been swiftly rebuffed by those who knew the answers. Well, what else had she expected? There were rules about these things. The name of the departed one could never be spoken lest the spirit should grow restless and return to cause trouble. The actual camp-site where a death takes place is avoided forever as a place in which to pitch by the relatives of the deceased.

Sorsha had never, until now, shown any interest in her forbears. Her present, unhealthy preoccupation with such matters was put down to her condition by King and his mother.

The single bit of information let slip by Aunt Dru, when questioned, was that the great-great-grandmother, whose name nobody dared to utter, and whose likeness hung on a museum wall in London, had died violently and horribly beneath the beech tree, on the triangle of green grass in the nearby village of Ashkeepers.

# Nina

It was said to be the hottest summer since nineteen seventy-six.

By the end of June there was a ban on the watering of lawns and gardens, the washing of cars was forbidden, showers instead of baths was a suggestion which was really an order, although how it could be enforced was difficult to see.

Night brought no relief from the heavy heat.

I sat for hours by the open bedroom window, while my neighbours crept surreptitiously through the darkness, running hose pipes and sprinklers unlawfully to grass and flower beds. I could hardly blame them. I watered the patio tubs and hanging baskets in the early morning. I considered it my duty to keep everything fresh and flowering for Lindsey and Darren, who had generously said that they did not mind at all about the closeness of the prison walls. I thought constantly about Francesca who was suffering badly in the endless heat. The baby was already two weeks overdue. A few more days, she had been told, and labour would have to be induced.

The legal details of my house sale and the purchase of the Toll House limped along at an irritatingly slow pace. I had, in the end, been obliged to lower my asking price in order to achieve what Poppy described as a firm sale. I went down to the estate agent's office and invited Ashley Martindale to laugh and say, 'I told you so!' But he was uncritical and kind and said that my hopes of obtaining a higher figure had been perfectly valid and understandable, and he was sorry it had not worked out. I now found myself regarding him with something close to affection. I even managed to leave his office without awarding him yet another alternative lifestyle.

The situation with George Barnacle was not so rosy. My attitudes towards him veered from mild annoyance to outright anger.

My solicitor complained about him. She was finding him uncooperative and sometimes obstructive. 'Anyone would think,' she said, 'that the wretched man didn't want to sell the Toll House.'

A date for the exchange of contracts had been set, optimistically, for mid-August. I was beginning to see why Mr Barnacle's friends had nicknamed him Monty. Apart from his uncanny physical likeness to the deceased Field Marshal, he had, when challenged, the same clipped, almost ill-mannered way of speaking, the thin-lipped expression of annoyance that Montgomery had shown in TV documentaries about the desert war. If he persisted with his delaying tactics, George Barnacle and I would be exchanging hard words. Meanwhile, my energy was drained by the continuing hot weather, and a growing anxiety about Fran's condition.

It was Niall who persuaded J. & B. Properties to loan us the keys of the Toll House for twenty-four hours, so that the extent of the much-needed renovations might be assessed. Imogen had packed a picnic lunch and we made a little holiday of that Sunday trip into the country. I asked for Imogen's advice on every aspect of the changes and decorations. I would not necessarily act upon her suggestions, but she no longer felt herself abandoned by my move out of the city and closer to Francesca.

Francesca! Every time I thought about her

now she was linked in my mind with a shadowy outline of Sorsha, who had, amazingly, been present in the ante-natal clinic, wearing the identical black and white dress and with the same look of weary resignation on her face.

As we arrived back at Imogen's house on that Sunday evening the telephone was ringing. Silly to say that a bell can sound meaningful and special, but this one did. We could hear Niall's deep voice answering, apprehensive at first, and then full of joy. He laid down the receiver and turned towards us, smiling.

'That was Mitch. Fran went into labour at midnight. She gave birth to a son at five this afternoon. Mother and baby are both very well!'

Imogen and I did sums in our heads, and reached simultaneously the same figure. 'Seventeen hours of labour,' my daughter whispered. 'Oh, my poor girl.'

'Well, it's all over now,' Niall sighed. He turned towards the drinks tray. 'I think we need a small reviver after such terrific news.'

Imogen, true to form, said at once, 'Not for you, darling. You have yet to drive Mother home, remember!'

I took the bottle from Niall's hand and filled the glasses to the brim. 'I'll walk home,' I said firmly. 'I'll stagger or crawl, if need be. But on this occasion, we will all three of us really push the boat out.'

# Sorsha

They had gone to a wedding on that Sunday morning, all of them, Manju and his family, Aunt Drusilla and her daughters, Sorsha's grandmother, parents, and her seven brothers and their families. They had roared away up Brickyard Lane while the air was still cool, the children waving from the cabs of Land Rovers and from brand-new brightly painted vans and pick-ups. Everyone had put on their finest outfits; the women had dressed one another's hair with ribbons and flower sprays; all their rings and earrings and gold sovereign pendants and brooches were on rich display.

Sorsha lay on the striped green-and-white garden lounger which Kingdom had recently bought from the Argos shop in the city. The silence of the *tan* was oppressive. From the trailer came the sound of Kingdom's heavy snoring. She could feel a scream welling in her throat. How dared he sleep so well when she lay wakeful through every night. She looked up into the shading branches of the oak tree to where a nesting pair of blackbirds came and went. She wondered if it hurt the female bird when she laid her eggs. Sorsha feared the process of childbirth more than fire or drowning; she told herself that the twinges of pain felt in the past few days meant nothing. She moved uneasily on the lounger. The pains were coming now, this minute; she willed them to cease. She had tried to tell Kingdom of her terror, but he had said that the baby inside her was growing bigger every day. If it stayed there much longer it would be too big to get born. She could see that Kingdom thought it was Sorsha's fault that the child was overdue. In the hours when she dozed the same nightmare always woke her. In her dream the baby had grown to the size of a two-year-old child who could speak its needs and was shouting from inside her to get out. The baby doctor had said often that she should come into the hospital to await the birth, and now the pain caught her unawares; it was not the dull backache or the twinges of the past few days, but a sharp agony which made her cry out for her mother. But her mother was gone, gallivanting up the country to a cousin's wedding party. Sorsha wept tears of chagrin and self-pity. She might have known that this was how it would work out. She had been abandoned in her darkest hour with only that lummox of a Kingdom to depend on. Perhaps she should have stayed in hospital like the doctor said, but the very thought of those brick walls made her feel sick. And to top it all, today was her seventeenth birthday.

Her second scream brought Kingdom tumbling from the trailer. His long black hair, fallen from its Presley quiff, hung in oiled locks across his face. Even in her state of terror she wondered how he could still look so handsome when dressed only in the Mickey Mouse patterned underpants she had given him at Christmas, and with sleep gumming up his eyelids. He stood white-faced and trembling beside the lounger. 'You can't have it now,' he shouted, 'not when there's only me here.'

His panic was a wonder to behold. It had the instant effect of making Sorsha calm and totally in charge.

'Steady up, you daft bugger!' she said coldly. She dared to swear only when her parents were absent. 'Wash your face, comb your hair and put your shirt and jeans on. I'll not go at all to that hospital with you looking like a toe-rag!' She eased herself with difficulty from the lounger and into the trailer where a small holdall was packed ready according to hospital instructions. Between pains she tied the lucky green ribbon in her hair, and pushed the silver-mounted hare's foot into the deep pocket of her dress. Having done all she could to ensure her own safety and that of the baby, Sorsha went out to sit beside Kingdom in the van.

She sat for several minutes while King attempted to fire the engine. The intervals between bouts of pain were growing shorter. King had her sitting in the driving seat manipulating knobs and levers while he messed about beneath the bonnet. Several times the engine spluttered, almost caught, and then died. King ran to the shed behind their trailer; he returned pushing the gleaming Harley Davidson motorbike that was the main love of his life.

'I can't,' screamed Sorsha. 'You wouldn't make me ride pillion, would you? Not in this state?'

They exchanged mutual glances of pure terror.

'There's no help for it,' King said. 'I can't birth a baby and that's that!'

'Oh,' she gasped, 'well now, you do surprise me! I would of thought your old mother had give you instructions how to do that, like she does about everything else.'

King meanwhile had straddled the bike, revved the powerful engine and was ready to go. 'Come on now,' he yelled, 'there's no other way to get you there in time!'

Sorsha lay in the high white hospital bed, her face turned towards the wall. Her tears soaked the pillow and the front of her night-dress. She was sore and aching; so sore and stiff she was certain that childbirth had ruined all her vital parts for ever.

She felt tenderised from head to foot as if she had fallen off a mountain and rolled over sharp rocks. All her resolve to be brave and silent in the *gorgio* hospital had been forgotten. She could still hear her own screams and swear words, the shameful grunting noises they had encouraged her to make. Courage and resolve had flown out of the window when the business really got started. The pains she had suffered while still in the *tan* were like pinpricks compared to the actual birthing. King had been invited by the doctor to stay and hold her hand and rub her back. She had said, between clenched teeth, 'Get him out of here before you have to pick him off the floor. I won't have him near me, no I won't!' She had become so hysterical that King had been pushed protesting from the delivery room; but not before she had seen the relieved look on his face.

He had come back when it was over. He had taken the news of a daughter with more fortitude than Sorsha had expected. He had kissed Sorsha's forehead and said she was his grand brave girl, and how much he loved her, and always would do.

'All right for you,' she had muttered, 'you haven't just had your insides tore out.'

He didn't understand what she had gone through. There were times when, for all his beauty, she couldn't stand the sight of King. She was shaken with a fresh burst of sobbing. The rest of them would still be at the wedding, not knowing or caring what had happened to her. By this time they would all be merry and dancing.

There were two beds in the room; the curtains were patterned with blue and pink flowers, there was a wash basin in a corner, and beyond an inner door she could glimpse a tiny bathroom. The other bed was empty, as was the cradle at Sorsha's side. She had held the baby for a minute or two when the birth was over, then the *chavvie* had been taken away by a doctor to be examined and have tests done on her. In those few minutes when the child was in her arms, Sorsha had gazed hard at the baby's face, fixing the tiny features in her memory, the thick black hair, the button nose, the rounded head, the blue-tinged colour of her. She had read the newspapers and watched on television the accounts of newborn babies who had been stolen from maternity units, or who got mixed up by careless nurses and handed out to the wrong parents. In the likely event that some evil thieving woman already prowled the wards, Sorsha made sure that she would knew her own daughter among a million others.

The door began to open, rubber-soled shoes squeaked across the floor, she closed her eyes and feigned sleep. A bright voice said, 'Well here she is, Sorsha! We shall have to do a few more tests, but as far as we can tell, she's a very healthy young lady.' The nurse went away. Sorsha opened her eyes, leaned over the cradle and checked that the baby was truly hers. She touched the tightly curled fingers, the downy head, and relief spread through her body making her weak and bringing on fresh tears. She slept uneasily, waking when the door opened once again to admit a trolley. She watched through half-closed eyes as the newcomer and her baby were installed in the far corner.

It was the girl she had seen in the antenatal clinic! It was the artist woman's granddaughter!

Well, it would be, wouldn't it? Such happenings were already set out in the Big Book where all the days of Sorsha's life were numbered.

The *gorgio* girl had long fair hair that hung down past her shoulders; she was very pale, there were dark smudges under her blue eyes. She was pretty, she was more than pretty; that fine-boned face would still be beautiful in old age.

Sorsha wanted to ignore her, but curiosity was stronger. Several nurses came and went; they said the girl would soon feel better, and cooed around the baby. Sorsha felt more than ever abandoned and isolated; she closed her eyes, turned her face towards the wall, and felt the sobs ache in her throat.

The nurses went away and the room was quiet. Sorsha moved uneasily beneath the single sheet, acutely aware of her *gorgio* companion. The girl said, 'You've had good news, haven't you, about your baby? I'm so pleased for you. It must have been an awful worry, all these months, but Mr Robinson is delighted with her.'

In the normal way of things Sorsha would have stayed silent, turned her head away, pretended not to hear. But this day was different from any she had ever known. Abandoned by her own, she turned towards the *gorgio*. Her voice truculent, her face scowling, she said, 'How come you knows so much about my baby? What is it to you if she's all right?'

'I'm a nurse. I work here.'

Sorsha rolled over and pulled herself upright on the pillows. She blew her nose on a hospital tissue and rubbed a hand across her tearful face. She said, 'You know for a certain fact there's nothing wrong with her? I thought they might be codding me, you know, just to keep me quiet.'

'They would never have brought her back and put her in a cot beside you if there had been a problem. She'll be monitored for a few days, and then you'll be able to take her home.'

The girl was nice. No 'side' to her, no airs and graces. Her name was Fran, which she said was short for Francesca; her baby was big although she was quite a small girl; a boy with reddish hair and blue eyes who weighed an alarming nine pounds three ounces.

Sorsha hesitated. She remembered the

many schools she had attended, the taunts, the put-downs. She lifted her head, stuck her chin out. 'You'd better know now,' she said, 'that I'se a regular travelling girl — a Romany — a gypsy. Me and Kingdom, he's my husband, we got our own brand-new trailer. He goes partners with his dad in their scrap and tarmacing business. We mostly stays put in the winter and goes travelling in the summer. 'Cepting this year we had to bide here because of the *chavvie* — this being a "lucky" hospital an' all.'

'Do you live far from the Infirmary?'

'It don't seem so far when I'm riding in the van. The van wouldn't start this morning, and King's mobile phone was on the blink. I come in here riding pillion on his new motorbike.' Sorsha giggled. 'We only made it just in time. You should have seen that doctor's face when he found out how I got here. Like I told him — you can't rely on my King for nothing.'

Sorsha's pale face reddened. 'I made a helluva noise when they got me on that high-up bed thing. I screamed the walls down. I can't hardly face them nurses.'

Fran laughed. 'Don't worry about it. There were three of us in labour today. We all yelled. It's what you're supposed to do, it helps things along. Did nobody tell you?'

'If they did I never listened. I was so sure she'd be born dead.' The tears welled again and rolled down her face. 'All the family stayed put this summer because of the bad news about the *chavvie*. Now that I've birthed her and she's good and strong — where are they? I'll tell you where. They're off to a wedding. When I really needed them this morning they was speeding up the M1.'

Fran said, 'The same sort of thing happened to me. For months my parents and grandparents have been calling in and phoning. But today of all days they went off on a picnic. Mitch has been phoning round for hours, but still nobody home.'

The *gorgio* father was the first to visit. He was tall, broad shouldered; his fair hair curled close to his head, his eyes a smoky grey-blue. Sorsha found him handsome; he smiled at her and asked how she was feeling. She smiled and nodded, too embarrassed to reply.

Mitch had brought Fran an arrangement of fresh flowers in a pretty basket. He held his son easily and confidently in one arm. He had been present through all the seventeen hours of labour. When the doctor had offered him the scissors and invited him to cut the birth cord, he told Fran how he could not see to do it for the tears that were falling from his eyes. The baby, who seemed already to recognise his father, made little chirruping noises like a fledgling bird.

There was a lot of laughter from that corner of the room. Sorsha thought that Fran and Mitch must have been together for a long time, they were so easy with each other.

When Kingdom came to visit he went straight to the cot and touched the baby's head. Sorsha lied. 'You can look but you can't touch,' she told him. 'Doctor's orders.'

King sat on a chair beside her bed, his gaze fixed on the facing wall. She could sense his nervousness, his near-panic in this place. He had spoken not a word since he came through the door. It was, she thought, the hospital, the room, the presence of the *gorgio* couple, and she and King being frightened and not fitting in. She also knew that this coldness, this distance, could not be allowed to grow between them. If they could not reach out to one another in this special time then perhaps they never would. She glanced across the room at the happiness of Fran and Mitch, she reached for King's hand. 'It's all over now,' she comforted him. 'It turned out to be a "lucky" hospital for us, just like the old ones said it would be.'

She hesitated, to apologise was not in her nature, but something needed to be said. 'I'm sorry,' she muttered, 'that it was not a boy. I'm sorry you can't call her Elvis.'

King tried to speak but no words came. He squeezed her hand so hard he almost broke her fingers. Tears rolled down his face and he turned away to hide his weakness from the *gorgio mush*. Sorsha noticed for the first time ever that Kingdom looked much younger than his nineteen years.

She said, 'We could call her Elvira if you like?'

Sorsha could see that Fran knew all about babies. She was a staff nurse in the Infirmary, which was a sort of boss's job; she told Sorsha about the three years of hard training, the difficult exams. Fran and Mitch were both aged twenty-five years, which seemed very old to Sorsha for them to be having a first child. When Fran or Sorsha needed to use the little bathroom, each mother stood guard above the other's baby. Although Fran was a nurse she showed the same deep distrust as Sorsha when it came to hospital security and the safety of their infants.

Fran did not need to be shown how to bath her baby. She had done it all before because it was her regular job. On the morning of Sorsha's instruction in the care of Elvira, both babies were undressed and bathed together. The senior nurse showed Sorsha how to test the heat of the water, to clean the *chavvie's* eyes and ears, to have ready in advance all the bits and pieces that would be needed. Seeing the two infants, undressed and side by side, the difference in their size and condition troubled Sorsha.

The boy, whose name was to be John, had a wide chest and shoulders and strong, kicking legs. He waved his arms, and made little quirky noises as if he was just about to speak. He had a lot of reddish spiky hair and very dark blue eyes. When he cried it was like the roar of an express train.

Looking at Elvira was like witnessing a miracle at first hand. After all the warnings and alarms she was here, all complete and better than predicted. Even so, seen against the *gorgio* baby, she was tiny. Barely tipped the scales at six pounds, the doctor said. When she cried the sound was no more than a kitten's mewling.

Sorsha asked Fran how long it would be before Elvira plumped up and lost her look of a skinned rabbit.

'Little babies usually grow faster than large ones. But you have to remember that she's a girl. She may grow up to be small and dainty, like her mother. As long as she gains weight regularly you won't need to worry. After all, she looks exactly like you.'

Sorsha had never thought of herself as being small and dainty. The notion pleased her. To be told that the child resembled her mother in looks was strange and exciting. She gazed and gazed at the little round head and thick black hair, the healthy pink skin and the tiny, perfect features, and felt a new emotion well inside her. The baby was really sort of nice, better than Sorsha had imagined. Mine! she thought. First time in my life I've got something that is all mine. I worked hard to get her. King is her blood-father, but that cost him only a minute of his time. I carried her all these nine months. I deserve her!

She felt the first stirrings of pride, and with it came a monstrous possessiveness that made her resentful even of the nurses who handled the baby, and the doctor who said that Sorsha and her child should stay for a few more days in the hospital, just to be sure that all was as it should be.

# Nina

I slept well that night for the first time in many weeks, and woke with a thumping head and dry mouth. Imogen and Niall, who are only ever party drinkers, had been able to produce nothing better than red wine and cooking sherry by way of celebration. I threw soluble aspirin into a glass of water and performed an unsteady but triumphant tap-dance on the bathroom floor. Francesca was safely delivered of a son, and I was a great-grandmother!

The telephone rang as I played with a slice of dry toast. It was Imogen. 'Niall and I are visiting Fran and the baby at two thirty this afternoon. We'll pick you up on our way in.' I gritted my teeth and said, 'How kind,' and forced myself to replace the receiver without actually snapping it in half.

For Heaven's sake! I can actually *see* the maternity unit from my bedroom windows.

Did my daughter imagine that I would be put off from enjoying this so longed-for moment for another six hours? I went up to my bedroom and selected my one really posh frock and my best high-heeled shoes. I looked in the mirror and was bound to laugh despite the headache. With my hung-over face and wispy hair, I looked like an elderly witch all dressed up for a garden party. I soaked my hair under the cold tap and combed it into order. I found and put on a pair of blue linen slacks and a white shirt. I informed Roscoe of my destination, filled his food and water bowls, and promised to walk him on my return.

But for my single visit with Fran to the ante-natal clinic, I had avoided entering the Infirmary buildings since the morning of Jack's death. I was told only minutes after he had died that I should return later on that day and collect the items which were in his pockets when he was admitted.

A blank-faced woman had pushed a sealed brown paper bag at me across a wooden counter. I signed a receipt for the wallet, the wristwatch, a ring of keys, a penknife I had given him on his last birthday. My fingers trembled so badly I could hardly hold the pen. It might as well have been a bag of groceries she disposed of; for her it was no more than a tidying up of loose ends.

I had sworn never to return there, no matter how desperate my need. Some days later, after the funeral, I hung thick lace curtains across those of my windows which overlooked the casualty department.

The maternity wing was newly built and approached from the rear of the vast hospital complex. The reception area contained a wide desk, and in a corner stood a glass-fronted outlet of Mothercare. The security cameras were placed high around the walls. Since the snatching of an hours-old baby from another city hospital, the nursing staff and newly delivered mothers were justifiably nervous and watchful. I approached reception and found it was unmanned. When the clerk finally returned from wherever she had wandered, I was all ready to complain about her absence from the desk, her lack of vigilance regarding my great-grandson's safety. Perhaps she sensed my anger, for she fixed me with an equally accusing stare. 'No visitors until two thirty,' she snapped, pointing to a printed notice I had carefully ignored. I had suspected as much since Imogen's phone call, and came prepared to lie and wheedle. I waved my bunch of flowers and packages. I said, 'Oh dear, and I've driven for most of the night — you see, it's my first great-grandchild, I'm so excited! I've come all the way from North Wales to see them.'

The skin of my face grow hot as I uttered these falsehoods, but the receptionist seemed not to notice. Her perfect makeup cracked into a near smile. 'Oh well,' she said, 'in that case I will make an exception.' She began to fill in the inevitable form and issue directions.

I walked to the bank of waiting lifts, and pressed the button which would take me to the second floor.

The doors were clearly numbered, the corridors were long. I paced many yards of cushioned flooring before I found Room 17. I tapped on the door and Fran called, 'Come in.'

As I stepped into the white, bright room, the first face I saw was that of Sorsha, the gypsy girl!

Just for a moment, recognition sharpened her pretty features and I thought she was about to speak. The unexpected sight of her in Fran's room shocked me into silence, which was just as well since Sorsha had obviously decided not to know me. I nodded, smiled, and said, 'Good morning,' politely, as I would to any stranger, and then turned all my attention back to Francesca and her beautiful child, who seemed even more of a miracle to me than had Imogen when first born, or even Francesca herself.

I kissed my granddaughter and congratulated her. I held my great-grandson. I photographed mother and son together, and then the baby, who was already waving his arms and kicking strongly. Fran told me about the birth, and all the time I was acutely aware of Sorsha's veiled glances in my direction, and her determination not to recognise me. Francesca was very pale and heavy-eyed, but joyful. We talked about names. Marcus was a possibility, but the lusty boy who bicycled the air and whose fists were never still, did not seem to me to be likely to grow into an intellectual and willowy Marcus.

The other choice was John. Now there was a strong name, short and to the point, full of character and charm. I was careful not to show enthusiasm in either direction. The child's most urgent need it seemed was not a name, but a few sets of Babygros in a size or two larger than his mother had provided. I remembered how Fran and I had once picked out tiny garments labelled 'newborn', or 'nought-to-three-months'. I went down to the Mothercare outlet and bought three Babygros in a size more likely to fit an infant of nine pounds and three ounces. When I returned to Room 17, Sorsha and her baby were no longer there.

'Where's your room-mate?' I asked casually.

'She and the baby are still having tests done. She's gone down for a final scan.'

'Complications?'

Fran looked concerned. 'They're both lucky to be alive in the circumstances. She was a *placenta previa,* and you know what that means!'

I didn't know, and being of a queasy disposition, I did not particularly want to; I nodded and tried to look intelligent, but failed to fool my granddaughter. 'It was a tricky pregnancy,' said Fran. 'She nearly miscarried at three months. *Placenta previa* is a condition in which the placenta is lying in a dangerously low position. A second scan was done when she was seven months pregnant. Mr Robinson tried and tried to convince her that she should come into hospital right then, because of the risk to herself and the baby, but she wouldn't listen.'

I walked slowly back across the busy roads which lay between the Infirmary and the house which was no longer mine. I stood among the half-filled packing cases and cardboard cartons in my bedroom, and experienced an exultation I had never previously known. I turned to Jack's photo in its silver frame and told him about his great-grandchild. 'Now I have something to plan for,' I told him, 'and very soon I shall be living nearer to them.' I felt, in that moment, that Jack was very close, that he approved my selling of the house and the move into the country.

I stood at a window which overlooked the Infirmary buildings, and pushed aside the heavy lace. I realised then that I no longer associated the hospital with death and loss, but with birth and the promise of a new life. I thought about Sorsha and remembered her fears, and was glad she had survived.

Fran and John came home after what seemed to me a dangerously short time in the maternity unit. Two weeks of what women of my generation had called lying-in had dwindled, it appeared, to a restless forty-eight hours in which the new mother had very little time in which to recover her strength, and to become acquainted with her baby.

I said as much to Imogen.

'Well at least Fran left with the doctor's

approval,' said my daughter. 'That gypsy girl discharged herself. The husband walked in with a suitcase, and one of those quilted nests for carrying a young baby, and they were off! It caused quite a commotion.'

'Oh dear,' I said, 'that wasn't a good idea, but so typical of Sorsha.'

Imogen pounced. 'You speak as if you know her!'

'Oh,' I could hear myself lying again, and this time in a weak voice that lacked conviction, 'it must have been something Fran said. How could I possibly have known her?'

I moved the conversation quickly to a less risky subject. My actions, wise or foolish, were strictly none of Imogen's business, but if the tale was told of my brief involvement with the traveller girl, I could imagine her reactions.

I said, a note of warning in my own voice, 'Fran thinks it will be a good idea if none of us visits them for the next week. She looks so pale and exhausted, she needs to rest. Mitch has taken a few days off work to be at home with her. They need time on their own to adjust to being a family, and to get to know John.'

Imogen said nothing, but from the mutinous set of her mouth, and her wrinkled forehead, I knew she would be ringing

Fran's doorbell long before the week was out.

I cast about frantically for a convincing lie that would thwart her visiting instincts, but could not find a single one.

I began to reflect on my worrying and growing habit of using lies to achieve my own ends, and resolved to tell nothing but the truth in future. Meanwhile, my house purchase had stalled, had become, in fact, stationary. The mid-August date for the exchange of contracts was moved on into early September. There was no good reason for this delay; except for the strange reluctance of George Barnacle to complete the transfer of the Toll House into my name and ownership. Lindsey and Darren, whose purchase of eighty-four, Infirmary Avenue continued to proceed without trouble, were anxious to move in, and who could blame them! For their sakes as well as my own, I was equally anxious to be gone. I began to dispose of surplus furniture and knicknacks to various dealers of second-hand goods. I had taken the precaution of having an illegal spare key to the Toll House cut in the twenty-four hours when Monty Barnacle had entrusted Niall with the original.

I had not known myself capable of such devious behaviour; but a serious dip had occurred in my moral values since meeting the little Field Marshal; and it might yet sink to even greater depths. As I travelled by bus to the village green of Ashkeepers, and walked the half mile to Homesteaders' Valley, I was pleasantly aware that I was about to commit the crime of trespass.

The morning was cool and overcast. A fine mist of rain was carried on the breeze as I walked slowly down towards Home- steaders' Valley. The greenness of the lawns, the freshness of herbaceous borders, the gleaming paintwork of second cars parked in driveways, was proof that hosepipe bans and Water Board warnings were ignored as blatantly out here in the country as in my part of the city.

The silence of the place was unnerving to a townie; even more unsettling was the ab- sence of people and traffic. The briefcase- carrying husbands had long since departed to railway stations and offices. The children had been ferried to school by their mothers in those well-washed Golfs and Peugeots, and I thought about John, child of the new millennium, who already had his own spe- cial travelling seat strapped into Francesca's car.

I studied the revolting 'kitsch', the gaudy

reds and greens of the Homesteaders' Valley stained-glass windows. The architect had managed to include every tasteless fakery of mock-Tudor and pastiche Elizabethan, obtainable by the liberal use of PVC, coloured chipwood, and glass. Stepping out of Pioneer way into Brickyard Lane, walking down the slope which led to the Toll House was to move back in time some two centuries or more.

Until today I had come here accompanied, first by Imogen, then by Imogen and Niall; and most distractingly of all by the owner of the house, Monty Barnacle. Seeing it now, in the blue-gray light of a rainy morning, my fingers itched for brushes and palette. Perhaps I would never catch that exact shade of honey-coloured stone, the red of the pitched roof, the massed colours of the trees and flowering borders, but I would surely try! The charm of the place caused a pain deep in my chest. If only Jack — ! But there was nothing to be gained by wishing. I allowed myself to admit that he too might have loved to return to this little house; then I put firmly aside the longing and the aching emptiness. I trod carefully on the old uneven flags of the front path. A broken leg at this point would confirm my city-bred daughter's fears that I would not be safe out here in the wilderness. I turned the iron key in the stiff lock, and the door swung inwards with a creaking sound worthy of a Hammer horror movie. I smiled at the thought; the tiny, dusty rooms stood quiet and innocent in the dim light from the dirty windows. I closed the front door and began to explore what was soon to be my fortress, my castle, the refuge in which I would remake my life.

It was still a two-room-up, two-room-down cottage; it differed from similar village dwellings in the wide single-storey addition which jutted out to one side, and which presumably would have been the working quarters and lookout post of the keeper of the toll gate. Niall had proposed that this spacious room be fitted out as a dining kitchen, and I had agreed. He also planned to knock out a connecting archway between the two small downstairs rooms, thereby creating a sitting room of reasonable size.

Of the two upper rooms, one had at some time been converted to a primitive bathroom, from which Niall would remove the huge, claw-footed iron bath and ancient watercloset, and install the very latest in coloured bathroom suites.

I roamed from upstairs to downstairs and back again, taking measurements for curtains and carpets, happily selecting which items of my furniture would fit the house.

Time passed. Birds sang, somewhere a dog barked, I heard the rumble of a distant tractor. I stood at what would soon be my new kitchen window, and felt the tension leave my muscles, the tightness loosen in my mind. I looked out onto a small paved area and beyond it a neglected lawn. I planned to buy a dovecote, new garden furniture, a few stone tubs in which I would plant spring bulbs. I would also buy a safe, non-electric lawnmower. I had not expected to hear the crying of a baby and so, for several moments, although my ears registered the new sound, my mind did not recognise it.

It was not the lusty roar of John who was in any case tucked up in cot or pram in his parents' house, and at least two miles away. Since I knew no other infants, the sound intrigued me. Some harassed mother from Ding-Dong Valley, I thought, was pushing a pram out in the lane, hoping to lull a fretful baby into sleep. I actually stepped outside, stood at the garden gate and looked up and down the lane. There was no mother to be seen, no pram, no sound of crying. I went back into the house and closed the door. At once the crying sound was audible.

I stood in the small dark hallway and listened carefully this time; it was the plaintive and exhausted wail of a very young infant who had been left too long alone. From time to time the sound would fade, only to begin again. It seemed to be coming from the bedroom, but how could it? I had been up there only minutes ago, measuring for carpets and curtains. I stumped my way irritably back up the stairs. The partly-furnished room looked exactly the same as when I left it. The crying was louder now. Feeling foolish, I opened the wardrobe door to find nothing but dust and a half dozen wire coathangers. I pulled out each drawer of a worm-eaten dressing-table, and the wailing continued. I became unreasonably anxious, and yet relieved that there was no witness to my odd behaviour, I began frantically to strip the damp and grimy counterpane and blankets from the bed and a strong smell of mildew filled the room. I sneezed several times, and with some difficulty I opened a casement to let in some fresh air. I went back to the bed, and shook the lumpy pillows as if I might find a baby concealed amongst the feathers. I peered under the bed and inside the cupboard section of a bedside table.

I was standing breathless and angry in the

middle of the threadbare carpet, convinced that someone was playing a monstrous trick on me, when, with a final, heartrending hiccough, the crying ceased. As I closed the bedroom window, I realised that the high wooden fence and close-planted conifers which bordered the rear garden effectively blocked out all view of Witches' Hollow.

Monty Barnacle had said that a family of travellers lived beyond the fence. I imagined a young mother, a girl like Fran, weary from the nightly feeds, lifting her crying baby from its pram.

The sound of that hopeless, weary wailing had disturbed me more than I was willing to admit. Relieved at finding so obvious a solution, I collected my handbag and left the Toll House, carefully locking the heavy door, and closing the garden gate behind me.

# Sorsha

King had told their relatives that 'husbands only' was the visiting rule in the maternity unit. Sorsha was secretly gratified that he had lied so that they might have these quiet few hours alone together. 'Just us, as a family, Sorsha,' he had said, stroking Elvira's little round head. 'Things are going to be different from now on. Your ma and mine, the grandmothers, they've got to leave us be, they must see that now we've got the *chavvie*, everything's changed.'

She had smiled and nodded at his new manliness, but still she sensed the boy in him, his need to lean on someone. She would not for worlds have admitted it to King, but she longed for the feel of her mother's arms about her, the loving words that would reassure her that she had done well; that she was a good girl; that Elvira was a miracle, a princess.

The strain of coping with indoors, with nurses and hospital routines was beginning to tell on Sorsha. When it came to caring for the baby, she was told what she must do at least three times over. Because she was Sorsha the traveller girl, and every nurse knew she lived in a trailer, a lot was said about cleanliness and strict hygiene.

Sorsha smiled inside herself at such times. Well, it was wiser to keep a still tongue while she was still dependent on them. But she longed to tell the nurses that their standards of cleanliness were not her standards. Hadn't she stood with her mother on some *gorgio* women's doorsteps and smelled the stench of their houses, glimpsed their nasty, greasy kitchens, the single bowl in the sink which was used for all purposes, and some uses she did not even care to guess at! She had watched them put men's and women's clothing together in the same washing machine. She imagined a similar practice in the hospital laundry, shuddered at the thought, and decided to go home.

King would not have thought to suggest it himself, but when she begged him to bring in straightaway her clothes and sandals, and the pink satin 'nest' trimmed with lace, made especially by Drusilla for Elvira, he was back within the hour.

Fran tried to persuade her against leaving. Fran was a good sort, the nicest *gorgio* Sorsha had ever met. But Fran was a nurse, trained to keep the hospital rules. Because they had shared the experience of first birth and the same room, it was only natural that Fran should say that Elvira still needed to see the special baby doctor. That Sorsha herself was not yet well enough to go home.

Sorsha knew, but could not find the words to say, that one more night spent in the airless smelly room, one more day of instruction from the nurses, and tests done by doctors, and she would go down into that dark place of the soul where it would be easy for demons to take possession of her mind, and destroy her altogether.

Every pulse in her body cried out for her mother, her father, her relatives; and later on, as the summer dark came down, for her and King to be together in the trailer, the doors and windows opened to the good air.

When King came back with the zipped bag, Sorsha dressed as quickly as her shaky legs allowed, while King made a clumsy job of easing the crying Elvira into her pink satin 'nest'.

She and Fran wished each other well. Sorsha gave Fran a lucky gemstone, which, she said, John should carry with him all the days of his life.

She and King ignored the pleading words of doctors and nurses; King thanked them for their good care of his family, and the two of them marched away head-high and close together, out between the clever doors.

It had been a 'lucky' hospital for them, and they were grateful. But the greater danger would have been to linger.

# Nina

The break in the weather after weeks of heat and sunshine was welcomed by everyone I knew. The onset of heavy rain meant that it was possible to sleep the night through. No more creeping about in the small hours carrying contraband water to parched flowers and lawns, or lying awake in the stuffy darkness, anticipating family disasters, serious illness, or one's own inevitable decline.

Two days after my visit to the Toll House a letter from my solicitor informed me that matters were finally on the move. Lindsey and Darren had been granted their mortgage for eighty-four, Infirmary Avenue; all paperwork for their purchase of my house was now completed, and they were ready for the exchange of contracts. After many letters and phone calls from my solicitor to Monty Barnacle, he had at last provided the information she required. The Toll House, I learned, had been in the possession of the Barnacle family for almost two hundred years. The title deeds had been difficult to trace, and Mr Barnacle himself had been bewilderingly unhelpful. However, it seemed that within the past two days certain 'lost' documents had been found, and we were now in a position to set a date for the exchange of contracts between Barnacle and myself; and would I please telephone her office.

I spent a happy hour with the telephone. A completion date was set with my solicitor for ten days hence!

I fixed a firm date for my move to Ashkeepers with a removal company, and was grateful for their offer of the loan of extra packing cases. I rang the two second-hand furniture dealers and arranged for the immediate collection of my remaining surplus bits and pieces.

Last of all I rang Imogen, who refused to get into an instant discussion of my news on the grounds that Niall needed to be present. Relieved, and surprised that she was so readily willing to share decisions concerning me with her husband, I said I would expect to see them around seven that evening. They arrived just before eight, for although specifically asked not to, they confessed to having just 'looked in' on Francesca and Mitch and the baby John.

'It was only for a few minutes,' said Imogen. My daughter and her husband were still showing the amazed and smiling satisfaction of first-time grandparents. Well, I knew the feeling. I recalled Jack's delight and mine when Francesca was born.

'So how are they?' I asked virtuously, thereby confirming that I alone had kept my word and neither visited nor phoned.

'Rather tired,' said Niall. 'The baby wakes to be fed at least twice in the night.' He smiled. 'Got to hand it to Mitch, though! He's absolutely wonderful at the nappy-changing and bathing. I was afraid to touch Francesca when she was tiny.'

When we reached the actual reason for this evening's visit, I could see why Imogen had needed Niall's presence as back-up.

'Mother,' she began portentously, and my spirits dived. 'You do realise, don't you, that when you exchange contracts with Mr Barnacle on the eighteenth, you will be technically homeless?'

'No, Imogen, not homeless. I shall be temporarily between houses. Believe me. I do understand my position. While Niall is working on my new place, I shall need to be elsewhere.'

'Exactly —' she broke in. 'Well, I'm relieved that you at last appreciate the problem. Of course, you'll stay with us while all the work is going on. It may even stretch out into the New Year, which would be lovely, wouldn't it? We could all spend Christmas together at our house. We've plenty of room. Fran and Mitch could stay over, bring the cot —'

I looked warningly and then beseechingly at Niall. But my son-in-law was studying the empty spaces in the room created by the second-hand furniture dealers.

'Imogen,' I said, 'I haven't quite decided where I shall be living until the Toll House is habitable. But I can tell you now, it will not be in your house.'

'— and there's all your furniture,' she continued, 'your clothes and personal possessions.' She spoke grandly, as if I was Her Majesty the Queen proposing to vacate Balmoral.

'Those arrangements have already been made,' I informed her tartly. 'The removal company have excellent storage facilities. Everything is to be kept in their warehouse until such time as the Toll House is fit to move into.'

This of course was lying on the grand scale. No such positive arrangements had been made. The legal business regarding both houses, having stalled for months, had moved with such speed that I had given not the slightest thought to my temporary housing or that of my belongings.

The astonishment on my daughter's face almost tempted me to chortle, but I maintained a dignified silence, while inwardly congratulating myself on a masterly piece of quick thinking.

'But where will *you* live?' She was game, my Imogen, but her certainty was fading.

The memory of a small hotel, glimpsed among trees as we had driven through Ashkeepers, came back to me even as she spoke. I said, 'Oh, there's a nice little place in the main street of the village. I shall stay there for the few weeks it will take Niall to do the essential work on the house.' I could be gracious and magnanimous in victory. 'You mustn't worry about me, darling! After all — Fran and the baby will also need you in the next few months.' I turned to my son-in-law who appeared to have taken his thoughts to a distant planet. 'Isn't that so, Niall? You and I between us will make very short work of sorting out the Toll House.'

He smiled. 'It's difficult to say, Nina. We have to be careful with a house of that age — and it's a listed building, remember. I've made some enquiries about the proposed alterations and it seems that the new kitchen window is the only item likely to be queried. But I must warn you now that the work will take longer than a few weeks.'

'Oh well,'; I could afford to be philosophical, now that I had made it clear that I would not be moving in with Imogen and Niall, 'just so long as I'm living there before winter starts.'

The Limes hotel had seven bedrooms, two of which were en-suite and situated on the ground floor. Dogs were not just tolerated by the proprietors but made positively welcome. My ground-floor room had trench windows which opened onto a vast lawn. After two days and nights in which Roscoe and I recovered from the move, and gradually adjusted to our new situation, Roscoe at least began to behave like one who had regained his youth.

Roscoe loved The Limes and all the pats and attention given him by total strangers; the tidbits slipped him by the kitchen staff. He loved Ashkeepers; every walk was an exploration of delight as he investigated strange and fragrant lampposts and tree trunks, and rooted blissfully in hedge bottoms.

Any doubts I might have had about my dog's reorientation quickly disappeared. As to my own ability to make the transition from town to country, I was no longer sure. I missed my early morning breakfasts in the café, and the exchange of news of family crises with Anna. In a worrying, unaccountable way I also missed the prison wall, the light from the security lamps which had shone for so many years into my bedroom. I found myself listening for the wail of ambulances and police cars, and hearing only the wind in the trees and the lowing of cows from the adjoining farms.

An appointment had been made with the house-clearance people to come out to the Toll House on Friday morning, since every room needed to be empty before Niall commenced work there on the following Monday. I turned my legal key in the lock and two burly young men named Gavin and Joe followed me in. The smell of mildew seemed stronger than ever. I noticed the tiny heaps of dust beneath chairs and tables which, said Joe, showed the presence of active woodworm.

'So what do you want us to move?' asked Gavin.

I hesitated. If any of these battered items was likely to cause a flutter of excitement among the experts at the *Antiques Roadshow*, I would just have to take the risk.

'Take all of it!' I said grandly.

'Carpets and all?'

'Carpets and all.'

In less than an hour the place was empty. I opened all the windows and swept the dusty floors. The transformation was amazing, the rooms seemed larger, lighter. My spirits lifted. I imagined the two small downstairs rooms linked by an archway, and could now see the ideal space which would take Jack's desk, and the long wall which would show the sofa and bookcase off to best advantage. I wandered through the house and out into the garden, and noticed for the first time the beauty of the morning.

I had forgotten autumn in the country; the colours of the changing season. The hedges which bordered my property were loaded down with scarlet hip, and the darker red of hawthorn berries. The trees had turned to shades of yellow, copper, and a tawny reddish-orange which would be interesting to reproduce on canvas. The sky was a cloudless duck-egg blue. I breathed in the clean air and listened to the silence. I reminded myself that I was not alone here. Fran and Mitch and baby John were now within walking distance. The village of

Ashkeepers was just a stop away along the main road. For amusement and diversion I had Ding-Dong Valley almost on my doorstep.

With the bulk of my furniture sold to dealers, and the remainder stored with the furniture removers; with my essential clothing contained in two suitcases, I felt light and unencumbered. I resolved that in future I would keep my possessions to an absolute minimum. No more hoarding of so-called family treasures and knick-knacks. Why should Imogen and Fran be burdened in their turn with the flotsam of previous generations?

I walked to a corner of the garden not previously explored. Behind a stand of laurel bushes, quite hidden from view, I found a neat little garden shed, the perfect home for the lawnmower and garden tools I planned to buy. I grasped the padlock which secured the shed and it fell open in my hand. I pushed at the door with a sense of satisfaction at the discovery of this unexpected bonus, only to find that the garden shed, surprisingly bequeathed to me by Monty Barnacle, was stacked from floor to roof with crates of old and mouldering books.

It was too late now to recall Joe and Gavin. Later on, perhaps, I could have a bonfire. I began to feel the rise of a boiling anger with Monty Barnacle, that elderly fop and poseur, who drove around in his vintage car, dressed like a fugitive from *Genevieve*, and leaving me to clear the rubbish from his house and shed.

I went back into the house. I resolved to phone Mr Barnacle that evening, to demand that he at once remove his disgusting, mouldy books from my garden shed. I stood in what I hoped would soon be my new kitchen and watched Roscoe's rootings in a weed-choked flower bed.

The crying began on the same sad and weary note, again as if the baby had wept for hours without attracting notice. I moved towards the stairs and then halted. There was no point in going up there. I knew the rooms were empty. Joe and Gavin had made sure of that. The crying continued, and I felt my stomach muscles tighten. The sound must be coming from the home of whoever lived beyond the fence in Witches' Hollow. I picked up my handbag and Roscoe's lead, stepped out onto the flagged path, pulled shut the front door and locked it. Perhaps I should investigate? On the other hand, perhaps I shouldn't? Halfway along the garden path I turned and gazed back at the Toll House, and as I looked a shadow seemed to pass across it. I stood among the fuchsia bushes in the mellow sunshine of that autumn morning, and felt deeply and unaccountably afraid.

The distance between Ashkeepers and Fran's house was greater than I had estimated. Halfway along the road I rested on a rustic bench provided for elderly walkers by a considerate borough council. It was clear that I should need to go into serious training if I was to do what I had boasted, and walk John out regularly in his pram.

Fran looked more ill and exhausted in her own surroundings than she had when lying back against hospital pillows. Her extreme pallor and heavily shadowed eyes alarmed me. There was nothing I could say or do except to offer any help she needed, but I could see without being told that Mitch had all things domestic well under control.

The baby, as is so often the case, continued large and lusty, and demanded to be fed two-hourly. I made rash promises to collect him and take him off her hands for a couple of hours, so that she might rest or take a bath, wash her hair, watch soaps on the television. I remembered, I told her, how it was with a first baby, the anxiety, the constant checking of pram or cot, never mind that she was a trained nurse. With one's own baby it was different.

Fran smiled and nodded and said little. She lay on the leather chesterfield as if welded to it. Inwardly I raged and fumed against a stupid and uncaring system which sent young mothers out of hospital long before they were fit and ready to take on the cares of home and family.

Back in my room in The Limes hotel I fed Roscoe and released him to wander in the garden. I had been obliged to take the return bus from Fran's village to the out-skirts of Ashkeepers; and I had thought my-self fit and active for one who was in the upper limits of late middle age! I turned to Jack's photo which stood on the bedside table and confessed to being over-optimistic, and foolish. I told him about the irritations of the day; the garden shed full of mouldy books, the mystery of the crying baby. I heard his reply as clearly as if he was there with me.

'Well at least your life's not boring any more. You are out of your rut, Nina. New home, new experiences, new people. And most exciting of all — a new baby in the family!'

I went to my bed that night feeling reassured. Jack could always be relied on to look on the bright side.

The autumn days stayed mild and sweet right into late October. My time at The Limes was extended week by week; I was comfortable there, but should the weather turn cold I would need to visit the storage unit in the city, and recover my woollies and a winter coat. Niall's estimate of three weeks' work on the Toll House had been wildly optimistic and made only to placate me; I could not complain, neither did I wish to harass him. The work he did was slow and painstaking, but well worth the wait. By the end of October all the rooms had been replastered, worm-eaten interior doors had been replaced, a new tiled kitchen floor laid down, and the tiny leaded-paned windows and their wooden shutters had been repaired and repainted. The roof and three tall chimneys had been put in order, and all timbers sprayed and treated for beetle infestation and similar horrors.

There remained the installation of a central heating system, and the fitting of bathroom and kitchen units. Imogen, as promised, was to accompany us to the builders' wholesalers to help me with the choice of styles and colours.

The days passed pleasantly enough. I found that by working in the garden I could observe the progress of Niall's work without being overtly intrusive. I also produced sandwiches and biscuits, and endless tea and coffee for my son-in-law and Wayne and Craig, his two assistants. I gave the lawn its final before-winter mowing. I cleared out overgrown borders, pruned roses, weeded paths, and gave the picket fence a fresh coat of white paint. The vegetable garden was a greater challenge. It was many years since I had wielded fork and spade. I was more than ever grateful for my en-suite bathroom at The Limes, and the constant supply of hot water in which I soaked my aching limbs each evening.

In between all this activity I explored Ashkeepers village, and observed, without enthusiasm, a few of my new neighbours in Homesteaders' Valley.

The village itself was familiar; I had been born and grew up there. It was a part of my past of which, since Jack was dead, only I was aware. I walked the streets, visited the church, wandered with Roscoe in the churchyard, and was not recognised by anybody. Thanks to the National Trust, which owned much of Ashkeepers, and the stately home which stood at its heart, the houses and shops, church and several chapels remained much as they had always been, simple and beautiful, built of the golden stone that was quarried from a nearby hill.

I sat on the low wall that surrounded the churchyard, and studied the single wide headstone which bore the names of my great-grandparents, grandparents and parents. In all the excitement and worry of selling my house in the city, searching for a suitable replacement, wanting to be close to Fran, but not too close, I had managed to evade the disturbing question of why I had come back to the place I had sworn, fifty years ago, never again to set foot in.

I suppose, if I were being altogether honest, I would admit that the presence of Fran and Mitch less than two miles down the road in Nether Ash had a lot to do with my decision to return. Not that I was conscious at the time of having deliberately decided anything. On that bungalow-seeking drive with Imogen, one road had led quite literally into another, and there we were, parked on the village green of Ashkeepers, and then driving into Homesteaders' Valley and confronting the Toll House. I had felt the old delight on seeing the magical cottage I had coveted in childhood; had remembered again the fascination of its history.

But I was almost elderly myself now; sixty years on and the past was dead. I could open the picket gate, walk up the path to the front door, step inside and with hardly a glance at my surroundings, say grandly to Monty Barnacle, 'I'll buy it!'

I could even pinpoint the exact second when all sense of reason and caution had departed. It happened in that moment when the iron-strapped oaken door swung open. A voice in my head had said then, 'I want this house — because I want it.'

I had found the pot of gold at the end of the rainbow.

A soft little breeze blew across the church-yard. The grass on my family burial plot needed cutting. Tomorrow I would bring the garden shears, a stone jar, and a few late sprays of Michaelmas daisies from the herbaceous border.

I thought about putting down roots, about belonging.

Home, for me, had been wherever Jack was. Again, I thought how the ownership of the Toll House, the return to Ashkeepers, was the first spontaneous decision I had made in half a century of living. I called to Roscoe; when we came to the lych-gate I snapped his lead on. There were still a few leaves on the churchyard trees. They clung precariously, golden and brown-veined. One sharp frost and all the branches would be bare.

First of November and still the days were calm and balmy. My host at The Limes talked about it being a St Luke's little summer. All at once the essential repair work was completed on the house, and we were discussing the final stages of what Imogen called 'the transformation'. I forgot all about the family graves and the Michaelmas daisies.

With my daughter's help I chose an all-white fitted kitchen, complete with eye-level grill and oven, and separate hub. The bathroom suite was to be a shade of pearly pink, like the inside of a conch-shell. The choice of colours, so different from my former browns and greens, was made at Imogen's suggestion.

Together we chose a soft lemon shade of kitchen wallpaper, and white-with-a-hint-of-pink emulsion for the bathroom walls and woodwork. For the rest of the house we decided on a scheme of warm cream walls and brilliant white paintwork. For the first time ever our tastes coincided. The harmony between us was so rare and unexpected that we both felt and looked a little embarrassed by it. It was a relief when we disagreed about the kitchen curtains. Imogen said Venetian blinds would be both practical and attractive; my preference was for blue and white checked gingham. In the end we compromised and I purchased both.

Back in my room at The Limes, and weary after the long day, I lay awake in the darkness and thought about my daughter. There were so many things she did not know about me; a history that I could never bring myself to tell her. It had been easy to keep my secrets in Jack's lifetime; he became skilled at diverting Imogen's childhood questions, so that as she grew older she accepted without question Jack's bland but misleading account of her mother's and her father's early lives. The day Imogen and I had just spent together had been pleasant, almost loving. The sort of day I regularly had with Fran. But the alarm bells ringing in my head warned me to be careful. Move too close to my daughter, and in my state of loneliness I might be tempted to grow confidential.

In the following days my presence was needed in the Toll House. The bathroom and kitchen were installed. The decorator arrived and painting and papering begun.

Niall considerately consulted me at every stage. He patted my shoulder and said how well we worked together. Not for the first time I wished that Niall was my son.

Ten days had passed before I found the time to return to the churchyard. The mild days were ended; that first frost had stripped the branches of their remaining leaves. I wore my linen slacks and a heavy sweater loaned by Niall, topped by a scruffy navy-blue donkey jacket borrowed from Wayne. As I walked briskly through Homesteaders' Valley carrying my bag of garden tools, several ladies on their way to a church coffee morning managed quite skilfully not to acknowledge me in any way.

I cut the grass and scraped the lichen from my family headstone. As the letters of each name appeared I was gripped by a mounting excitement. So here they all were, at rest in this village where they had lived out their quiet, uneventful lives. My great-grandparents, Josiah and Pennina. My grandparents, Pennina and Henry. And my parents, Imogen and Paul.

Taken together the inscribed dates on the weathered stone covered a span of one hundred and twenty years, and bore witness to the existence of six people of whom Imogen and Fran knew nothing.

I filled a jar with water and arranged the sprays of Michaelmas daisies and placed them to stand in the centre of the grave. As I stood back to admire the improved state of the plot, I became uneasy. Someone was watching me. I looked slowly around the churchyard, ostensibly calling to Roscoe, but seeing no sign of the observer. And then, as Roscoe came trotting obediently to my side, a shadow moved down by the lych-gate. A slight, black-garbed figure slipped through the entrance. It could have been a small thin woman wearing a long black skirt. Or it could have been the vicar.

That first frost had pitched us headlong into winter long before Niall and I were ready for it. To go to the furniture store in the city and ask for the sealed unit to be opened, so that I might grab a few warm clothes, seemed even more than ever ridiculous and at this point, self-defeating. While I wore the strange collection of borrowed male and female heavy garments, I hardly needed to argue my case with plumbers and decorators for haste. Even so, I eventually moved into the Toll House in a snowstorm, with paintwork still tacky, and the newly installed radiators making ominous rumbling noises which Niall assured me was normal and would soon settle down.

With the large items of furniture set in place, and the labelled packing cases put in the appropriate rooms, I made coffee for Niall, Craig and Wayne, and the removal men, and after a minor celebration around the kitchen table I sent them all away.

Roscoe chose his permanent place beneath a kitchen radiator, standing beside the warm spot and gazing expectantly at me until I dragged his basket into position. I watched his small, rough-coated, white and black body curl up contentedly on the tartan blanket. Roscoe was a smart dog. I noticed again how he had mastered the knack of instantly accepting changed homes and circumstances, even though he was no longer young. I stacked the coffee mugs in the washing-up bowl and walked into the sitting room. Niall had worked a miracle here; the creation of an archway had brought in light from the two windows, and given me, at the one end, a front view of the garden and the distant roofs of Homesteaders' Valley; and to the rear a sight of the fence which concealed Heaven knows what!

Imogen had been right about the moss-green carpet. It set off beautifully the warm cream walls and the flowered-chintz loose covers on chairs and sofa. Jack's mahogany desk looked at home in its allotted space. I began, halfheartedly, to unpack lamps and pictures. I stood at the front window and watched the falling snow, large fluffy flakes that settled in minutes to colour the world in white. The noise from the radiators diminished to a barely audible hum. The silence of the little house was of such a denseness that if I had reached out a hand I believe I could have touched it.

In the course of renovation, Niall had uncovered a lovely old rose-pink bricked fireplace. I pulled an armchair into position beside it, and placed a low table close at hand. I plugged in a lamp, switched it on and set it on the table. I sat down, and like Roscoe, I tried out my chosen place.

When I woke it was late afternoon; snow had drifted halfway up the windows, Roscoe was whining to be let out, and I had not even made up my bed.

The bedroom was tiny. Niall had built a run of wardrobes and storage fitments on the longest wall: in the remaining space stood my bed and a single bedside table and the dressing-table set before the window. I found the packing case labelled BEDDING and pulled out sheets and pillowcases, duvet and pillows. Imogen had failed to rouse my interest when it came to decorating this room; we had settled in the end for cream walls and a tweedy beige carpet, which looked well enough with my old and faded yellow bedlinen and duvet cover.

There was just enough space for Roscoe's basket in a corner.

I hauled it upstairs together with his blanket. He followed me, his paws still damp from his trip into the snowy garden. He stood in the doorway, barked at me, but did not enter.

I returned to the kitchen and heated the casserole, thoughtfully provided by Imogen. The central heating was efficient, the little house grown warm and cosy. Perhaps it was the unaccustomed heat, the comfort of the hot food, but in spite of the afternoon nap, I was overcome by a weariness I could not fight. I checked the door locks, switched off the lights, and although it was only six o'clock, I knew that I would have to go to bed.

I expected that Roscoe would follow as he always did, but I returned from the bathroom to find his basket empty. I stood at the top of the stairs and called him, and he came up reluctantly, but again no further than the bedroom door. I spoke sharply to him but he did not move. In the end I picked up the basket and took it back to the kitchen. He snuggled down contentedly enough, but I felt uneasy about him.

As I drifted into sleep I thought about the contrariness of Roscoe, who was not normally contrary. I began to count up all the jobs which needed to be done. The unpacking would take several days; I wanted desperately to see Fran and the baby; change-of-address cards needed to be sent, and people notified of my new telephone number. Before getting into bed I had pulled back the window curtains, although, since the room was so small, I now saw that I could almost have twitched them shut or open while lying back against the pillows. The snow had ceased to fall. From the kitchen window I had seen moonlight reflecting off the whiteness of the garden, the dark line of conifers and the wooden fence which sheltered Witches' Hollow.

A family of gypsies lived down there, according to Monty Barnacle, who ought to know. Well, that was no surprise. Travellers, my father once told me, had been pitching regularly in the Hollow since the days of stagecoaches and highway robbers.

My last conscious thought was of the Toll House and its history, and the people who had lived here; and that one day when every packing case was empty, and the snow gone, I would go to the local history library and check for any mention of it.

# Sorsha

Sorsha had come home to find the sort of welcome that more than atoned for the hurtful neglect of her family at the time of Elvira's birth. Since that morning when Kingdom had driven at speed into the *tan,* and yelling from the van that Sorsha would stay no longer in the city hospital, and would somebody help him to pack a bag with her clothes and the baby's shawl-thing, amends had been made and apologies offered.

Her family had not understood the seriousness of her condition, or the risk to the unborn child. Well, how could they since she had never told any of them; not even King. But after the birth the hospital doctors had talked to King about it all, and he had told her parents; reproaches had been uttered but, as Sorsha pointed out, their knowing the bad news in advance would not have changed the outcome. They should in fact be grateful to her for sparing them unnecessary worry.

They were grateful for this first grandchild and great-grandchild. King's consideration and tenderness towards the convalescent Sorsha and the baby Elvira was noted by her parents and brothers; his round-the-clock, hand-and-foot devotion to his 'two lovely girls' began to change their view of King.

For the first weeks, and while the warm weather continued, Sorsha lay for hours on the garden lounger, shaded by the oak tree, Elvira sleeping in the navy-blue pram beside her.

Visitors came, bearing gifts. Sorsha felt important and valued. Motherhood had changed her status, in a way that marriage never could. The experience of childbirth had admitted her to that world of women which men could not enter. Encouraged by her grandmother and mother, her aunts and those cousins who were themselves mothers, she told and retold the agony of her labour, the long hours of terror, her fears for her own life and the life of the baby. And with each telling the residue of horror in her mind grow less, the trauma eased a little; the reality took on the glamour of a television drama in which Sorsha had played the starring role.

She could even joke about having a little brother or sister for Elvira; but not for a few years yet, of course. As it was, the trailer which had seemed spacious for the two of them, was already overcrowded with the baby's gadgets.

Sorsha loved the trailer. It had been the wedding gift of her parents and brothers, custom-built and done out in her favourite shades of green. All the carpets were a dark-green, the curtains a fern-green velvet; the window-blinds were made of white silk with pulls and fringed bobbles of the same delicate green. The kitchen was fitted out with white units and dark-green floor tiles, the bathroom likewise. The brass wall-lamps had amber shades, and the window-glass was etched with a lucky design of horses' heads and horseshoes. The bedrooms, one large, one small, had dark-wood cupboards and wardrobes, and bedcovers made of a pretty pale-green cotton sprigged with white and yellow daisies.

Elvira's room had come ready-fitted with bunk beds, which were already piled high with the gifts and toys from relatives and friends. Elvira, of course, slept in King's and Sorsha's bedroom, in the old polished-wood rocking-cradle which had been carved by a great-grandfather and used by all the babies of the family.

King had wanted to buy a brand-new cradle, factory-made, draped with a lace canopy and so shoddy that it would likely last them out for only the one baby. Sorsha had explained to him the importance of heirlooms and family treasures. Never mind that the wood of the old rocking-cradle showed the tiny toothmarks of Sorsha's father, who as a baby was noted for his fearsome biting habit. Those toothmarks meant that Jem's memory would live on through all the generations of new mothers who would use the cradle, and tell the story of his sharp teeth to their children, and their children's children.

King had not really tried to understand, but then his was a more loose-knit family than her own, with members scattered up and down the country. King had no first-hand experience of strong traditions. All he had was the top cupboard in the bedroom in which he stored the guitar and the other foolish mementoes of the singer Elvis Presley, who might or might not have come from a travelling family.

The *gorgio* nurse, Fran, had foretold that Elvira would grow faster than her own large boy, because she had been born smaller. And so it was! The luck for which the Infirmary was well-known among travellers had followed Sorsha and her baby. Elvira grew plump and strong; she was a happy and contented infant, even though Sorsha had, from the beginning, been obliged to bottle-feed her.

In early November, King and her father and brothers would go north to work on a new important road. They would be gone for about six weeks. Elvira's christening, in the 'lucky' church in Nether Ash, had been booked for the second Sunday before Christmas.

As the days grew cooler, Sorsha and Elvira no longer spent time beneath the oak tree, but were glad of the warmth and comparative quiet of the trailer; although the peaceful time did not last long. As King reported when the noise first started, all hell had broken loose in the shabby old house on the far side of the fence. Builders and plasterers, plumbers and decorators, hammering and shouting, the day long. Sorsha wondered who would want to live in such a place. On more than one occasion she had seen the shadow of the *mullo* which haunted the house; she had felt the sadness of the spirit, heard a baby's cry.

Nothing in the world, no promise or persuasion, would make Sorsha walk alone through Brickyard Lane, in daylight or in darkness.

# Nina

The continuing snowfall came as quite a shock after three successive mild winters which had brought nothing more than a token sprinkling of white in our part of the country. After searching through bin bags and packing cases I finally located my gumboots and thick gloves. As well as the mouldy books, Monty Barnacle had left me a shovel in the little wooden shed. I cleared the flagged front path each morning and uncovered a patch of loose earth for the benefit of Roscoe. He was only a small dog and did not take easily to floundering up to his armpits in deep snow.

There was an ancient bird-table within view of the sitting room window. I made a note to buy wild-bird seed when I next went into the village. Imogen phoned every morning, and yes, I reassured her, I had survived the night, had eaten breakfast, and was about to begin my daily task of unpacking and putting things into drawers and cupboards, which would all, of course, later prove to be totally impractical and need to be rearranged. My freezer and cupboards were stocked with sufficient food to feed a regiment. The television set and the radio were both in perfect working order. If conversation became an urgent need I had Roscoe to talk to, and there was always the telephone!

I called Fran who was not yet back to her old bubbly and energetic self. Mitch had returned to work, leaving her alone with John who slept a lot; she admitted to a lot of daytime viewing of television soaps and chat shows, and a wise disinclination to venture out into the snowy world. In a way it could be said that the severe weather had done both of us a favour. In the case of Fran, a time of much-needed rest was being imposed upon her. As for me, confinement to the Toll House meant that I was becoming thoroughly acquainted with every corner of it.

Not that it was spacious; but it was very different from the city house I had shared with Jack. Different too from the house I grew up in. There were unexpected nooks and crannies, little cupboards set into the foot-deep walls; a baking oven far back in the old brick fireplace, its rusted metal door impossible to open. The part of the house which was now my kitchen must, according to Niall, have been the hub of the toll-keeper's business, the office from which payment to use the good road was demanded. I looked out towards Homesteaders' Valley and tried to imagine the queue of stage-coaches and farm carts which had once waited to come through the toll gate. But all that came to mind was the present gravelled driveways which held Volvos, Golfs and Peugeots; their owners confident in their Bally shoes, their uniform of Aquascutum skirts and cashmere sweaters. I transferred cutlery from a low drawer to a high drawer, reasoning that too much bending would give me backache; I placed the bread-crock on the kitchen counter and hung two flower-prints on the wall. Well, I had a few smart outfits of my own. It might be interesting, when the roads had cleared and the sun shone, to saunter through Pioneer Way wearing something less unfashionable than Wayne's old donkey jacket.

I wondered, too, how I would respond if the ladies of Ding-Dong Valley ever deigned to recognise me!

And so the days passed, and a week was

gone in which, on reflection, I had achieved a great deal. The thaw set in overnight. I awoke one morning to sunshine and the sounds of water dripping, and the roar of powerful engines out in Brickyard Lane. I did not investigate the noise of the passing traffic, even though it was unusual. Since moving to the Toll House I had fallen into the habit of watching breakfast television. It was a poor substitute for Anna's conversation, and those crack of dawn breakfasts in the café; in fact I felt thoroughly decadent, eating toast and drinking tea, still wearing dressing gown and slippers, in the company of a TV presenter. I was especially riveted on that morning of the thaw. The first item of news was a dramatic account of yet another kidnapping of a young baby, in a small town on the far side of the county.

I was tempted to push the OFF switch and fade out the newsreader's concerned face and voice. A year ago I would have done exactly that, reasoning that such a tragedy did not concern me, and that my knowing the details could not help anybody. But that was then, and this was now.

A year ago there had not been a baby who was my great-grandson, living down the road in Nether Ash.

A year ago, and the very name of

Ashkeepers was no more than a submerged and manageable memory; a place in which I had been born and suffered my personal heartache. A village to which I had sworn I had no intention of ever returning.

The newscast was brief. The baby, asleep in her carrycot, had been stolen from an unlocked hatchback, in the few minutes it had taken for her mother to buy nappies at a local chemist's shop. Passers-by were asked to contact the police. People shopping in the area, and questioned on the spot, said they had noticed nothing unusual. Young mothers lifting carrycots from cars were a common sight in these days, and they all wore jeans, didn't they! I shivered and pulled the dressing gown tight around me. It had always been easy for a determined woman to steal a child, if that was her intention.

It was even possible for an infant, sleeping in a pram on an autumn evening, to be taken from its home while the unsuspecting mother fetched logs to mend the fire.

I felt an urgent need to visit Fran; wearing heavy walking shoes and dressed in dark trousers and a warm, orange-coloured jacket I set out for Nether Ash. It was good to get away from the house, to step out along the main road, to breathe in the fresh air. If

Fran was agreeable, John might also benefit from an airing in the mild and pleasant morning.

It was many years since I had wheeled out a baby, and the navy-blue pram which, by some trick I did not understand, would also turn into a carrycot or pushchair, had double wheels like those on supermarket trolleys. I found the whole contraption difficult to manage; for like supermarket trolleys, the pram veered alarmingly in directions I did not wish to go, while the baby, almost hidden under shawl and blankets, slept sweetly through it all. He had recently been fed and I planned to keep him out for at least two hours. Fran had looked nervous when I told her of this plan. But surely she could see that, apart from Mitch, Imogen and Niall, I was the most responsible, the most suitable person in the world to have charge of her child.

But was I? If Fran had heard about the latest kidnapping she did not say so. I struck out along the main road which led back to Ashkeepers. I began to think about the early morning television newscast, the baby who had been stolen from his mother's car, while that car had been parked beside a shop, and people passing on the pavement. Audacious but simple, the newscaster had said.

People rarely walked these two miles between the villages; there was a thrice-hourly bus service, and the majority of country dwellers possessed their own private transport. I imagined a car pulling up beside me, the rear door opening and some respectable-looking young woman asking directions of me. Between the passing of one heavy lorry and the next, how easy would it be for that woman to reach out to the pram, snatch the sleeping child, and for her accomplice to drive them swiftly away. I admitted to myself that in the event, I would be too old and feeble to fight them; to save John.

All at once the blue sky, the mild sweet air, the singing birds, seemed like a lure which had led me into danger. I looked back and forward along the straight and level pavement. I had reached the midway point between the villages and could see their respective church steeples in each direction, but apart from the passing traffic, not another living soul. I turned the pram around and walked swiftly back towards Nether Ash. I had the frightening sensation of being useless and stupid; too vulnerable, too old and ill-equipped to protect Fran's precious child should danger strike. A certain shakiness in my legs warned me of just how foolish I had been. I gripped the pram handle and now found it to be a superior kind of Zimmer frame, which helped me to recover. My breathing slowed, and, eventually, the thumping of my heart. By the time I reached Nether Ash I was strolling confidently, as befitted a great-grandmother who was wheeling out the youngest member of her family. I returned the smiles of other pram-pushers. But the fear stayed with me. I could not rid my mind of the thought of thieving hands, outstretched towards a sleeping baby. On future expeditions with John I would stay within the comparative safety of the village streets of Nether Ash.

I was woken in the early hours of the next morning by the desolate crying of the neglected baby. It was the first occasion on which I had heard it since moving into the Toll House. Having once been wakened I found it difficult to sleep again. I dozed uneasily until daybreak, and went wearily down to the kitchen to make coffee and toast as the first streaks of light showed pink across the eastern sky.

I sat in the rocking chair beside the kitchen radiator and watched the sun rise, a sight which had been denied to Jack and me in Infirmary Avenue, hemmed in as we were by the roofs of the hospital and the prison wall.

Gradually my irritation lessened. So what was a broken night when set against the many advantages of living in the Toll House? And all babies cried, didn't they! There was every chance that John, in his time, would disturb the sleep of Fran's and Mitch's neighbors, if he had not already done so?

And yet my uneasiness persisted. The crying I heard was never the lusty, angry demand of a hungry infant, but always that weak despairing wail of a baby who knows itself to have been abandoned. The time had come, I decided, to visit my so-far unseen neighbours who lived beyond the fence.

I made my bed, washed the breakfast dishes, fed Roscoe and told him he must stay at home and I would walk him later. The barking of dogs had sometimes come from the far side of the fence when sound was carried on a north wind, and Roscoe had delusions of grandeur when it came to fighting mastiffs who were three times his size. I put on the orange-coloured coat and gumboots and went quickly from the house.

I closed the garden gate carefully behind me, taking my time, feeling the crusading zeal which had brought me this far ebbing fast away. I stepped out into the lane, and into wide, water-filled ruts which must have been made by the recent passage of heavy vehicles, and I remembered the traffic sounds I had heard on the morning of the newscast about the stolen baby.

The air was crisp and cold, my breath plumed out and up into the leafless branches; the sky was a delicate duck-egg blue. Just for a moment I was the child I had once been in this lane, roaming in a forbidden place, creating my own magic. I slithered down through mud and slush towards Witches' Hollow. As I negotiated the bend in the lane I saw for the first time the tall and heavy wooden gates which ran parallel with the fence and prevented entry to the Hollow.

I gave the left-hand gate a tentative push and it swung open. I took two steps inside and was conscious of the gate closing silently behind me.

The scene before me was equally quiet, and so unexpected as to halt me in my tracks.

'Gypsies live down there,' Monty Barnacle had said. I had imagined a few old-fashioned wooden wagons, a couple of dogs, half a dozen coloured ponies grazing the tough winter grass.

What I saw was a grouping of a dozen custom-built modern trailers, gleaming white with silver-coloured trim, and each positioned on its own hard standings of concrete. Neat tarmac paths led up to each trailer. A block of red-brick buildings stood in a far corner. Two tethered lurchers and an elderly greyhound observed me but did not make a sound. A Landrover and a yellow van were parked close to the gates.

I stood for a long time, confused and unwilling to move further. The fence, seen from this side, seemed higher and more than ever divisive, closing off effectively the inhabitants of the Hollow from their neighbors in Homesteaders' Valley, and also from the Toll House. The tips of the conifers waved even higher than the fence, reinforcing the division. Not all prison walls were built of red-brick and monitored by long-distance video cameras! Someone, at some time, had made very sure that this particular minority group and their culture should never impinge upon the village of Ashkeepers.

The silence was oppressive. I became aware of eyes that watched from behind the pretty ruched-silk window-blinds. I had never been so conscious of being the intruder in a private place. From within the compound it was difficult to believe that the

Toll House and its garden stood only feet away on the far side of the fence.

My reason for coming here no longer seemed valid or important. I began to back away towards the gates. As I moved, the tethered dogs began to growl and yelp. At the same time the door of the nearest trailer was thrown open, and a girl stood poised upon the threshold, and I saw the pretty kitten-features, the tumble of long black hair, the now slim, almost too-thin figure of Sorsha, and somehow I was not surprised.

She beckoned me to her and I moved as if spellbound past the van and Landrover and the tethered dogs, my gumboots making no sound on the tarmac path or the flight of metal steps that led up to her door.

She stood foursquare in the doorway. I remained on the middle step which, since I was the taller, brought her gaze level with mine. I took in the closed windows, the solid chassis of the trailer, the height of the fence that reared up behind it, and I knew that even if Sorsha's baby had cried the whole night through, there was no way I could possibly have heard it.

She spoke in the gruff, uncompromising voice that I remembered. 'You'd best come in, seeing as you're here.' She indicated a strip of carpet which was taped to the top stop. 'And you can take your mucky boots off before you do!'

I kicked off my gumboots to reveal bright yellow socks which had an all-over pattern of Pink Panthers — a joke Christmas gift; typical of Imogen.

Sorsha stood aside to let me enter, she looked down at my feet and I saw the grin she did not try to hide. The door led directly into her kitchen. I tried not to stare, to show my amazement, but could not hold back from saying, 'But this is — well, it's — it's so —'

'Not quite what you expected, eh?' Her tone was sharp, amused, gratified by my astonishment.

'I don't know. It's the first time I've seen the inside —'

'Our trailers are different from the *gorgio* tourers,' she cut in, 'custom-built to suit our fancy. Special.' She moved from the kitchen into the living room; she watched my face as I took in the elegant brocade-covered sofas, the cabinets which held displays of Crown Derby china, and Waterford cut glass; the Chinese silk rug which covered much of the floor space.

I could see now why Sorsha had insisted that I remove my wellies!

It was difficult to admire the trailer and

its sumptuous fittings without sounding patronising. So I enquired about the baby and was taken at once into the bedroom, where she slept in an old carved rocking-cradle.

'Is she still waking in the night?' I enquired.

'Never did,' I was told. 'Sleeps right through. No trouble.'

'Are there any other babies in the Hollow?'

'Never a one. Spoilt rotten she is.'

'Yes,' I said thoughtfully. 'Well, she would be. All those aunts and grandmothers and cousins. Where are they this morning? I thought when I came through the gate that no one was at home.'

'The men went north days ago. A special job. The others are gone to the city. There's just Elvira and me and my grandfer and the dogs here, on our ownsome.'

I heard the drag in Sorsha's voice. The girl was lonely. I also saw the wariness in her face. I had chosen the right morning for my visit. But for her isolation, the need for diversion, she would never have invited me in.

She made tea, serving it in old thin china, with chocolate biscuits on a plate. We eyed one another from facing sofas. 'Funny,' she said, 'me making tea for you, this time.'

'Yes,' I said. 'Last summer seems an age ago. A lot has happened since that day you knocked on my front door. You've had your baby. My granddaughter has had hers.' I paused, not quite knowing how to continue. She and I had not acknowledged each other when in the hospital room. I had thought I was respecting her privacy, but perhaps she was offended?

'How is she? Your Fran?' Sorsha smiled, revealing small white pointed teeth. 'How's that whopping big boy of hers?'

'Fine,' I said. There was an air of complicity between us now which gave me courage. 'But he still wakes twice in the night to be fed.'

'Just like a fellah. Never satisfied. Anyways — he'll take some filling up, a *chavvie* that size.'

I was struck by the wisdom of her reasoning. I drank my tea and placed the valuable china carefully down on the glass-topped coffee table.

A cry from the bedroom brought Sorsha upright and running. She returned with the baby in her arms.

'Her name is Elvira. Hold her for me while I warm a bottle.'

I parted the folds of the shawl; the crying ceased abruptly. Huge dark eyes looked out of a kitten-face; a fluff of thick black hair curled upon her head. She was a very pretty baby.

When Sorsha came back with the bottle I said, 'She's your living image.'

'So everybody tells me. Well, that's a good job. Daughters ought to look like their mothers. Your Fran now — she don't look a bit like her mother and her father, nor you for that matter.'

'No,' I said slowly. 'Fran looks like my husband — her grandfather.'

'I bet that pleases him.'

'It did, when Fran was younger. My husband died seven years ago.'

'Sorry,' she said and then formally, sounding like a polite child, 'I'm sorry for your loss.' She looked down at Elvira who was feeding eagerly. 'Greedy little monkey,' she said proudly and then, without looking up, 'What brought you to my door, missus? What do you want with me?'

The memory of the disastrous drawings lay heavily between us. I, from embarrassment, could not bring myself to raise the subject now. She, I suspected, from superstition and a sense of dread, also chose to stay silent.

I said, 'When you came to my house in the city last summer, I was on the point of moving. Well — you told me so, didn't you. A bungalow you said, remember? So I moved just recently, and not to a bungalow but a little old house just up the road from here.'

Comprehension widened her eyes. 'That's you!' she said. 'That's you in the place with the crooked chimneys! That's you that's been making all that racket, hammering and thumping day and night!'

I thought she exaggerated somewhat, but could not deny that a certain amount of noise had been made. 'I'm sorry,' I said. 'It couldn't be avoided. The house was in a bad state. A lot of work needed to be done. But it's all finished now.'

She continued to look doubtful. 'You like that place, that house?' There was something in her tone that made me feel uneasy. I recalled the shadow I had seen, the unexplained crying of the invisible baby.

My answer was more vehement than I intended. I needed to convince myself as well as Sorsha.

'I love it! I really love it! And it's not as if the place was strange to me. I was born in Ashkeepers. I knew this lane, the little old house and Witches' Hollow, when I was a child. When I saw that the Toll House was for sale I knew right away it was what

I wanted. There is also the fact that Fran and Mitch live in Nether Ash. I'm not a young woman, Sorsha. I want to see as much of my family, especially John, as I possibly can.'

Family sentiments made good sense to her. She nodded her approval. 'Yes,' she said. 'I can see all that. But wouldn't you have been better off in one of them new houses?'

'No,' I said loudly. 'I would have hated living in among those yuppies! Definitely not my kind of people.'

The smiled spread wide across her face. 'I likes to hear you say that,' she said. 'It was the builder of them houses that put that great high fence up. Like we was not fit to be seen, or something! He threatened to get us moved off from the Hollow, but Uncle Manju foxed him! He straightway laid down tarmac, put in drains and piped water, and built the shower and laundry block. Council *mush* couldn't find fault no more when he came spying on us.'

She laid the baby across her shoulder and patted the little pink-clad back. ' 'Tis a *kushti* place, the Hollow. I was born down here, in my grandma's wagon.'

Something stirred far back in my mind. 'Your grandma? She'd be about my age, wouldn't she?' And then I remembered her, the skinny, pretty girl with the glossy black ringlets that I had so envied; her dark and penetrating gaze, and abrupt voice and manner. We had sat together in Miss Evan's classroom in the winter months when the travellers were pitched in the Hollow. My father had treated their chronic bronchitis, persuaded them into hospital for more serious illness. I had carried medicines to my father's gypsy patients. Now I became aware of Sorsha's keen gaze.

She spoke abruptly. 'I don't know how old my grandma is. How old are you, missus?'

'Sixty-eight.'

Sorsha thought about it; she began to display the natural hesitation of the traveller to pass on intensely personal information to anyone who was a non-gypsy. It was only her contact with Fran that had so far been my passport to her confidences. I sensed her withdrawal, her fear that she had already been over-friendly.

I said, 'Your grandmother's name is Estralita, isn't it? Your mother is also called Estralita. So how did you come to be called Sorsha?'

I wanted to smile at her shocked face. Without considering consequences she blurted, 'My father is an Irishman. Sorsha was his mother's name.' I saw her arms tighten around the baby's sleeping form. 'What do you know about my grandma and my ma?'

I spoke gently, wanting to reassure her, to prove some slight credibility of my own. 'My father was the village doctor in Ashkeepers. He took care of your family when they were pitched here. Your grandma came sometimes to the village school. I knew her well.'

'They was rotten to her in that school! They called her *diddecoi* and hedge-hopper and dirty gyppo!'

'I know they did, Sorsha. It was very cruel. But there will always be ignorant people who name-call those who are different from themselves. She was a clever girl, so they were jealous of her. She was pretty too. You look very much like her.'

A tentative smile eased the tension of her features. 'Why for you never told me all of this till now?'

'I didn't know myself, did I? It really hadn't occurred to me that the same family would still be pitching here in the Hollow. It was a long time ago, Sorsha. Sixty years. A lot has happened since then, not all of it good. And my memory is not what it was.'

'She'll want to see you — my grandma.'

'And I would like to see her.' I paused. 'It's amazing, isn't it, the way a family like-ness is sometimes handed down. That morning last summer, when you came knocking at my door, I knew right away that you reminded me of someone, but I couldn't remember who.'

She nodded. 'I told you then that you hadn't seen the last of Sorsha!' She laughed. 'What a story I got to tell them when they come home!' She rocked Elvira in an ecstasy of mirth, and then suddenly sobered. 'But they'd best not know I went into your house. 'Tis hard to tell it now when I didn't tell it then.'

Oh, I knew exactly what she meant! 'Don't worry,' I said. 'It shall be our secret.'

As a seal of our friendship she handed Elvira to me. 'You can put her down if you like.'

As I carried the tiny girl to the rocking-cradle I realised with great pleasure that the child in my arms was Estralita's great-grand-daughter. I also realised again that the baby in my arms could not possibly be the one who cried so heartrendingly in the region of the Toll House.

I agreed in the end to spend Christmas

with Imogen and Niall, but on Christmas Eve I developed flu and so passed the next week in bored isolation. By the time my temperature was normal and the worst of the symptoms were subsiding, I was heartily sick of all television and radio programmes, and had reread all the best books in the bookcase. To add to my frustration, the weather, which had before Christmas been so cold and snowy, was now mild, with unseasonal sunshine.

From the kitchen window I could see clumps of early snowdrops, and the green spears of daffodils, and the tips of what might turn out to be crocus and chionodoxa. I put on a heavy coat, a scarf, and warm boots. The air, as I stepped out onto the flagstones, was so clear and sweet I felt intoxicated. But the weakness in my legs betrayed me. I have to admit the truth, I tottered no further than the garden shed, went inside, and sat down to recover on a crate that was full of Monty Barnacle's mouldy books. I sat for several minutes; when the world ceased to spin I began to look around. On the shelves, among the balls of green twine and boxes of plant food, were stacks of other, larger books. There was one, bound in green leather, the lettering on its spine picked out in peeling gilt.

I lifted it down, glanced idly at the title, and almost dropped it from surprise.

I opened the stiff and speckled cover and found I was, in fact, holding *The History of the Village of Ashkeepers* by Montague George Barnacle.

Back in the house I made a pot of strong coffee and laced it with the remaining inch of good cherry brandy left over from a long-ago Christmas. I sat down close to the log fire and waited for the spirit to take effect. I was thankful that Imogen could not see me at that moment. I had refused to allow her to visit over Christmas on the grounds that there was nothing she could do to help, and contact with me might result in her passing on my germs to John. It was the final argument which convinced her, although she still phoned me every day.

The book lay unopened on the coffee table, its green leather binding disfigured by the patches of blue mould. This Montague George Barnacle must have been a most dedicated village historian. The book was a thick one, the leather and gilt an endearing indulgence by a writer who had been determined to see his life's work privately published.

In the warmth of the room the smell of mould became unpleasant. I fetched a damp cloth and a dry one and began to wipe away the fungus. In spite of my best efforts faint brownish stains remained. I thought about phoning Monty Barnacle and informing him that I had found his ancestor's valuable testament, and did he wish me to post it to him, or would he prefer to collect it?

But the very thought of Barnacle and his curious reluctance to finalise the house-sale, the inconvenience caused by the rubbish he had left *in situ*, made me angry and brought on a return of the weakness in my legs. I lay back in the chair, the book heavy on my knees, and knew that however valuable it was I would not voluntarily return it to its owner.

After all, I reasoned, he must know of its presence in the tool shed. If he wanted it back he could come and claim it!

In any case, I wanted very much to read what exactly it was that this particular Montague George Barnacle had written about Ashkeepers back in the eighteen nineties.

I was sleeping in my chair when Imogen arrived. I woke to find her looming over me.

'Your door was unlocked, Mother! I know this is the country, but even so you shouldn't take unnecessary risks. Fran always locks her door, you know! It's impossible to be too careful these days.'

'Fran,' I muttered, 'has an irreplaceable baby who might be stolen away. She has good reason to be careful. It was I who warned her to keep her doors locked.'

I looked up to catch the curious expression on my daughter's face. 'Nobody,' she said gently, 'is going to steal John, Fran's is only a small cottage, and the baby is never left alone. You mustn't worry so much. It's not good for you at your age.' She began to strip off her coat and gloves. She picked up the half-full coffee pot and took it to the kitchen, saying over her shoulder, 'I'll just revive this for us, shall I?'

She returned with the reheated coffee; I thought she might mention the brandy content, she could hardly have failed to notice the smell, but sometimes, when I least expect it, my daughter is capable of great tact.

She sat down in the facing armchair and at once pounced on Barnacle's book. She stroked the fine green leather, and touched a finger to the gilt.

'Oh my,' she said softly, 'now isn't this something! Would this be the same — ?'

I nodded. 'His grandfather,' I said.

'So where did you find it?'

'In the tool shed. Rotting away among a pile of rubbish.'

'But that's criminal,' said Imogen, who has a proper respect for books. 'Don't give it back to him. He doesn't deserve to have it. At least, not unless he comes here and demands it. This must have taken half a lifetime to complete. Seven hundred and forty-nine pages. Oh, mother! What a find!'

She turned to the first printed page and began to read.

'The village of Ashkeepers, known formerly as Moors End, gained its present title in or around the year seventeen forty-nine due to the custom of the local inhabitants of collecting and keeping the ashes of witches, who had recently been burned at the stake on the village green. It is fabled that every hovel, cottage and farmhouse had its lidded terracotta pot standing in a corner of the kitchen, in which reposed a goodly handful of what they believed to be the "magic dust" which they trusted would protect them from evil.'

Imogen shuddered, closed the book abruptly and replaced it on the table. 'Nasty,' she said, 'doesn't bear thinking about, does it? He writes about it with a sort of relish — "a goodly handful" — ugh!

I don't think I would have liked Montague George Barnacle.'

'You wouldn't be crazy about his grandson Monty, the estate agent, if you knew him,' I told her. 'However, he left this book, and I'm sure it's a pretty rare one, so I'll forgive him much.'

'You intend to read it? All of it?'

'Of course,' I said. 'But I don't suppose that opening paragraph is typical of the whole book. It'll be crammed with boring historical detail, like the date and time of day the horse trough was installed on the village green, and lists of the names of church incumbents going back to the year dot. But there might be a few small nuggets of riveting interest. It's got to be better than the current TV programmes.'

I gazed intently into the corners of the room. 'There must,' I said, 'at one time have been a vial or two of witches' dust placed strategically in this house. I must check with Niall, ask if he found any little lidded pots — ?'

'Mother! Really — sometimes I wonder about you!'

And well you might, my dear daughter. And well you might.

That one springlike day turned out to be what country people call 'a weather-breeder'. The snow returned, bringing blizzard conditions and serious drifting. Mercifully our power and telephone lines remained in place, and my stocks of food, and logs were still more than adequate.

I looked upon my enforced isolation as being a time of necessary convalescence. And for entertainment there was always Barnacle's book.

I began to read the word of Barnacle on a January afternoon, with snow drifting halfway up the windows, Roscoe snoring by my feet, and a full wine glass of Harvey's Bristol Cream standing at my elbow. I was prepared for boredom, my jaws already primed for yawning. I skimmed through the first gut-gripping paragraph which had so upset Imogen and which was headed Preface. '— Ashkeepers, known formerly as Moors End — the custom of local inhabitants of collecting and keeping the ashes of witches — burned at the stake on the village green —'

Old Montague George had certainly known how to grab his readers' attention on the first page. He continued: 'In preparing this history of the village I have been sorely tempted to omit the more startling and unedifying aspects of the nature of some of its populace. But to do so would be to deny truth, and to vitiate the purpose of my labours, and so, dear reader, I make no apology for any startling disclosures which may appear in the following pages. I will commence with the sparse information available to this historian, and relating to the hamlet known as Moors End which consisted in those days of three farms and a sprawl of hovels which housed labourers and their families. The low-lying land was unproductive, the hamlet flooded and unapproachable in winter. Even in summer, in times of drought, the only path down to the farms was narrow and unfrequented. The place itself and the handful of people who lived in it were spoken of, even then, in whispers by their distant neighbours. It was said that these farmers were ungodly men who prospered only by means of chicanery and evil, and who deliberately cultivated their isolation as a cover for their misdeeds. Witchcraft was hinted at but not confirmed.

'In recording these facts it must always be remembered that the time of which I begin to write is the mid-eighteenth century, an era of great wickedness and corruption when Satan stalked the land, and an unrecognised amount of power lay in the hands of highwaymen and witches. This unchallenged power permitted them, initially, to terrorise and plague the simple country people, and to rob any man or woman who dared venture unprotected onto the King's highway.

'When some belated measure of summary law and order was finally accomplished, a significant amount of justice was then seen to be meted out on the gibbet and stocks on the green of Ashkeepers village.

'In the following pages I shall tell the stories of those times as they were told to me when I was a young man, by my grandfather Barnacle, who was a mighty raconteur, and accomplished in the expressive oral tradition of his time.

'I have no reason to doubt the absolute truth of these tales, and have verified many of them by diligent research of my own.'

Montague George Barnacle
The Toll House. Ashkeepers. May 1928

# THE HISTORY OF THE VILLAGE OF ASHKEEPERS

## Chapter 1

I have found it difficult to determine which came first, was it the toll road, or the village proper? It may well be that the presence of the one promoted the growth of the other. I suspect that certain papers pertaining to these matters have long since been destroyed. It is a matter of record that two coaching inns were built in the vicinity, between the years of seventeen fifty and seventeen fifty-five. At around the same time a triangular strip of greensward seems to have become established on the high ground beyond the turnpike, around which cottages, a blacksmith's shop, a dairy and bakehouse soon evolved. Eventually the remains of a long-defunct church were resurrected, and two further chapels built. A community was gradually coming into existence, where formerly only sheep had grazed.

I believe it was also at about this time

that the valley known as Moors End was renamed Witches' Hollow, and deservedly so, in view of the unspeakable acts which were performed there. The village which stood above the Hollow was soon to earn itself the doubtful *soubriquet* of Ashkeepers, and is known by that title to this very day. In the year of seventeen fifty it was proposed that certain interested persons should subscribe towards road repairs, and a toll be exacted for the use of such a road.

According to my grandfather's tale, the first toll house was no more than a rough wooden shack, thrown up hastily beside a swinging metal turnpike gate. The wealthy gentlemen who had risked money in the financing of these road improvements wished to measure the return on their investment before raising a more permanent and expensive dwelling. I have no information as to the type of man who inhabited that first toll house. Whatever was known of him became quickly overlaid by the dramas and tragedies which attended the sojourn of his unfortunate successor. In the year of seventeen fifty-two the wooden shack was demolished and a tidy little toll house built of local stone, the walls of which were one foot thick and the windows mullioned and with leaded, diamond-shaped panes. There were two downstairs rooms and two up, plus a single-storied extension which was artfully angled to give a comprehensive view of all traffic which approached on the gateward and leeward sides.

The former metal turnpike was replaced by a heavy gate of wooden manufacture.

It was required of the toll-keeper that he be a man of unblemished character and honest reputation, willing to man the gate and extract the tolls both by day and night. His reward was a stipend of fifty pounds per year, and sufficient ground for the stabling of a horse or two, and the keeping of a house-cow, pigs and hens; he and his family also occupied the Toll House at no extra costs to themselves.

The job of turnpike-master, set out in these terms, would appear to be a sinecure. But the isolated nature of his task, the contentious, sometimes dangerous aspect of the work, seemed to attract a certain type of individual. This second 'Pikey' of Ashkeepers was typical of his kind; morose, foul-mouthed, short-tempered, and sadly ill-favoured as to looks, having a wall-eye, sparse hair, and a bilious complexion.

The mystery was that a beautiful young woman like Pennina could bring herself to marry and go to live with him in the lonely Toll House.

Pennina herself was also somewhat of a mystery!

She had appeared out of nowhere, seeking work in the Three Choughs Inn. Her looks alone had secured her immediate employment. She was tall and slender, yet voluptuous withal. Her lustrous black hair fell in ringlets across her forehead and cascaded to her shoulders. Her skin had the whiteness more commonly seen in that of a high-born lady. Together with her full red lips, her dark and flashing eyes, it could truly be said that such a beauty had never been seen or dreamed of in the whole of our County. Pennina not only increased by fourfold the business of the Three Choughs, she added an atmosphere of class to what had formerly been a rough and simple pot-house. Coach-masters and postilions whose language had once been punctuated with the foulest oaths, become meek and quiet-spoken in her presence. Yet such was the coldness of her composure, that for all her smiling welcome, no man ever dared to lay a finger on her.

With hindsight it was soon plain to see that her arrival in the village had been carefully timed to coincide with the raising of the stone-built Toll House, and the installation as 'Pikey' of Ezra Lambton.

Now Ezra was not a true drinking man. He belonged to that school of reluctant imbibers who can sit for hours beside an inn fire, nursing without intention of calling for a refill the same half-pint pot. Like many a lonely and unsociable man he craved to be among his fellows, but not in conversation with them. There was also the nature of his work which made visits to the inn infrequent. Imagine then the amazement of all who witnessed the first approaches made to Ezra Lambton by that remote and lovely woman, Pennina.

On those evenings when a stand-in could be left to man the toll gate, Ezra made for the Three Choughs and sat as close to the bar-room fire as safety of his person would allow. On such occasions, Pennina herself fed the fire with dry logs, and enquired tenderly as to the state of Ezra's health and comfort. It was soon observed, though spoken of only in whispers, that Pennina would sit for a full half-hour, chatting and smiling with the 'Pikey'; and misanthrope and confirmed bachelor that he was, even Ezra began eventually to respond to Pennina's charms. He appeared ever more frequently in the ale house. He sported a red silk cravat; a smear of scented oil adorned his sparse hair. But no amount of fine feathers could ever have concealed the crabby nature of the man, and yet Pennina gave every sign that she found his character and person fascinating.

It came as no great surprise to the patrons of the inn when the first wedding to be celebrated in the newly resurrected church was that of Pennina and Ezra Lambton.

It was always at this point in his tale that my grandfather Barnacle would pause and draw his thoughts together. For now he was on the point of returning to a far distant past which must, for the sake of the descendants of those concerned, be accurately reported.

The following extraordinary account of kidnap, murder, and allied evil deeds came down to my grandfather's grandfather from his own dear father, who had often told the tale when his family were seated around the fireside on a winter's night.

These facts, passed on by word of mouth down several generations, are now to be here committed to paper for the first time ever.

Little Georgie Barnacle had no recollection of his parents, or indeed of his dire beginnings in this hard world. His first clear memories began at the age of six or maybe seven years when he was taken from the poorhouse to the newly raised Toll House to work for his master Ezra Lambton. Georgie's tasks were the chopping of wood, the sawing of logs, and the constant tending of the fire; for the 'Pikey' was a man who complained of the cold even in the height of summer. Georgie took charge of the livestock, feeding, and cleaning out the habitations of horse and cow, pigs and chickens. He prepared the rough and ready meals that were eaten by his master and himself. He slept, summer and winter, on a heap of straw in the barn. When Ezra Lambton embarked on what can loosely be described as his courtship of Pennina it was young Georgie who was left alone to man the heavy toll gate and collect the tolls. The boy was never to forget in all his long life the arrival of the new Mrs Lambton in the turnpike kitchen.

Pennina, it would seem, had never prior to her marriage, set foot in the place which was to be her home. Ezra had taken her outright refusal to visit a bachelor in his living quarters, and unchaperoned, as being yet another proof of her purity of soul and her good breeding.

The wedding had been celebrated on a Sunday, and in the springtime of the year.

The 'Pikey' was not a popular man; his only witness was a potman from the inn, while the landlord of the Three Choughs accompanied Pennina.

A handful of ragged urchins sent up a cheer as the couple emerged from the church door and made their way back on foot down the flinty road towards the turnpike.

Georgie's knowledge of the fair sex had been limited to the toothless crones who administered the poorhouse, and the rare glimpse of an elegantly gowned lady as her carriage swept through the Toll House gate.

Imagine if you can the child's astonishment at his first sight of Pennina Lambton in her wedding gown of crimson lace, her glorious black tresses twined around with fresh spring flowers; the smile on her lovely face that was for him alone. As she bent towards him and gently stroked his face, Georgie knew that should it be necessary, he would happily die for Pennina.

It was Ezra who was to feel the first lashings of her tongue! Having touched Georgie's thin pale face, she then turned upon her new husband. 'You didn't tell me I should find a half-starved child here! Is he the "servant" you referred to, the "man" left in charge when you came up to the Three Choughs?'

Ezra, unprepared for this sudden change of mood in his beloved, stuttered that yes, Georgie was indeed that one.

'Then shame on you,' cried the new bride. 'Just look at him. He's naught but skin and bone, and stinking dirty with it.'

'He tends the livestock,' muttered Ezra, 'he's bound to get a bit of muck on him. But don't you worry, my love, he sleeps and eats out in the barn. You won't even have to look upon him if the sight offends you.'

It was this final statement that truly enraged Pennina; she stood, hands on hips, in the middle of the kitchen and looked about her. She spoke in the low tones that Georgie came to know as presaging trouble.

'Husband,' she said, 'the state of your house resembles the filthiest pig-sty, the stinkingest midden I have ever witnessed. If something is not done immediately to remedy matters — then I too shall sleep this night alone and on straw, and in your barn!'

She turned back to Georgie. 'Water,' she ordered, 'heat it on the fire — and quick about it; and bring the broom and shovel.' She reached up to the clothes line where the tollmaster's shirts aired above the stove. She began to tear the flannel into strips.

Still dressed in her wedding gown, the flowers wilting in her hair. Pennina thrust shovel and broom into her husband's hands and commanded him to clean the floors, while Georgie heated water, and she herself used strips of shirt to clean the piles of greasy pans and dishes that lay on every surface.

When the kitchen was scoured to her satisfaction the rest of the house received the same attention. The evening was well advanced when Pennina, the damp curls clinging to her neck and forehead, the bridal gown now stained and bedraggled, called for more hot water with which to scrub her husband and the weary Georgie.

There remains no record of how Ezra Lambton felt about the dousing. But Georgie, in his old age, greatly enjoyed the telling of this first bath taken in his young life; and how, wearing a clean pink flannel shift which belonged to Pennina, he was bedded down that night in luxury on a quilt beside the kitchen fire.

There is no record of the bedding of Ezra. But I think it may be safely assumed that exhaustion rendered him incapable of anything more that night save grateful sleep.

# Nina

Spring came slowly that year. Hard frost alternated with bitter winds; and then towards the end of March we had a few of those tender days when a lemony light and the stilled air tempted us to walk in our gardens to exclaim with delight over lingering snowdrops and crocus, and daffodils which trembled on the brink of flowering.

I visited the churchyard. I could not have said why, but the place had begun to hold a fascination, a drawing power, which would not allow me to pass by the lych-gate.

On the path which led to the Lambton graves I met the sexton. He remarked on the small bunch of flowers in my hand. 'Snowdrops have lasted well this year. It's all due to the cold, of course. Worst winter we've seen in Ashkeepers since nineteen sixty-three.'

'Yes,' I said. 'So people tell me. I moved

here last September, from the city. I had forgotten what winter was like out in the country.'

He gave me a measured look. 'You'll be the lady who bought the Toll House?'

'Yes.'

'That place stood empty for a long time.'

I had the strong impression that his words were intended to convey a concealed message. I had sensed the same veiled hostility, almost threat, when speaking to the milkman, the butcher, the grocer, the woman who served in the bakery. The only truly welcoming face among the tradespeople of Ashkeepers was that of Mr Patel, who owned the newsagent's shop on the village green.

Until this moment in the churchyard I had let the matter ride. But on that balmy morning I grew angry.

'Why,' I demanded of the sexton, 'why do you think the Toll House stayed empty for so long? Is there something I don't know about it?'

He had not expected to be challenged. He shuffled his booted feet and did not meet my gaze.

'Well, come on now,' I persisted, 'out with it! Am I likely to suffer death-watch beetle, or subsidence? Or perhaps you are trying to tell me that the place is haunted?'

It was the final word that spooked him. He touched his cap, bid me 'G'morning,' and moved swiftly off towards the south door of the church. 'So what sort of ghost do I have?' I called after him. 'Is it a headless lady or a mad monk?'

He half turned and spoke across his shoulder. 'Do you ever hear a baby crying, Miss Lambton?'

I recognised him then by the sly tilt of his head. Oh yes, I remembered James Luxton, the school bully.

I began to say that my name was Franklin, but there was no point. In my arrogance, and convinced that in fifty years of absence people would have forgotten about me, I had believed that no one in Ashkeepers would recognise Nina Lambton, the doctor's daughter. But the sexton and I had sat at the same wooden desk in the village schoolroom. He had been a police cadet in nineteen forty-nine, when my firstborn daughter had been stolen from her cradle.

I stood for a long time, the foolish snowdrops clutched in my cold hand, unable to move or switch my gaze from the south door of the church through which the sexton had disappeared.

Some people react to extreme shock by

behaving as if nothing extraordinary has happened. They continue to go about their daily business showing no emotion, no distress. Sometimes they are heard to laugh, to make inappropriate remarks, unlikely observations.

I am one of those people.

Like Imogen and Niall, I am really only a Christmas-and-birthday-party drinker. On the morning of Jack's funeral I drank a third of a bottle of Bell's whisky. Drank it straight down, not having eaten any breakfast. I stood stone-drunk at the graveside, only partially anaesthetised by the strong spirit, showing nothing but a blank face, not weeping, not slurring my speech or staggering, but dying quietly inside, where nobody could see.

You think, when you are young, that certain moments are indelible, that no matter how long you live, or what happens in your life, you will never forget the exact contours of your just-born baby's face; that startled, slightly crumpled first gaze; his first cry.

I thought I would remember forever the baby we had not yet named. What I actually recall, still recall after almost fifty years, is her scent, that unique baby-smell that is said to be a trick of nature, intended to bond together child and mother in the days immediately after delivery.

In the weeks that followed her abduction, I could not be parted from her pink cot blanket. I slept with my face burrowed into its softness, I carried it everywhere with me in those awful days, so that I might still breathe in her baby-scent, and believe that whoever had stolen her would take pity on me.

I walked down to the Lambton graves. The Michaelmas daisies were brown and shrivelled; I threw them into the waste bin, filled the jar which had held them with fresh water, and arranged the snowdrops. The shock of the sexton's recognition of me had made my movements awkward. I spilled water on my coat, skinned my knee on the sharp curb of the gravestone as I leaned over to position the flower jar. I had planned to walk to Nether Ash that morning. Instead, I sat down on the bench beside the lych-gate. Before seeing Fran, before any further contact with John, my great-grandson, I needed to sort out my thoughts.

The horror which had happened all those years ago *had happened*.

There was nothing I could do to change things.

While I lived in the city it was possible to believe that those terrible events were a secret agony known only to Jack and me. But half a century of self-delusion had insulated me against reality. By cutting all ties, refusing all contact with my family and childhood friends, I had believed myself invisible. I had imagined that those who might have remembered me were either dead or senile. I sent flowers, but had not attended my grandparents' or parents' funerals; not even the funeral of Grandma Franklin.

I had not immediately known James Luxton. How many other old acquaintances and friends had I glanced at without recognition? They had clearly known me in spite of the passage of years and my changed appearance.

I thought back to the way I had looked at the age of eighteen; tall and slim, but rounded where it mattered most. My dark hair had swung at shoulder-length in the curled-under style that in those days was known as 'page-boy'. My father had once said that I was pretty; but after all — he was my father.

I remember laughing a lot; smiling because I was happy. I touched a hand to my short silver-white hair and thin lined face. Something about me had triggered someone's memory of those days, and the very thought of their knowledge sliced into me like the first cut of a surgeon's scalpel. I could feel old wounds, which even if never healed had partially closed over, begin to gape wide again, to throb and ache.

I began to recite the mantra which I had once believed would bring her back to me safe and sound.

'She is not stolen — only borrowed.'

It had never worked then. It would not work now. I should not have returned to live in Ashkeepers. I could see now that the subconscious longings which had drawn me back here were misguided, dangerous even!

What had I been thinking of? What lunacy had made me imagine that I could reinvent myself; my life? I had dreamed of turning back the clock; walking out again on the Nether Ash road with a baby sleeping safely in its pram. A child with fair hair and blue eyes, who looked exactly like his great-grandfather, Jack. For a whole year after Jack's death I had not believed that he was gone. I would come back to the house after only a short absence, and even as I turned the corner into Infirmary Avenue the conviction would grow that this time he would be there — waiting for me. As I put my key into the lock and turned it, I would feel his presence, waiting patiently in the hallway.

And then, on the first anniversary of his death, it seemed as if his spirit had departed, and a part of me was relieved, and another part bereft.

I had never once been aware of the spirit of my lost child.

In the days and weeks that followed her abduction I would sit in the nursery, holding the pink blanket and willing her to come to me, at least in spirit.

She never came, in spirit or in body, and I took this to be a sign that she was still alive. All these years on, and I still believe that my daughter lives.

I walked out of the churchyard and paused, chilled and indecisive, in the village street. From where I stood I could see the green sloping down towards the main road. Its stately old trees had looked magical at Christmas, their branches strong with tiny coloured lights. In February, in the time of snow and severe frost, the silver-rimed boughs had possessed a delicate unearthly beauty. Today, when it was almost April, and some hint of spring expected from them, those same branches showed no sign of green. The grass beneath them was still rough and weary-looking; even the clumps of daffodils which had pushed optimistically upwards through frost and snow, had all their buds discreetly closed against the interminable winter.

I began to move slowly down the gravelled path that led past the iron railings which were intended to protect the ancient stocks and whipping post from the attentions of present-day graffiti artists. Again I halted, and stood before the stone trough with its embossed date which proved that in eighteen eighty-seven the people of Ashkeepers had taken pity on and made provision for their thirsty horses.

The houses which stood around the green were all familiar to me. Their occupants had been my father's patients. I wondered who lived now in those attractive cottages, and how many of the elderly villagers who had been my contemporaries had already recognised me as being the girl they had known in the nineteen forties, the former Pennina Lambton, spinster of this parish. I decided it hardly mattered anyway. Jimmy Luxton, gossip and sexton of this parish, would long since have spread among them the news that I had returned and bought the Toll House.

I could not go to Nether Ash that morning. The effort of presenting a smiling face, of carrying on a normal conversation with Francesca, was beyond me. I would phone my excuses, plead a headache.

I turned toward Homesteaders' Valley as a light rain began to fall.

According to Imogen, who has a psychology degree and works as a counsellor, there is a simple and valid explanation for every quirk and deviation of human behaviour. I have wondered whether, if the point arose, Imogen could give me a convincing explanation as to why one woman should want to steal another woman's baby.

My daughter's favourite theory concerns her mother. She believes, and frequently says, that my state of mind is always reflected in the degree of attention I pay (or do not pay) to my personal appearance.

Imogen has noted that during buoyant optimistic spells I am at my most presentable. It is at such times that I visit the hairdresser, and use cream on the rough skin of my hands. It is also, presumably, that only when high as a kite for some unexplained reason, do I fish out my good clothes from the back of the wardrobe and pay attention to my make-up. In my ebullient states, according to Imogen, I am sufficiently well-groomed to appear publicly with my elegant daughter.

On my allegedly 'low' days, she actually

tells me to get a haircut, use a dash of lipstick. A general sorting-out takes place, a gentle weaning-away from old shoes and wellies, comfortable anoraks and woolly hats.

On one memorable occasion, having caught me unawares in a sweater, the elbows of which had started to unravel, Imogen concluded on the spot that I was already deep into a serious depression and needed some professional help. All of this is of course pure bunkum!

Imogen herself, who is as temperamental as a racehorse, invariably wears high-heeled shoes, a frilly apron, and a pale dramatic make-up when cooking the Sunday roast.

I rest my case!

On the morning of my meeting with Jimmy Luxton I was lower in spirits than I had been since moving to the Toll House. Theoretically, if Imogen's assessment of me was correct, I should have been wearing my gardening trousers, and the shabby duffel coat that was minus all its toggles. As it was, I had put on my 'good' black and white tweed suit and white angora sweater. Over it I wore a Burberry raincoat, one of Imogen's cast-offs, which although well-worn still proclaimed its pedigree to those who professed to recognise quality when they saw it.

I walked slowly into Ranchers' Close, still thinking about Jimmy and hardly noticing that the light rain had become a downpour. As I turned the corner into Pioneer Way a large dog leapt a garden hedge and charged towards me. I tried to sidestep, he swerved, both of us moving in the same direction. Collision was inevitable. The Dalmatian and I rolled together on the pavement. A woman's voice shouted 'Gorbi — Gorbi! You bad boy,' and then to me, 'oh, I am so sorry. Are you hurt? Let me help you up!'

I looked up to see a large well-corseted lady, her improbably blond hair already losing its style in the heavy rain.

There is no way at my age to rise gracefully from beneath a Dalmatian, especially when lying on a slippery wet pavement. The dog licked my face while his owner struggled to pull me upright. Shaken, but otherwise unharmed, I regained my feet and, still swaying, I hung on to the plump shoulder of my saviour. I attempted an embarrassed smile. 'I thought,' I said, 'for a minute there that he was going to bite me!'

'Gorbachev?' Her pencilled eyebrows almost vanished into her hairline. 'Oh, he's a sweetie, aren't you, precious! Gorbi wouldn't hurt a fly.'

The dog wagged his tail and pushed a wet nose into my hand.

'Haven't I seen you walking a dog?' the woman asked. 'Aren't you the lady who bought the Toll House?'

I said 'yes' to both questions, and my body stiffened involuntarily as I braced myself against further quizzing. I gave her a hard stare, suspecting her of being yet another faction of a village witch-hunt against me. But her face expressed no more than mild concern as she began to lead me towards her garden gate.

'You're looking awfully pale,' she said. 'You really must come in and rest for a moment.'

I wanted to resist, to walk away and reach the solitude and quiet of my own house. I needed to think, to work out exactly what was happening to me. But the unpleasant truth was that I felt faint and slightly nauseous. As I climbed the three steps up to the woman's front door, I felt a trickle of blood below my left knee. The fall had reopened the graze I had suffered in the churchyard. I allowed myself to be led into a warm and cheerful kitchen, and parked upon an upright chair beside the table.

'Hot sweet tea, I think, don't you? Best thing in the world for shock.'

Almost at once a thick blue mug of Ceylon's best was plonked in front of me. I was reminded irresistibly of Sorsha, and that morning last summer when she told my fortune. I drank the tea and immediately felt better. I began to look further than my tea mug. A large tray, decked out with embroidered lace-edged cloth and cups and saucers of fine china, was placed at the far end of the table. Several dollied plates held sandwiches and fairy-cakes and an assortment of biscuits.

Noticing my interest, my hostess explained. 'It's my turn to do the coffee-morning. We're organising a bring-and-buy in aid of aged horses.'

'You're attached to the church, I expect?'

'Oh no!' Her face and voice could not have been more outraged if I had accused her and her friends of organising a session of sadistic practices and unholy rituals. 'We're a very select little group, you know.' Her laughter was self-conscious. 'We Homesteaders don't consider ourselves to be any part of that village.' She waved a dismissive hand in the direction of Ashkeepers. 'Not that we didn't try, mind you. Oh yes, we all made heroic efforts when we first moved here.' Her voice took on a hard edge. 'Oh, you'll soon find out for yourself when you try to integrate with them. You not only have to have been born here. Your family name has to be on every other headstone in the churchyard, going back to the Flood and further.' She shrugged. 'We Homesteaders decided in the end that it wasn't worth the bother. We ladies have our bridge club, and our mother and baby group, and of course our coffee mornings. The children have pony club and little discos. The men belong to the same golf and sailing clubs. We are a very close little community. Well, we have our own standards, don't you know. Standards are important, don't you think? Wherever would we be without standards?'

I nodded weakly, but she scarcely noticed. She was fluffing up her damp hair and pushing her feet into black patent court shoes that were a size too small. She checked the tray and the loaded plates, and turned up the central-heating thermostat by several notches.

I half rose in my chair. 'You've been very kind,' I said. 'I'm feeling much better now.' It was not altogether true, but the prospect of meeting a flock of lady Homesteaders was more than I could face. But I was too late.

A chiming doorbell which played the first

bars of 'Una Paloma Blanca' sent her scuttling into the hall. Squeals of delight and welcome faded and I could hear her explaining my unexpected presence as the guests were ushered into what she called the lounge. My hostess came back into the kitchen. 'You can't possibly go now,' she whispered. 'You must come and meet the girls.'

Her gaze flickered across me for any latent signs of unsuitability. She had already checked the label in my raincoat as she draped it to dry across a chair. The black and white suit and fluffy jumper had been mentally priced before I was invited in. My shoes, which were from Marks and Spencers, would not quite pass muster, but in view of my injury, she had obviously excused my lack of taste in footwear.

I had, rather meanly, allowed her to believe that my bloodied knee was all the fault of Gorbachev. But then, I no doubt lacked her high moral standards. I followed her into the lounge. A dozen pairs of eyes assessed me. 'I don't know your name?' my hostess whispered. I forced a smile. 'Nina,' I told the Homesteaders, 'new owner of the Toll House.'

Their relief was palpable. Not only was I an incomer, but my Burberry now hanging on a peg in the hall had no doubt been noted and filed in a dozen well-coiffed heads. Their mass insecurity amazed and appalled me. As I sat down and accepted a cup of coffee and a fairy cake, there was a general relaxation of tense muscles and faces. A small birdlike woman who wore a scarlet cashmere sweater and appeared to be in charge of the meeting, sat forward in her chair and proceeded to introduce her friends. She had one of those penetrating voices which would, without effort or benefit of microphone, reach the rear wall of any town hall. I took in only one name. My hostess was Primrose, better known as Primmie. I was invited to tell them 'a little about myself'.

I had, I said, recently moved to Ashkeepers from the city to be nearer to family, since my granddaughter and her husband and child lived in Nether Ash. I was, I said, a widow. I had one married daughter. I liked to read, to sketch and paint. I had a small dog named Roscoe.

Smiles of approval spread from one face to another. The scarlet cashmere lady nodded and quivered like a demented robin. Her band-saw whisper echoed round the room: 'Could be quite an asset? Ask her to join our sketching group?'

I shrank back into my seat and busied myself with drinking coffee. Talk became general. Without moving my head, my gaze swivelled left and right around the room, which could be described in the one word: beige. Someone, some publication, perhaps *Homes Beautiful* or *Graceful Living*, had told Primmie that beige was tasteful and fashionable. She had taken the advice too literally. Beige carpet and curtains. Beige sofas and armchairs. Beige wallpaper and paintwork. Even the dried-flower arrangements and photograph frames were in toning shades of fawn and sand.

Photograph frames! My gaze returned to a large coloured studio portrait which stood on a side table, and which had been partly obscured by the arm of a generously built lady, dressed from shoulder to ankle in Stuart tartan. As she moved to make her choice from the plate of chocolate biscuits I looked, closed my eyes, and looked again at the smiling photographed features of estate agent Ashley Martindale.

Primmie noticed my interest, if not my shock. 'My grandson!' she said proudly.

As I walked into my house the telephone was ringing. It was Fran, worried by my failure to show up that morning. I blamed my absence entirely on the tussle with Gorbachev, and gave her a quick rundown on the Homesteader ladies, and their chagrin at being shunned by village society.

'It's not like that here in Nether Ash,' said Fran. 'At least, if it is, I haven't noticed.'

'But this is Ashkeepers,' I said. 'It's always been a very clannish sort of place. Secretive. Unhealthy. There's a kind of power thing that is passed on over here among the old village families. They don't take kindly to strangers. Or to those whom they believe to have transgressed.'

The line from Nether Ash was silent for several moments, and I began to fear we had been disconnected. And then Fran said, 'Grandma? Are you okay? You don't sound quite yourself.' She paused. 'You seem to know quite a bit about Ashkeepers?'

I don't know why I told her; I certainly hadn't meant to. Perhaps the meeting with James Luxton, and my subsequent acceptance into the Fellowship of Homesteaders, had unhinged my usual barrier of caution.

'I was born here,' I said quietly, 'and there are times when I almost wish I had died here.'

In my normal cheerful voice I added, 'I'll see you tomorrow morning then! Have John ready and in his pram for around ten o'clock. I'll bring a bag of stale bread, and we'll feed the mallards down by the duck pond.'

When I was a child growing up in wartime Britain I would first eat the cabbage and potatoes, and save the precious egg or slice of Spam till last. The fact that the special treat had grown cold at the edge of my plate did not seem to matter. I would eat it slowly, savouring each mouthful.

I found myself applying the same trick of anticipated pleasure to my reading of Barnacle's book.

The events of the morning had left me shaken and more disturbed than I wished to admit. The heavy rain persisted into afternoon, making gardening impossible. I put a match to the laid logs, pulled my chair closer to the fire, wrote two long and overdue letters to distant friends, made a pot of tea, and turned finally to the writings of George Montague. I imagined him bewhiskered, wearing a frock coat and high collar, penning his manuscript seated at a roll-top desk.

# BARNACLE'S BOOK

## Chapter 2

We have no way of knowing just what it was that Ezra Lambton expected of marriage. He was not a young man. The church records of Ashkeepers show Pennina's age on the day of her wedding to be twenty-two years; she is described as a maidservant. Ezra admitted to thirty-nine years, and his father had been a shoemaker. They were in every possible way an ill-matched couple. One would have imagined the misanthropic Ezra to be more suited to the bachelor state; while the benefits of such a union to the young and beautiful Pennina are indeed difficult to see, at this point.

It would seem, from my grandfather's tale, that the main beneficiary of Ezra's nuptials was the poorhouse child, Georgie Barnacle. From the moment she crossed the threshold of the Toll House, Pennina had shown herself to be both mistress and master of the place. Whatever her origins, somebody, somewhere, had taught her well the domestic skills that were necessary to a country housewife. In those first weeks of her occupation, she scrubbed and polished, washed and mended; and most important of all from Georgie's point of view, she produced hot meals, succulent roasts and sweet puddings, the like of which he had never known in his young life. In spite of Ezra's objections the boy continued to sleep beside the kitchen fire. When travellers came in the small hours, knocking at the door and shouting 'Wake up there, Pikey!' it was no longer Ezra who stumbled half asleep into the office, but Georgie who took the top money, issued the ticket, and opened up the heavy gate. His reward was a good hot breakfast the next morning, and a smile and a touch of Pennina's fingers on his cheek. Make no mistake about it, dear reader! Georgie Barnacle was, and always would be, her willing and devoted slave. For this Pennina Lambton was a very clever young woman.

The Toll House of Ashkeepers, under her direction, became a model of its kind; its keeper always prompt and fair now in his weighing of vehicles and livestock, and the pricing of tickets. Ezra himself, although still taciturn, was no longer truculent. After six months of Pennina's cooking he had obviously gained weight. With the increased girth had come a certain mildness of manner, a disinclination for argument and strife. It was observed by the regular users of the toll road that the Pikey looked to his devoted and beautiful wife for guidance in all matters.

It was also around this time that Pennina, who had never previously mentioned family, began to have visits from brothers, cousins, aunts and uncles.

They came on horseback, handsome and flashy characters, all of them possessing Pennina's same charm and persuasive tongue. The second bedroom was almost always occupied. The visitors were carefully obsequious to Ezra, and treated Georgie to good-natured chaffing. The child looked forward to their presence in the house, and scurried to assist their comfort. The comings and goings of such agreeable and colourful characters added zest and diversion to his somewhat lonely and secluded life. Georgie noticed, and in his child's way, half understood why Pennina herself sparkled and laughed when with her family, as she never did when alone with Ezra.

Having no family of his own, and knowing

nothing as yet about the ways of men and women, he was not surprised or shocked at the amount of kissing and cuddling, the amorous horseplay that went on between Pennina and her kin; but never, he noticed, in the presence of the keeper of the Toll House. For yet another change in Ezra's life had been his wife's insistence that he would pay regular visits to the Three Choughs. Too much time, she told him, spent away from the jolly company of their neighbours made him a dull fellow in her eyes. With herself and Georgie at home to man the gate, Ezra, so she said, owed it to himself to have a little leisure time, to enjoy the rewards of his hard-earned money; to at least take a sip or two of the excellent local cider. Pennina, so Georgie noticed, was always sweet and attentive to Ezra when he staggered back late at night from one of these drinking adventures in the Choughs. Georgie wondered sometimes why a clever young woman like Pennina should encourage the keeper of the tolls to absent himself periodically from his post, and indulge in the taking of strong drink, when to do so left him fuddled and incapable of working. If such a practice should come to the notice of the gentry and professional men who had invested their good money in the building of the Toll House and the laying down of a metalled road, and its subsequent upkeep, Ezra Lambton could well find himself and his wife swiftly out of house and job; and Georgie himself would be back in the poorhouse. But it seemed that Pennina by some magical means was always apprised well in advance of a visit by the trustees. Whenever those gentleman were due to come out from Exeter by the Quicksilver coach, Ezra was sure to be found sober and industrious, his accounts in good order, his young wife meek and subservient to him, and dressed as neatly and modestly as any Quaker lady.

Spring led into summer, and all went well with the inhabitants of the turnpike. Georgie's main task was the cultivation of the fruit and vegetable gardens. With Pennina's help the strip of land behind the house was more productive than it had ever been. Likewise, the hens now laid regularly; the pig would soon be fat enough for winter slaughter. And yet, at the very nub of things, it began to be obvious that all was not well with Ezra Lambton. By nature a solitary man, the almost constant presence of one or more of Pennina's relatives was becoming irksome to him. He would sit, when business was slow, on a wooden stool in his office and watch the road on the leeward side, as if longing for the diversion of a shepherd and his flock, a stagecoach from Frome or Shaftsbury; or some carter on his way to market.

His unwanted guests were not Ezra's only problem. There had been a sudden, recent increase in robbery on the King's highway. Several stagecoaches had been stopped and plundered; two business gentlemen had been shot dead on the road into Ashkeepers when they refused to hand over their purses. Not a single perpetrator of these crimes had as yet been apprehended. A shotgun and a brace of pistols now hung on Ezra's kitchen wall. A fierce dog was chained to a post beside the office door. Caught as he was between the roistering young bucks who were Pennina's kin, two or three of whom now seemed in almost permanent occupation of the second bedroom, and the threat of violence from without, he was finally forced to speak to his young wife.

Georgie remembered well the occasion of that first quarrel between his master and mistress, and the revelation it brought to Ezra and himself of a very different Pennina.

The trouble began on a Sunday evening in September. Business had been slow as it usually was on the Lord's Day. The Exeter stagecoach had come through, and when the toll was paid and the gate opened up by Ezra, Pennina came strolling out, as she often did, for a word or two with the coach-master. Georgie thought how fine his mistress looked that evening, in her dress of yellow silk, and with a single marigold plucked from their little flower-patch and tucked into her dark hair. The gown had been a gift from her cousin Jacob, bought in Exeter, and carried in his saddlebag to the Toll House. Somewhere along the road the dress had caught a small red stain upon the hemline, which Pennina had tried in vain to wash out. Ezra had scowled and said that such finery was quite unsuitable for a toll-keeper's wife. He had not quite forbidden her to wear it, but his meaning was made clear. Imagine then his anger when she openly defied him on that autumn evening. Not only was she, for the first time in their marriage, flouting his expressed wish; but with her hair dressed high, and the gown low-cut, she was deliberately flaunting her charms before the passing traffic.

Ezra listened in silence to the bantering exchange between his wife and the coach-man. She chaffed him about the servant-girls at his next stopping-place, wherever that might be? He said there was not a single one that took his fancy at the Swan in

Frome. She asked him about the state of the roads between Ashkeepers and the Swan. As long as the rain held off, he said, he should make good time and be tucked up in one of the inn's soft beds by ten of that evening. Coach journey times were improving. London to Edinburgh, which only two years ago had needed ten days, was now down to five; while Pickfords and their 'flying wagons' were covering the distance from Manchester to London in just over four days. Several new toll roads were under construction. Travel was the coming thing. People were finding out that there was another world beyond their own village green.

As the stage pulled away, Ezra closed the gate behind it with unaccustomed force and marched into the house, where he remained for many hours, sequestered in his office.

It was early in October when another kind of traveller rolled into Ashkeepers. They came with four flat-carts pulled by horses, two donkeys, and half a dozen coloured ponies. Eight men and six women, and several children. Georgie asked Pennina what manner of poor people these were, who had no proper roof above their heads save the leafless branches of the trees in Burdens' Wood.

'Gypsies,' she told him. 'They come here every winter. Did you never see the like of them before?'

He reminded her that the children in the poorhouse were put to working from first light till bedtime. Since coming to the Toll House, and especially since the advent of Pennina, Georgie had found time to witness more wonders of the world than he had ever dreamed of. At least four times in every week he was entrusted to carry a sealed note from Pennina to the landlord of the Three Choughs; his route to the inn lay through a long and muddy drovers' track which marked the western boundary of Burdens' Wood.

He had first seen the people known as gypsies as he walked to the Three Choughs in the dimpsey light that falls between afternoon and evening. As he turned into the drovers' track he had spied them coming towards him, but still a good way off. He at once dropped down into the ditch and crouched behind a whinberry bush. His heart almost ceased to beat as their thin and strange-looking dogs sniffed around him; though to his great relief they did not bark, but merely pushed at him with their cold wet noses, and then loped off after some imaginary rabbit. He watched the passing procession, wide-eyed and scarcely breathing.

He had thought, since coming to the Toll House, that he was man-of-the-world when it came to experience of strangers. Georgie Barnacle had seen them all! Or so he believed. There were the stagecoach masters; for the most part gallant fellows of skill and courage who flirted with the maidservants at all the posting-inns between Exeter and Bath, and then boasted to Pennina of their conquests.

And then there were the passengers who rode the Quicksilver line, and travelled to such distant places as Sherborne, Yeovil and Chard. Not that Georgie saw more of them than a quick glimpse through a stagecoach window of a pretty profile under a fancy bonnet, or a stern visage below a tall hat, as the wheels rumbled through the toll. But at night, wrapped in his quilt beside the kitchen fire, he dreamed of one day riding on the box beside the coachman; of seeing for himself Yeovil, Frome, and Taunton town.

Oh yes, Georgie had witnessed a wide variety of this world's men and women. But never before had he seen such a people as those who passed before him now. Unlike the drovers and carters who came through the toll gate, these people did not chaff and shout to one another, but walked in dignified silence. Except for one young woman whose flaming red hair hung down below her waist, they were all black-haired, dark-eyed, and with skin the colour of a polished walnut. The men led the horses which pulled the flat-carts. The women walked together in the rear, leading what he now observed to be three nanny-goats, as well as the two donkeys, and a half-dozen mettlesome ponies. The children were already scattered deep into Burdens' Wood. He could hear them calling to each other.

The procession veered off into a clearing between the beech trees. As the carts and their owners wheeled sharply to make a left turn, Georgie was granted a closer view of the gypsies, and what he saw was both alarming and yet fascinating. He realised, even at that first sighting, that these were a singular breed of people. No previous experience of human kind had prepared the boy for women who went barefoot and yet strode out straight-backed and head high, as if they were princesses. Neither had he witnessed men of such wild and yet handsome looks. The clothing of the group was a mixture of finery and rags, brightly coloured but ill-fitting, yet worn with as much confidence and style as ever was displayed by the original owners of the garments.

They did not penetrate far into the woods but halted in the clearing. The horses were unharnessed from the flat-carts and led away together with the ponies towards an adjacent paddock. The nanny-goats were tethered to an ash tree; and still no words had passed between the gypsies. Each one had a particular task. They did not crash and stamp about in the clearing as did the villagers when in the woods, but moved silently like apparitions, or people witnessed in a dream.

Georgie, although stiff and chilled, remained crouched beneath the whinberry bush. He could not bring himself to climb out of the ditch and continue with his errand to the Three Choughs, although failure to appear at the required hour might well earn him a beating from the owner of the inn.

He watched, open mouthed, as the four men, having first attended to their horses, came back to the clearing and proceeded to cut out long supple hazel wands from the surrounding bushes. They then made holes in the soft ground, using the sharp point of a black iron tripod.

The women, meanwhile, were unloading the flat-carts. The men pushed the hazel into the prepared holes, bending the wands over to make perfect arches. The women laid strips of blanket across the arched boughs until all was covered to make a number of little bow-shaped brown tents.

It was at that point that the children returned, appearing silently between the trees, their arms filled with brushwood and dead branches. It was not until the children came close to their parents that any speech passed between them, and then only a mattering and mumbling of which Georgie understood not a single word. Darkness had come down meanwhile, and the gypsies were now no more than shadows in the clearing, when the whole scene was lit up by the sudden flaring of their fire.

I have been told, dear reader, that even when a very old man Georgie Barnacle still told this story with as great a sense of wonder as he experienced when a child on that October evening. For, seen by firelight, these were a people both beautiful and terrifying. Their movements were graceful, like those of dancers. A tripod, the same one that had been used as a tool to make tent holes, was fixed before the fire, and a cooking-pot suspended from it above the flames. Water, also brought by the children from a nearby spring, was poured into the pot, and

what looked like potatoes and joints of rabbit added to it. To one side of the clearing
two boys milked the nanny-goats into a tin
pail. More brushwood was brought and laid
inside the little brown tents to make a dry
bed.

One by one, their tasks completed, the
company gathered to sit around the fire.
The last to join them was a young man who
carried a fiddle across his shoulder. As the
group settled down to await their supper,
Georgie came slowly back into himself. He
became aware of the undelivered note still
in his pocket, and the passage of time which
had been considerable. He climbed out of
the ditch and began to hurry towards the
Three Choughs.

As he ran down the grassy drovers' trail,
the wild, sad notes of the gypsy fiddler's
music reached out to him and touched his
very soul, and he knew that he would return
to Burdens' Wood as soon and as often as
he was able.

We shall never truly know what passed
through Ezra Lambton's mind in that winter
of seventeen fifty-three. It will not however
be presumptuous of us to guess, dear reader,
that by the onset of Advent, even Ezra must
have realised that the 'honeymoon' period

of his marriage was over, and never to return.

We are, of course, utterly dependent on the views and judgements of young Georgie for our information on this subject. But since the tale was told in the sere and mature years of his own life, I believe that Georgie brought his own gathered wisdom to the relating and interpretation of the worsening situation in the Toll House.

The onset of shorter days and longer nights meant an increase in his daily tasks, and yet less time in which to perform them. Georgie woke regularly at five of the morning, as had been compulsory practice in the poorhouse. It was to be his lifetime habit to rise at dawn, occasional inebriation and advancing years notwithstanding.

His first task of the day was to mend the fire and set the kettle to boil. Having put on his outer garments, and stowed away his quilt, he would check that the outside lamp was still burning and then make his way up to the barn.

These small hours were the best time of his whole day. He would light the lantern and hang it on a nail beside the cow-stall. He would speak first to the house-cow which had been named Arabella by Pennina, who had a habit of naming any animal that was unlikely to end up on their dinner table. He then addressed a few words to Pennina's bay mare, Nancy. Ezra disapproved of his young wife's foolish track of bestowing human status on brute creatures, although little had been said on that subject lately. With his head tucked into the cow's warm flank, and his fingers pulling milk down into the pail, Georgie thought about the changing, worsening situation between his master and mistress.

From the very beginning, Pennina had shown herself smarter than Ezra, more capable in every skill that counted in the business of the Toll House. Not that Ezra Lambton was a fool. Any man employed by the trustees of the turnpike needed to be able to read easily the many notes and forms involved in daily business, and to reckon up the weights and measures, and the cost thereof of such goods passing through the toll gate.

But Pennina was quicker!

And when a long line of stagecoaches and assorted wagons, interspersed with a herd or two of sheep and cows, awaited their turn to pay for the issue of a ticket to pass through the gateway, why then, speed was of the essence!

While the pedantic and slow-witted Ezra worked out on paper the cost of tonnage of live weight, in either animals or people, not to mention vehicles, Pennina had reckoned it all up in her head, and had the answer at her fingertips.

She was popular with the coachmasters and the drovers. Ofttimes there would be a clutch of eggs or a little posy left on the doorstep. But her popularity never strayed beyond propriety. There was no special word or gesture of familiarity between his wife and her admirers to which Ezra could take exception.

Not that he didn't try! Ezra grew daily more suspicious, more watchful; less than ever inclined to allow Pennina to work with him at the turnpike, even when his customers shouted and argued, and clamoured to be allowed to pay for the ticket that would permit them to continue with their journey along a good road.

So obsessed was he with his wife's success in what he rightly deemed to be man's business, that Ezra failed totally to notice what was happening inside the Toll House walls, and underneath his roof thatch.

But Georgie, who had learned a thing or two lately about the ways of men with women, from the lewd talk of postilions and cattle-drovers, had begun to eye with great unease the amorous antics of her many relatives when visiting Pennina. He had also noticed, when entering the barn that morning, two fine black stallions tethered in the corner stalls. His milking finished, he walked over to survey them.

The horses showed signs of severe exhaustion. Their coats bore a scum of dried-on lather, their eyes were dulled. He fed them, along with Arabella, and spoke gently to them. He wondered which members of his mistress's family had chosen to seek sanctuary with her this time.

# Nina

My reading was interrupted by an unsolicited phone call from a double-glazing salesman. The telephone was in the kitchen. Having slammed the receiver back onto its stand, I stood, quite still, acutely conscious for the first time of my own actual physical location in the house in relation to the past. I don't know why it had taken so long for this awareness to develop. But I had, from the moment I decided on purchase of the house, been concerned utterly with the changes I would make; the colours of wallpaper and paint, the installation of conveniences of twentieth-century domestic life, without which I imagined I could not exist. That first reading of Barnacle's book had merely skimmed the surface of my mind. This second instalment had begun to pull me inwards and back. Far back.

I had known of course that the single-storied room I called the kitchen must once have been the office from which the turnpike did its business. But knowing is not feeling. Today, I felt the shade of Ezra.

I stood before my stainless-steel, double-drainer unit, fitted with the mixer taps which, according to Imogen, were an indispensable aid to modern living. The window under which this miracle was installed was the one from which Ezra Lambton had watched the approach of cattle-drovers and their herds; and the stagecoach drivers of whom he was becoming jealous and mistrustful. Unlovable as he had been, I sensed his bewilderment and pain.

I looked out on to the narrow winding track which I had always known as Brickyard Lane. This lane would have been an old packhorse trail, green in summers, its lower reaches flooded in winter. It would still, in Ezra's time, have been one of many approaches to the toll-road; to that good, wide, well-drained, flinty thoroughfare which led to Ashkeepers village.

And it was down this road that Pennina must surely have often gazed with longing, while she issued the tickets which assured the travellers of a swift, if uncomfortable, journey. I asked myself yet again just what had she been doing in Ashkeepers to begin with? And exactly what had been her position in life before she came to work at the Three Choughs inn?

And why, given her looks and winning ways, as described by the first Georgie Barnacle, was she married at the age of twenty-two to a charmless dolt like Ezra Lambton?

I began to experience a fierce and protective feeling towards this Pennina, from whom I might even have taken my name and my dark looks. The other, less attractive side of the coin was my certain blood kinship with Ezra, from whom I, and several previous generations, had inherited their surname.

An inheritance, I now realised, which had ended with my father, William Lambton, who had only produced a daughter.

I stepped back and turned towards the run of white-fronted cupboards and drawers which now occupied the rear wall of my kitchen. I imagined a desk or a table which held stacks of tickets, and a wooden drawer or till which would contain the silver coins stamped with the profile impress of George of Hanover, the ruling King, with his craggy features and long nose.

There would have been the wooden stool on which Ezra sat when business was quiet. What had been his thoughts and fears, his probably well-justified suspicions of his young wife? And what of Georgie Barnacle?

In a time when the average life expectancy was less than thirty years, he had survived to what was then a great age, to pass on his tales to children and grandchildren. I looked down at the pattern of the carpet tiles laid by Niall, and imagined the original floor of beaten earth, and the child George, wrapped in his quilt asleep beside the fire.

I returned to my armchair and sat for a long time, with the heavy leather-bound book closed and resting on my knees. The house seemed to settle around me, protective and reassuring, like a shawl around the shoulders. I closed my eyes and almost slept. And then, softly into the silence, there began that hopeless, muted wailing of a very young baby.

I no longer sought the source of the crying but let the sound penetrate my consciousness, piercing and wounding as it was meant to do by whoever or whatever spirit wished to punish me by this means.

Spring continued to play a tantalising game that year.

A primrose-yellow day with mild sweet breezes and hazy sunshine would again be followed by a week of pelting rain which turned first to hail and then sleet.

I abandoned my self-imposed habit of walking to Nether Ash, and crept gratefully onto the bus. While a floor-level metal grill beside a rear seat blew out warm air on to my frozen feet, I listened in quite shamelessly to the village people's conversations. On Fridays the bus was filled with elderly couples on their way to do weekend shopping. I saw their closeness, their comfortable devotion, and felt a sharp stab of envy. If only Jack — !

My thoughts were broken into by a voice which reached every corner of the crowded bus.

'May I sit beside you? There's not a lot of room, is there, on a market day?' She had exchanged the scarlet cashmere for an expensive dark-green guernsey and toning skirt, topped by a Burberry which was much newer and cleaner than my own.

Without waiting for an answer she continued, 'I don't usually travel on public transport, you know! But my Audi has gone in to be serviced. So annoying, especially in this inclement weather.'

From her disdainful tone we might have been riding on a farm cart, recently used for the purpose of muck-spreading.

'Oh,' I said pointedly. 'I rather like the

263

bus. Of course, I prefer to walk in fine weather. So much healthier, don't you think? All this riding around in cars — so destructive of the environment; and so many women drivers quite unfit to be at the wheel at all!' The slur on women drivers was a blatant lie, but she was not to know that.

She said, her decibel rate slightly lower, 'I take it that you don't drive?'

Conversation among the other passengers, which had been brisk and noisy, now dropped to a low murmur. In a deliberately pitched voice which almost equalled that of my new friend, I said cheerfully, 'Never have driven. Never wanted to. As I said, I love the bus ride, especially on the top half of the double-deckers. Such lovely views! So panoramic, don't you agree?'

My desire to score points had led me into rashness. She saw her chance to pounce, and did so.

'Ah,' she bellowed, 'I was forgetting, you are an artist, aren't you? We were wondering, the girls and I, if you would care to join our sketch club? Only a small group, don't you know, but *select* and *nice*. Landscapes. Dogs and horses. Pretty cottages.'

'Ah!,' I cried, loudly disappointed, 'Well, isn't that unfortunate. You see, my favourite subject is the human figure. Male. Nude.'

'Unclothed?' She almost achieved a whisper.

I nodded. 'Sorry about that.' I was saved from further tricky explanations since the bus was already pulling into Nether Ash and the site of the Friday market. The expression on her face was one that would comfort me in times of self-doubt. As I stepped down into the driving rain, several senior citizens from Ashkeepers, who had never before acknowledged my existence, were grinning broadly in my direction.

Ah well. Even marginal acceptance was welcome; for whatever reason.

Fran's kitchen is blue and white with antique-pine units fitted by Mitch. They have this heavy farmhouse table large enough to seat ten people, and a kitchen dresser crammed with willow-pattern china. The working surfaces are tiled in blue and white. Fran had sewed the neat gingham curtains. Some kitchens make a happy statement about their owners. Fran and Mitch were homemakers.

In the time it took to walk from the bus stop to Fran's cottage, the rain had slowed and almost ceased. She took my damp raincoat, and then handed me a mug of tea. The washing machine, loaded with baby garments, hummed through its programme. Upstairs, in the lemon-painted nursery, John slept.

Fran had lost weight; a lot of weight. But her face no longer showed that awful pallor, or the dark rings round the eyes that had so alarmed me. She had regained much of her energy, her sense of fun. Incidents and conversations which I would not dream of telling to Imogen can be enjoyed a second time around with Fran.

I told her about the lady Homesteader met that morning on the bus, and the invitation to join the select and proper sketching group, and my refusal of the honour.

'I didn't know you used nude male models, Grandma?'

'I don't. I wouldn't know where to find one even if I needed such a subject. I made it up. I lied.'

Fran laughed. She said, 'Well, I can understand why! But don't you think it might be a good thing to take up painting again this summer? Not with Primrose and her gang, but on your own, the way you used to do? There must be subjects in Ashkeepers and district that you would enjoy sketching?'

The unasked question hung between us.

At her mention of Ashkeepers, we both remembered the phone conversation in which I had said, 'I was born here, and on one occasion I almost wished I had died here.' And Francesca, who was closer to my heart than any other woman, could not bring herself to ask the questions which were in her mind.

As I braced myself to speak, a cry from the nursery had Fran making for the stairs.

'John's awake,' she smiled, 'and the rain has stopped. You'll be able to walk with him, after all.'

The village green at Nether Ash has a duck pond, and swings and a climbing-frame scaled down for the use of toddlers. John hated to wear the yellow, warm and thickly padded snowsuit that restricted his freedom of movement, but once in his pram and away from his mother's concern, he ceased to struggle. But still he looked un-happy underneath the navy-blue hood, as we walked towards the water.

The mallards and coots, ecstatic from the recent rainstorm, quacked and waddled through the mud, and dived repeatedly into the swollen pond. To begin with the baby viewed them without interest, and then a group of a dozen or more of the wild ducks came waddling and bobbing around the pram. John leaned across the apron, sud-denly alert, his small face solemn and puzzled. I watched intently, wondering what thoughts were in his baby's mind. And then he began to laugh as I had never heard him. A great chuckling belly-laugh, that told me more surely than any words that he found them comic, and I began to laugh with him, until we were both of us red-faced and convulsed.

The laughter had the curious effect of binding us together, never mind an age gap of sixty-seven years. We had shared a private joke, and as we walked away from the duck pond, John would look up at me from time to time and begin again that fat, delicious chuckling sound that negated, at least temporarily for me, the sad wailing sound of the nonexistent baby who lived in the bedroom of the Toll House.

I slept well that night, and awoke with my head full of plans for a pleasant day of gardening. The outside temperature had risen overnight. I adjusted the central heating thermostat and opened a few windows. After switching on the kettle, I unlocked the kitchen door and let Roscoe out into the garden. I stood for a moment breathing in the soft air, and then turned back into the kitchen. It was only then, with the morning sun making this the spring day we had all been waiting for, that I looked down and saw the shiny black carcass of a dead crow, which someone had placed carefully in the centre of my doorstop.

There is a brand of nastiness that leaves a stain, and not only on the doorstep. Roscoe began to investigate the carcass, and I shooed him away to his regular relief-spot at the far end of the garden.

I collected newspaper and a brush and dustpan, and pulled on a pair of rubber gloves. But even protected from direct contact, a shudder of pure horror zinged through me as I manoeuvred the dead crow onto yesterday's *Daily Mail*.

As it lay I could see how the bird's head lolled at an unnatural angle. Its neck had been broken. The visible eye still seemed to hold a malevolent gleam, the feathers to catch a horrible semblance of remaining life from the brilliant sunshine.

It was when I began to roll the newspaper bundle together that I first smelled and then saw the scorched tail feathers, and the twist of string protruding from the shorter feathers of the neck. Gently, as if the bird was still capable of feeling, I teased out the frayed ends which hung from the little noose. I knew then that the burnt feathers and the loop of string was the special message I was meant to find. This was not just a dead bird.

It was not even a dead crow which just happened to draw its last gasp on the Toll House doorstep.

This bird of ill-omen was intended as a warning, and as a reminder that in times past the punishment of women for certain crimes had been death by simultaneous hanging and burning.

I pushed newspaper, crow, and rubber gloves into a carrier bag, and then sought a temporary hiding place for them, out of Roscoe's reach, and the sight of visitors. I turned on the hot water tap and scrubbed my hands in disinfectant until the skin burned. I placed the padlock key from the garden shed on a high shelf in the kitchen. All desire to spend a day working in the garden had vanished.

I sat in the kitchen and drank cup after cup of hot sweet tea and considered my options. For half an hour I allowed my imagination full rein. I visualised this shadowy someone, at first catching the crow and killing it, then looping the tiny noose about its neck, and burning the tail feathers. I forced myself to admit to the presence of that someone, quietly lifting the latch of the garden gate, approaching in darkness and stooping to lay his or her 'gift' on my door-step.

The degree of malevolence required to go through with the bizarre performance meant that somebody in Ashkeepers hated me or feared me; or maybe both.

I ruled out the Homesteaders, whose knowledge of witchcraft and ill-wishing was almost certainly restricted to a little genteel trick-or-treating on Halloween night.

Which left me with a choice of any man or woman in the village aged sixty-five years or over. Or possibly the sexton, Jimmy Luxton, about whose gender the village had never been quite certain.

It had always been the women who cold-shouldered me, who blamed and condemned me. Fifty years on, and either singly or collectively, some woman or women meant to drive me once again from Ashkeepers.

For what reason I could not begin to imagine. The past was a closed book. What had happened — happened. I posed no threat, could no longer be a source of embarrassment or shame to any living person.

If a lifetime of grief and tears can ever pay for a moment's youthful inattention, then surely I had paid my debt a thousand times over.

I considered going for a long walk, but walking would only lead to thinking, and today at least I could not face my thoughts.

At eight thirty in the morning, with my bed unmade and dirty dishes stacked in the washing-up bowl, I sat in an armchair and once again opened up Barnacle's book.

# BARNACLE'S BOOK

## Chapter 3

Georgie Barnacle was never to be certain of his exact age. Like many a male infant, abandoned by its mother and left in darkness on the poorhouse doorstep, he was named for the reigning monarch. The origin of his surname was, and remains, a mystery to this day.

It was Pennina Lambton who bestowed upon him an age and a birthdate; she who nurtured him, gave him an identity, and his own place in the world.

On the first anniversary of her marriage to Ezra she declared that same date to be Georgie's birthday. After a thoughtful examination of his physique, she declared him to be thirteen years old.

Georgie privately believed himself to be two years younger, but there was no denying that the last twelve months of good food, warmth, and a lightening of heavy duties had seen an amazing change in him. He was a whole foot taller. His chest and shoulders had broadened. His hair, cropped close to his skull while living in the poorhouse, had been allowed by Pennina to grow out into red and springy curls that tumbled to his shoulders. His face had the high and handsome colour that bespoke rude health and good living. He no longer cringed and shambled, whined and begged, but at Pennina's insistence Georgie walked tall and spoke up for himself, as befitted the son of the house he now saw himself to be.

His newfound confidence had been marked by his master and disapproved of.

'You make too much of that boy,' Ezra grumbled to Pennina. 'He's getting above hisself.'

'Would you have him still creeping about the place like a whipped dog?' Pennina patted her husband's shoulder. 'Boys work harder when they're well fed and cheerful. A full belly brings better results than a beating.'

'But it costs more.' Ezra moved away from her consoling touch. 'He's eating us out of house and home. As for them boots and clothes you bought him! Whoever heard of a workhouse bastard going fine in velvet, and leather shoon?'

'But he only wears the best clothes for church on a Sunday,' said Pennina. She had a special voice when reasoning with Ezra. She used it now. 'Husband, dear husband,' she bowed her head and linked her hands together, 'you must know by now that everything I do is done only for your sake. You must say that the Toll House is considerably improved since we wed. Why, you are held up by the trustees as an example to other turnpike masters. Everything is shipshape here, and Bristol fashion! You and I go well shod and looking decent, and Georgie is your assistant. How could you let people see him going about the place barefoot and in rags? He's a handsome child. Why, I've heard strangers mistake him for your own son.'

'You're a mite too fond of him,' Ezra muttered. 'You spoil him.'

'Ah!' cooed Pennina, 'so that's it. My dear old shaggy bear is jealous, is he?'

Georgie, lurking and listening behind the kitchen door, grinned hugely in his enjoyment of the altercation.

'You know you are my own true love,' Pennina whispered.

'Hmm. Well I don't know so much 'bout that either! There's all them young fellahs — your cousins and suchlike. Seems to me you're overfond of them too.'

'Oh, oh, oh!' Pennina wailed. 'Whatever shall I do with you, my sweetheart?' She held him by the shoulders and shook him gently. 'Don't you remember how, from all the men who gave me the eye in the Three Choughs, it was you and only you I chose?'

'Yes. Yes, I remember well. And that's something else I've wondered about lately.'

'No need for wonder, dear husband. I knew from the first moment I saw you, that you were quality. When I asked about you I was told how you were held in high esteem by his lordship up to the big house, and by the city gents in Exeter who formed the trust that built the toll road. Only men of spotless character and good conscience are chosen to be turnpike masters; which is as it should be. Just look at the responsibility you carry — all that toll money, Ezra! And you so brave and fearless too, living out here in this isolated spot, and only the gun on the wall for your protection.' Pennina paused and kissed her husband in the middle of his forehead. 'I looked for a long time, Ezra, for a man of your experience of the wide world. I am sorry if my silly ways upset you. I mean nothing by it. It's just that I find

the life here lonely after the hustle and bus-
tle back at the Three Choughs.'

Ezra, halfway to forgiveness, slipped an
arm about her waist. She began to stroke
his face. 'I'll tell you what I'll do. I have a
poor old aunty in Exeter city who'd benefit
from a week or two of good country air. I'll
send her a note by the next postboy that
comes through. She'll be company for me,
and nothing at all for you to fret yourself
about.'

Georgie busied himself around the barn
and garden. His relief at the reconciliation
between Ezra and Pennina was profound.
His whole future depended on the marital
harmony of these two adults. He considered
their recent argument and his own place in
it. The notion that strangers had mistaken
him for Ezra's own son was a doubtful
honour and almost sure to be untrue. Of
Ezra's resentment towards him there was no
question. One false step, one rash word, and
in spite of Pennina's support the Pikey
would send him packing, and be glad of the
excuse.

He thought about the way Pennina had
spoken up for him against her husband's
anger, and his boy's heart almost burst with
gratitude and pride. As he bent his back
that afternoon to the lifting of long rows of

turnips, Georgie renewed his vows of eternal love and lifelong devotion to Pennina Lambton.

In the days before Christmas a frost came down upon the land such as had not been seen in living memory. Only the hardiest of souls dared to travel in the bitter temperatures. Business at the toll gate slowed to a trickle. The failure of Pennina's elderly aunt to arrive when expected was put down to the weather. There was a sudden increase in the number of notes carried by Georgie Barnacle between the Toll House and the Three Choughs.

Two days before the eve of Christmas Ezra Lambton was informed by the Exeter trustees of the robbery from a toll house near Frome of one whole month's takings, and the death by shooting of the tollmaster, who had attempted to defend himself and his family, and the money which was in his care.

Extra vigilance was recommended. Ezra instructed Georgie in the use of the gun. He also ordered him, on pain of thrashing, to stay wakeful and watchful through the night hours.

When Georgie confessed to Pennina that he sometimes fell to sleep towards morning, she gazed long and hard at him and seemed at first disinclined to speak. He grew uneasy beneath her gaze. Thinking she blamed him for such weakness, his eyes filled up with tears.

At last she spoke. 'Georgia,' she said, 'what I say to you must not go beyond the two of us.' She looked from the office window and towards the gate, where Ezra was arguing with a cattle drover. 'Sleep easy, boy. I will see to it that Ezra does not leave his bed at night to check on whether or not you are at your post and wakeful.' And now she came close, and gazed directly into his eyes.

*'There is no danger here, to us.* Remember that! *We are quite safe.'* If he was tempted to ask how she could be so certain of their safety, if such an awkward question even came into his head, he did not pursue it. Such was his trust in her that he accepted her words, and from that time forward he slept the night through.

Burdens' Wood had been a regular stopping place for gypsies for as long as anyone could remember. It was always mid-afternoon when Georgie, the folded note for the landlord of the Choughs pushed deep into his breeches pocket, made his way along the drovers' track which led to the clearing among the beech trees. He no longer paled at sight of the gypsies, although his fear of them was great. He had watched them, but at first only from some distance, as they gathered mistletoe and holly from the trees and hedges in these last weeks before Christmas. He became bolder and more curious, adept at avoiding discovery by them, heeding the warning signs of their approach, the slap of their bare feet on the frozen iron-hard ground, the muttered sounds of their strange language. It was on the very eve of Christmas that Pennina summoned him urgently from his work in the barn, and pushed the note into his pocket.

'Fast as you can,' she told him, 'and give it straightway into Jacob's hand, and nobody else's. Make sure that none sees you give it to him.'

He had ran through the dirty yellow light that threatened snow. Speed on the outward journey would allow him to dawdle on the return. His mission at the Choughs completed, Georgie came again into the green track and dared, for the first time ever, to try to penetrate the thicket of brambles that partially concealed the circle of little brown tents, and the smoky unattended fire. Having forced his way to the edge of the clearing, he crouched behind a blackthorn bush and watched. He could have approached directly from the drovers' track, but that would have risked being seen by any gypsy who lurked within the camp.

As it was, all his stealth counted for nothing.

The boy was a whole head taller than Georgie, but rake-thin. His arms were full of brushwood and a single rotted log. The black hair stood up in wild tufts on his head; his skin was the darkest Georgie had ever seen. His eyes had no colour at all, but seemed to be transparent; they glittered with the kind of madness that Georgie had once witnessed on a bolting horse.

The boy did not speak but jerked his head towards the fire. He walked away and Georgie followed, fear and curiosity preventing him from running for the safety of home and Pennina. The gypsy tossed the brushwood onto the grey embers and stirred the fire into a blaze. He placed the log carefully among the flames, and hung a large black kettle on the tripod.

Georgie moved closer to the warmth, uncomfortably aware of that strange, light gaze fixed upon his face and person.

The boy said, 'What do you want with us?' A dog which had until then lain silent also crept closer to the fire and began a low growling which was not unlike the gypsy's tone of voice.

'Nothin',' said Georgie, 'nothin' at all.'

'Just as well you don't, then! Us got nothin' for the like o' thee.'

The first flakes of snow began to fall, and Georgie became shamefully aware of his thick woollen breeches, his good broadcloth coat and stout boots. The boy's bare feet stuck out from the bottoms of patched and filthy trousers which were secured about his bony frame by a bright yellow scarf knotted at the waist. The top half of his body was only partially covered by a shabby waistcoat of brilliant brocade from which every button was missing. He moved around the fire, pushed the dog to one side, and stood very close to Georgie. He reached out a dirty finger and touched the red and springy curls, the high colour which stained the skin across Georgie's cheekbones.

'Ah, *dordi, dordi,*' he muttered, 'our Estralita'll be wantin' take a look at thee.'

'Who's your Estralita?'

'My mother's sister.'

'What would your mother's sister want with me?'

'She's away to the town, hawkin' the last of the mistletoe and holly. Only me here now, mendin' the fire and catchin' the supper.' He clamped a strong hand on Georgie's shoulder, gripping so hard that the smaller boy cried aloud. 'Be here after nightfall. They'se'ull all want to view thee.' He shook his head in a kind of wonder, 'But mostly Estralita.'

Georgie backed away slowly from the fire, and then turned to run between the beech trees. As he went he could hear the gypsy's shout. 'Be here! If not, I'll come and fetch thee!'

His return to the Toll House went unnoticed by Ezra and Pennina. In Georgie's absence, the aunt from Exeter had arrived on the Quicksilver coach. While he hung his good coat on a hook in the kitchen, and put on the sackcloth apron and old boots he wore when working, he could hear the angry conversation in Ezra's office.

'But there's nowhere else for her to sleep, Ezra. 'Twill only be for a few nights. We can't turn Cousin Giles out of the little bedroom — he pays well to stay here, and the extra silver comes in handy.' Pennina's voice took on its confidential tone. 'You don't think I'll enjoy sharing our marriage bed with Aunty, do you? I'll miss you every minute of the night. But you've seen the state the poor old soul is in, especially after her long journey. Please, please, Ezra!'

'And where am I supposed to sleep?' asked Ezra bitterly.

Pennina said, 'There's that broad settle in the good room. If I lay a couple of sheepskins across it, that'll make you a soft bed. Georgie can bank up the fire so that you don't take cold. Oh, my sweet, sweet man, you don't know how much this means to me.'

Georgie milked the house-cow, fed the hens, the pigs and horses. He did not have a single glimpse that night of the aunty who had already retired to rest.

Pennina was being especially attentive to Ezra, who was still showing a dangerous ill-temper. After supper was eaten and the dishes cleared, she whispered to Georgie, 'Leave us on our own for a while, lover. Master's not quite himself this evening.'

He put on his good coat and boots, and took care that none in the house witnessed his departure. He had never before been abroad on his own after true dark had fallen. But this particular night was not really so dark; a full moon sailed in a clear sky. The snow had ceased, leaving a wisp white covering on fields and paths. He turned into the drovers' trail and the gypsy boy appeared like a ghost, out of nowhere, to walk beside him. They did not greet one another but moved fast through the beech trees and towards the clearing.

A great fire had been built against the bitter night; its flickering glow lit the hard proud faces of the assembled gypsies. At sight of them a sharp pain twisted deep in Georgie's chest, and he experienced a longing he did not expect or understand. But there was fear too, and at that moment he would have turned and fled back down the green lane, but the boy held his upper arm in an iron grip. He pushed Georgie forward to stand fully in the firelight. He spoke at some length in the strange language, and was answered in the same tongue by the oldest of the women present.

There was a silence in which every gaze of the seated company was fixed on the stranger. The very old woman was the first to speak. She beckoned him to stand before her, and looked close into his face.

'What name dost thee go by, cheel?' she asked him.

'Georgie Barnacle, ma'am.'

'Who give thee that name?'

'Parson Jenkins, ma'am.'

'Him up to the poorhouse?'

'The same, ma'm.'

'How came thee to the poorhouse?'

'I know not, ma'am.'

The logs on the great fire shifted suddenly, causing the flames to leap high and bright. The old woman's face was momentarily etched against the surrounding darkness, showing every wrinkle in the walnut-hued skin, the deep furrows which ran from nose to mouth, and the black glitter of her eyes.

She leaned forward and stretched out a skinny claw to touch his face. Her hand then moved to grab his red curls. She said, 'Didst thou ever know thy mother and father?'

'I did not, ma'am.'

Her grip on his hair was so fierce that he flinched in pain. When she relinquished her hold he staggered with the effort to remain upright. She began to speak again in her own language, and a young woman came to stand beside her; the same young woman he had seen on that day of the gypsies' arrival, the one with the red curls hanging to her waist.

Georgie and the woman gazed at one another, and he saw the tears start in her eyes. Again he felt the yearning which was both a pain and a pleasure. All at once an argument broke out among the gypsy men. There was a lot of shouting and gesticulating, of which Georgie understood only the two words of his own name.

Fear grabbed him by the throat, stealing his breath away. He had overheard talk in the Three Choughs, that gypsies put spells on people, ill-wished them, stole their children and sold them in the city to be slaves.

He cursed the foolish curiosity which had brought him back to Burdens' Wood. The gypsy men were now enraged to the point of throwing punches at each other.

Seizing his moment, Georgie turned and fled down the road which led to home and Pennina.

At Christmas Georgie attended morning service with Pennina and Ezra. The resurrected church looked very fine. For the use of the gentry there were private pews with little carved entrance doors and embroidered kneeling hassocks. Flowers and candles beautified the altar. The Lambtons' pew was somewhere in the middle of the church, since they were neither aristocracy nor needy poor.

Ezra wore the suit of black in which he was married, lightened by a cravat of blue silk at his scraggy neck. Pennina glowed in a new gown and cape of burgundy velvet which set off her creamy skin and dark hair.

Georgie, his red corkscrew curls newly washed, was proud in a smart green jacket and breeches which Pennina had ordered to be especially made for him in Taunton Town.

The gypsies also came to church at Christmas. They wore their usual assortment of once fine, but now shabby garments, which included brocade gowns and silk-fringed shawls among the women, and fancy waistcoats and plumed hats for their menfolk.

Their children, unaccustomed to restraint of any kind, rolled and fought and played across the marbled aisles.

The gypsies had entered with a flourish, marching in through the west door and passing without a glance the humble rear seats; their bare feet slapping on the coloured tiles. They found the pews reserved for his lordship unoccupied, and seated themselves with great assurance. From which favoured position it seemed that no man present had the courage to evict them.

In the grey light of that December morning those faces had lost none of their fascination for Georgie. As they settled into their chosen places, adjusting hassocks and cushions to their liking, his gaze moved from one dark-skinned visage to another, lingering at the haughty features of the oldest woman, pausing at the sharp bones and strange, light eyes of the boy met in the woodland clearing. He looked finally and long at the young woman with the red curling hair, which was somewhat like his own recently grown locks.

Georgie had seen his reflection but the once, mirrored in the surface of the duck pond on the village green. But that had been long ago, when his head was shaved and his body skinny.

He had no true inkling of his present looks.

The two small children who sat close to the woman had the same bright cheeks and red hair as their mother. Pennina also watched those children, but with an anxious gaze which puzzled Georgie.

The turn of the year brought drenching rain and its resultant mud. It took sixteen heavy horses to pull a bogged-down stagecoach out of Witches' Hollow. The incidence of highway robbery continued to increase. Ezra ordered a brace of pistols to be sent out from Frome, and bartered half of a cured ham for a mastiff puppy.

Ezra, who slept hardly at all on the uncomfortable settle, now needed a lengthy afternoon nap in the bed he once shared with Pennina. It was in these hours, Georgie noticed, while the tollmaster was absent from his office, between noon and the fall of dark, that the secret and illegal business of the Toll House was enacted.

Even Georgie, naive and inexperienced boy that he was, could not help but be aware of the nods and winks, the whispered consultations that were made when Pennina was in charge. Pennina herself had changed in many ways since the arrival of her elderly aunt. When questioned by Ezra about her pale face and heavy eyes, she also complained of her inability to sleep peacefully in the same bed as old Aunt Lizzie, who suffered, she said, from nightmares and tossed and turned the night through. The carrying of notes to Jacob at the Three Choughs had now become an almost daily occurrence. The green lane had deteriorated to a quagmire in that month of January; and Georgie's safest route to the inn lay over the higher, drier ground through Burdens' Wood.

Such a change of direction brought him into closer contact with the gypsies. He would pass them by with just a nod on the outward journey. But on his return he would be persuaded to linger; especially in the company of the light-eyed one.

'So what do they call thee?' the boy asked.

'My name is Georgie. But you already know that.'

The boy began to laugh; he held his sides and doubled up with mirth. 'What sort a' fancy handle is that, then? Among our people the name we are given and the name we are called by is not always the same thing. I was named for my father.'

Georgie said, 'So what do they call you?'

'I was named Silvanus, but I answers to Silva or sometimes Anselo. Then there's my secret name what I never tells to any soul.'

'Well, I got but the one name, and that is the same as the King of England!'

'He was thy father? The King of England?'

George laughed at the gypsy's ignorance. 'Never had a father what I know'd about, nor mother neither.'

'How come thee to the Toll House?'

'The master called for a smart boy and I was the lucky one.'

'Don't look much like luck to me.'

'You don't know Mistress Pennina, my master's wife.'

'Good to thee, is she?'

'Good as gold! Well — look at me. I wants for nothing.'

Silva spoke quietly. 'Nothin' save thy own

291

family. Them as is thy own kind.'

'Don't need nobody.'

'But what if thee was to find thy own dear mother? Thee was never born to this Toll House woman! Dost thou never think on these things? Mother — father — brothers — sisters?'

Georgie felt a stirring in his heart. He had never even thought about, never mind spoken the word 'mother'; as for finding her, every child reared in the poorhouse knew that he or she had been abandoned. His life with Ezra and Pennina was as near to family living as he could ever hope for. Sometimes, lying curled up in his quilt, between sleep and waking, he would try to see himself as their child, the son of the Toll House. But the picture always blurred and faded, and was it any wonder? Love, whether given or received, was so far beyond his boy's experience that he could not envision it, even in his private dreams. He treasured the odd, affectionate gesture from Pennina as a miser hoards his gold. But lately he had suspected that her kindness might have other, deeper motives than true fondness for him, and that his loyalty might be the coin of his eventual repayment. The love of the gypsies for their children was fierce and protective and freely given. Chastisement was rarely practiced.

He remembered the beatings, the near-starvation, the isolation in the dark cell that were the favourite punishments in the poorhouse.

Here, in this woodland clearing, among the little brown tents, and beside the fire that was more than a fire to these people, but also a home and a comfort, and the place where they all came together; here it was that Georgie Barnacle first witnessed the closeness of the Romany families, the love of the parents for their children.

He watched the red-haired Estralita, and Silva's sisters, Faithina and Orphilla, and knew them for a very different brand of woman than the hard-eyed, strong-fisted matrons of the poorhouse, or the sweet-talking but deceitful Pennina. The lot of the gypsy woman was a hard one. They reminded him of the wild cats which lived deep inside Ezra's hayrick; those reckless and beautiful creatures which were ever ready with teeth and claws to protect and defend their young.

The men of the tribe, Pentecost and Mackland, Silence and Ambrose, Comfort and Ferdinando, were quite unlike the sour-natured Ezra Lambton. Oh, they were quick-tempered, handy with their fists when they had drink taken, especially towards their wives. But they were tender with their children; they played jokes on one another, were by turns high-spirited and cast down. But never morose; and never deliberately evil.

His initial fear of the Romany people had quite gone. He began to learn a few words of their language, to look forward with longing to the time spent in their company around the fire. They, in their turn, behaved towards the orphan boy as if he were their own.

In the short days of winter, when the daytime was shortlived, and candlelight and firelight the sole means of illumination, many lapses of correct dress and even token cleanliness were inclined to pass unnoticed. With the return of lighter mornings Georgie saw how Ezra had taken to appearing in his office, nightcap still in place upon his head, slippered and unshaven, and never seeming to be properly awake. His temper, never sanguine, had become a cause for fear among drovers and travellers alike. No longer did a coachman dare to make his usual imperious shout of 'Pikey!' when approaching the Toll House after dark; or the even briefer, and more lordly demand of 'Gate!'.

Such high-handed orders were likely to be met nowadays by a scatter of shot from Ezra's gun, and he was known to be careless of his aim. The queue of traffic wishing to pay the toll and pass the gate would on some days stretch away out of sight into the hills. Restless sheep and cattle would become uncontrollable and wander away into green lanes, and the many side roads used by packmen and their horses.

The village of Ashkeepers, always a place of ill-repute, now became known as a good place to avoid.

Georgie Barnacle, his thoughts and heart in Burdens' Wood, went about his daily chores unhearing and unseeing, careless of the chaos growing daily more severe within the Toll House. He closed his mind to the open warfare waged on each other now by Ezra and Pennina, the shouting, the arguments, the occasional exchange of blows. The elderly aunt from Exeter continued to occupy Ezra's rightful place in his marriage bed. The young and flashy cousins made brief appearances and swift departures on their sweating and hard-ridden horses. Ezra sustained a cut cheek, caused by a slap from one of Pennina's heavily beringed hands.

It was on an evening in late March when Georgie, returning from the Choughs and the partaking of a supper at the gypsy fireside, saw a dark-garbed figure moving ahead of him down the drovers' lane. It was the dimpsey time of day when outlines are blurred and angles softened; he could just make out the long full skirts and distinctive widow's bonnet of Pennina's Aunt Lizzie. But this was surely not the old bent figure who pattered and muttered about the Toll House? This woman strode out with energy and speed; her bent back somehow miraculously straightened. His curiosity aroused, he began to run silently across the damp grass. As he drew near he could hear the merry tune she whistled, even though to whistle like a man was said to bring ill luck on a woman.

All at once Aunt Lizzie's progress slowed and then halted. Fearing she had seen him, Georgie dropped down behind a blackthorn bush which was in full flower. When he dared to peer out he could scarcely believe in what he saw. Pennina's aunty was hoisting her long black skirts to waist height and unbuttoning the flies of a pair of men's trousers. She then proceeded to relieve herself from a standing position and against the bole of an elm tree. All the hoisting of skirts and the straightening and rebuttoning of trousers had knocked her lace-trimmed bonnet well askew, revealing the stubble of her close-cropped head.

A muttered oath and an irritable adjustment of the bonnet, and Aunt Lizzie was once more on her way.

Except that she was not, nor could she ever have been, Pennina's aunty.

For the first time since the new Mrs Lambton had moved into the Toll House, Georgie experienced true fear. He walked slowly back towards the turnpike, and entered the barn by a rear door, exhibiting a caution he did not yet fully understand.

He lit the lamp and forked hay into the manger. Arabella, long past her regular milking time, her udder hard and painful, lowed reproachfully at him as he settled down with stool and pail. In the quiet of the barn the pounding of his heart eased into a more steady rhythm. He began to work out the implications of what he had just seen in the lane. Pennina's aunt was in fact a young and agile man. On that thought came the realisation that the same young man was sharing Ezra's marriage bed with Ezra's wife, while the keeper of the toll slept downstairs on the settle.

He pondered, for the first time, the nature of the correspondence carried by himself between Jacob and Pennina; the unlikely silken gowns, the velvet cloaks, the golden rings worn that winter by the spouse of a simple turnpike master.

He thought about the sudden increase in highway robbery, the murder of packmen who were foolish enough to travel singly; and the sweating horses often tethered in Ezra's barn.

Ezra Lambton, befuddled as he was by his love for a young and beautiful wife, retained as yet sufficient wit to see that he was being taken for a fool. He had not yet become aware that he was also a cuckold, a deception which was practised upon him with such audacity as had knocked the breath from Georgie Barnacle's young body. If Ezra should ever discover the true identity of 'Aunty Lizzie', yet more murder would be committed in the parish of Ashkeepers.

Since he did not dare, or even wish to reveal the extent of his own knowledge of affairs, Georgie decided that he had no other recourse than to be watchful and wary.

Watchful of Pennina's safety; and wary of Ezra's evil temper.

The only moral guidance which had come Georgie's way had been gleaned from the thunderous sermons preached in the Ashkeepers church. The parson's warnings of hellfire and eternal damnation meant nothing to him. Georgie believed that the sins of envy, gluttony and lust were luxuries reserved for rich folk. The poor, and these included gypsies and workhouse inmates, must look for their own brand of salvation, their own way into Heaven. With every man's hand set against them, they could not be expected to heed the well-fed, well-clothed, well-housed parson's dire predictions.

He and Silva had spoken about that very subject on the day that two of the Lovell family had been taken up for vagrancy.

'They was caught sleeping in a farmer's hayrick,' said Silva, 'doing no harm to nobody. Estralita is 'specially cut up about it. Ambrose and Wisdom is her brothers, and her closest kin. They two have been good to her through all her troubles. Much use to her they'd be now, on the prison ship bound for the Americas. Seven years' deportation is a lifetime. Not many men lives through that sentence to see their relations once again.'

Georgie had never known Silva quite so low in spirits. The troubles of the Lovell family had begun to touch his own heart in a way that the strife within the Toll House never could.

In April the gypsies made ready to depart from Burdens' Wood. The harsh judgement of the magistrate made on Estralita's brothers had silenced their music and their laughter, so that even the warm winds and sunshine could not raise a smile from any of them. Estralita's rosy face had grown pale, the red hair hung in tangles about her shoulders. Even the children, normally so boisterous, were now subdued.

He would always remember that last evening in the green wood. He had performed his chores with speed, filled the log-baskets, milked Arabella and fed and watered the rest of the creatures in his care. The final Quicksilver coach expected on that Saturday night had already passed the gate. Georgie had taken his quilt into the barn, explaining to Pennina that since the nights were no longer cold, and Ezra snored and muttered on the settle until daybreak, he actually preferred to sleep among the hay-bales. In fact, having doused the lamp that hung by the barn door, Georgie slipped silently away into the shadows and made his way up to Burdens' Wood.

The Lovells would be pulling out in the morning. Since the deportation of Ambrose and Wisdom, they feared to remain so close to the village of Ashkeepers. Further charges of vagrancy could be brought against any one of them, at any time. No crime need have been committed. To argue with the law that they were no charge on the parish, that their bender tents were more than equal to the thatched roofs of the *gorgio,* was to whistle in the wind. They were to travel to a place called Norton Fitzwarren which was close by Taunton Town.

Georgie had been invited to leave the Toll House and journey with them.

'Thee is more'n welcome,' Estralita Lovell told him. She reached out a hand to smooth his red curls, but then drew back as if the touch might burn her. 'Thee could travel along wi' me and my *chavvies.* Since my brothers is lost to me I got no family man to help me.'

Georgie said, 'I'm no man, but a boy still.'

She shook her head. 'No boy, no more! Thee is near to fifteen summers old.'

'You can't ever know that. I was left in the poorhouse from my birth. Nobody can tell me my true age.'

'Fifteen years old,' she repeated softly. And then, as if the words were torn from her throat, 'Didn't I give birth to thee in Shepton Mallet gaol? Dost thou think I would not know my own flesh and blood?

I held thee in my arms. I named thee Manju for thy father, then the gaoler tore thee from me and said, "Thy child is dead, was born so, never drawed a single breath." I was turned away from that prison the very same evening. All these years I have mourned thee, Manju, and yet in my heart I believed thee still to be alive; didn't I see the rise and fall of thy little chest?'

At her words Georgie felt the strength go from his legs. He sat, agape and aghast upon the grass. He saw how the rest of the Lovells, including Silva, had drawn well back from himself and Estralita. The woman who said she was his mother came closer to him. 'Hast thou never seen thy own face, Manju?'

'No.'

She reached into the pocket of her skirt and pulled out a square of shiny tin which she pushed into Georgie's hand.

'Look well,' she cried. 'Look first into thy face and then into my face and then go see my other two *chavvies*. Measure them beside thy own self. We is all four of us as like as peas from the one pod.'

She waved to the group who sat apart on the far side of the fire. 'They have all of them 'marked on it. Silva know'd the very first minute that he saw thee, that thee was my lost child and none other!'

She held out her hands toward him. 'Come with us, Manju! Thou art my lost boy — found after fifteen years of mourning.'

Georgie gazed at his own mirrored features and then at those of the woman and her children. The likeness between the four of them was not to be denied. He saw her pain, her yearning. He longed to ask. 'If you are my mother — then where is my father?' But to pose that question would commit him, would take him halfway towards belonging to her.

She said that he was fifteen years old; that his real name was Manju Lovell. That he was once pronounced dead in the Shepton House of Correction, and yet was here, living and breathing and ready to be claimed as her very own. Such a happening was the dearest dream of every orphan child, but in the event it was all too much for Georgie to take in. His thoughts turned towards Pennina.

He recalled the air of excitement in the house that night. Four horsemen had arrived at midday. They had spent the afternoon drinking at the Choughs. Pennina and 'Aunt Lizzie' had whispered together in the office while Ezra slept in the upper room.

Some evil was afoot within the Toll House!

Pennina was the dupe, the unwitting accomplice of her relatives. There were two sides to this business of family living, and one of them not good.

Estralita Lovell waited for his answer.

He said, 'I am bonded to the Toll House master. If I run away now, I'm sure to be apprehended by the law and punished. In a year from now I shall be free. Next springtime, I will come with thee.'

# Nina

As a means of diversion from the finding of a dead crow on the doorstop, Barnacle's book had a lot to recommend it.

I was no longer sure that the author was writing the simple but dramatic truth, or if the whole panorama of highway robbers, gypsies, orphans and cross-dressing lovers was the product of his overheated and re-pressed Victorian imagination. And if so, did it really matter?

It was turning out to be a thundering good tale!

I began to cast the roles in the drama. Should Hollywood ever take an interest, Margaret Lockwood would make a wonder-ful Pennina, while Clark Gable (minus moustache) would be a riveting Aunt Lizzie. The finding of a child-prodigy to play the part of Georgie proved more difficult. It occurred to me then that Lockwood and

Gable, even if still living, must by now be very old, at least in their eighties. I quickly substituted Emma Thompson and a young fellow name of Cruise, or was it Hanks? I find the names and faces of contemporary actors as interchangeable as their AC/DC morals and their confusing hair-lengths.

The sad thought of an aged or deceased Lockwood and Gable brought me smartly back to the dead crow. Instinct told me that somehow the book and the bird were linked, but try as I might I could not fit both into the scenario of Georgie Barnacle and his adventures.

That bird could not remain for too long, either on my mind or in the garden shed, without creating an unpleasant odour.

I sat upright in my chair and in a fit of revulsion hurled Barnacle's book across the carpet, and watched it slew sideways to fetch up against the stone curb of the fireplace.

Something terrible was about to happen between those pages, and I simply could not bear to read about it! Life was due to deal a rotten hand to every one of them. Events were all set to transpire which by comparison would make my poor old crow look like the gift of a birthday present from a secret admirer.

I began to wonder if Georgie was really

Estralita's lost child? And just supposing that, let us say, in nineteen forty-eight a stolen baby had not been murdered, but had miraculously survived, would it really be possible, years later, to identify the lost one by her adult looks?

I stared down at the book, the skilful binding and gilt lettering, and imagined the gentle handling which had preserved it in its present pristine state for sixty-eight years. Filled with remorse, I lifted it tenderly, checked that no damage had been sustained, and replaced it on the table. Later that day I bought a bush of flowering cherry from a nearby garden centre and dug a hole deep enough to accommodate both its roots and the corpse of the crow. I worked in the garden on those days when I did not visit Fran or walk out with baby John. From the vegetable patch I had a view of passing traffic both from Witches' Hollow, and the neighbouring houses in Homesteaders' Valley.

I continued to feel threatened. It took courage in the early morning to open the door and take in the bottle of blue-top skimmed, left by the milkman. When I paid him at the weekend, he gave me an odd look, but made no mention of the deceased bird, which he must certainly have noticed.

★ ★ ★

The squatters' arrival in Ranchers' Close had been so unobtrusive that they had been in occupation for some days before the neighbours registered their presence.

So great was the shock and sense of outrage among the Homesteaders that it brought Primrose Martindale knocking at my door early on a Monday morning. She was over the step, through the tiny hallway, and into the kitchen before I had so much as thought of inviting her to enter.

The short walk from Ranchers' Close had left her breathless and temporarily speechless. I pulled out a chair and she sat, plump shoulders hunched, while I switched on the kettle and spooned instant coffee into two mugs. I was irritated by her intrusion which would mean my late arrival at Fran's house. Nothing less than the four minute warning of nuclear extinction could justify the way she had barged in without a word of explanation. The longer I live alone the more territorial I become. Except for family, I grow increasingly resentful of unexpected callers.

I poured boiling water onto instant coffee granules and pushed mug, milkjug and sugar bowl in her direction. She was looking very pale, and after all, she had ministered tenderly to me after my collision with her dog Gorbachev.

She stirred milk and sugar into her mug, and took several sips before speaking. 'Did you see them?' she demanded. 'Did you see them arrive?'

'Quite possibly,' I answered, 'but it would help if I knew who and what you are talking about.'

'The hippies,' she gasped. 'The ones who are living in number forty-eight. We thought you might have seen them moving in. You're always in your garden, or looking out of your bedroom window. You'll have a clear view from there of the rear of the Simpsons' home.'

'But surely it's up to the Simpsons to decide on what sort of people they invite into their house?'

'Squatters,' she said loudly. 'The Simpsons are on holiday — Bermuda — and, oh dear, their three-piece suite is loose-covered in white linen! The carpet is pale yellow. All those dreadful people trampling over everything in their big black boots, spilling food and drink on the furniture; blocking up the sink and probably the loo!' Primrose drank deeply, and I observed with horror that tears were rolling slowly down her cheeks. She pushed her empty mug towards me. Bemused, I automatically gave her a refill. I could at least still recognise desperation when I saw it.

'You see,' she said, 'I feel so responsible. I have the Simpsons' keys. I promised to look in every day, pick up their post, water the houseplants. See that everything was *ALL RIGHT.*'

'And you didn't?'

'Well — no. I can see their front windows quite clearly from my house; I didn't think it was necessary to go over, not every day. And I was busy, you know how it is. It wasn't until last night that I began to feel just the teensiest bit uneasy. April Simpson had left all the curtains closed, so as not to have the sun fade her wallpaper and carpets, but when I looked across I noticed that the bedroom curtains had been pulled back. The drive was empty so I knew they hadn't returned from Bermuda unexpectedly. I was afraid to go over there on my own, so I telephoned for Ashley — he's my grandson, you know — to come with me. Ashley is an estate agent, he knows all about property, and the law. We knocked and knocked and almost wore out the doorbell, but nobody answered. Then Ashley tiptoed around to the back of the house and looked through the kitchen window, and there they all were,

310

giggling and drinking beer and wine straight out of cans and bottles. When Ashley questioned their right to be on the premises, they shouted at him to go away and mind his own business. They wouldn't open up the door and speak face to face as any honest person would have done.' Primrose paused and drained her coffee mug and set it back on the table with a force that would have cracked a less sturdy object. 'But while he was talking to them, Ashley recognised two faces. He went back to his office and looked at the computer records. The girls he had recognised were, as he suspected, the two who had been looking, with a view to buying, at various city properties for some months past. He went through the list of houses they had viewed, and sure enough, the Simpsons' was the most recent property they had asked to see. One of Ashley's sales negotiators had shown them over number forty-eight just before the Simpsons set off on their travels.'

'They were casing the joint?' I asked. Not for nothing had I watched *Columbo* on the television.

'Exactly, Nina! But here is the most remarkable coincidence of all. Ashley found that those same two girls had also looked over your house — the one you sold before

311

you bought the Toll House.' Again she paused and pushed the mug in my direction. I switched on the kettle and hoped that I had left the bathroom in good order. Before too long Primrose would be asking if she might use it.

'You see,' she continued, 'Ashley says it would help him enormously if you would be willing to identify them.'

'I can't see how that would help to get them out of number forty-eight.'

'It would show intent. It would prove to the police that they had been looking for some time for a suitable property to squat in.'

I said, 'I hadn't noticed a FOR SALE board on number forty-eight.'

'Well, no. The Simpsons are very private sort of people. They didn't want any old Tom, Dick or Harry knocking at their door asking to be shown over. Ashley has a photo, of course, and details of the property displayed in his office windows.' Primrose clutched at her refilled coffee mug like a shipwreck victim grabs a lifebelt. 'A much more dignified way of selling one's property, don't you think? Less likely to attract the wrong type of people.' She sighed. 'I promised Ashley that I would come and see you. After all, you actually knew April Simpson.

She told me how the two of you discussed art together on the village bus.'

Resisting the urge to point out that the wrong type of people, in spite of all precautions, had succeeded in invading number forty-eight, I made myself another coffee refill.

In the end, having used the bathroom twice, and after extracting a promise from me that I would help her if I could, Primrose drove me into Nether Ash.

I needed to think, and pushing a pram which holds a sleeping baby offers very few distractions. I walked slowly in the cold May sunshine, around the posh and the not-so-posh areas of Nether Ash. When he sleeps, the rosy colour leaves John's cheeks, and in the deepest period of that sleeping his face is waxen. I always grow frightened at this point, and need to resist the urge to nudge him, or gently shake him awake, if only to dispel my own terrors. On that morning I watched him with extra care; noted the occasional twitch of his eyelids, the regular rise and fall of the little chest, the soft tremble of his mouth in sleep. I wondered what his dreams were? I wondered what Primrose Martindale had meant when she said I was frequently to be seen standing at my bedroom window. My heavy mahogany dress-ing-table, wide and triple-mirrored, stands directly before that window, blocking it completely. And then there were the two girls. Oh yes, I remembered them! The ele-gant one with the trilling laugh and her hair in a French pleat. Her friend, chunky in floating chiffon and Dr Marten boots. Both of them in deepest black from neck to toe, performing their duo act like the good de-tective and the bad one.

Smart of Ashley to have recognised them and traced them back on his computer. Un-fortunate for me that he should have a rec-ord of their visit to the house in Infirmary Avenue. Already I felt myself being pulled into the drama that was brewing in Home-steaders' Valley.

Back in Fran's kitchen, drinking hot chocolate, with John still sleeping peacefully in his pram in the garden, I told her about my crack-of-dawn visitor; about the Simp-sons' white linen sofa-covers, and the squat-ters who at this moment were probably spilling cola and coffee on them.

Fran pointed out a few truths that had not occurred to me.

'You were very lucky, Grandma. They were obviously looking for a large house, and yours was, for some reason, considered unsuitable as a squat.'

I remembered the giggling and whispered conversations. I now believed that my house had been rejected only after keen discussion; as a squat it would have had many attractions. Situated in a quiet side road. Neighbours who made a religion out of keeping themselves to themselves. Large rooms on three floors, all of them well furnished. To gain illegal entry would have been easy. I lived alone. I could at any time have arrived home from shopping or a visit to my family to find the outer doors locked, the squatters already in occupation and impossible to evict. Except for that good old prison wall, and the long-range video cameras; except for the frequent passage of police vehicles through Infirmary Avenue, about which the girls had clearly not possessed previous knowledge; I had been saved from homelessness by the very features which had been a hindrance to purchase for many home-seekers. Unfortunately for the Simpsons their house had possessed all the tempting features of my old home, plus the virtues of a protracted absence of the owners, and a total lack of police surveillance.

Fran said, 'So what happens now?'

'I don't know. Primrose had the Simpsons' door keys and was supposed to be keeping an eye out. She's consumed with guilt, and determined to involve me in the whole mess. I don't know what the legal position is on squatters. I have a nasty suspicion that once they are in possession of a property it takes legal action on the part of the owner to get them evicted.'

Fran said, 'Don't worry about it. It's not your problem, is it?'

'It might be.' I hesitated, not wishing to burden her with my fears, but I had, of course, already said too much.

'Tell me!' she said.

So I told her about the crow on the doorstep. I did not explain the full significance of such a gift, neither did I mention the several people in Ashkeepers who might, with malice aforethought, have donated it. I spoke instead about two of the squatters, and my suspicions of them.

'They've been in the Simpson house just long enough,' I told Fran, 'to have recognised me, and perhaps watched me working in the garden, or walking Roscoe.' I explained how, all those months ago, I had felt the antagonism of the chunky girl.

'I admit I argued with her; but she was so unpleasant and aggressive. I remember thinking at the time that she would probably bear grudges. She was definitely the stronger character of the two. I can just imagine her creeping into the garden after dark, enjoying the prospect of the fright I would get when I took in the morning milk.'

I became conscious of Fran's quizzical gaze.

She said, 'This business of the crow seems more like the prank of a few mischievous schoolboys. I think you're attaching too much importance to it. Oh, I know it was nasty, but, Grandma, don't let it spoil the Toll House for you.'

I looked at her sweet and serious face and could not tell her all the tale. 'You're absolutely right. I shall have to watch myself. Paranoia is a symptom of advanced senility. Those girls were city-bred. Wouldn't know a crow from a jackdaw or a rook. It must have been, as you say, a silly prank by schoolboys from the village.'

Because of the delayed spring and the unseasonable cold, the green of Ashkeepers was still that shade of intense emerald usually seen in early April. Clumps of daffodils still bloomed underneath the beeches and horse-chestnut trees. In cottage gardens I could see the pinks and whites of cherry and almond blossom. I sat on a comfortable bench and gazed surreptitiously around me.

I had chosen a time of day when the senior citizens would be having their after-lunch nap, and the youngest of the pupils were not yet released from the mixed infants school behind the church.

I unpacked my sketchpad and the tin in which I kept my charcoals. Just to touch the old leather school satchel, which had once belonged to Imogen, was to be reminded of Jack and days spent beside a river, he fishing, I drawing.

I thought about Fran's troubled look as I had left her that morning. She had put her arms around me, hugged me hard and kissed my cheek. I hugged her back, and thought even as I did so that Imogen and I had never been able to exchange such a gesture of concerned affection. But my state of mind had worried Fran, who should not have the whimsies of an elderly grandmother laid on her young shoulders. It was a role reversal I could not allow to develop any further. *My* function was to help *her*.

Roscoe sat sedately beside me, acting for all he was worth the part of protective dog who could turn dangerous if the need arose. Although the Green was deserted I felt as conspicuous and foolish as a lone performer on a lit stage. I began, self-consciously, to outline the great chestnut tree which stood in the centre of the Green. There was no planned composition; I drew, almost doodled the single object which filled my vision. As I worked, I began to relax, the tension left my neck and shoulders. I fell into a state of mind that was close to dreaming. My fingers moved the charcoal across the surface of the paper and I watched the emerging outlines as objectively as I might have viewed a film or a television sequence. Feeling curious, but with no great sense of surprise, I saw that although the chestnut was in full and glorious leaf, the fingers which held the charcoal were sketching in bare branches. To the right of the tree I added a gibbet, and surrounding it a series of open wooden galleries like football stands. The crowds of spectators, some of them standing on farm carts, stretched away into surrounding fields. I added the cottages which stood around the Green, and the church with its tall spire. Off in the distance, at the very edge of the emerging scene, I sketched in the drovers' track and the Toll House and its three crooked chimneys.

I began to add detail: stalls which sold gingerbread and oranges, gin and muffins. The picture took on the atmosphere of a carnival; I could feel the excitement of a populace determined to enjoy a rare public holiday. Most of the faces I drew were vacuous and ugly, but among the foremost of the mob who had gathered to watch the execution were two figures which bore a recognisable likeness to the descriptions in Barnacle's book of Ezra Lambton and his young servant Georgie Barnacle.

Ezra and Georgie stood apart from one another, both faces blank of all expression as they looked upwards at the gallows. Georgie, both hands clamped across his face, peered out at the gibbet from between spread fingers.

The hanging man wore a skewed, beribboned bonnet. A pair of narrow-cut trousers were just visible beneath the long full skirts of the gown as described in Barnacle's book.

I wiped the charcoal dust from my fingers and became aware of the leafy chestnut tree, the cold spring sunshine. The mixed infants, released from school, came whooping down the Green. The senior citizens were making for the newsagent's to collect their copies of the evening paper.

I forced my gaze back to the drawing. A little way off from the chestnut tree I had sketched in a tall stake surrounded by heaped straw and faggots of split wood. The woman, bound by her hands and feet, was attempting to lean away from the encroaching flames. She had the tall, voluptuous figure and black ringlets of Pennina Lambton.

Ashley Martindale came knocking at my door that same evening. We smiled nervously at one another, remembering our heated exchanges of last summer. Seeing him now, away from his blue and silver office, I felt more kindly disposed towards him. As he sat on the sofa, drinking a small Scotch drowned in water, I noted his open-necked sports shirt and crumpled cotton trousers, his mud-spattered loafers. He pushed his fingers through fiery hair that would have been improved by a radical cutting. His fingernails were in deepest mourning.

Catching my amused look he said, defensively, 'I'm planting out seedlings in my grandmother's garden. I'm on holiday at the moment.'

'No need to explain,' I assured him, 'the casual look suits you better than your "office" image.'

He grinned, and I warmed still further towards him. He said, 'You'll have heard the full story of the squatters in number forty-eight?'

'Your grandmother was here, and in some

distress. She seems to blame herself for the whole disaster.'

He nodded. 'I've told her there was nothing she could have said or done to deter a bunch of dedicated squatters. They've obviously been involved in this kind of thing before. Those two girls — they knew exactly what kind of property they were looking for. At the point when our sales negotiators were becoming suspicious of them, they promptly disappeared.'

'Only to resurface on the Simpsons' doorstep.'

'Yes.' He drank his watered whisky and looked thoughtful. 'I hesitate,' he said, 'to involve you in this mess. But it would be enormously helpful if you were prepared to identify those two as the people who once looked over your house with an alleged view to purchase. If it comes to a court case —'

'Ashley,' I interrupted, 'if it comes to a court case you can count me out. I feel sorry for your grandmother. Anybody who has to explain away spoiled white linen sofa covers to April Simpson has my deepest sympathy. But I simply will not get involved.'

'I don't blame you. It's really not your problem. But would you be willing to make a statement to the police? Just the facts as you know them?'

'I might go that far.'

His relief was so obvious that I felt ashamed; but not quite sufficiently to change my mind.

'You see,' he said, 'since my grandfather died, my grandmother has had difficulty in creating a life for herself without him.' He waved a hand toward Homesteaders' Valley. 'This little community here, the friends she has managed to make, it means everything to her. Now she feels that she has let April Simpson down very badly —'

'Look,' I said, 'I'll do anything I can to help, short of a court appearance. I'll — I'll go around again and see your grandmother in the morning, if you think she would like that?'

'Will you? Oh, that would be kind of you. I'll tell her.'

He left me, still expressing gratitude. I locked the doors and went upstairs, after making sure that Roscoe was comfortable in his kitchen bed. It had been a strange day. I stood for a moment before the triple-mirrored dressing-table, which blocked the window from which Primrose Martindale had said she often saw me gazing out. My hair needed trimming. A visit to the hairdresser would be a wise move, before Imogen should interpret my present shaggy state as a sign of incipient madness.

I leaned further in towards the mirror. Surprisingly, considering the traumas of recent days, I looked unusually cheerful. There were no new wrinkles, no dark shadows, no drooping of the lips. In fact, if I hadn't disliked the word so much, I would have described myself as looking perky.

My visit to the city, the first in many months, was made on what people were hailing as the first day of summer. The winds, which had blown persistently for months from the north-east, had swung around overnight, bringing warm air from the south. There was a mood of gaiety aboard the bus. The older and more cautious among us still wore our dark and heavy winter garb. After all, it was still May, wasn't it, and not yet wise to cast a single clout. But umbrellas were no longer carried, feet no longer sought the warmth that blew from metal grilles. The talk was on the single subject of the squatters. In spite of their professed sympathy, there was a certain hint of *Schadenfreude* among the lifelong citizens of Ashkeepers, a quiet satisfaction that if such misfortune had to strike the village, better that it should have fallen on the incomers rather than the genuine inhabitants.

Guesses were hazarded, and opinions aired. There was a faction among the vicar's flock which claimed to recognise the squatters as an offshoot of the Moonies. When questioned, nobody quite knew what the Moonies did, except that it was bad. I remembered my own, very similar suspicions last summer, about the girls in black. But before I could voice them, old Mrs Vinney tossed her bombshell into the discussion.

'Witches!' she said loudly. 'Them's a coven! You mark my words! Next thing you know there'll be a plague of frogs, and dead birds on people's doorsteps, and devil worship. They'll be dancing naked in Burdens' Wood.'

My blood quite literally ran cold. I felt the shiver right down to my toes.

From the back of the bus came a further comment on the Moonies, but from whom I never knew. A man's voice spoke up loud and clear. 'The Moonies steal away little children. I saw a programme about it on the television.'

I stood up, rang the bell, and left the bus two stops short of my intended destination.

The city traffic seemed louder and heavier than I remembered. The press of hurrying bodies on the pavements forced me back to stand against the plate-glass window of a shop. I felt homesick. Not for the house in Infirmary Avenue, but for the café and Anna, and our early morning confidences across the cappuccino. I began to walk fast towards Museum Walk.

Anna greeted me as if I were a relative, long-lost. The lunch rush was over, the café almost empty. Anna came to sit at my table. She looked closely at me.

'You are looking better, Nina! More life in you!'

From the ebullient and tempestuous Anna, this was praise indeed. 'It's been a challenging winter,' I said, 'and the spring has had its moments.'

'But that's good,' she cried. 'All those years in that dark old house. You might as well have been living on the moon, or across the road locked up in the gaol.'

I paused, coffee cup halfway to my mouth. She was right!

'So what has happened to you since you moved into the country?'

I smiled. 'You wouldn't believe me if I told you.'

'Try me,' she said. 'I was born in a little village in Tuscany. It is in those small communities that life is really *lived*.'

So I told her about Sorsha and Kingdom; about the Homesteaders and their Sunday supplement-style houses; about the finding of Barnacle's book in the garden shed, and its amazing contents.

Anna clapped her hands together. 'But how wonderful! To be able to read about your ancestors, and so far back — that is really something!'

'I'm not so sure. They seem to have been a pretty wild bunch of people. The book is really about the Barnacle family, but the Lambtons figure largely in the story. It's beginning to look as though the first George Barnacle was, by birth, a Romany gypsy. As for my descent from Ezra and Pennina Lambton — well, I can't imagine how that ever came about. A less likely brace of parents would be hard to find.'

Anna said, 'The child, and there must have been one, you agree? Well, that child need not have come from Ezra. This Pennina, she had many lovers, yes? Maybe all you had from Ezra was his last name?'

'Ye — es,' I said. 'I think that's very likely.'

Anna looked at me, her head at an angle, curiosity in her eyes. 'How much of this story have you read?'

'Oh — I'm still in the first chapters.'

'How can you bear not to read it all at one go? I would sit night and day and read until the end. I couldn't stand not to know what happened to them all.'

I said, 'I have to take it slowly.' I hesitated. 'There are things about me, about my life, that you don't know and that I can't tell you. Already, this book begins to frighten me. There are parallels in that old story that match up with happenings in my own life. I can't quite begin to see the pattern yet, but I know in my bones that it will be there. Sometimes I am afraid to turn the next page — terrible things are about to happen —'

Anna held up a hand. 'Okay — but this was how long? Two hundred and forty years ago? And who knows? You might learn something good from this book.' She laughed. 'These old ones, they can't have been all bad. You carry their blood, and look at you, you are not a bad woman.'

Just for a moment I took comfort from her words, but almost at once my doubts returned. Even so, when I left the café I felt more hopeful. I wandered through the city and down to the newly built and prestigious shopping centre. The summer colours for children's clothing were lime green and navy blue. I selected shorts and tee-shirts, socks and a sun hat in what I hoped was John's size. He was growing so quickly; already when standing on tiptoe he could see over the windowsill, and watch traffic passing in the main street of Nether Ash. I had said to Fran when she bought his first pair of proper shoes, 'He'll walk away from you now.'

My first little girl had never walked away from me. She had been taken. Stolen.

I once heard a woman, the mother of eight children, describe how she still grieved, twenty years later, for the loss of her firstborn child. It was as if, she said, he had been her one and only.

I think I had always known that Jack and I would marry. His father was a local farmer, mine was the village doctor. We attended the same schools, played musical chairs at the same birthday parties. We had both lost our mothers in childhood. Jack's mother had died respectably in an influenza epidemic.

Mine had absconded with a travelling salesman who drove up to the house one winter's evening offering, on deferred payment terms, a complete edition of the *Encyclopaedia Britannica*. That blue and gold set which he left in exchange for my mother stands in the bookcase to this very day.

It was never paid for. Not even on deferred terms.

Our motherless state was not mentioned by our respective fathers. We were born, Jack and I, into an age of reserve and stoicism; of stiff upper lip, and the promise of Winston Churchill that the best we could hope for in that time of war was a life of 'blood, sweat and tears'. Our lives were ruled by, in my case, a succession of uncaring housekeepers, and in Jack's by a martinet grandmother. We were aware, he and I, of each other's loneliness, although such feelings were never talked about between us or acknowledged by the adults in our narrow world. In fact, we were considered fortunate. We had each our homes and one parent. We lived in the country so were not evacuated. The nature of our fathers' occupations meant that they would not be called for Army service.

My father's house stood on the edge of the village. Our rear garden abutted onto the Franklins' grazing meadows. We attended the village school. When Jack, at the age of eleven, was moved to the large school in the city, I could hardly wait for that two years to pass until I could join him on the early morning bus.

I became aware only slowly of the changes in the Franklin household. Mary Franklin had died, and my mother absconded, both on the same snowy winter's night. The drama in my own life overshadowed for a time the tragedy in Jack's. It was summer when I finally went once more through the wicket-gate that linked our garden to the Franklins' meadows. In the distance I could see Jack, at work with his brothers, raking the loose hay up to dry in long, straight windrows. There was something about those four boys, their silence, the way they bent to the task without once looking up, that prevented me from crossing the field and speaking to them. I walked on, and even as I approached the house I began to feel uneasy.

When electricity was brought to Ashkeepers village, the march of the pylons was halted two hundred yards short of the Franklin farm. Jack's father saw no advantages in new-fangled gadgets. He bred sheep and cattle, and the fields were down to arable and meadow. In those years between the wars, and up into the late nineteen forties, the farm was still worked exclusively by horses.

The large and rambling house was kept in good repair but lacked charm and comfort. Jack's mother had done her best. In her lifetime the gloomy rooms were bright with flowers in summer, and with arrangements of leaves and berries in the winter.

She had the gift of knowing where to place a few coloured cushions on a window seat, and to hang a pair of cheerful curtains. But even Mary could not change the Franklin inheritance of scorning what was termed 'soft living'. The stone floors struck chill even in the hottest summer. The few carpets were thin and holed. There was one room, opened only for weddings and funerals, and known as the parlour, which as a child I was never allowed to enter. Family life existed solely in the kitchen and the scullery. When the Franklins sat down it was not to rest but eat, and those straight-backed wooden chairs discouraged any inclination to relax or lounge.

Amazingly, I remember Mary Franklin more clearly than I recall my own mother. Jack's mother was tall and slim, pale-skinned, blue-eyed, and with a mass of fluffy, yellow hair. She smiled a lot, and even when not actually laughing, her lips curved up, as if she found the Franklins irresistibly amusing.

Jack was his mother's image, and not only in his looks. They both had the gift of merriment, a lightness of spirit I never encountered in my own home.

When I climbed up the steep fields on

that June morning, and smelled the sweetness of the mown hay, it was for Jack's mother that I grieved, and not my own.

I walked through the yard where a few hens scratched idly in the white dust. The dogs came fussing around me. I came into the huge, dark scullery which had not changed in any detail in my absence. The egg-crates were still piled high in one corner; the mud-caked boots in varying sizes still stood in a long line. The dolly-tub and washboards, the ironing boards and rack of flat-irons were in their accustomed places, close to the soapstone sink and soggy wooden draining board.

The overpowering smell was, as always, of paraffin oil.

Jack's grandmother, who had until recently lived alone in a small stone cottage called the Toll House, up in the high fields, was now in full-time occupation; she ruled the house, the farm, her son and the four grandsons. If she mourned her dead daughter-in-law she never said so. But neither did she comment on the departure of my own mother, the doctor's flibbertigibbet wife.

Grandma Franklin was a tiny birdlike woman, fierce, unsmiling, dressed in summer and winter in an ankle-length black dress and white apron, a shawl around her shoulders, her white hair scraped hard back from her face, and secured at the back of her head by tortoiseshell combs.

Her only greeting that morning was to ask if anyone had thought to give me breakfast. When I said no, and anyway I wasn't hungry, she pushed me firmly towards the kitchen table and began to spoon hot porridge into a bowl, which she thumped down before me with the order, 'Eat that!'

From that day forward, in return for my acceptance by Jack's grandmother, I washed eggs, cleaned out chicken coops, ironed sheets and shirts and pillowcases. At haytimes and harvests I helped her to fill baskets with sandwiches and rich dark fruit cake, and bottles of cold tea, and carry them down to the fields. I wondered sometimes where she obtained the ingredients for those cakes, since rationing was strict throughout the nineteen forties.

I did not know it then, but from the age of ten years I was under training by old Mrs Franklin to be a farmer's wife. Jack's wife. It was from her I learned how to cook on a temperamental, coal-fuelled iron range; how to fill the oil lamps, trim the wicks, and clean the glass funnels with a wedge of screwed-up newsprint.

When, years later, Jack and I were ostracised by the people of Ashkeepers village, she was to be the only one to believe, unconditionally and unreservedly, our version of those terrible events.

There were aspects of life as lived by the Franklins that, as a child, I accepted without question. It was much later, when Jack and I were living in the city, that I thought back on those times, and the strange, oppressive atmosphere of that farmhouse, and the sense of sorrow that had never eased since the day Jack's mother died.

Jack's brothers tolerated my presence in the house and around the farm with the same silent indifference with which they bore the long hours of heavy toil, their father's frequent criticisms, and his rare and grudging praise. They were in most ways their father's sons: dark-haired, dark-skinned, of medium height and stocky build, they possessed the tenacity of their grandmother Franklin, and their father's unshakable conviction in his own sour judgement of the world. The only feature handed on to them by Mary Franklin was their blue eyes.

It occurred to me now, thinking about them for the first time in many years, just how completely we had lost touch. I had not informed Jack's brothers of his sudden death. Since moving back to Ashkeepers I had kept away deliberately from the east side of the village and the house that had been my father's.

I had not enquired whether any member of the Franklin family still lived and worked up at Sunshine Farm.

The month of June brought the first of the settled warm days. Overnight my lilac trees came into full flower, the fuchsia bushes in my little front garden were weighted down by pink and crimson blossom. The squatters at number forty-eight discovered the Simpsons' garden furniture, and their state-of-the-art lawnmower. I watched, amazed, standing with Primrose at her bedroom window, as the black-clad group mowed front and rear lawns and even trimmed round the edges of the flower beds and weeded. They then trooped back and forth from the Simpsons' four-car garage, bearing white wrought-iron chairs and table, flowered parasol and padded loungers, which they arranged in a companionable grouping. At last it was possible for us to take a head count of them. In all, there were fifteen young persons on the Simpsons' lawn; as far as we could tell, eight of them were male and seven female.

Primrose was less impressed by their sheer weight of numbers than their unexpected mowing and weeding, and complete at-homeness. Just for a moment a gleam of hope shone in her eyes. 'You don't suppose,' she murmured, 'you don't suppose the Simpsons actually *invited* them to care-take? April could have forgotten to mention it in all the rush of leaving and getting to the airport?'

I shook my head.

'No,' she said. 'Perhaps not. But the fact that they are taking care of the garden is a good sign, isn't it?'

I pointed out that those young people were actually being rather clever. With the Simpsons away and proving *incommunicado*, there was, as the police had pointed out to Ashley Martindale, no proof that they had not, as they declared when interviewed, been invited to stay in the house and take care of it by Fiona Simpson, who was, they said, their chum from college, and fellow Soul of God. With Fiona accompanying her parents on what now appeared to be a world tour involving six months of uncharted travel, proof, as the Detective Constable said, was going to be a bit of a problem.

I could not stand to see Primrose so downcast.

I said, 'But you're absolutely right about their care of the garden being a good sign. It could mean that they are being equally respectful of those white linen covers and that pale lemon carpet.'

Primrose shuddered, genteelly. She gestured backwards, towards her king-sized, four-poster bed with its dazzlingly white lace hangings, ruched silk coverlet and massed blue scatter-cushions.

'Can you imagine,' she whispered, 'what those awful people are getting up to in April's master bedroom, on her four-poster bed?'

Until that moment I had never given a thought to such wild possibilities. Now, fighting back lewd laughter, I said, 'Do you mean that you and April both have similar four-posters?'

'Identical in every detail,' she said proudly. 'Unknown to one another of course, we both took ideas from that trendy magazine, *Beautiful Homes and Gardens*. Our bathrooms are identical too. We both have the same make of Jacuzzi —' She continued to list the items over which she and April had been of a single discerning mind.

My attention wandered. Between the trees

I could see my own narrow, lead-paned bedroom window, the front door of the Toll House, and a flash or two of crimson and purple from the flowering fuchsias.

Even as I looked, the tall, thin figure of a white-haired woman stood motionless inside my bedroom window. She looked down into the garden; then raised her head and across the intervening space, she gazed straight at me.

Some sound of alarm must have escaped my lips for Primrose came at once to stand beside me. Her gaze followed mine; she bridled. 'There you are!' she cried triumphantly. 'Didn't I tell you I could see you from your —' Her voice trailed away, the sentence left unfinished. She looked back at the window and then at me.

'But you are here with me,' she said unnecessarily. 'So why can I see you over there?'

'That's not me, you fool!' I really shouted at her. 'Somebody's broken into my house. I expect that I now have my very own bunch of squatters — oh, I'll do anything to be in fashion!' Shock and fear were making me hysterical and silly. 'If that woman's age and appearance is anything to go by, there must have been a breakout from the Eventide Rest Home down the road.'

Primrose looked sad and sympathetic at the same time.

'No,' she said gently. 'I don't think so, Nina. That woman stands in your window every day.'

Primrose refused to allow me to go home by myself.

Before leaving her house we drank, between us, a large pot of strong tea, laced liberally with Gordon's gin. To give us courage she said, although I suspected that it had long been her ambition to ply me with strong drink and then look over my house, and this was an opportunity not to be passed up. We walked, not altogether steadily, past the Simpsons' lawn, where the exhausted Souls of God were now resting from their labours on the Simpsons' sunbeds and recliners.

Several languid hands were lifted in greeting as we wove past. We both waved back, with rather more enthusiasm than was called for in the circumstances; but that's how gin affects a lady of mature years who is not a regular imbiber.

I unlocked my front door, tripped and almost fell across the doorstep, and called loudly up the stairs, 'Come out, come out, whoever you are. I know you're up there, you lousy squatter.'

Primrose giggled. She said, with what appeared to me at that moment to be remarkable acumen, 'Nina, it's no use calling out, is it? Let's face it, your house is haunted.'

I nodded. 'You may be right, Primrose. As a fatter of mact, I know you are!' I leaned confidentially towards her. 'Somebody,' I whispered, 'recently left a dead crow on my kitchen doorstep.'

Primrose said, 'You're drunk.'

'So are you.'

She began to cry. 'I often am,' she sobbed. 'Don't tell Ashley, will you. He's a bit prim and proper. A regular killjoy, if you must know.'

'Is that why you failed to notice the squatters in the Simpsons' house? Because you were blotto?'

She nodded. 'I have these days when nothing seems to matter. You must know what I mean?'

'Yes,' I said. 'When it happens to me I put a slog of cherry brandy in my coffee. Not often, you understand. My daughter Imogen has a keen sense of smell. She already believes that I am more than a bit dippy.'

Primrose spoke with exaggerated gravity. 'Whatever you do, don't tell her about the ghost at your bedroom window. You do agree it was a ghost, don't you, Nina?'

'Oh yes. Well, it has to be.' I was articulating carefully now, fearful of further spoonerisms. 'You see,' I said, 'my dressing-table stands right flush with that window. No space for anything human to get between it and the windowsill.' I half rose from my chair and then subsided. 'I would take you up and show you,' I assured her, 'but I don't think either of us could manage the stairs.'

We viewed one another with mutual and unexpected fondness. 'You know,' I told her, 'I didn't like you much when we first met. But you improve upon closer acquaintance.'

'Thank you,' she said. 'I didn't like you either; neither did my Ashley. But now we are both agreed that you're a damned nice woman.'

Gin doesn't suit me; it makes me sleepy and ill-tempered. Primrose must have left my house at some point. When I awoke in the small hours of the morning, stiff and cold and slumped across the kitchen table, the door was open but there was no sign of my new friend. I didn't worry about her. The fact that she had been even capable of walking proved either that her head for gin was much stronger than my own, or that she was, as she had hinted, a regular imbiber of the sloe-juice. I groped my way towards the light switch, and then clapped a hand across my eyes against the painful brilliance. Roscoe, from his basket, eyed me with disgust.

'You knew,' I accused him. 'You knew from the first night we moved in here that there was something funny in that bedroom. Call yourself a guard dog, do you?'

I awoke the next morning, fully dressed and lying on top of the bedspread, and with the worst headache I had ever known. I lay quite still for several minutes. I smiled, imagining Primrose, similarly indisposed, sprawled among her blue, embroidered scatter cushions, and under the canopy of white lace. With the gin fumes still swirling in my heard I got myself into the shower and turned the temperature gauge at first to lukewarm and then to cold.

Dressed in a clean cotton nightdress and wrapper, I crawled around the house closing all the blinds and curtains against the morning sunlight. I felt almost convalescent. Even so, I shuddered as I caught sight of my reflection in the hall mirror. There was nothing for it but to lock and bolt both doors against possible callers. Particularly

Imogen. I made a large pot of strong coffee and added to the tray a glass of water and a pack of soluble aspirin.

Primrose, I decided, would have to be watched in future, when in depressed mood. She was not an alcoholic, of course she wasn't! But an occasional tippler who did not like to drink alone.

I lay back in my comfortable chair, swallowed coffee and aspirin and felt my head settle back, more or less, upon my shoulders.

I began to think seriously about Primrose, to whom there was considerably more than met the eye. She had let slip one or two fascinating bits of information last night, when in her cups. Although she was technically a widow, Mr Martindale had abandoned her long before his final exit from this world. He had been what Primrose politely termed a ladies' man but, as the evening progressed, a more detailed rundown of his exploits made it clear that he had been randier than a rampaging billy-goat.

But it was Primrose who had triumphed in the end. She had never divorced him. On his demise she inherited all his worldly goods, his car, and a proportion of his company pension. 'If one must fall in love with a bastard,' she advised me, 'it's just as well to make sure he's a wealthy bastard, and then outlive him.'

I remembered Ashley's touching account of her grief at her husband's death, and subsequent difficulties in the rebuilding of her life. Ashley had clearly believed in every word that he was saying.

I pondered a while on the false face we sometimes show our children and our grandchildren, believing, perhaps mistakenly, that we have a duty to protect them from awful truths.

I began to wonder what indiscretions I might also have let slip last night, when in my cups. Not much, I told myself. After all, reticence had become my prop and mainstay; so ingrained in my nature that I thought twice about imparting the most trivial personal information.

Those of us who have much to hide must be constantly watchful of our secrets.

I lifted Barnacle's book from its place of honour on the coffee table, and balanced it on my knees but did not open the covers. Beyond the closed curtains I imagined the beauty of the June morning; the mist not yet burned off in the hollows of the Franklin fields, the scent of mown grass and the almond fragrance of late may-blossom; and Jack, a gangling boy waiting for me by the gate in the home field.

I remembered his father and mine; the farmer and the doctor. Two dedicated men who never noticed the loneliness, the sense of abandonment suffered by their children.

Harry Franklin's devotion was to the land which had been in the possession of his family for generations. My father's single aim was to care for and mend the bodies of the men and women who worked that land and depended on it for their existence.

In Ashkeepers, in those years of my childhood, every family had some connection to the local agriculture and horticulture. Even I, in times of harvest, was allowed to work alongside Jack and his brothers, to perform the menial tasks thought suitable for a girl; like keeping the chaff-hole clear on the threshing machine and milking the house-cow.

I suppose my father had some inkling of my whereabouts in those long school holidays, and at weekends. Since younger doctors had been called up for active service on the war fronts, his daily surgeries and rounds covered not only the population of Ashkeepers, but also that of Nether Ash and the several outlying farmsteads. He never asked how my days were passed, and I never volunteered to tell him. Looking back, I can feel a certain understanding, a sympathy for that moody, overworked doctor whose failed marriage had left him with a silent daughter who needed a mother, and a gloomy, echoing barn of a house managed by any housekeeper who could be persuaded to stay longer than a week or two.

In my own way I abandoned him just as surely as had my mother, who as doctor's wife and helpmeet had been an unqualified failure. Flirtatiousness was not called for in a ministering angel, and she was very attractive. She was also a city girl who made no effort to attempt the transition from town to country living.

The heels on her crocodile-skin court shoes measured at least four inches. When she walked down the main street of Ashkeepers, housewives who were brushing dust from their doorsteps were likely to aim their sweepings over my mother's elegant feet.

I can see her now, the blonde shingled hair peeping from beneath the cloche hat; the sweet curve of her powdered cheek against the fur collar of her well-cut coat. And that dazzling smile; the upward glance of pure coquettishness from beneath mascara-ed lashes; the way her whole body would lean invitingly towards the chosen man. I remember my own unease when witnessing her inability to behave like other children's mothers; the lurch and dip in my stomach when I saw the jealous expression on my father's face. A few years on, when I began to notice boys in a particular way, I deliberately monitored my behaviour towards them; willed myself to show an indifference and a coldness I did not always feel.

Only with Jack did I dare to be openly affectionate and loving. With him there was no need for flirtatiousness, for coyness. As for the attitude adopted by the people of the village, 'like mother, like daughter' was their predictable assumption. As I came into the teen years and my looks improved, I became aware of the gossip, the whispers and sideways glances. I learned from the current housekeeper that my friendship with Jack was 'talked about', as was my association with the gypsy girl, Estralita Lovell.

Ashkeepers held its judgemental breath and waited for the day when the doctor's daughter would, in her turn, play the harlot.

Jack also had his family problems. The Franklins had always been known as a secretive, unsociable people. In the time of Jack's mother some bridges had been built. She had been an active member of the Mothers' Union, had provided a produce stall at village fetes. But from the day of her funeral the gates of Sunshine Farm had been closed to all comers except the vet, the doctor, and the doctor's daughter. When Jack moved to the grammar school in the city, I waited for him at the bus stop each afternoon, and walked with him through the village and up to Franklin's farm. Jack and I did our homework together; we drank his grandmother's pale, milky tea and ate scones warm from the oven. We listened to the war news from London as it crackled through the brown Bakelite wireless set which stood on a high shelf in the kitchen. It was the only modern gadget in that spartan household and was switched on twice daily; for the farming news at six every morning, and again at six in the evening for reports from the war fronts.

Those long litanies of how many of our aircraft had bombed German cities, how many tons of explosive had been dropped on the populations of Hamburg and Berlin, had no relevance to our own quiet, rather boring lives. We half listened, but without really understanding, to the plummy precise diction of the radio announcer, and looked for reassurance to one another across our school books. Jack had won a scholarship to the city school, but his father, who did not believe in education, had made it clear that on his sixteenth birthday Jack would be expected to join his brothers and work full-time on the farm.

My father, from what I now believe to have been sheer inertia and disinterest, was equally indifferent to my future employment prospects. It was tacitly assumed that on leaving school I would replace the house-keeper and part-time receptionist, and take up the duties at which my mother had so spectacularly failed. He allowed me, for the sake of appearances, to have the final two years of my so-called education at a small private school in Nether Ash; where I learned nothing of importance.

It was on those twice-daily walks to and from the private school that I first met Estralita, who herself dropped in and out of the education system according to the dic-tates of her father and the wandering habits of her tribe. Estralita Lovell. Beautiful and clever. A Romany gypsy who had attended a variety of schools in places I had never even heard of. The teachers in the Ashkeep-ers school found her bewildering and dis-ruptive. Her mind was greedy for all the teaching they could offer; she learned at speed, always aware that tomorrow or next week her family might pull out from their 'atchin in Witches' Hollow, and head for some horse-fair, some market; or field work on a distant farm. And yet she rejected the moral teaching of our little church school. She would speak out in the husky voice that became a growl when she was angry, against the narrow-mindedness, the bigotry, the unfair treatment of her people by the *gorgio*.

Her father came only once to a parents' evening. A dark and brooding presence in the shabby little schoolroom, he towered head and shoulders above the rest of the fathers.

When Mr Matthews the headmaster told him that if sent to school more regularly, Estralita would be 'university material', his laughter could be heard up and down the street.

'University?' he roared. 'What would my maid want with university learning? Her husband is already picked out. She'll be wed on her sixteenth birthday.'

Depression. The very thought of it frightens me. Oh, I know I joke about it. I confess to the occasional dash of cherry brandy in the pot of coffee, and laugh at Imogen's nervousness when I neglect to have my hair trimmed. But I know and she knows that I am liable to regress, to suffer again the bouts of utter weariness during which no matter how long I sleep, when morning comes I lack the strength of will to leave my bed.

Imogen watches me. I watch Imogen watching me.

Behind the casual phone-calls, the drop-in visits, the little morale-building treats and outings, she is monitoring my mood. Checking my potential for lapsing once again into melancholy. Lovely word — melancholy.

Say it slowly and it sounds like music.

Except that the experience is anything but lovely. Or musical.

I do not deserve Imogen.

Here and now I need to make this fact absolutely clear.

On the night that she was given to me, thrust so unexpectedly into my arms, I could not believe that she was mine to keep. I have never dared to love her unreservedly. Always I hold something back, knowing that should she one day learn the truth, she would despise me even more than I despise myself.

Barnacle's book. It rests as heavily on my knees as on my mind.

Anna says that it must be wonderful to read about my ancestors, and so far back! But how can I be sure which one of those young men who spent time at the Toll

House actually impregnated Pennina Lambton? And does it matter? How many of us, even the aristocracy with their well documented family trees, can be certain beyond doubt that their blue blood does not have a tinge of red from some handsome long-dead footman or groom? Some low-born serf?

Or some whistling gypsy?

# BARNACLE'S BOOK

## Chapter 4

The prevailing winds hung in the north that springtime. It seemed to Georgie Barnacle that this year the hedges never would green over, or the birds sing. On his daily errand to the Three Choughs he lingered in Burdens' Wood, stood in the clearing and gazed long and thoughtfully at the ring of field stones which had once made safe the Lovells' fire. Already the holes which had held the bent wands that formed the bender tents were silting up with mud and stones. A thin pale grass had begun to push up through packed earth that was beaten iron-hard from the passage of the gypsies' bare feet.

In his head Georgie thought he heard the staccato rhythms of their strange language; he imagined the aromas of roast pork and rabbit stew, cooked at times when the dogs had been fleet of foot around the warrens;

or when some farmer for whom they worked had a generous heart.

He could not believe that in so short a time all traces of their habitation had been obliterated. He wanted them back, longed for the leaping flames that had lit and warmed the winter's evenings, ached for the feeling of belonging he had experienced among them.

He fell into a kind of melancholy, ate and slept but poorly, and went indifferently about his day's work. He was also conscious of changes in his body; his bones had lengthened so that he now stood taller than his master Ezra. A bristle of red hair sprouted on his chin and upper lip. He fell to daydreaming at inconvenient moments of the day. On one grey April evening he found a scrap of white lace caught upon a thorn bush, and knew it to have been torn from Coralina Lee's skirt as she searched for firewood in the thicket. He knelt beside the bush and lifted the lace with great tenderness from the sharp thorns. He smoothed it flat, laid it for a moment against his face, and then folded it carefully so that it was secure between the skin of his chest and his flannel shirt.

He had not noticed Coralina when he first met up with the Lovells. But in those days of winter she had also grown, from child into almost-woman, and the change in her was such as to stop the heart from beating. He had not dared to ask Silva anything about her, or to show the least spark of interest when in her presence. The Romany men were jealous of their women, and Georgie had marked that Silva also looked with longing on Coralina.

Even so, it was Georgie Barnacle who was favoured by her shy smiles.

April ran into May, and still the sun was pale and weak. The men of business came out from Exeter to look at their investment. Forewarned of their arrival, Ezra and Pennina, alarmed that they might lose their secure situation, called a truce on their quarrelling; and, outwardly at least, appeared to live in harmony together. Business at the Toll House, quiet throughout the months of winter, began to increase as the hours of daylight lengthened. Most drovers and cattle dealers were obliged to drive their flocks through the gate on the way to Shepton market. The carriage trade increased by tenfold. Ezra spoke of the need to employ an extra man, but characteristically made no move to find one. Pennina's 'aunty', his true gender still unsuspected by Ezra, had departed for Exeter. Or so it was said.

Georgie, lonely and restless since the Lovells' departure, and inclined to wander for an hour before bedtime in Burdens' Wood, witnessed on one dimpsey evening two horsemen in the drovers' trail who, on reaching the lane-end, reined in and dismounted, and were soon locked together in a passionate embrace.

George studied the taller, broader of the pair, and from the set of his head and shoulders knew at once that the rider was Pennina's 'aunty'.

The smaller, slighter man also seemed familiar, but Georgie could not identify him.

Any surprise he might have felt that two well-dressed gentlemen should behave so peculiarly together was lost in his conviction that the men were well known to him and bent on mischief.

He made with all haste back to the barn, and hid in the hayloft, and as he expected the riders came within the hour, their horses' feet swathed in burlap so that they made not the faintest sound across the cobbled yard that might alert Ezra to their presence.

The men, having unsaddled their mounts and tethered them into the stalls, began to speak to one another, but in tones so low that Georgie could not make out a single word.

A shaft of moonlight from a dusty window lay across the barn floor. By its light an astonished Georgie watched the small man strip off his bulky caped riding jacket, kick off his boots, and remove his breeches. As his cocked hat came off a tumble of dark curls fell to his shoulders. From the shadows the taller man produced a silk gown and slippers. The dress was pulled over the long ringlets and its hooks adjusted with a great deal of fumbling and giggling. A turn of the silk-clad shoulders into the moonlight and Georgie, no longer surprised, recognised the face and figure of Pennina Lambton, his master's wife.

He hardly noticed the couple's departure from the barn. All his doubts and suspicions of the past year could no longer be denied. He leaned his back against the stacked hay and remembered Pennina's extravagant spending. The gowns and jewellery, the good clothes for himself that could not possibly have been bought from the one pound weekly of a tollkeeper's wage.

In his heart he had always known these things, but could not bear to acknowledge Pennina's perfidy. Even now, he still saw her as a pliant woman who was led into crime by the young men who said they were her relatives.

Georgie pondered on this business of 'family'.

It seemed to him that relatives made ill use of one another; abused trust, exacted loyalty on the strength of the frail link of a shared bloodline. Better to be an orphan, raised in the poorhouse, never to know from whom or whence he came!

And then he remembered Estralita Lovell; the longing in her face when she looked at him, the way she had called him 'Manju' and claimed him as her lost boy.

Even though he believed not one single word of what she said; even though he thought her to be driven to lunacy by her time in the Shepton House of Correction and the death there of her newborn infant, still he could feel the warmth in his chest on hearing her words of love for him.

He knew nothing about human mothers. Among sheep, the ewe would only accept and feed a substitute lamb when that lamb was wrapped in the pelt of her dead off-spring; and then not always. Estralita laid claim to Georgie only because of his red hair and blue eyes. But such colouring was common among the people of the west country. Every shade of red was to be found between Frome and Yeovil; from strawberry to ginger, and the ruddier hue known as chestnut or canker.

But not among the Romanies!

Silva had pointed out this difference when they had argued on the matter.

'Only one rusty-poll shows up on us lot among many thousands,' Silva boasted. 'That's why the *gorgios* call us the "dark ones". We came out of Egypt three hundred years ago. We were the kings and princes in our own land.'

Three hundred years was a span of time which Georgie could not imagine. As for kings and princes?

'So why did your people leave this Egypt place if you were so well off there?'

Silva leaned towards him. 'I'll tell thee a secret. 'Twas a gypsy blacksmith what made the iron nails that fixed Jesus to the Cross. For that mistake the rest of us is made to suffer, to wander the world till the end of time with every man's hand set against us.'

He had punched Georgie lightly on the forearm. 'Make no mistake about it, thee is Estralita's first-born.' He paused. 'And that makes thee my cousin, and cousin to Coralina Lee.'

The month of June brought summer to

Ashkeepers. Georgie's fair skin burned and freckled in the sudden heat. Pennina stitched a light muslin shift that would protect his arms and shoulders; she purchased a salve from the wise woman who lived in Nether Ash, an expensive ointment which was guaranteed to prevent blistering. These signs of Pennina's concern for him brought him ever lower in his spirits. He carried his knowledge of her misdeeds, her deception of Ezra, as uneasily as he carried hay-stools across his scorched back.

The lawlessness in this corner of Somerset had reached such proportions that ever stricter sentences were ordered at the quarter sessions. The main administration for the punishment of wickedness and vice lay with the Justices of the Peace who were appointed from among the local gentry. These gentlemen were responsible for keeping order in their district; it fell to them to read the Riot Act when necessary.

Only those offences which involved the penalty of death were remitted to the assizes in Taunton.

Georgie listened to the talk of coachmasters and postilions, and the bar gossip in the Three Choughs. It was rumoured lately that the misdemeanours once thought to be committed by individual ruffians and rogues were not after all the spur of the moment crimes that were usual in such cases, but the work of a large and well organised gang. Rewards had been offered by the Lord Lieutenant of the county for information which would lead to the apprehension of the felons.

A sum of twenty guineas had recently been awarded to a farmer who had informed on his brother, a counterfeiter.

After a long hot day spent beside the toll gate and working in the garden, Georgie sat in the cool of the evening beneath the beech trees in Burdens' Wood. All through that day he had pushed away fearful thoughts of Pennina, but now in the stillness, memories came crowding on him. He remembered her arrival at the Three Choughs, the wonderment shown by the regulars at her beauty and regal bearing; the refusal by Jacobs the innkeeper to talk about her origins, or her reasons for working as a humble barmaid. And then there was her marriage to Ezra, which made no sense at all no matter how you viewed it. The only benefit gained, if benefit it was, could be said to be the entry it gave her to the Toll House, and the inside knowledge gained of the movement of traffic on the turnpike. From that point in his reasoning all other mysteries were made clear. Georgie Barnacle was nobody's fool. But for his devotion to Pennina, he would have come much sooner face to face with the painful truth.

The young men who professed to be her cousins might well be exactly that, but they were of course also a part of the thieving band who were terrorising the surrounding villages and countryside. Terrible tales were related by coachmen and packmen about the woundings and murders committed by the gang. Brave efforts had been made by the local militia to apprehend them, but it was said that many times, when almost on the point of capture, they vanished when in the vicinity of Witches' Hollow and Ashkeepers.

He remembered the two horsemen seen in the drovers' trail; their passionate embraces and subsequent arrival in Ezra's stable. He recalled his own lack of true astonishment when the slighter of the two was revealed to be Pennina.

He had known then exactly what she was, although his boy's mind had found the truth impossible at that point to accept.

The knowledge of who she was had been offered to him that afternoon by a drunken packman in exchange for a free passage through the turnpike.

'His lordship's youngest daughter is her ladyship Pennina,' the man had whispered from behind his grimy hand. 'That don't sit well, I can tell you, with his high and mighty Lord Lieutenant of this fair county. Frightened witless he is, lest she be found out. But there's naught he can do about it. Wild she is, and always was so, and in with a bunch of young hellions from London who think it great sport to rob us simple country folk!'

The packman had swayed and nodded, and pushed a dirty finger at Georgie's chest.

'You mark well what I'se a-tellin' you, young 'un! That'll all end in murder. And what will my Lady Pennina do then, when she stands accused at the assizes, and is put up before us all to be judged-on by her father and her uncles!'

The shadows grew long and the air still. A mutter of thunder sounded high above the beeches; raindrops big as spade-guineas fell onto Georgie's head and shoulders, cooling his body but not his mind. He had heard about but never seen the lordship's castle, its gardens and lands, the many servants needed for its upkeep. He put a hand to the cotton shift sewed for him only yesterday by the lordship's daughter. He remembered her unfailing kindness to him, and wondered again what craziness possessed her soul that she could live and work in a humble Toll House, wedded to old Ezra Lambton.

It was time to look truth foursquare in the eye.

Pennina was a highway robber; a woman who committed her crimes disguised in men's clothes. She was the close companion of footpads, thieves and murderers; and Georgie Barnacle's only concern was that she should never be apprehended.

Summertime had its usual disturbing effect that year on the young members of the rural population. The return of the sun saw a loosening, and then an abandonment of proper Christian virtues. Such behaviour may have been caused by the liberating effect of their casting off the heavy and constricting layers of winter flannel, and the donning of flimsy muslin garments? But when boys and girls, men and women, worked side by side in the haying and harvest fields, a certain lack of modesty among the females ensued, which was deplored on a Sunday from the pulpit in Ashkeepers church.

Immorality on a grand and pagan scale began with the drunken merriment of May Day celebrations, and continued henceforth throughout the months of summer. A rush of weddings was always to be expected from around September up to Christmas. Mass baptisms of the resulting infants were a feature of the first weeks of the following year.

It seemed to Georgie Barnacle, isolated as he was by his living and working in the lonely Toll House, that parson's weekly warnings applied to over two-thirds of the more fortunate worshippers there present; the rest of them being excluded from blame on grounds of great age, infirmity, or like himself, by a woeful lack of opportunity to sin.

On balmy summer nights, while waiting on the arrival of the Quicksilver coach from Shaftesbury, he would fall to dreaming about Coralina Lee, and wishing he had broken his bond to Ezra Lambton and travelled with the gypsies on their summer wanderings. But then he would remember the strict laws of her people; the way they guarded the purity of their young girls and women, marrying them off at an early age to preserve their physical and moral safety.

Marriage would be his only route to Coralina Lee, and he had nothing to offer save himself.

And what exactly was that self?

He had learned from Silva that a marriage

between a *tatchi Romanes* and a *gorgio* was rarely permitted by the elders of the tribe. Estralita Lovell had claimed him as her own child, but how could she be sure?

How could he be sure? And did he really want to be a part of their wandering uncertain lives, with the hand of every house dweller turned against them, and the gibe of *diddecoi* ringing in his ears?

Pennina Lambton had given Georgie a sense of pride in his own worth. She had taught him in the long winter evenings how to read and write like a proper scholar. He was capable now of managing the turnpike single-handed, and frequently did so. He would, said Pennina, one day be a toll-master in his own right.

But there were days of heat and dust, when ill-tempered Ezra, out of sight of Pennina, would bring his stick hard down across Georgie's ribs for some small error in his reckoning, or his tardiness in manning the gate.

Georgie Barnacle, at this point, did not so much *think* as *feel* his way through life. And his feelings were powerful lately, and difficult to control. At the age of sixteen, going on seventeen, his shoulders broadened, his voice deepened. There came a day when he stood beside the landlord of the

Choughs, who had until now been the tallest fellow in the district, and realised that he actually topped Jacobs by several inches. Such knowledge changes a young man's view of himself. Knowing he had the ability to lift Ezra by his scrawny neck, and dash his brains out against the wall, conversely removed all Georgie's desire to do so.

Pennina still treated him as if he was the undersized child he had been on her arrival at the turnpike. She tended his blistered skin when he took sunburn; dosed him for coughs and upset stomach; chided him on wet days for lying down to sleep still wearing his soaked clothing. She trimmed the corkscrew curls with her silver scissors when they grew long enough to obstruct his vision.

He allowed all this without complaint. In fact, in a certain way he enjoyed the occasional regression into a childhood he had never known. But more and more, as he came to understand the world around him, Georgie longed to speak to Pennina as one adult challenges another. His opportunity came when a traveller, bleeding and shaky, rode up to the turnpike very early on a Sunday morning. The man, in his middle years and richly dressed, had, he said, been riding out last evening intending to find his married niece who lived in the vicinity of Ashkeepers.

He swore several oaths as he dismounted stiffly and hitched his horse to the wooden rail. Georgie moved swiftly to assist him but as Pennina came out from the house, the man turned away from Georgie's helping hand, and sketched a token bow in her direction. Georgie saw the look of recognition that flashed in the man's eyes.

'It seems,' he said sharply, 'that I must once *again* throw myself upon your mercy, ma'am! As you know I have been set upon by villains. Robbed of every penny, and beaten for good measure. I cannot pay the toll but must with all speed reach my brother's house. I give you my promise that if you will allow me to pass through I will reimburse you fourfold on my return journey.'

Even as he spoke the man swayed and stumbled. Georgie looked to his mistress for guidance and though sensing Pennina's reluctance to speak further with the stranger, he nevertheless led the bleeding man into the Toll House and sat him down on Ezra's chair.

'I could go by the back lanes and the drovers' trails,' the man lamented, 'but I fear further attacks. I shall feel safer if I can remain upon the toll road.'

Georgie applied a wet cloth to the blood-ied head, while Pennina looked fearfully towards the staircase. Ezra, still sleeping, was unlikely to appear before noonday, but still she was uneasy.

Georgie, also equally disturbed, asked in a hushed tone, 'So whereabouts were you when you were struck down, sir?'

'Up at the crossroads, close by that cesspit of a place known as Witches' Hollow. Oh, they were a clever bunch,' the man said bitterly. 'I was attacked soon after midnight, which meant it was already Sunday.' Again he turned towards Pennina. 'And as *you* well know, ma'am, the victim of a highway robbery has no redress in law if robbed on a Sunday.'

'But no, sir.' Pennina spoke coolly, all her confidence regained, 'I did not know that article of law. Why ever should I?'

'I understand that you have legal connections, madam.'

'Then you have been woefully misinformed sir! I am, as you see, a toll-keeper's wife, and a generous one who is prepared to allow you pass the gate without payment, due to your injured condition.'

'You are well spoken madam, for one of lowly position.'

'I was once lady's maid to a duchess.' Pennina smiled. 'I picked up my employer's ways of speech.'

Georgie continued to dab at the oozing wounds on the man's face and bald head, but the hand which held the cloth began to tremble. This was no simple wayfarer, anxious to be on his way. Battered though he was, the fellow spoke with all the authority of one who is accustomed to giving orders, and those orders being obeyed. He sat quietly and suffered Georgie's ministrations.

'I think,' the man said to Pennina, 'that you learned more than your refined ways of speech from that duchess. But I must warn you, madam, of the dangers inherent in being too clever. I speak to you now as if you were my own dear daughter —'

'But I am not, sir! I am not your daughter, dear or otherwise!'

'Even so, I shall have my say, and I beg of you to listen. The situation in these parts concerning serious crime has become unbearable in recent months. There are rumours. And because of my *position* — my *responsible* position, I am forced to heed those rumours. I am quite sure you take my meaning.'

Georgie saw the altered expression on Pennina's face. The curious exchange between these two had now shifted to a more serious level, and the reason for this was far beyond his simple comprehension.

'It is said,' the man continued, 'that witchcraft is rife in this quarter of the county. As you will be aware, madam, since you have also studied history, that Joan of Arc, a *woman* who rode out wearing *male apparel,* was eventually burned at the stake as a *proven witch.* For a female person to don breeches and other male clothing is a dangerous departure from normality, and liable to misinterpretation. Remember that advice, ma'am, I do implore you. I do not give it lightly!'

In the silence that followed the stranger's warning every smallest sound was magnified for Georgie. He heard the rumble of carriage wheels in the far distance, the scratching sounds around the midden made by the claws of the barnyard fowls; and the pad of bare feet overhead which meant that Ezra had risen from his bed.

Pennina spoke sharply. 'I thank you for your concern, sir, although it is ill-judged and quite unnecessary. And now I think it is time you were on your way. Because of your condition you may pass, as I have already said, without payment of the toll. My assistant tollmaster will help you to your horse.' She paused and curtsied deeply before the injured man. 'May I wish you safe journey, sir, and please to give my very worst regards to your noble brother! I trust you will find him in poor spirits.'

Georgie heard and saw with great alarm the triumph and mockery in her voice and on her face. 'You may also deliver this message to him. I will see him and his kind rot in hell yet! And that curse includes you, my lord! Now be on your way before I am tempted to finish you off altogether.' She smiled. 'If you wish me to keep silent about my father's crimes, you will tell no one of your meeting with me.'

The man tried to rise from Ezra's chair, but found it impossible to walk without assistance. Georgie led and half carried him out to his horse and saw him safely mounted. The sun was already clear of the horizon and growing hotter. The man looked pale and close to fainting.

Georgie ran to the well and returned with a filled pitcher and an iron ladle. When the man had drunk his fill he said, 'What is your name, boy?'

'Barnacle, sir. George Barnacle.'

'You are a good fellow, Barnacle. What you are doing in this nest of vipers, I know not! But that is your own affair. You have shown me Christian charity this morning. But for your presence here, I do believe she would have killed me. I owe you my life, assistant toll house keeper!' The man pulled a ring from his finger and pushed it into Georgie's hand. 'I would give you a guinea but I have none. My name is Roehampton. If I can help you at any time I will do so. I sit regularly on the bench, and should you ever need me you will find me at the quarter sessions.'

Georgie opened the gate and watched the rider out of sight down the straight road. He did not go back into the house but went slowly to the barn and began to milk Arabella. With his head pressed into the cow's flank and his fingers easing down the warm mills, the pounding in his head grew quiet and his heartbeat steadied.

All that day he remained outside the house. He avoided contact with Pennina until hunger drove him indoors for his supper. Even then he could not bring himself to face her, but ate swiftly, his gaze upon the wooden platter, his thoughts in turmoil. Pennina was equally withdrawn. Ezra too, although usually silent and morose, appeared that evening to also have even darker matters on his mind.

As was his habit, the tollmaster, having

finished his meal, took up a clay pipe and tobacco, left the house and seated himself on the bench before the gate, in order to enjoy the cool air of the evening.

Georgie also rose to leave, but the need to challenge Pennina was stronger than his instinct to remain silent and thus avoid conflict. If he did not speak now he knew that he would never again find the courage.

He stood before the window which gave a fine view of the gate and good road. He thought about the man, no longer young, who had that morning sat fainting and beaten in the saddle. The man who had given him a gold ring, and promised help if George should ever need it.

Without looking at her face he asked Pennina, 'Was that wounded gentleman your father?'

She did not answer straightaway. When she spoke her voice was low so that he must strain to catch her answer.

'No,' she said, 'not my father but my uncle.'

'Then it is true what they whisper about you. You are the lord lieutenant's daughter? You are a high-born lady?'

She nodded slowly, and then the words broke from her in a bitter stream. 'But I do not count any of them as being relatives of mine. I have cast them off. They are no longer my family.'

'But why?' asked Georgie. 'Why would you leave a castle for a toll house? Why would you wed an old man like Ezra Lambton?' His voice fell to a whisper. He found the next words nigh impossible to speak. 'And why would you join with a band of highway robbers and murderers, my lady? You must know that you risks your own life every time that you rides out?'

The face she turned towards him was all at once merry and dimpled, and yet full of such a terrible mischief that it was almost a distortion. 'But don't you see, George? That is the beauty of it all! The risk, the danger, the raffish company I keep — oh, believe me, it all goes much against the grain when my noble family hear about it. Oh — and I take a care that they hear *all* about it, never fear! And make no mistake, I am not yet done with them. There is more sport yet to be had with the Roehamptons.' She paused. 'Revenge is very sweet, George. Let no man ever persuade you that it is not. And now you have had your say, we will never speak of this again.'

She began to clear the supper table, gathering up the dishes and platters in her usual tidy fashion, her features once more composed in their regular calm beauty. In spite of her dismissal of him, Georgie longed to speak further with her, but the words and the courage would not come. He had so far in his young life no experience of bitterness and hatred. No understanding of revenge.

He left the house and began to walk without notice or intention towards Burdens' Wood. He stood in the clearing and watched the shadows lengthen beneath the beech trees. The rich greens of summer had a healing quality which cooled his agitated spirit; he bent down and touched the ring of firestones left by the Lovells as if this sign of their existence was the only security left to him. The last seven years of his life had been made safe and easy by Pennina; she had made a fair scholar of him, had named him to her uncle as being her assistant toll-keeper. She had given him a pride in his own self. And who was he to stand in judgement on her?

He knew her to be by nature compassionate and tender. This family of Roehamptons must have wronged her grievously to have driven her to marriage with Ezra and a life of crime.

And thus did Georgie Barnacle, young and innocent, prevaricate and make excuses for Pennina Lambton because of his devotion to her.

Although, to be perfectly truthful, dear reader, I doubt that any words of his would have prevented that final disastrous outcome of events.

In August, because of the heat and drought, the first leaves fell early from the maples and beeches; the grasslands around Ashkeepers were burned off to a pale dust. The new hay and straw was already being fed to sheep and cattle. Watering holes were almost dry and the pond on Ashkeepers Green was no more than a muddy puddle.

For the first time in his life Georgie suffered an aching pain in his head, and not from the long days spent underneath the hot sun, but from the turmoil of his feelings.

At night he spread his blanket beside the open barn door; he watched the brown moths flutter around the lit lantern, and listened to the rustling of the dry leaves. Off in the meadows thirsty cattle lowed. An owl hooted, a dog barked. He lay watchful and waiting, like an anxious father whose only daughter has not yet returned from trysting with her lover, underneath the moon.

Lying on his side, his ear pressed to the beaten earth of the barn floor, he caught the first faint vibrations caused by horses' hooves as they galloped down the drovers' trail.

Pennina was no longer careful to muffle the sounds of her approach. Ezra, long since abed and in a drunken stupor, could be trusted never to waken even though the Toll House and its gate should burn down around him.

Georgie rose and gathered up his blanket; he moved from the door and went into a dark corner of the barn. On other nights the riders had come laughing into the lamplight, exhilarated from their night's adventures, congratulating each other on yet another bold escape from the militia. On this night not a word was spoken. Pennina, wearing men's garb, was the last to dismount, lifted down from her horse by the two young bucks who were said to be her cousins. Georgie heard her moan of pain as her feet touched the barn floor; saw her stumble and then regain her balance. Still silent and subdued the three moved haltingly towards the house.

The horses had been tethered in their stalls, their distress ignored. Georgie went to each in turn, speaking gently, stroking and calming the trembling creatures, wiping the lather of sweat from their coats, checking fetlocks and hooves for injury. He came last of all to Pennina's mount, and although the horse had itself taken no damage, a hand run across its flank came away wet and dark with blood. Pennina's blood.

When the eastern skies were streaked with the first grey light of dawn, the lamps still burned brightly in the Toll House windows. A dozen times in that long night Georgie had approached those windows and then backed away. He remembered Lord Roehampton's warnings to Pennina. As the first small birds began to chirrup in the hawthorn hedges he rose, folded his blanket as Pennina had taught him, and placed it on a high shelf in the stable. Methodically, head still aching and body weary, he began the first tasks of the day. As the sun rose higher in a clear sky his sense of foreboding increased. Three times he went to the pump, slaked his thirst and soaked his face and head in the sweet cold water. He glanced frequently towards the silent house, where the lamps burned palely now in the brilliant morning. With Ezra never altogether sober, and Pennina injured, the coming weeks promised little time for dreaming of Coralina Lee.

Pennina was very sick. He longed to see her but she lay out of sight, all visitors forbidden entrance to the bedroom above the kitchen. Once again Ezra slept on the settle in the good room, while his wife was tended by the cousins who had brought her, faint and bleeding, back to the Toll House on that fateful evening. The management of the turnpike now rested entirely in Georgie Barnacle's capable hands. Without consultation he took it upon himself to employ a poorhouse boy, even as he himself had once been chosen. He showed the same merciful kindness to the child Jem as he had received from Pennina all those years ago.

As the days went by and no visit was made to the Lambton household by the militia, he began to believe that Pennina's injuries had been, as her cousin Hugo stated, purely accidental; at least until that morning when Pennina came slowly and with difficulty down the narrow staircase; in fourteen days he had never glimpsed her, and now she was so changed that Georgie scarcely knew her for herself. Gone was the straight back, the poised head, the translucent skin underlaid by the pink flush of health. Pennina, white as a bedsheet, stooped as a crone, clung with both hands to her cousin's arm, to lie back exhausted in the cushioned rocking chair, beside the fire.

In a quiet spell when the gate could be

safely watched by the new assistant, Pennina called Georgie to her side.

She motioned him to sit on a low stool.

Seeing her close up and full face he could not conceal his shock at her appearance. The bruising around her jaw and eyes was fading to shades of yellow and plum, but the swelling of her lovely features had only just started to subside. Her right leg, beneath the long skirt of her gown, was thick with a bandaging of ripped-up bedsheets, which extended downwards to her ankle and foot. Her right arm and hand were similarly swathed.

In his new-found confidence as acting turnpike master, and secure in his own physical strength, Georgie faced Pennina finally as her equal, and in some measure, her superior.

He leaned forward and gazed into her eyes. He said, in a gentle and compassionate voice, 'What happened to you, my lady?'

She looked away, through the window and beyond to where the crenellation of the castle turrets showed grey against the blueness of the distant hills. When she spoke her voice was soft and dreamy. 'You have first and foremost to understand, George, that my father is an evil man. He uses his high office to hide his many crimes, the worst of which is murder. This habit of concealment is not unusual among the judiciary of this fair county of ours; criminals are not always chained in prison ships and transported to a far place; many of them sit in judgement and pass sentence on men far less wicked than themselves.'

She paused. 'My father became enamoured of a very young woman, the daughter of a bishop; a foolish girl but one who was clearly beyond his usual evil methods of procurement. She was like a sickness in his blood. He persuaded me, in my innocence, to befriend her, to have her pay month-long visits to us at the castle. My mother,' and here Pennina faltered, 'my mother treated her as if she were her own daughter, and all that time — all that time, that vixen was my father's whore. In the end it was not enough for them to make a cuckold of my poor dear mama. There came a day when my mother suffered an accident. Except that her death by drowning was no mishap. It was cold-blooded murder.'

'Can you be certain of that, ma'am?'

'I saw it happen, George. It was very early in the morning. I was riding through the coppice on the far side of the castle lake, when I saw my father crouching at the lake's edge and rolling a long dark object into the water. In the time it took for me to ride down towards him, he became aware of my approach and since concealment was by then impossible, with great haste he made some effort to retrieve the bundle. As I reined up beside him I saw that the sodden object lying half in, half out of the lake was the body of my mother. A great dark bruise marked the left side of her forehead, and there was no life in her.

'I said to my father, "This is your work. You have killed her."

'We looked long and hard at one another. He saw in that moment the hate I bore him. He made me no answer because he could not.

'I turned from him and mounted my horse, and still he made no sound. I returned to the castle. I packed my own and my mother's jewellery, and as much gold as I could lay my hand upon. I rode over to the Three Choughs and took the Exeter stage, having first bribed Jacobs to say nothing, should my father make any enquiry for me. Once in Exeter I sought out my cousins Peregrine and Hugo. Their mother and my mother were devoted sisters. Their feelings of grief and anger on hearing of my mother's murder were equal to my own.'

Pennina's head fell back onto the cushions. Her face was deathly white now. Two pitchers stood on the table, one of which held wine and the other water. George poured a measure of each into a tumbler and put it to her bruised lips. When the faintness passed he said, 'No more, ma'am — you have talked enough for one day —'

'No, George! I will tell it all. I could not bear that you should think ill of me. For your own safety you must know the truth. My uncle Roehampton will no doubt attempt to bribe you with gifts and pleasant words, but he is my father's poodle. It was he who swore on oath at the assizes that my mother's death was accidental; having first of course paid the surgeon to confirm that she had, for a long time past, been suicidal, suffered spells of vertigo and loss of memory. All of which I knew to be untrue.'

Georgie sat head bowed, his gaze fixed on his clasped hands. 'It is a dreadful tale, and I well understand your feelings, but what I cannot understand, ma'am, is your marriage to Ezra, your lawless style of living in the past years.'

'I do not altogether understand it myself, George, and believe me I have agonised about it. The death of my mother, my father's subsequent marriage to his whore, worked great changes in my head and heart. It was as if my former life had been lived with stopped-up ears and closed eyes. In those few minutes at the lakeside, my mother's drowned body lying at my feet, I saw clearly for the first time the selfish hearts, the wickedness of my father's family and all their kind. I remembered the stinking hovels in Ashkeepers, the ragged barefoot children, the hunger and sickness suffered frequently by my father's tenants, and a kind of righteous madness came upon me. I vowed to avenge these wrongs; to rob the rich and give succour to the poor. Most of all I sought vengeance for my mother's blood. I knew my father's cast of mind, his need to be admired and looked up to by others of his own sort. The greatest harm I could do him was to bring disgrace upon his name. I could have publicly declared him to be a murderer, but who would have believed me? I knew the power he possessed, the way he gloried in the greatness of his many titles. He had taken me with him on occasion to the Taunton assizes, so that I might see and admire him in his scarlet robes, and know him for a judge of men, a God-like person who could order the death by hanging of some simple illiterate peasant who had stolen a loaf or a piece of cheap ribbon. Even then, when I was still a child, I questioned in my heart what manner of man my father was, that he could end so easily and without compunction the lives of his fellow human beings.'

Once again Pennina faltered, and George held the tumbler to her lips. When she had drunk a little of the wine and water her voice grew stronger. 'I know what is in your mind, George. You are thinking that I too have not been altogether blameless with regard to Ezra and my treatment of him. And you are quite right. But you are very young, and still ignorant of the ways of men and women.' She sighed. 'When I left Exeter my plans were uncertain. The jewellery I had pawned brought in very little money, and I refused to be beholden longer to my aunt and cousins. I needed a safe haven from which to operate my revenge. I persuaded Jacobs to employ me at the Choughs. It was not an inn that was likely to be frequented by the Roehamptons or their servants. I went unrecognised by all save Jacobs. But I hated the bar work; for all my fine sentiments, I could still not quite forget that I had been born in a castle.

'It was Hugo, my cousin, who first spotted Ezra. Poor Ezra, lonely and unloved, loathed by his fellows because of his disposition and his authority as the turnpike. But in many respects he was fortunate, having a neat new house which stood by itself amid woods and meadows, a regular stipend, and land enough to grow all the food he could ever eat; and most important from my point of view — a barn and roomy stables. For my purpose, Ezra could not have been improved upon.

'I proceeded to court him. At first he resisted — he believed that I made sport with him. It was I who proposed marriage. I promised to be a good wife to him, and I kept that promise.'

The colour rose in George's face. 'I found it hard,' he stammered, 'to think of the two of you together. That didn't seem decent to me, you being so young and him so old.'

The bruised lips stretched into a wry smile. 'Ezra was never a complete man in the way you mean. A few kisses, a cuddle at bedtime kept him happy. And you must admit, George, life in the Toll House has been more comfortable since my coming, for both you and Ezra.'

'Comfortable, ma'am, but not safe. Ezra is neither deaf nor blind, and I too have all my senses. I have heard the tales told in the Choughs and by passing drovers, of the highwayman who robs only the wealthy travellers and makes gifts of gold to the poor folk. I have tended to your mistreated horses when you return here close to dawnlight.' He stumbled a little over the next words, but spoke them all the same. 'I have also watched your loving ways with your cousin Hugo; the one who was your 'aunty' to begin with. Ma'am — I have no liking for Ezra Lambton, but you have brought danger close to the Toll House. He fears that he will lose his house and his living if you should be apprehended. He drinks to dull his misery and fear. Mayhap I am speaking out of turn, ma'am, but it don't seem right to me that you should use him so, when he has done you no wrong.'

'You are right, George. As soon as I am well I will make amends to Ezra. In these past months my actions have been those of a crazy woman. My only thought was to bring disgrace upon my family name. Each time I robbed my father's wealthy friends I half-wished to be caught by the militia; to be arraigned for all the world to see, to stand before his judgement at the Taunton assizes.' Pennina gestured with her good hand at the injured arm and leg, her battered features. 'Instead, I received a thorough beating from a rival villain who said I was poaching on his territory; and what have

I achieved? My father cares not a fig about the little scandal I have raised.' She smiled, a smile so terrible that Georgie's blood ran chill. 'But I have lain abed, thinking, these last two weeks, and the time has not been wasted. There is a way, George, in which I can destroy my father and his whore, cause them more heartache than they ever dream of, and I shall not need to ride out at midnight, nor carry pistols. Sometimes,' said Pennina, 'the simplest plan can be the most effective.'

Pennina healed slowly but not completely. By the end of September the cuts and bruises, the swellings had all but disappeared. But she remained severely lame in her right leg, her right arm was weakened. Her cousin Peregrine returned to Exeter; Hugo stayed. Ezra made valiant efforts to pull himself together. The boy Jem turned out to be a willing worker. Pennina resumed her old sweet ways with Ezra. Between them all the Toll House regained its former good reputation for prompt service and fair dealing.

But for all these improvements Pennina was not her ebullient and merry self. Her black silences could last a whole week. She began to collect a curious assortment of objects, which she hid in a cupboard in the barn; a large wicker basket which had carrying handles, a number of well-boiled soft white sheets and two crocheted blankets.

George felt the heart turn within his chest at the sight of her limping painfully about the house and garden. As to her thoughts, he knew them to be bitter, vengeful. A sense of brooding hung about her, a threat so powerful that they were all, in their separate ways, affected by it.

It was at Michaelmas that a postilion, from his high seat on the London stage-coach, called out to him late one afternoon that Georgie's gypsy pals were coming into Ashkeepers. 'Saw them a-roving down through the back lanes,' he shouted, 'with their goats and donkeys. They've got the little dancer with 'em. The one you got your eye on!'

Georgie wondered how it was possible that a postilion from London should know the secrets of his heart. The gossip in the Three Choughs must be more reliable than usual. The knowledge that Coralina Lee was but a few fields distant lent speed to all his actions. His chores completed, he excused himself from the supper table, washed at the pump, put on a clean shirt, and with his hair still dripping wet, he set out for Burdens' Wood.

They came into Ashkeepers as dusk was falling, driving slowly through the blue-gray dimpsey light which hid the shabbiness of their lightweight creaky carts, and the weariness of the ponies and donkeys which pulled them.

The familiar outlines of the flat-carts, the designs of brightly painted flowers and leaves which covered every inch of wood-work, once again stirred a sweet nostalgia deep in Georgie's chest, a longing for a style of living he had never known. He remembered that first time he had witnessed their entry into Burdens' Wood; the way he had hidden behind the blackthorn bush, nervous and astonished.

This time was different. He still watched from a concealed spot, but with keen attention and without fear. It was important to him on that autumn evening that on this occasion he should learn and remember every smallest detail of Coralina's people and their peculiar customs. He noted how the carts were loaded high with bedding; with the bundled straw and bracken and the coarse brown blankets, some of which would form the coverings of the bender tents. Suspended from the sides of the carts and from the tailgates were kettles and tripods, buckets, bowls and baskets. In the panniers carried by the donkeys would be the precious fiddles and tambourines by means of which they made a precarious living; and their few bits of valuable china, brought, it was said, centuries ago from a land called Egypt.

They travelled light.

Nothing was stored and saved against a rainy day.

When they ate, the food was devoured to the last crumb. When they drank, the vessel was emptied to the final drop. Silver was for the spending. Gold came their way but seldom. Life was for living. For who could tell how long or short that life would be?

They needed no cupboards, drawers, painted cabinets or oaken chests. No locks or keys.

Yet they were not an improvident people. Every aspect of their lives had a logic, a rhythm, a pattern. They had somehow managed to survive centuries of persecution at the hands of the *gorgio*. And still they roamed away in their season; and still they returned, rattling along on their painted carts through the leafy lanes of springtime, and across the brown and golden fall of autumn leaves; striding and riding across the wetlands, and the parched fields, impervious to heat or cold.

A tough, indomitable race, known for the nervous hardness of their temperaments, for tenaciousness and uncertain temper, and always watchful. Always poised for sudden flight.

They turned into the path that led to the clearing between the beech trees. Silva had said that this was a good pitch, sheltered and isolated, with the stream of sweet clean water running close by, and their safety guaranteed by Lord Roehampton; just so long as they obliged him in certain matters. Georgie could not imagine what possible business there could be between the castle and the Romanies, but Silva, his finger tapping the side of his nose, assured him it was so.

In the rear of the flat-carts the young women walked together. They passed him by so closely that from the cover of the whinberry bushes Georgie heard clearly the slap of their bare brown feet, and the quick chatter of their strange language. They moved with the long, lithe stride of women who are accustomed to walk great distances over rough terrain. If he had dared he could have reached out a hand to touch the brilliant stuff of Coralina's skirt as she swung by. But this was not the time or place for his first advance towards her, especially after the long parting.

Which, come to think about it, could hardly be counted as a parting, since they had scarcely known each other.

Several days elapsed before the time and place were suited to his purpose concerning Coralina. He had carefully avoided all contact with Silva. Because of Georgie's great height and breadth of shoulder, and the fierce red of his hair, it was not easy for him to pass unnoticed in any location, especially a woodland where he lacked the Romany skills of silent movement, and crashed and blundered through copse and grove like any *gorgio* lummox. He feared to meet Silva lest he should learn that Coralina was already wedded. And so he hovered and watched and waited, and finally the moment came.

It was in the blue and early twilight of mid-October that he found her in a safe situation; she was gathering wood and walked apart from her sisters and cousins, yet with her family still close by and within safe hailing distance. As a young and *gorgio* male, Georgie knew he dared not compromise her. He appeared on the woodland path, but placed himself at some distance so as not to cause her fright. Unlike the loose girls of Ashkeepers, the gypsy rawnies observed the rules made by their menfolk.

He said, remembering the words he had learned from Silva, '*Sar shin*, Coralina.'

She looked swiftly back across her shoulder at her chattering sisters and then, reassured, she answered '*Sar shin*, Manju.'

He bent to take the bundle of faggots from her, but she would not allow it. 'No,' she said, 'you are a man, and this is women's work.'

He needed to detain her, if only long enough to learn if she was wed. 'Then rest awhile,' he pleaded. 'Let us wait here for your sisters.'

She sat down on a mossy log, and he stood a little way off, his back leaned against an elm tree. He had forgotten how beautiful she was; or maybe time had worked a miracle in her. The half-child she had been in springtime had changed over summer into a young woman whose loveliness caused the blood to pound behind his eyes, and the breath catch in his throat.

He could not speak for gazing at her, and he thought she knew it. As her sisters came closer Coralina bent her head to the faggots, sorting long from short, thick from thin, as if she was unaware of Georgie Barnacle, propped against the elm's bole, and gazing at her with his great sheep's eyes.

Her skin was the soft shade of dark amber, her hair was thick and straight, blue-black in colour and combed sleekly to her head, to fall in two heavy braids which hung to waistlength. Her earlobes were pierced by two copper hoops which swung enticingly against the slim stem of her neck. Her eyes were the same translucent no-colour opaline as those of her cousin Silva. He wanted her to look up at him, to acknowledge his presence, and since she was the first girl he had ever courted, the only ways he knew were simple and direct, and lacking guile.

'Art thou wed, or promised?' he asked abruptly.

The tawny skin of her face became suffused with a deep pink. She ceased the business with the faggots. Her left hand crept up to her left earlobe and began to twist the copper ring. Georgie noted the gesture, taking it as a sign that she was disturbed by his question; but still she did not answer.

'Betrothed, then?' He strove to keep his voice level and unconcerned, but the ragged edge of it came through.

At last she took pity on him. 'I was promised,' she murmured, 'to Ambrose Lovell. But he don't keep me to it, not no more, seeing as how he'll be gone away for seven years to transported-man's country.'

The relief spread from Georgie's head and chest into his legs, causing him to slump against the elm, and then slide slowly downwards. From a seated position among the dry leaves he said, 'He was the one that was put aboard the prison ship?'

'Aye, Manju,' she said. 'He was thy uncle, thy mother's brother.' His instinct was to deny all connection to the Lovells, but the words jammed in his throat. Coralina believed that he was family, the lost son of Estralita Lovell. As Georgie Barnacle he would not be acceptable as a husband. As Manju Lovell there was still a chance that he might be permitted to wed Coralina Lee. He clenched his fists until the fingernails bit into his calloused palms.

'What must I do to offer for thee? And if I offer, wilt thou take me, Coralina?'

She looked up at him then and he met the full power of her fascinating, no-colour eyes. There was no coquetry, no artifice in her. 'If thou offer for me and my Daddus say so, I will gladly take thee, Manju.' He saw her smile for the first time; saw her shine from within like a storm-lantern on a wild night. He wanted to turn cartwheels, to swing like a child from the low branches of the tree; to announce his joy with a chorus of great shouts that would echo down the groves of beech and ash. But her sisters were stepping lightly now through the sapling oaks, smiling and nodding, as if they had held back in anticipation, judging their moment to appear.

It came to him then that this meeting might not after all have been solely of his contriving. But what did it matter! She had said yes, without a second thought.

Now he must seek out her father; claim his belated kinship with the Lovells; inform her family that he was not a penniless poorhouse boy with nothing of value to bring to the marriage, but a man with prospects.

At North Town in Taunton a new toll house was under construction. The investors in the almost completed toll road had spoken privately to Georgie. The position of turnpike master was his for the taking, but they preferred he should be established, a married man.

He said to Coralina, 'I will come on Sunday. I will speak to your father.'

She rose and went to stand among her smiling sisters. He watched them slip silently away among the trees and thought how little he knew of the ways of women.

If Georgie had been less in thrall to

Coralina, he might have noticed the change which had recently come over Pennina. But so concerned was he with his own plans for the future that he quite failed to register the high, almost frenetic spirits of his master's wife, her increased energy, her sudden sense of purpose.

Even when he came again upon the wicker basket which still lay concealed in the old wooden chest in a corner of the barn, he only half noted the addition to its contents of several baby garments. If he gave the matter any thought at all, it was to assume the collection to be a gift by Pennina intended for some poor village wife, soon to be a mother.

His offer for Coralina Lee was made on a mild still night in late October. The whole company of Lees and Lovells were aware of his purpose in coming among them. A young wild boar had been snared, killed and cooked with onions and turnips. As he came up to the fire, the smell of roasting pork mingled with the scent of burning applelogs. The faces which turned towards him were smiling, welcoming; even that of Silva! They called him Manju. The woman Estralita, who said she was his mother, held both his hands as if she would never let him go. The children who were said to be his brother and sister danced around him, brought him hot sliced pork on a wooden platter, and the fragrant tea to drink, which was more costly and more highly prized among the Romanies than ale or porter. The business was done in a few words.

Coralina's father, a small dark man who played the fiddle, took Georgie to stand apart from the feasting, and asked him what his intentions were towards his daughter.

'To wed with her,' said Georgie.

Silence Lee answered with a slow nod of his head. 'So be it,' he said after some thought. 'Thee art big and strong, and will be a good help to us. It is a wonder and a magic that thou art given back to us, Manju, after all thy hard years lived among the *gorgio!* My Coralina will bring with her a good pony, a donkey and a spanking new flat-cart. What treasure brings thee to this marriage? Though if it be no more than thy ownself it will be enough.'

Georgie looked to the group which sat around the fire; he saw the keen expectant faces of the Lee family, the joy of Estralita Lovell, the general air of approval at a good bargain struck. It was only then that the realisation came to him that as far as the Lees and Lovells were concerned, marriage to Coralina would mean that he became one of them, travelling in the seasons with flat-cart and pony, snatching a doubtful living by whatever means he could.

Instinct warned him that this was not the time to inform Silence Lee that his daughter, once married, would be living in the newly built toll house in Taunton town, sleeping beneath a house-roof, wearing shoes upon her feet, and with good food on her table every day. He walked back to the fireside and sat down beside Coralina.

She held his hand and smiled shyly at him.

The wedding, she said, would take place in four weeks, since word must be passed on to those who were now travelling up and down the country. If Georgie was like-minded she would need, as well as their own style of Romany marriage, to have a blessing from the parson in the Ashkeepers church. After that would come the dancing and feasting. Georgie nodded his consent while all the time in his heart he grew faint and troubled. The matter was more complicated than he had imagined. In his innocence of the ways of women he had imagined himself and Coralina after their wedding, wandering hand-in-hand into the sunset to live happily together in Taunton.

On his way back to the Toll House, he

trod the extra mile which brought him to the Three Choughs. He was not a drinking man but on this occasion he needed some company other than his own, and a drink that was stronger and cheaper than the gypsies' tea.

The meal of roasted pork had made him thirsty. He drank a measure of ale and listened to the excited talk of Jacobs and his cronies. They asked if he had heard the news? A great event up at the castle! The birth of a male heir to Lord Roehampton! The son his lordship had waited for all these many years.

'Big celebrations,' said the blacksmith, 'all Roehampton's tenants and workers are to be invited. Plenty of ale, plenty to eat. There'll be music and dancing. Them gypsies out in Burdens' Wood 'ull be up at the castle, playing their fiddles, singing their wild songs and banging away on their tambourines; and pinching the silver if they gets a chance.'

The gossip became general; arguments broke out regarding the mystery of the death of the first Lady Roehampton.

'Daft as a cuckoo she were,' said the farrier. 'That come as no surprise to nobody when she chucked herself in the lake.'

'And what about the daughter?' asked a

farmer from Nether Ash. 'Vanished in thin air, she did. Nobody have seen her since the day her ma' died.' He gazed thoughtfully into his tankard. 'Mayhap 'twas she pushed her mother into the water. She always was a wild one, that Pennina.' He looked around the smoky room, but failed to recognise Georgie Barnacle in his dark corner.

'They do say,' the farmer whispered, 'that Lady Pennina is still in the district. That her goes about dressed in breeches like a man and have took to witchcraft.'

Jacobs said sharply, 'And how would you know about that, William? Did you see her with your own eyes?'

The man laughed, uneasy at the confrontation. 'Well no, landlord. Even if I did see her I wouldn't recognise her, would I? Reckon none of us would. We was never on visiting terms with the high and mighty Roehamptons. Us never took tea with Pennina.'

Jacobs laughed. 'They do say she's plain as a pikestaff. Well, her nose'll be proper out of joint now. There'll be nothing for the Lady Pennina to inherit, now she've got a baby brother!'

Georgie heard but did not really listen to the banter of the drinkers. All his thoughts were of Coralina and his coming marriage;

and how soon after that marriage he would dare to tell Silence Lee that his daughter was lost to him forever, and would henceforth live with her husband as a *gorgio,* never more to travel the winding roads of Somerset and Dorset, or pitch her tent and light her fire in Burdens' Wood.

There are times, dear reader, in the penning of this narrative, when I could wish to have Georgie Barnacle here, sitting at my side, so that I might ask him what he thought and how he felt in certain situations.

And yet! Whenever this longing to have him present and accountable comes over me, it is promptly followed by the most utter certainty that he has, at that very moment, popped into my head to inform me of all I wish to know.

He should have been happy, but with each day that passed his sense of unease deepened. There had been no courtship between himself and Coralina, only shy and longing glances, nods and sighs; not even conversation, and yet each had seemed to know the mind and heart of the other.

It was only now, with approval given, and Georgie accepted as a future son-in-law, that he began increasingly to discover the many complications which are attendant upon true love.

He had not, for instance, known until told by Silence Lee that Coralina was the principal dancer in the entertainments given by the gypsies at the great and noble houses of the West Country; and since he had never witnessed the dancing of young women, he was not too sure of what the term entailed. Georgie had a muddled recollection of the Morris men who stamped and cavorted around Ashkeepers green on May Day. He remembered the guisers who performed in their curious mummers' costumes. But he could not believe that the gentry would hand over their gold to watch such clumsy antics from the Lees and Lovells. It was to Silva that he turned for accurate information, and the subject was not difficult to raise, since the talk in Burdens' Wood was all about the coming celebrations up at the castle, at which the Lees and Lovells were commanded to perform.

'So how many of you has to do this dancing?'

Silva laughed. 'All of us — 'ceptin Silence and Jai, and Tawno, what plays their fiddles for the music. Can't dance without music, surely even thou knows that?'

'Don't rightly know what dancing is,' admitted Georgie. He studied Silva who was skinny as a larch-pole and head and shoulders shorter than himself; they moved into a flat patch of the rideway where they stood in conversation, and Silva raised his arms high, his arms and fingers curved inwards to his head. He began to rotate very slowly, stamping his bare heels on the ground in a steady rhythm. The thin body, ramrod straight, whirled faster and faster. The heels beat an impossibly rapid tattoo. A series of wild cries came from Silva's throat; the no-colour eyes had a crazy light, the upraised chin and tilted head began to turn in a curious jerking movement. The curving fingers snapped and clinked. Georgie fully expected that Silva was about to fall down in a convulsion, but the madness ended as abruptly as it had begun. Silva seemed to expect an admiration Georgie did not feel.

'That's dancing?'

Silva nodded. 'That's the finest dancing thee is ever likely to chance upon. 'Course that is only half the dance without Coralina.' He sighed. ' 'Tis nothing wondrous without her, and the fiddle music, and the tambours playing, and the wearing of my special shoes with the square nails in heels and toes what makes for a good loud tapping.'

'Coralina stamps and shouts in that wild fashion?'

Silva gave Georgie a hard look. 'Nobody dances like Coralina. 'Tis a gift not vouch-safed to many *racklis*. Coralina earns more silver for the family money-bag than all the rest of us *chals* put together.'

It was a thought he did not wish to dwell on, but distraction was not hard to find. News of the child born in the castle, the celebrations planned by the Roehamptons, had reached the Toll House and Ezra Lambton.

'We're all invited,' her husband told Pennina. 'Toll House'll have to be closed for the whole of that evening.'

'Not possible,' said Pennina, 'there will still be a Quicksilver stage or two to clear, even on a Sunday. I shall stay here and do my duty, Ezra. The rest of you are welcome to join in my Lord Roehampton's junket-ing.'

Ezra argued and pleaded, but she would not relent, and so it was Ezra and Georgie, Hugo and Jem who set out on that afternoon early in November, to ride on the farm cart to the castle on the high hill.

The dry hot summer had cooled only slowly. In these first days of November many trees still waited for the first frosts to strip them bare of leaves. The warmth that lingered in the baked earth made the shorter days pleasantly mild and still. Georgie wondered at the necessity for the thick caped greatcoat worn by Pennina's cousin, but before he could remark upon it other matters came to trouble his mind.

Pennina had for days past been in a strange mood. The wicker basket full of sheets and baby garments had vanished from the barn. A young woman with a days' old infant had been moved that very morning, without explanation, into the Toll House. Pennina's cousin was ominously silent and quite unlike a young man on his way to a joyous celebration given by his uncle.

Georgie pondered on these mysteries until Ezra nudged him with a bony elbow. 'We're coming into Roehampton country,' he said briefly. 'All you can see from here to sunrise and sunset belongs to that one family.'

It was an awesome sight. Hundreds of acres of green and rolling parkland set with stands and groupings of fine trees gave way to dense, impenetrable forest. The gravelled drive ran straight and true up to the finest, largest edifice that Georgie had even seen. Bigger than the poorhouse, or Ashkeepers church, its gardens and lawns lit with coloured lanterns, its mullioned windows glowing in the fall of twilight, he needed to remind himself that it was here Pennina had been born; from here she had ridden out, never to return. On the shore of this silver lake she had watched as her father pulled her mother's drowned body from the water. He remembered her bitterness and hatred as she had told him the story. Among those present here today, only Lord Roehampton and Georgie knew the truth about that death. And now the new young wife, the bishop's daughter, had given birth to a healthy son; a child who would inherit every stone and acre.

Grassland had been set aside for the standing of carriages and carts, and the tethering of horses. The sounds of merrymaking drifted on the night air. A broad terraced area at the rear of the main gardens formed an open-air theatre. Here it was that the Lees and Lovells were about to begin the entertainment of the evening. Bewildered by the magnificence of his surroundings, Georgie saw but did not appreciate the grandeur of the place. It would be later, much later, that his stunned mind would recover sufficiently to remember details.

Meanwhile, his greatest anxiety was for Coralina.

Coralina the dancer; who was turning out to be not at all what he had in mind when he offered for a wife.

A great fire had been lit at the rear of the paved terrace. In the foreground, in the light thrown by its flames, the Lees and Lovells were grouped according to their skills. The women and young girls who would dance and play the tambours stood together on the right-hand side. To the left, the musicians waited, fiddles under chins, until Lord Roehampton gave the signal to begin.

The Romanies were dressed in a style that was even more colourful and strange than their usual garb. The men wore tight black trousers tucked into high boots, topped off by loose silk shirts in brilliant colours and each with the red and yellow *diklo* knotted at the throat. Golden earrings swung low enough to touch their shoulders. Oil glistened on their slicked hair. Such was their transformation that Georgie hardly recognised them as the raggle-taggle crew who raced their flat-carts through Ashkeepers, and lived in poverty in the wild woods.

As for the girls and women, he could only gaze and marvel. Gone were the tattered skirts and bodices, the scraps of shabby finery begged from the kitchen door of some big house. In their place were ankle-length dresses of scarlet and black, frilled and beribboned; black shoes were worn on feet which went bare in summer and winter, and over their oiled and gleaming hair were pinned long lengths of black and heavy lace.

Coralina alone wore a dress of emerald silk; Silva a shirt of matching colour. They stood motionless together in the centre of the terrace, the red light from the fire shining on them.

A silence fell across the assembled crowd. The darkness of the night seemed to grow deeper. Georgie glanced, first to his right and then his left, at Ezra and then Hugo. But Hugo was no longer with them. It was at that moment Lord Roehampton, from his raised seat in the foreground, lifted his hand and gave the signal to commence.

The music began so softly and slowly that it was difficult to hear. The male dancer proceeded to move stealthily around the female. Coralina stood, head bowed, gaze lowered, as if unaware of the predatory Silva; and then the single thread of fiddle music was joined by two others, the bells of the tambourines chimed softly, raising the tempo. The dancers responded;

Coralina moved until she too was caught up in the encircling dance begun by Silva. The soft roll of a drum was a signal for the beating of tambourine-skins to commence. The nailed shoes on the feet of the two dancers began the rapid tattoo that Georgie had witnessed in Burdens' Wood. They swayed, hands and arms curved high above their heads, whirled and dipped and circled one another, without ever touching; and yet the erotic message of the dance was clear for all to see. Georgie thought the performance would never end.

He felt the prickle of sweat break out across his face and shoulders. He could not complain that the movements were indecent; he had seen more blatant displays, much closer coupling of men and women, in the lanes and meadows around the Toll House.

As the dance achieved its climax, wild cries broke from Silva's throat, to be echoed by the shouts of the fiddle and tambour-players. A great sigh passed across the watching crowd; the cheering was loud when Coralina finally knelt before Silva, head bent in submission as he placed a possessive hand upon her shoulder.

The music ended, the gypsy band regrouped. Accompanied on the fiddle by

Silence Lee, a young Lovell man began to sing a sad song in his own tongue. Coralina and Silva moved into the background to clap softly in time with the song.

Georgie, more disturbed than he had ever been in his young life, edged away from Ezra and began to walk slowly towards the field where the farm cart waited.

He needed to be quiet and on his own.

The girl of the dance had been a wanton, a jade.

Perhaps he had been too quick to offer for Coralina?

But even as these doubts pounded in his head, his attention was caught by a horseman riding dangerously fast towards the road. A shaft of moonlight revealed the set features and heavily-caped figure of Pennina's cousin Hugo. The horse was a bay mare which almost certainly belonged in the Roehampton stables.

The militiamen rode up to the Toll House while Ezra and Georgie were busy with the Exeter coach and its passengers. There was an urgency about the soldiers' movements as they dismounted and approached Ezra Lambton. Their orders, said the sergeant, were to search the house and its outbuildings and to question the occupants. On the previous evening a terrible crime had been committed at Roehampton Castle. While the celebrations were in progress, the infant boy in whose honour the party had been given was stolen from his cradle, and his nursemaid cruelly murdered lest she should recognise and later name the thief.

It was Pennina who spoke up to the militiamen. 'Before you go into the house I will tell you that we do have a young child here, but he is not the one you seek. A few days since, a poor girl came to us seeking shelter for herself and her newborn baby. My husband, like the good kind soul he is, gave permission for her to stay awhile until she regains her strength.'

The sergeant, impressed by Pennina's speech and bearing, was now reassuring. 'Fear not, ma'am. The infant we seek is not hard to identify. He has a thatch of pure black hair, and a small brown birthmark on his forehead.'

The search of the house and barn was less than thorough. Georgie, asked if he had witnessed anything untoward up at the castle on the previous evening said, with truth, that all his interest had been fixed on the gypsy dancers.

It was later that morning, when the militia were many miles away, that he climbed up to the hayloft and found the wicker basket artfully concealed behind the heaped-up hay.

He had guessed that the child must be hidden in some place beyond the house, and he marvelled at the cleverness of the deception. It was Hugo who had stolen Roehampton's heir, and murdered the nursemaid. It was Pennina who had planned and connived to bring the young woman and her baby into the house to act as decoys for the militia, and for the mother to act as wet-nurse for Roehampton's son. He looked down at the sleeping infant, at the thatch of pure-black hair, which was so like that of his half-sister Pennina, and the small brown birthmark on his forehead.

There was evil here and he could not condone it. Neither could he betray Pennina. He stood for a long time; he thought about the neat little toll house which could be his in Taunton Town. He thought about the Lovells and the Lees who wished for nothing more than to claim him as their own. A great shudder passed over his body, leaving him weak but his mind made up.

He turned away from the makeshift cradle and the sleeping baby, walked from the barn and the only home he had ever known. When he reached the drovers' trail he paused and looked back at the sloping roof and the three tall chimneys, at the little house built of honey-coloured stone, with its leaded-paned windows and oaken door. He tried hard to put all thought of Pennina from his mind.

For a moment Georgie hesitated; then he turned, squared his shoulders and marched with purpose towards Burdens' Wood, Coralina Lee and marriage.

# Nina

There must have been a moment when Jack and I looked at one another in a different way. A point at which the dependency of two lonely children upon each other had deepened into the greater needs of adult love.

We had always been aware of one another's dreams and longings, but our feelings for each other were kept hidden. The desire to belong, to a person, a family, a tribe, is as powerful as the basic animal needs for food and warmth and shelter.

I remember the first time he kissed me.

It was springtime, the hedges creamy-white with May blossom. I had lived all my life in Ashkeepers, had walked the fields in every season, but never before had I noticed in a romantic way the lavender-blue shadows cast by the beeches and chestnut trees, the delicate foliage of the aspen and silver birches. As we walked in Burdens' Wood in that April twilight I knew that this was to be the time and place.

If Jack could not be tempted to kiss me in the springtime, when could he?

I don't know why we submitted so easily to our fathers' will. There had still been no discussion of the future, no flicker of rebellion from either of us. At the respective ages of sixteen and eighteen, having taken School Certificate, we were settled obediently into a life which, had we been consulted, neither of us would have chosen. Within days of taking over the running of a medical household I knew exactly why the turnover of housekeepers had been so rapid. But even those housekeepers had been allowed one afternoon and evening off duty. It became the only point on which I dared to make a stand against my father. I argued with him that I really needed one half day each week for essential shopping in the city, and to change my library books.

I chose Monday afternoon, leaving the doctor to fend for himself with the remains of the Sunday roast, and cold apple pie and custard. I had discovered the cinema; sitting alone in the red plush seats of the Odeon or Gaumont, I learned about life; about love between a man and woman, about romance in the nineteen forties, Hollywood style.

There was a taint about being an abandoned child. Jack and I both felt it, recognised it in each other. We were bruised, cowed, as if we had failed to live up to expectations, to give satisfaction. Only bad children lost their mothers.

The damage showed up in our spiritless acquiescence to the wishes and demands of others; in our delayed adolescence, our fears. Jack, who had the example of his three elder brothers constantly before him, accepted the yoke more easily than I.

I lied to my father about my reasons for visiting the city. Using one shilling and ninepence of the housekeeping money I spent those Monday afternoons in blissful forgetfulness of the real world.

I queued for two hours in drenching rain to see *Gone with the Wind*. From Scarlett O'Hara I learned what a mature and determined woman can achieve. From Vivien Leigh I took lessons in the ways of love, the art of kissing. I began to practise the uplifted face, the moistened, slightly-parted lips, the wide-eyed gaze, before my dressing-table mirror. But Jack seemed unaware of my new Tangee lipstick, the imploring way I gazed up into his face. My long dark hair, released from its tight plaits and draped alluringly across my right eye, seemed to make him nervous rather than amorously inclined.

We were country children; the process of procreation was no mystery to us. But we were too well known to one another, we lacked the mystery and excitement of strangers meeting in a new situation. We lacked romance.

On that April evening I recognised that I would have to make the first move. As we strolled beneath the beeches, the toe of my sandal just happened to snag upon a tree-root. I stumbled and was caught up, as I had intended, in Jack's grasp. When he made to release me I flung my arms about his neck and held on, face uplifted, lips moistened and half-parted. The scarlet colour flooded to his hairline, and still he hesitated. My heartbeat thundered in my ears. If I had been mistaken in his feelings for me how could I ever bear the shame? There was one way only of finding out. Rejecting all thoughts of my harlot mother, I pulled his face down to mine and, awkwardly at first, and later passionately, we served our apprenticeship in kissing.

We expected family disapproval, protests from our fathers, orders to remain apart until we were old enough to 'know our minds'. It never happened. Life went along as it had always done. The only outward change being that Jack and I now walked hand-in-hand instead of leaving half a yard of space between us.

Grandmother Franklin had flashed us a single grim smile when we returned that evening to eat the nightly bread-and-cheese and cocoa supper. It was the closest she could permit herself to expressing satisfied approval. As the months went by I began to realise the changed relationship between Jack and me meant different things to different people.

Grandma Franklin was old and tired; she was more than ready to hand over the household management of Sunshine Farm to the chosen girl, the one she had trained up into her own ways, to be a fitting wife for Jack. All these years later I can see that John Franklin's greatest fear was that his sons would leave him, although he had done nothing to ensure their love or loyalty. He knew me for a quiet, reserved and biddable girl; not the wandering kind, but one who could be relied upon to live her whole life in Ashkeepers. Married to me, Farmer Franklin was sure that his youngest and dearest son would never leave the homestead. As for my father, it was clear from his casual observations that he fully expected that Jack and I would one day live with him in his house. Plenty of space here, he said. No need for you to ever leave your comfortable home, Nina! And what is more — whatever would I do without you?

The war ended on my seventeenth birthday. Servicemen came home, were demobbed, and returned to civilian life. Something called National Service was introduced. Young men of a certain age group were to be conscripted, put into uniform and sent overseas. The sons of farmers, especially the younger ones, were no longer considered exempt from serving king and country. Three weeks after Jack's nineteenth birthday his orders came to report to Catterick Barracks, in Yorkshire. Three months of training and he was aboard a troopship bound for Palestine.

For the next two years all I had for comfort were his thrice-weekly letters, and the sapphire engagement ring which never left my finger.

When we married I was nineteen years old, and Jack was twenty-one.

The two years of waiting for Jack had not been wasted. The status of engaged person gave me sufficient courage to insist that I intended to begin married life in my own domain, or not at all. To her credit, Jack's grandmother, after the initial shock and disappointment, saw the wisdom of my decision. It was her suggestion that she and I should open up her old cottage on the edge of Burdens' Wood.

I had not entered Brickyard Lane since my mother left. It was the place I most associated with her although I don't imagine we could have walked there very often. Country rambles were not her style.

On that wet spring morning, with the talisman engagement ring on my left hand, and Jack's most recent letter in my raincoat pocket, the old enchantment of the place was overwhelming.

From some way off I could see the low roofs of the cottage, the three crooked chimneys, the picket fencing. As we came closer the dark clouds parted and a shaft of sunlight glinted off the ancient golden stone and diamond-shaped lattice of the window panes. It was almost biblical, and I saw it as a favourable omen.

The little gate squeaked loudly as I pushed it open. I remember saying, 'I'll bring the oil-can when we come again.'

Grandma Franklin said, 'No, Nina! A squeaky gate warns you in time when strangers are coming — and not only strangers! In this wicked world you can never be certain who your friends are.'

She had a stock of these gloomy sayings, so I hardly listened. I oiled that gate, and exactly two years later I was to bitterly regret my action.

But on that May morning the fuchsias were coming into bud, and Jack was due home in a fortnight. The wedding was planned for early August, which gave us three months to decorate and furnish the Toll House.

It was taken for granted by our families that Jack would return to his work on Sunshine Farm, and I, though wed, would continue to act as my father's receptionist, and part-time housekeeper. But for the fact that Jack and I would be married and together, it had been assumed that nothing else would change.

Even I believed that I could turn the clock back ten years, to the time of innocence when I had held my mother's hand, and the fuchsia bushes had reached higher than my shoulder. Jack's oldest brother Alan was also to be married that summer, to a girl from the city who had not as yet been introduced to any of his family. When searching for our own engagement ring, Jack and I had spied, and were spied by Alan and his girlfriend who were also studying the display trays in jewellers' windows. But such was the relationship between the brothers that neither one of them had ever referred to the matter; and so it came as a severe shock to the rest of the Franklins when Alan finally informed his family that he was about to marry a nurse from the city hospital, and they would like to move into Grandmother Franklin's old cottage straight after their August wedding.

It was the kind of misunderstanding which is bound to happen in a household which meets only around the kitchen table, and where conversation is not allowed at mealtimes; and because of the nature of farming, each brother worked mostly on his own. I was angry at Alan's news, embarrassed, and filled with unjustified guilt. Jack's homecoming, which should have been joyous, would be spoiled by the tension which was sure to be felt between himself and his brother.

Grandma Franklin refused to discuss the matter. Her cottage had long been promised to Jack and me; if Alan had chosen not to talk about his marriage plans he could hardly expect to take over her property on a moment's notice. In any case, there was another small house on Franklin land, un-inhabited and needing repair, but that would be no problem. A firm of builders was contacted, and the work put in hand. All would be ready for Alan and his wife by the end of August.

Without any real discussion or explanation, any soothing of his hurt feelings, Alan Franklin, oldest son and his father's prop and stay, was awarded a damp and isolated gamekeeper's cottage which stood in that far stretch of Burdens' Wood which leads on into proper forest.

To the best of my knowledge he accepted the gift with gratitude. As to the opinions and feelings of the new wife who would share that home, well, they were disregarded by her in-laws. When I raised the point with Jack, when I suggested that perhaps he and I should offer to take the inferior forest cottage, he said that it had all been sorted out, and it was not for us to interfere in matters already settled by his grandmother and his father. And so, once again, we behaved like obedient children; seen but not heard, our lives arranged by those who thought that they alone 'knew what was best for us'.

For some reason I have never understood, Alan's wedding day had been fixed to coincide with ours. The mistake could not, in this instance, have been from lack of communication. Even Franklins showed interest in these first weddings in their family. The thirtieth of August had long been ringed on the big calendar which hung on their kitchen wall as being a special day set aside for Jack and me.

Alan's choice of date must have been deliberately provocative. It succeeded only in dividing further a family which had never been close to begin with.

Roy, second son, was to stand as Jack's best man.

Derrick, third son, was to stand for Alan.

Farmer Franklin, morose and unwilling in his Sunday suit, attended the city wedding of his rightful heir.

Grandmother Franklin, bossy as ever and almost smiling, took the place in Ashkeepers church of my absent mother, who was hardly missed.

Two years away from his family had changed Jack. But for his acquiescence in the matter of the cottages, which was, after all, to our advantage, he was no longer prepared to bend to his father's will.

He announced at the wedding reception

that he would not be returning to work on Sunshine Farm, but intended to take full advantage of the government's offer to ex-servicemen of further education. I can see him now, champagne glass in hand, white carnation in the buttonhole of his new gray suit, his fair hair not quite yet recovered from its final Army haircut.

'My wife and I,' he said, smiling down at me, 'have talked it all over. I intend to do now what I should have done when I was younger. I've been offered a college course. I have a notion to be a schoolteacher; to teach perhaps in the village school or in Nether Ash.'

It was Grandma Franklin who spoke first. 'But you've already been away for two years, boy! How long is this course going to run, and what about Nina?'

'Nina supports me all the way, Grandma. It's a one-year course and I can take it in the City University. I'll be home every weekend.'

I was proud of Jack that day, impressed by his courage at leaving the safe haven of the family business for the riskiness of a new venture.

It was much later that I realised he had been careful to make his initial announcement regarding the future in his father's absence; and also that the house we now lived in was, reassuringly, the sole property of Grandmother Franklin, who could be trusted, even should we ever displease her, never to evict us.

My father's wedding present was a sizeable cheque and a two-week honeymoon in Dawlish. I had needed his signed permission to marry Jack, since in those days majority was not attained until the age of twenty-one. It is only now that I realise how young, how inexperienced I was in all departments. But for the once-weekly trip to the city cinema I had never left Ashkeepers. I had never ridden on a train or stayed in an hotel. Lovemaking with Jack had gone no further than kissing, and what was then termed 'heavy petting'; and he was my one and only boyfriend. In those first weeks of September I was dizzy with the kind of happiness that comes but once in a lifetime, when every experience is fresh and shining, and life promises to be forever and perfect.

I remember the clothes I wore; the wedding dress of heavy white satin, discovered at the back of a spare room wardrobe and sewn into a protective bag made from a bedsheet. The dress smelled of old lavender and had been my mother's. It fitted me

430

perfectly, and I prayed that my father would not recognise it. (If he did he never said so.)

My going-away dress was powder-blue, with a corsage of gardenias, and a silly little hat with a veil that felt scratchy on my nose and cheeks, but was oh so chic!

The family had come with us to the railway station. As we boarded the train Grandma Franklin pushed a parcel into my hands. 'For later on!' she whispered, 'not to be opened until bedtime!'

Nervously I opened it at bedtime, not knowing what I should find. When the brown paper and tissue fell away I lifted up two scraps of pink and white chiffon which turned out to be a see-through nightdress and matching wrap.

I remember Jack's shocked expression and then the laughter which convulsed us. I have it still, that touching little handful of romance. Where she obtained such daring lingerie I shall never know. Perhaps from a mail-order catalogue? I could not imagine her going into a city shop and choosing such garments.

I could never bring myself to thank her for her gift, to do so would have caused acute embarrassment on both sides. But when Jack and I returned from Dawlish she

431

brought bread and milk and eggs down to the cottage, and one of her special rich dark fruit cakes.

'Nice holiday then?' she asked, and I thought I saw a twinkle in her eye.

I busied myself with the groceries and averted my red face. 'Very nice, thank you, Grandma,' I said demurely.

'Wonderful!' said Jack. 'Amazing stuff — that chiffon!'

Imogen approved of Primrose, for many reasons. The most important of which was the relief my daughter felt when she realised that her mother had finally found a 'respectable friend'.

On the day I introduced them Primrose was at her very best; the golden hair was newly washed and set; while the Tory-blue suit, worn with a single rope of pearls and a diamond brooch pinned to a lapel, made her look like a cross between the Queen and Lady Thatcher. She had drunk sufficient gin to give her confidence, but not enough to render her indiscreet.

Even I was impressed.

We sat in my garden, in the shade cast by the apple tree. I had made an effort; mostly for the sake of Imogen, who had lately caught a whiff of something not quite right in the Toll House, and needed to be diverted, and if possible, reassured. I had also visited the hairdresser, and had retrieved a seldom-worn silk dress from its dry-cleaner's shroud. I wore a new pair of silver-coloured sandals, which for some obscure reason delighted my daughter. I served home-made scones warm from the oven, with clotted cream and strawberries.

They got on together like a house a-fire!

I came out from the kitchen where I had been replenishing the scone-dish to hear Primrose saying 'Yes — it was a terrible time. My grandson Ashley was only six years old when he lost his parents. My son Tim, and Lucy his wife, were killed instantly when their car skidded on an icy road. Ashley was mercifully thrown clear. But it marked him, you know, that sudden loss. I brought him up as well as I knew how. I tried to be both mother and father to him, but it was very difficult on my own. You see, dear, Mr Martindale and I were already divorced when the tragedy happened. There is another grandmother — Lucy's mother, living here in Ashkeepers. But she's very strange, almost a hermit.' Primrose tapped her forehead. 'After the accident she refused to see Ashley. Chased us away from her door, in fact, when I took him to visit. I couldn't believe she could be so cruel — Ashley being the only remaining link to her poor dead daughter. People tell me that she has worn deepest black since the day of Lucy's funeral. She's said to be always hanging around the grave in the churchyard, but will speak to no one. Oh well! Ashley and I have managed very well without her. He's a truly fine young man, and the loss is all hers.'

Imogen made suitably sympathetic noises and patted Primrose's diamond-laden fingers. Talk about fools rushing in where angels fear to tread! While I had considerately refrained from questioning Primrose on the subject of her bringing-up of Ashley, even though my curiosity about him was intense, Imogen had obviously asked the direct question and been answered fully. From the moment I first saw Ashley in the estate agent's office, I had felt strangely drawn toward him, had imagined a variety of lifestyles for him. Now I hovered at a discreet distance from the tea table, hoping for further revelations, but Primrose dabbed at her mascara with a wisp of lace and said, 'Now, Imogen dear — do tell me all about yourself and your lovely family!'

I sat down, took a scone, split it, slathered it with cream and irritably peppered it with strawberries. Imogen was telling Primrose about Fran and Mitch, and John; about Niall and his renovations of old houses. About her own job and her considerable ambitions; information about her personal life which had never been confided to me, her mother.

I bit into the scone, a large bite which saved me from joining in the conversation. My mind began to wander back to the mystery of Ashley, and his beginnings. *'Killed instantly when their car skidded on an icy road . . . It marked him, you know — that sudden loss.'*

*'There is another grandmother — Lucy's mother — she's very strange. Worn deepest black since the day of the funeral — always hanging about the churchyard.'*

A memory began to flicker at the edge of my mind. What I needed to know was the name of Ashley Martindale's other grandmother. I opened my mouth to ask the question, and at that very moment Fran arrived with baby John.

He came walking determinedly down the lawn towards us, legs akimbo and slightly bandy to accommodate the nappy; a miniature John Wayne, his arms waving excitedly when he saw Roscoe. He was so beautiful I felt the heart melt within me. All thoughts of Ashley and the past were lost.

John was here and now.

He was my present and my future.

When they had said their goodbyes and driven away, Primrose and I remained sitting in the lengthening shadows.

She said, 'We're lucky to have them, you know! I have Ashley, and you have Imogen and Fran, and the baby.'

I said, 'Imogen and I are not close.'

'Yes,' she said, and then with unexpected insight, 'I could feel a shadow lying between you. You both try too hard to pretend it doesn't exist. What is it, Nina?'

I was on the very edge of telling her, but the habit of fifty years of silence was still too powerful to break.

I laughed. 'Oh, it's nothing dramatic. Imogen was always more Jack's child than mine. It just happens that way sometimes.'

'Don't leave it too late,' she said, and then, obviously thinking of her dead son and daughter-in-law, 'I've wished so often that I had told them while there was still time how much I loved them. But how many of us expect to outlive our children?' And now the tears began to roll unchecked down her soft and powdered cheeks.

'It's one of the very worst nightmares of

any parent,' she sobbed, 'to go on living, year after empty year, while one's child is —'

I felt the tears burn hot behind my own eyes. The scream in my head was so loud it made me dizzy. Don't tell *me* about it, Primrose! I know better than you how it feels to lose a child. You at least saw your son grow up and marry; have a child of his own. I had only hours, a few days, of my baby daughter.

'But of course I still had Ashley,' she was saying. 'Without him there would have been no reason to go on living.'

She shivered, and began to clear the table. 'It's getting cold out here,' I said. 'Why don't we move into the house. I'll make some coffee.'

'Yes,' she said, attempting a smile. 'That would be very nice,' and then, 'I don't know why you are so kind to me, Nina.'

It was a statement rather than a question, and I realised for the first time that although Primrose belonged to all the snobbish little clubs that proliferated among the Home-steaders, what she actually lacked was a woman friend of her own generation. Some-one in whom she might confide; admit her fears. I began to feel deeply ashamed of my intolerance of her; of the way she dressed, her obsession with her house and its contents; her need to be stylish and contemporary.

As I poured a generous slug of cherry brandy into the freshly brewed coffee, I began to look affectionately on the Tory-blue suit, the Thatcher hair-do, the lapel brooch.

Primrose was apologising. 'Sorry about all that crying in the garden. It was seeing your daughter, and Fran and the baby. It made me think of what might have been, if only —' She sighed. 'I really enjoyed talking to Imogen.' She looked meaningfully at me. She said again, 'You're so lucky to have her, Nina'.

We came into a spell of settled weather, hot dry days which seemed to merge confusingly, one into the next. The lawn turned brown; watering again became a nightly duty. John celebrated his first birthday. Fran and Mitch hired the church hall, trimmed it with streamers and bunched balloons, and on that Sunday afternoon I joined a large group of young parents and their babies in singing 'Happy Birthday — John!'

Although the hall was over-warm, I could see the wisdom of an indoor venue for the party. Some small guests walked strongly, others toddled, while many were still at the crawling stage. The parents were all well-known to one another, they sat together in a doting half-circle watching compulsively the antics of their young.

Imogen, and Mitch's mother, Joanna, took turns at hugging the birthday boy. Fran and Mitch dispensed tea and coffee and lemonade from the hatch of the church hall kitchen. I, on a roving commission, camera at the ready, recorded John's rolling baby-cowboy gait, his predilection for the prettiest of the tiny girls, his vain attempts to kiss a particular one who was more interested in eating her sandwich. Already he was a miniature person in his own right, with his individual likes and dislikes. He hated the taste of cheese, but loved bananas. He favoured his mother's looks until he smiled, and then he was all Mitch. The one clearly enunciated word he had so far spoken was 'MORE!'

It was Fran who said, as we were sweeping up the debris of burst balloons, streamers and bread crusts, 'I can hardly believe it's a year since I was in the Infirmary, giving birth.'

'Yes,' I said, 'it must be Elvira's birthday, too!'

'Tomorrow,' said Fran. 'Sorsha's baby

was born after midnight. Do you ever see them, Grandma? Are they still living in the Hollow?'

'I catch a sight of them sometimes, driving in and out. They wave and shout hello. Those two families have had a stopping-place in Ashkeepers for three hundred years or more. History repeats its patterns. Sixty years ago I sat in the village schoolroom with Sorsha's grandmother, Estralita. A few more years, and John and Elvira will be starting school on the same day, sitting in the same classroom.'

Fran said, 'I like the idea of that! Continuity, links, a sense of belonging.' She hugged me, impulsively. 'I'm so glad you came back to Ashkeepers. I can't really understand why you ever went away.'

Primrose and I had avoided all contact for a month at least. When we finally came face to face in the village post office, sufficient time had passed to allow the embarrassing dust of rash confidences to settle. We could pretend, as we stood among the racks of birthday cards and chocolate bars, that nothing of importance had ever been said.

She invited me to go back to her house for coffee, and I was glad to accept, although

I made a silent resolution to avoid any offered drink that was even mildly alcoholic.
Settled in her beige-on-beige room, sipping
cappuccino (Primrose has what she calls a
'state of the art' machine), and eating a most
expensive brand of chocolate biscuit, I could
feel myself relaxing both physically and
mentally.

It was I who raised the subject of the
squatters.

'Still there,' said Primrose. 'The police
come around from time to time, but it seems
there is nothing they can do.'

'But surely people can't just move into a
house and — and purloin it, take it over?
How can that be legal?'

Primrose sighed. 'They know the law,
these young men and girls. There was no
forced entry, you see! So no crime has been
committed. They have also been careful to
avoid damaging any of the Simpsons' possessions. In fact, but for them the garden
would by now be in a sorry state. They even
clean the windows regularly and wipe the
outside paintwork.'

'So,' I said, 'it could be argued that the
Souls of God, as squatters go, are a positive
asset to any long-term holidaymaker who
needs a house-sitter?'

Primrose giggled. 'Perhaps they should

advertise their skills; come recommended by the travel agents.'

'Well,' I said, 'I am pleased to see that you are no longer in a state about it.'

She patted her hair, and studied her ruby-red fingernails. 'Sergeant Drew keeps in touch,' she said coyly. 'He's been awfully reassuring. He explained about squatters. The law, it seems to me, is very much on their side. Did you know for instance that they are legally entitled to a water supply? They will, eventually, be billed for it, of course, but as I said to Drew — that bill will certainly never be paid! The same rule appears to apply to gas and electricity.'

I said, 'There will be trouble when the Simpsons arrive home. In their position I would borrow a brace of rottweilers and a shotgun and go in mob-handed.'

'Oh no!' said Primrose, who does not watch *Columbo*, and was unconsciously mimicking the voice and words of Sergeant Drew. 'A house owner who uses threats or force to repossess his property is committing a criminal offence. All a squatter needs to do to make his position legal is to pin a notice to the front door warning the house owner not to enter. The police actually warn owners not to take action themselves, since they could so easily be charged with criminal damage, or assault against the squatters.'

I said, 'I don't believe this, Primrose!'

'It's quite true. In fact, the Simpsons have already made a fatal mistake. The police finally made contact with them last week, told them about the situation here and advised them to do nothing at the moment, since the local force were watching the situation on a daily basis, and there was nothing to be gained by precipitate action.'

Primrose sighed. 'But you know how forceful April is. She telephoned me — and then she phoned the squatters. Sergeant Drew also had a call from the Souls of God later on that day. They told him he could call his watchdogs off. That they had spoken with Mrs Simpson, and everything was sorted out. They had explained to her how her daughter had invited them 'to drop in any time they were passing' which was exactly what they had done. Having found the garden in danger of regressing to a wild state, and the house unguarded, they had done the decent thing and decided to caretake until such time as the Simpsons should return. It seems that April, calling expensively from Hong Kong, neglected to ask how they came to have a key, or how they managed to deactivate the burglar alarm.' Primrose giggled. 'Oh, Nina! You should have heard the language used by Sergeant Drew when he heard about that phone call. If it comes into court, he said, it could be argued that April had implied her consent of the squatters' occupation by negotiating with them, and by admitting knowledge that they are living in her property and doing nothing about it.'

'But what *can* she do about it?'

'She could fly home, I suppose, but they've paid thousands for this world trip.'

I looked at Primrose's flushed face and shining eyes. I said, 'You're enjoying every minute of this, aren't you?'

She wriggled her shoulders like a guilty child. 'I don't feel so bad about it all now that Drew is in charge — and you must admit, Nina — April Simpson is a very uppity sort of woman.'

I smiled. 'Tell me about Sergeant Drew.'

She settled more deeply into the cushions of her chair. 'Well — he's a widower. Lives alone. Has a married daughter. He's due to retire next year. He's a — homely sort of man, a bit overweight, and gray-haired, likes gardening and home decorating. You should just see his bungalow, Nina —' She halted in mid-sentence, realising that she had just admitted far more than she intended.

I said gently, 'I'm so glad you've found a

good friend, Primrose.'

She looked grateful and complacent. 'Yes,' she said, 'what began as a catastrophe has turned into something that is really rather pleasant, romantic even!' She rotated a nylon-clad ankle, and smoothed the skirt of her fashionable dress. She leaned forward to ram home the point she wished to make.

'It does pay, you know, Nina, to take care of one's personal appearance. You know what I mean. One never knows when love may come knocking at the door. On that evening when Drew first interviewed me I was wearing my lilac two-piece and the bronze shoes. I could tell straight away that he was — well, appreciative and impressed.'

She looked meaningfully at my navy-blue trousers, bagged at the knees, and the washed-out shirt and canvas shoes.

I knew exactly what she meant. But I was not waiting for love and romance to come knocking at my door, was I?

As I walked slowly homewards I asked myself a few uncomfortable questions.

I was certainly waiting for something.

Waiting for something to happen.

Something significant and instant, a revelation in which bells would ring and veils fall away, and all the pain and mystery of the past fifty years would be made good, and clear.

September is the richest month, the time of thanksgiving for the hard-won harvest.

Our first daughter was born in the month of September, and stolen from us before we had even given her a name.

If you love a baby deeply enough, fiercely enough, that child is never altogether lost, no matter how long her absence or for what reason. I have to believe this. For half a century I have clung to the certainty that my child still lives. That one day I shall meet her, hold her. It is so easy to steal a baby.

Perhaps because it is a rare theft, because the right of an adult to have possession of an infant is hardly ever challenged; it is assumed that the pusher of the pram, the bearer of the swaddled bundle is the rightful owner.

And who should know that better than I.

John is walking now. He wears that first pair of little leather shoes, strapped and buckled and so heart-breakingly adult in appearance that it saddens me to see his chubby baby toes constrained so early; and yet I know the shoes are necessary to save his feet from damage in a stony world.

The navy-blue pram has been judged redundant, and in any case he no longer fits comfortably into it. He now has a pushchair called a buggy, upholstered in blue and red tartan and fitted with strong straps and a stiff and complicated buckle which I find difficult to release, but which reassures me. Anyone attempting to snatch John from his buggy would be defeated, at least briefly, by its child-proof lock.

Babies are stolen by two types of woman. The unbalanced and vindictive. Or the truly grieving and bereft. The result is the same in either case; the parents of the lost child will, for the rest of their lives, secretly or openly, blame one another for an agony which never ceases.

When something unbearable happens we either die of heartbreak, or bury the experience so deeply that it can never resurface. Jack and I did not die of heartbreak, although there were times when this seemed a desirable option. We covered our sorrow with the weight of years, moved from village to city, changed our life's plan.

But the unbearable remained unbearable, no matter how deeply buried. The stain of it drifted upwards, marking us forever. We never talked of what had happened in Ashkeepers. Never speculated, after that first year, as to the reason or the identity of the culprit. For there must have been a culprit. There must have been a reason. A baby who is ten days old does not rise and walk away on her own two tiny feet; and who needed her so desperately that they would take her from us?

The suddenness of Jack's death, the massive coronary which stole his speech, and killed him within hours, meant that even if he had wished to break that long corrosive silence between us, he was robbed of the opportunity; the final easing of his share of our mutual torment. 'It's good to talk,' they say on the British Telecom commercials. But how is it possible to talk when there is nothing left to say?

This ancient dwelling, this house in which I now live second time around, has seen many tragedies, many bitter heartbreaks. I felt then, and still feel, that the place known as Grandma Franklin's cottage, and later, when historians had done their homework, as the Toll House, was a part of the horror.

Sometimes I wonder how I can bear to stay here. But it was idyllic to begin with; those first two years of our occupation were the happiest of all my life. My father's wedding gift enabled us to buy essentials. New line for every floor, and not the cheap stuff which ripped easily into holes but the expensive cork-based kind which was guaranteed to last a lifetime. We chose a light-brown wood-block pattern which simulated parquet. Over it we laid the handmade woollen rugs I had pegged while Jack was in the Army. We retained the faded velvet curtains left by Grandma Franklin. Our furniture was an unmatched collection of pieces donated by my father, from a house which had always been over-furnished. I cooked on an iron range, heated water for washing clothes and bathing in a brick-built copper which took up one corner of the kitchen. Lighting was by candle and oil-lamp. Warmth came from log-and-coal open fires.

That cork-based line justified its guarantee. It was still there, intact all those years later, underneath the cheap fitted carpet laid down by subsequent owners of the house; as fresh and indestructible as my memories of those days.

In a year of strange discoveries and see-saw emotions I seemed to have gained nothing more than an endearing and sometimes boozy friend; and an old book of improbable stories.

But now it was September again, the golden time when the sun is kinder; when mornings are chill with a low mist, and nights bring a great red moon to hang in the western heavens. I had a premonition last night when I saw that moon, of something momentous about to happen.

We were happy in that long-ago September. Jack and I were creating for each other the home our parents had never managed to make. Every smallest new addition was significant and precious. Our first baby was due on the last day of the month. Jack was about to take up his first teaching post in the village school at Nether Ash.

It was a time of fresh starts, of high hopes. We had finally overcome our tentative attitudes to life; we had confidence in one another, we believed that the good times were all before us. I even imagined that I might change the uneasy situation between Jack and his brother Alan. I thought about ways of getting to know Dinah, the sister-in-law who had never been properly introduced; and then I met her unexpectedly one September morning in the main street of Ashkeepers. We came face to face, both wearing the dark expandable skirts and flowered cotton smocks that were the only maternity wear available in those post-war days. Neither one of us had known for certain that the other was pregnant, and so brief had been my glimpse of her beside the jeweller's window all those years ago, that until she spoke and said, 'Hello — I'm Dinah,' I might still have passed her by. I remembered her as being small and slender, pale-skinned and with a mop of dark curly hair. Well, she was no longer slender, and neither was I. We viewed one another's unwieldy bodies with mutual sympathy, and moved without a word towards the bench beneath the copper beech tree. But I could sense her antagonism, and it shocked and upset me; and then I began to think about the past two years, and she a city girl, living with the dour and silent Alan in their isolated woodsman's cottage. I looked more closely at her, I turned towards her and saw her white, drawn features, the dark puffy shadows underneath her eyes. She looked to me to be severely anaemic, and that puffiness surely indicated kidney problems. I was not a nurse, but my father was a doctor, and I had picked up bits of amateurish knowledge along the way.

I said, impulsively, 'Are you looking after yourself? Are you taking your iron pills and your orange juice? What does your doctor say about things? You need to eat well for the baby's sake.'

She gave me a long and measured look, and I felt my face glow hot and red with shame. I knew what she was thinking.

'You've got a bloody nerve,' she said softly. 'What do you care about me or my baby? We could die out there in that awful forest, and not one of you Franklins would give a damn. We'd be a heap of bleached bones before any of you came looking for us.'

The tight control in her gentle voice was far worse than any shouting or screaming, any fishwife-style vituperation; and now I could not bear to look at her; instead I gazed upwards into the sheltering branches of the copper beech.

The quiet relentless voice continued to accuse me. 'You've got it all, haven't you, Nina. You married the favourite son and grandson. You and Jack were given the best of the houses. Your father is the village doctor. You don't know what it's like to be poor; to have a drunken mother, a runaway father. I've heard you went to a private school. Everything handed to you on a plate — and you've never appreciated any of it.'

Alan must have talked to her about me, and not kindly. I tried to turn the conversation. I said, 'So how did you and Alan meet?'

She shook her head. 'You don't even know that much?'

'Well — no', I said. 'Jack and his brothers, they never really talk to each other. It's the way they've always been. There's nothing to be done about it.'

'They're jealous of each other. Can't you see that? Have you never noticed the way they watch one another? Why, when they were children, Alan says they even monitored the amount of food put on their plates, in case one was given more than the other.'

'Not Jack!' I said swiftly. 'He was never like that!'

'Didn't need to be, did he? Daddy's favourite. Grandma's darling. The only one who featured his dead mother. And of course he was the youngest, the baby of the family. It's tough,' she said, 'to be the oldest son in a family like the Franklins. Alan still gets the shitty end of the stick even though he works his guts out on the bloody farm, and obeys his father's every order.'

I said, 'Look — I'm sorry that you —'

But she continued as if I had not spoken; as if the bitterness of years had finally spilled over and could not be contained. 'I hear that Jack's a schoolteacher these days. No more getting up at crack of dawn on freezing winter mornings, eh? No more sweating in the hay and harvest times for gentleman Jack. No more risk of catching a hand in the machinery because you're so bloody exhausted you don't rightly know any more what you're doing. You asked how I met Alan. I was the nurse who helped to sew his fingers back on in the Infirmary casualty department when he trapped his hand in the grinder. Not that it did him any good. That hand is virtually useless now, and that's bad news for a farmer.'

'I didn't know,' I muttered. 'I didn't know about Alan's accident, or that you were a nurse.'

'Why should you? I've seen your sort before. Wrapped up in your own imaginary little troubles. Feeling sorry for yourself for no good reason. You don't live in my world, or in Alan's. Just as well you don't. You'd never survive the first five minutes. Weak and useless — that's Jack and you. Nothing bad ever happened to either of you, and if it ever did you'd go right under.'

I said hesitantly, 'We both lost our mothers when we were young.'

She laughed, with what sounded like genuine amusement. 'Mothers!' she said, 'who needs 'em? Mine fell down blind drunk in the street one night, and was run over by a number twenty-two bus. Best thing that could have happened — for her sake and mine. Barnardo's did a damn sight better job on my upbringing than she ever could have.'

A silence fell between us. People went in and out of the shops around the Green, they paused and stood in little gossipy groups as they had always done. A drayhorse clopped in through the blacksmith's gate, on its way to be reshod. It was all so normal and peaceful and reassuring.

I stole a sideways glance at the girl called Dinah, who was, I realised belatedly, now a close relative of mine.

There seemed nothing more to say, and yet I felt compelled to say something.

'Dinah,' I began, 'we shall both be giving birth in a few weeks. Our children will be cousins. Couldn't we put all these bad old feelings behind us for their sakes? Make a fresh start with a new generation? Try to get along with one another? After all — the Franklins' problems shouldn't really be allowed to touch you and me. Couldn't we be friends, and then perhaps our husbands would gradually come around — feel differently towards each other.'

She sighed. 'You haven't taken in a word

I've said, have you? Next thing you'll be suggesting is high tea at your house on a Sunday, a double christening in that snooty little church there! Don't you understand? I love Alan Franklin. What hurts him, hurts me, and things have been done to him across the years that can never be undone. Especially by you and Jack.'

I saw hatred flash in her dark eyes and then I knew she would harm me if she could. 'I don't forget,' she said, 'how you and Jack ran away when we were looking in that jeweller's window. Didn't want to know us, did you?'

She half rose to go, and I tried once more to establish some kind of normality between us. Desperate to detain her just a little longer, I said, 'When is your baby due?'

'Last day of this month.'

'So is mine,' I told her. 'Who is your doctor? Which hospital are you booked into?'

'No doctor. Like I told you, I'm a trained nurse, I know what I'm doing. As for a hospital — how are we expected to get to the city from where we live, especially if I go into labour in the middle of the night? But don't you worry about us, Nina. Alan and me will do what we've always done. We'll handle it ourselves, and owe nothing to the bloody Franklins.'

Later that same day Grandma Franklin came to see me, basket filled with windfall apples, two pots of her special gooseberry jam, and a dozen still-warm homemade scones. The gifts were a poignant proof of Dinah's bitter accusations. I folded the white, starched cloth and laid it back in the basket.

I said, as artlessly as I knew how, 'I hear that Alan's wife is also expecting.'

Equally artlessly, her head turned away towards the window, Grandma Franklin said, 'I heard the same rumour.'

'Alan must be very pleased.'

Her thin lips tightened. 'If he is, he never says so. He's exactly like his father. Close-mouthed and stubborn.'

I tried again. 'It must be lonely for her, living up in the woods and Alan working all hours.'

'You've seen her.'

'Yes. I met her on the Green. She looks terribly ill, and she's very unhappy. I wish there was something I could do to help her.'

'Do you think I haven't tried?' Her fore-head flushed crimson with the force of her anger. 'They're a lost cause, those two. Alan was a difficult baby, a naughty child, and a resentful and jealous young man. He's got a chip on his shoulder as big as an outhouse, and all for no reason.'

'Perhaps,' I said diffidently, 'if you could all sit down together and talk about it — ?'

'Talk! What good did talking ever do except make bad trouble worse. Best left alone, Nina — them and their problems.'

I believed that she was wrong in her judgement of the situation. But even I, who was a Franklin only by marriage and who told Jack everything, good or bad, that was on my mind, on this occasion kept my own counsel and said nothing.

Towards the morning of the following day I went into labour. Three weeks earlier than had been predicted.

She was perfect.

So exquisite that even now, forty-eight years on, I cannot bear to think about her. Six pounds, two ounces; dark hair, blue eyes. I had worried in the months before her birth that, like my own mother, I might also lack maternal instinct. I need not have doubted. When I held her in my arms for the first time, touched her tiny hands, the rose-leaf skin, I knew that if necessary I would die for her; do murder in order to protect her.

Jack felt the same way. It was no longer

enough that we loved one another; the baby became a part of our charmed circle. We talked about nothing else but the future we would make for her; argued cheerfully about names, and then decided there was no need for a hasty decision. Six weeks could elapse before we were obliged to register her birth.

You might think that in almost half a century I had told this tale so many times that I could tell it parrot-fashion. Like a nursery rhyme. Like a poem learned by heart.

But the strange truth is that I have never told it to anybody, and now I don't know how to begin.

Where to begin?

I could tell it in six short sentences. Perhaps that is how I should confront it? Get it over quickly, like the pulling of an aching tooth.

But the time will come when I must reveal the past to Imogen and Fran. I owe it to them. So consider this confession as a rehearsal; an exercise in clarity and bitter truth.

I came home from the hospital still shaky and subdued from the nineteen fifties' iron rule of maternity ward-sisters, and the obligatory ten days of lying-in which were considered proper in those days for the newly confined.

Confinement. Lying-in. How dated, how antiquated it all sounds now. I can imagine how Fran will smile when I tell her this first part of the story. Layette is another old-fashioned word. No expandable Babygros in those days, no disposable nappies, but a regulation six dozen towelling and muslin squares, a dozen long cream-coloured winceyette gowns, embroidered and beribboned; a dozen hand-knitted matinée jackets. Bootees and mittens, bonnets and shawls; all in cream or white, of course, no colours allowed for the first six months. Fifty years ago a baby *looked* like a baby, and not a miniature adult dressed in dungarees and floppy hats. We were as Victorian as hansom cabs and jet jewellery. But who can say now which way was the best, the safest?

In the ten days of my absence the weather had turned cooler. There was a carpet of fallen leaves beneath the beech trees on the Green. My father drove us home from the hospital. Grandma Franklin was waiting at the garden gate. I remember walking down the flagged path, the baby in my arms, and pausing to show the fuchsias to my daughter, as my mother had once shown them to me. I remember placing her in Grandma

460

Franklin's arms, and seeing those grim, un-smiling features melt with tenderness and love.

So much love.

For such a short time.

But we were not to know that, were we?

Jack had lit fires in every room. The scent of burning applewood filled the cottage.

*These rooms. This cottage. This same cottage.*

'If walls could speak,' was a favourite saying of Grandma Franklin. My house knows exactly what happened in those last days of October. I believe that in dwellings of great age the dramas which occurred within them are absorbed into their fabric. Beneath the recent decoration of pale wallpapers and paintwork is the memory of those browns and golds that were fashionable in the nineteen forties. My eyes see the room as it is now, but the mind behind the eyes positions the little blue folding pram with its bright chrome mudguards in the corner close to the window. A satin-bound pink blanket which covers the baby has the furry cut-out of a rabbit appliqued on it. A fluffy yellow toy duck is suspended on a ribbon and pinned to the pram's hood. It is early evening and the lamplight casts a soft glow over the imitation-parquet linoleum, the bright hand-pegged rugs, the worn but comfortable armchairs. From the kitchen comes the aroma of a meat and vegetable casserole slow-cooking in the oven of the black iron range. The baby sleeps that long and necessary slumber of a child who has arrived a little too early in the world.

The mother of the baby, who is twenty years old and still sees herself as being a girl, despite motherhood and responsibility, looks around her domain, her castle, and is still amazed at the wonder of it, the rosiness, the charm of it all. Her name is Nina Franklin and the house stands close to Burdens' Wood, which is itself an annexe to deeper ancient forest. The sounds of the night, the wind roaring in the high trees, the sharp cries of small rodents, do not disturb her. She is a country girl. It is city traffic, city people, that alarm her. She has lived her life in a world of mutual trust, of simple faith and ways, of kindly people. She has never dwelt behind locked doors. Somewhere about the place there is a heavy iron key which locks both front and back doors of the cottage. But if required to do so she could not readily put her hand upon it. She checks the time by the wall clock, and thinks about the father of the baby who is conscientious and absorbed in his new position as teacher in the school of Nether Ash. He cycles to and from his work. He is late home on Monday evenings. He has volunteered to help the headmaster with a newly formed scout group.

The baby stirs and sighs and sleeps again. The girl sets the supper table with a white linen cloth, and the plated-silver cutlery which had been a wedding present. In the centre of the table she places a pottery jug filled with Michaelmas daisies. She takes extraordinary pleasure in these small touches of domesticity, the style of which her flibbertigibbet mother had never even attempted.

She looks again at the wall clock, and then into the log basket. The remaining two small logs cannot last out the hour which will elapse until her husband's return, and the baby is small and must be kept warm. She moves to the pram, lifts a fold of the shawl and smiles down at the sleeping face of her tiny daughter. Names trip across her tongue; Felicity, she whispers, Josephine, Susan, Christina? They cannot decide, but there is still no hurry. They have another four weeks yet before the registration must be made.

She picks up the log basket and goes out through the kitchen door to the woodshed which stands at the far end of the garden.

There is no moon, but she can find her way by starlight. She fills the basket with small logs; the wind whips up her long dark hair so that it streams sideways across her shoulder like a brave flag flying. As she re-enters the kitchen the swathe of hair falls across her eyes, obscuring her vision. She stumbles, almost drops the basket, and then recovers her balance. She takes a moment or two to tie back the loose curls with a silk cord found in her apron pocket, and then she carries the logs to the sitting-room fireplace, kneels down before it, and begins to mend the fire.

She has placed three logs in a pyramid position when the feeling comes to her that something is wrong in the room. Her first thought is for her child. She looks sideways towards the pram. The fluffy yellow duck stills hangs by a ribbon from the pram's hood. The satin-bound pink blanket and its appliqued rabbit lies neatly tucked in just as she had left it, around the small mound that is the baby. The pram hood is still raised to shield the sleeping child from draughts and lamplight.

But even so she is uneasy.

She opens the door which leads into the tiny front hallway. The air is much colder out here, which does not surprise her since the heavy wooden outer door is not quite closed. She pushes it shut and hears the latch click. The wind, she thinks, must have blown it open. But surely the strongest gales could never have moved that great slab of black oak? She looks down and sees still-damp muddy footprints on the tiled floor; large fresh prints, the kind made by a Wellington boot. A man's boot.

To begin with she is puzzled. Jack wears shoes these days that are suitable for his new profession, new and black with smooth leather soles that leave no imprint. And in any case, if Jack had arrived home unexpectedly early he would have called out; guessing that she was fetching firewood or washing from the clothes line, he would have come into the garden, searching for her.

Grandma Franklin never ventures out after dark, and certainly never wearing boots of that size.

She supposes her own father, making a late visit to a patient, might have called in. He sometimes needs to wear gumboots when attending a farmer's family; all those muddy driveways, farmyards. But her father, finding her absent from the house, would not have gone away without a word. He too would have come into the garden, shouted her name, waited for her answering call.

She turns back towards the warm room, and as she goes in through the door some aspect of the pram, seen from another sharper angle, causes her to pause. Beneath the blanket, the tiny mound which is her baby daughter has a slightly altered shape, a different outline. Even as she walks towards the corner close by the window, a terrible fear like a knife slash rips through her body, opening her up to panic and hysteria. Even before she lifts the blanket and sees the little lace-edged pillow lying in the place where her child should be, she is moaning and keening like an animal. Like a crazy woman.

She snatches up the pillow and the mattress, as if the child might have somehow slid beneath them. She begins to search the room, peers behind curtains, as if the baby might have grown tiny wings and flown. She runs to each armchair, pulls out the cushions, runs her hand along the gaps in the upholstery as if the baby might have slipped down into that concealed space where combs and coins, handkerchiefs and scissors habitually vanish. She raises the corners of the tablecloth and looks under the table. She opens and closes cupboard doors; pulls out drawers and slams them shut.

Someone is playing a trick on her. A cruel trick meant to punish. Someone is demonstrating, in the most wicked and agonising way, that she should not have left her baby alone in the house, not even for the few minutes it had taken to refill the log basket. Somebody is showing her that she is not fit to be a mother. But who would do such an awful thing? And why?

For a dizzy, terrifying minute she imagines her own long-lost mother returning to Ashkeepers, old now and repentant, wanting a second chance at motherhood; creeping into her daughter's house, and stealing away on impulse the grandchild she had not expected to find.

But her mother had never wanted the baby Nina.

So why should she now burden her aging self with Nina's child?

She goes back to the pram, and remembers the careful positioning of the pillow, made with intention to deceive. A part of her mind, the corner that is still capable of reasoning, is able to work out that whoever stole her baby had done so quite deliberately. With malice aforethought. With evil intent.

The thought is so destructive that she feels a kind of numbness around the region of her heart that is like a death. The awful keening ceases. She is silent now, hand clapped across her mouth. It had been so easy. The cottage isolated, invisible among tall trees. Front door on the latch, and never locked. Curtains never closed. Someone had watched. Watched and waited for the new, inexperienced mother to be quite alone in the house. Waited for her need to fetch logs for the fire, or to bring washing in from the garden, or take rubbish to the dustbin, or use the lavatory; knowing that it would take only seconds to lift the small sleeping bundle and escape into the darkness.

She fetches a stool from the kitchen and places it beside the pram. She sits on the stool, knees and hands pressed tidily together like a good child hoping to avoid inevitable blame. Then she lifts a satin-bound corner of the pink blanket, and is almost destroyed by the unique, unbearable waft of fragrance that is compounded of brand-new baby and talcum powder. But whoever has stolen her child has at least left Nina the pillow, the blanket. Tenderly, she lifts both items from the pram and wraps the one in the other. When her husband returns this is how he finds her; hugging the blanket-wrapped pillow, holding it close to the damp milky patches which are spreading all across the front of her blue blouse.

She has heard the sounds of his arrival, knows his every movement; first the shiny new bicycle put safely away in the garden shed, then the removal of his bicycle clips, the way he combs his thick fair hair with his fingers before he steps through the door to greet her; the four strides of his long legs which will take him to the pram.

But although he is a man and not expected to be intuitive, on this night he also senses something wrong within the house. As he comes through the sitting-room door his face is already stiff with apprehension.

He sees her rocking to and fro beside the pram.

He says, 'What is it? Is she ill? All evening I've had this bad feeling — ?' He puts an arm about her shoulders, looks down into the empty pram. He pulls aside the blanket she is holding. He sees the pillow, the damp patches on her blouse, the crazy look of her, her dead eyes.

'Nina!' His whisper is urgent, fearful. 'What happened here? Tell me, for God's sake! *Say something!*'

She tries to speak but nothing comes. She lifts the pillow high, mutely offering it to him. She points to the empty pram, bows her head in shame. He runs to the stairs, leaps them three at once; she can hear him rush from one bedroom to the other. Wardrobe doors are dragged open and slammed shut. A faint anger stirs in her. What does he think she is doing? Playing some silly game with him of 'let's hunt the baby'? Her voice returns with her growing resentment at his lack of perception.

'She's gone,' she screams. 'Somebody came in and stole her.' She looks down at the blanket still clutched in her hands and the full horror of what has happened finally strikes her. 'And she's only dressed in a gown and matinée jacket, she'll die of cold and exposure. They hadn't even got the sense to wrap her blanket around her.'

The police arrive.

But not as they would come now, in the nineteen nineties, with blue lights flashing, wa-wa sirens moaning in that dying fall of sound which flips the stomach over; tumbling from their cars as if every split second might make a life-or-death difference to the eventual outcome.

Fifty years back, when informed of a possible case of child abduction, it is our elderly Constable Hackett, a leftover from the war years, who should surely have been retired long ago, who comes cycling out from the village through the wild night. He stumps into the house none too pleased to be dragged from his fireside and slippers, and his tripe-and-onions supper.

His initial suggestion, having peered into the empty pram and cot, and shone his torch briefly round the garden, is that young Mrs Franklin might have 'put the babby down somewhere and somehow mislaid it'. He becomes anecdotal. It could happen. Had happened. New mothers were known to be absent-minded. Why, his own daughter had once left the pram which contained her month-old son standing outside a shop, and had gone home without it. Realising her mistake, she had run all the way back to find the pram and the baby still parked where she had left them, and no harm done.

He goes on to relate other instances of maternal forgetfulness. He makes a joke of it all; as far as he is capable of skittishness, Constable Hackett is skittish as a young colt.

But at last their stony looks, their silence, cause him to change tack. He finally recalls with whom he is dealing.

These two are not village youngsters, pranksters known to him from childhood. They have never knocked on cottage doors and run away, or ridden their bicycles without lights.

The boy is Farmer Franklin's youngest, and that family are a serious bunch, not given to joking. Some would say miserable. As for the young woman, well, she is doctor's daughter.

How many times has she counted out the constable's arthritis tablets into a pillbox in her father's surgery. How often has she visited his house to apply fresh dressings to his wife's bad leg.

Hackett squares his shoulders, tugs at the worn and shiny serge of his uniform jacket. His gravity is now deeper than his former levity was high.

'I'll go straight back and phone headquarters,' he says importantly. 'There'll be somebody out here from the city at about first light.'

The girl begins to weep hysterically; and now he remembers certain things about her; that her name is Nina; that her mother ran away when she was little, with a salesman who travelled in encyclopaedias. That she has never mixed much with the people of the village. That even when working with her father she has seemed aloof and quiet. Now he is visibly embarrassed by her raw emotion, her lack of proper control. He finds such behaviour unseemly in one who, until now, he had considered to be ladylike.

He begins to wonder about her, and his uncertainty shows in the way he backs out of the front door and advises the young couple to 'get some sleep, m'dears. It'll all get sorted out in the morning.'

'As if,' sobs the girl when he is gone, 'as if we had reported a lost kitten.'

They do not come at first light. It is mid-morning when the small black police van drives down the track which leads to the cottage. It is Saturday, so no school. Jack is at home. But he would have stayed with her anyway. They have not slept, have not even gone upstairs, but have passed the night fully dressed and in speechless terror, neither of them willing to voice the awful fears that twist their hearts.

Long before the first light streaks the sky Jack and Nina begin to search the garden, the outbuildings, the hedges and ditches. They blunder about, dazed and confused, faint from lack of sleep and food. It has not occurred to either of them to inform their families of what has happened.

The policemen introduce themselves as Detective Sergeant McKay and Constable Dove. They are considerably younger than the village bobby, which is reassuring, isn't it? Jack assesses them as ex-Army, ex-redcaps lately returned from the war and following a new career. They wipe their muddy boots on the doormat and remove their caps before entering the house, but still there is that military air about them, as if they are operating under martial law.

To begin with it is all very low-key.

The policemen sit down, pulling out dining-room chairs and placing their caps and notebooks on the table's polished surface. They write down names and ages. As if any of it mattered. Questions are asked. About Jack and Nina. About the baby.

Nina, who is less intimidated by this arm of the law than is her husband, says shouldn't they already be out searching, too much time has already been wasted, and how can people's family histories make any difference — ?

They stare at her as if they are longing to be back in the Army, and still with the power to put her on a charge for insubordination.

Nevertheless, they put away their notebooks, return to the van and release a large black and tan Alsatian dog. They ask for an item of the baby's clothing, something that will carry the child's scent. She shakes her head. All in the wash, she tells them. The older policeman reaches out a hand to take the pink blanket she is cradling in her arms, but she will not give it up. When he persists she smacks him hard across the face. Jack apologises for her. She is not herself, he tells them. Jack loosens her fingers one by one from the pink wool, and hands the blanket over. They must have it, he tells her. The dog needs to get the scent before they can start looking for —

'The body?' she screams. 'That's what you all think, don't you? You believe she's dead, that's why you're in no hurry to start looking for her.'

Again it is the older policeman who speaks up, and this time his tone is silky-soft, insinuating, hateful. 'And why should you think that, madam? Why should you assume that Baby Franklin is dead? Do you have any reason for that conclusion? Is there perhaps something you've neglected to tell us?'

She feels sick and confused. The question is a barbed one; it holds a hidden meaning which is supposed to frighten her, but she cannot work out what that meaning can be.

So she says, with as much dignity as she can muster, 'Don't call her Baby Franklin. It's not her name!'

'What is her name?' the younger policeman asks.

'She hasn't got one,' screams Nina. 'She's

475

nameless, and now perhaps she always will be.'

Jack says over and over, 'You are not to blame for any of this, Nina. Nobody blames you.'

But she blames herself. She thinks she will die of guilt; hopes to die of guilt, and quickly. If only she had not left the room, the house. If she had only waited for Jack to bring the logs in. If she had not paused in the kitchen to tie her hair back; perhaps in those few vital seconds? But what? She tries to imagine a shadowy figure lifting the front door latch, slipping into the room, bending over the pram. But the image lacks substance; it is as naive and ludicrous as the policemen's questions. Was it possible, they had asked, that a relative or friend, or a considerate neighbour, might have come to the house, and only wishing to be helpful, had taken the baby off her hands for an hour or two?

But what friends?

What neighbour?

And so late in the evening, with an autumn gale blowing? And without the pram, the blanket? And if so, why had they not yet returned her?

Oh, you'd be surprised, say the city detectives, the daft things people do.

A whole day passes in fruitless searching.

Several unsavoury items are discovered in hedges and ditches. A rusty bicycle. A split feather mattress. A sackful of rude magazines hidden in a rotting tree-trunk. A dead dog tied up in a flour sack.

Let nobody say that the ex-redcaps and their Alsatian are not trying. But Jack and Nina are not surprised when the search does not turn up their daughter. Their sense of foreboding grows deeper with every hour that passes. They cling to one another as if they too are lost. What does surprise them is the apparent stupidity of the police, who are much more diligent in their questioning of Nina than in their searching of the woods and village.

Jack mentions the word 'kidnap'.

The detective-sergeant is scornful. Kidnap, he says, happens only to rich folk's children, film stars, millionaires.

Who does Jack think he is? Rothschild? A member of the aristocracy? Or a scion of the Royal Family? (God bless 'em)!

The grieving couple, dazed and sick at heart, look at these hard-faced men and cannot believe their insensitivity, their cruelty. But how can Jack and Nina say so?

The officers in blue are all they have.

In their innocence the parents of the missing baby still believe that the police are there to help them. What they do not guess, but are about to discover, is that when a child is missing from its home it is always the parents who are the first to be suspected of its murder. Although they do not know it, Jack is already in the clear; alibied by his headmaster and twenty-seven boy scouts.

After thirty-six hours of fruitless searching, a high-ranking officer with pips on the shoulders of his uniform jacket comes out to the cottage to question Nina. It is not until Jack cannot bear to watch this persecution, when he shouts, 'Why don't you leave her alone? Can't you see she had nothing to do with it?' that she finally realises the only suspect in the disappearance of her baby — is herself. The mother, who had not bothered to give her child a name.

The police, it seems, have moved into the cottage and do not intend to leave. Their jackets are draped on the backs of chairs, their caps hang on pegs in the kitchen. Their folders and notebooks cover the dining-room table. The nails in their heavy boots are leaving scratches on the fake-parquet pattern of the expensive linoleum. She feels vaguely annoyed at the prospect of all the polishing and tidying she will have to do when they depart. But what else will she do with her time? There will be no baby to care for. Already her body is accepting its permanent loss. Her milk has almost dried up without the help of tight binding or medication. As for her mind; she is so far gone in confusion that when her father and Grandma Franklin walk into the room, she hardly recognises them.

And still the questioning continues.

Again and again they take her through the days and nights since she left the hospital. How often in that time had she left the house?

And over and over she explains how the unfamiliar routines of feeding and bathing, of dressing the baby; the endless washing of nappies and baby clothing in addition to her usual household duties, had seemed to take up every waking hour.

So you didn't leave the cottage, even for five minutes? they persist.

Exhausted and bewildered she screams at them. 'Look at the pram wheels if you don't believe me! One trip up that muddy track into the village and those white rubber wheels would be filthy.'

'You could have washed them, Mrs Franklin. Or carried the child in your arms.'

'But why would I?' she moans.

The policemen stare her down. They allow their silence to answer for them.

She and Jack are expected, it appears, to feed and water the interrogators. Jack stokes the fire with coal and logs. He brings them trays of soup and sandwiches, for which he is not even thanked. The fact that Nina eats nothing does not seem to concern them. Perhaps they prefer their victims weak and on the point of fainting?

The same questions keep coming at her, but phrased in a dozen different ways.

Who else but she and Jack had been in contact with the baby? What did she think about the alleged abductor's failure to wrap the days-old infant in its blanket?

Why was she being so stubborn about telling them what had really happened? She was, after all, the only person present at the time.

Surely she must have heard or seen something?

The young policemen and their dog go away, and Nina and Jack are left alone with the senior detective, who returns again and again to the subject of the pink blanket. The fact, he says, that a very young infant was exposed to cold gale-force winds dressed only in a gown and nappy, is open to only one interpretation. He turns to Jack, and asks, in an oddly pleasant and conversational tone, what he thinks that interpretation might be.

Jack says there could be several reasons.

The baby had been snatched in great haste. The need for a warm covering had been overlooked. It could have been a planned abduction with a car waiting in the lane? The policeman shakes his head. 'Not in *such great haste*,' he points out. '*Someone* had found time to carefully, artfully, arrange the pillow and tuck the blanket around it in order to make it appear that the baby was still sleeping in the pram.'

*Or so they had all been told by Mrs Nina Franklin.*

'But it's true,' cries Nina. 'Why would I lie about it? I was fooled for a few minutes, and that few minutes gave the — the abductor extra time to get away.'

'So you would have us believe, Mrs Franklin. But let us suppose there was no abductor. Let us suppose this whole business is *a family matter.*' In the same conversational tone, as if he is discussing the state of the weather, he says 'You see, it could be reasoned that a dead infant would not need a blanket.'

He pauses and looks kindly at her. 'Why

don't you tell us how it really happened?'

Her father is sent for. She sees by his manner, his lack of understanding that her predicament has put her in the same shameful category as her mother. She is an embarrassment; to be avoided. He administers a sedative and leaves her. Jack wants to stay with her but she insists that he reports for work as usual on that Monday morning. There is nothing he can do. The sedative calms her, but she is aware that something dangerous is happening in her mind. She thinks that her father's coldness has brought her to the edge of madness. She needs to be alone, if only for an hour or two. She treads on quicksand, one false move now and she will be forever lost. There are things she feels impelled to do, like concealing in cupboards every item of baby equipment, packing into drawers the furry, fluffy toys; scouring and disinfecting the little house as if it has been visited by plague. She works in a frenzy of random activity, as if to erase every sign than an infant ever lived there. And still the policemen come and go. They are more gentle with her now. They try to sit her down, to talk quietly to her, but she simply works around them as if they are invisible.

Military policemen they might once have been, accustomed to terrorising tough men, but in the face of this silent wild-eyed girl they are finally defeated. They attribute her frenetic behaviour to guilt. But still she does not fully comprehend what they are thinking. They continue to play a waiting game, confident that sooner or later she is bound to crack.

It is mid-afternoon when the mud-spattered van pulls up at her gate. The police have gone away, and in her right mind she would have been amazed at the arrival of the male faction of the Franklin family. As it is, she wonders vaguely if the brothers have been sent by their grandmother, and then she sees that their father is with them. It is the first time that any of them has crossed the cottage threshold. This is clearly not a social occasion.

They troop past her in blank-faced silence. She scarcely knows how to greet them. They are dressed in what passes with them as their Sunday best; moleskin trousers, corduroy jackets, cravats tucked into open-necked flannel shirts, and heavy brown brogue shoes. They are large men; when she invites them to sit down they jostle awkwardly around the dining table, the leather-patched elbows of their jackets resting on its newly polished surface, their faces turned towards her as if she is the visitor and expected to initiate the conversation.

Farmer Franklin is the first to speak.

'Bad business,' he mumbles. 'It's a full week now, and still no news.'

She nods, wondering at the obviousness of his statement. Especially when made to her.

'The whole village has been questioned,' he continues. 'Every man Jack of us — the women too. Not good for Alan's wife Dinah, and her about to give birth any minute now.'

She bows her head at his aggrieved tone. She looks at Alan who is tense and pale. She hears herself apologising.

'I'm sorry, Alan, for all the upset. How is Dinah?'

'Not good. What with the police, and their dogs beating about the woods, and all their questions we can't answer! We could do with a bit of peace and quiet at this stage. It's not fair that we should be having all this upset.'

She begins to study the four faces, and sees not a flicker of pity or understanding among them. She accepts then that they have not come to commiserate with her, to offer their support, their help. They have come to accuse her. Of what she is not certain. Their hostility is sharp-edged and impossible to comprehend.

And now, slowly but surely, her carapace of misery is finally pierced. The shield she has placed between herself and the rest of the world begins to shatter. She remembers how, in the past two days, even her father has questioned her severely about her feelings towards her newborn daughter. She reads the same doubt in the eyes of Jack's father and his brothers. *They believe it is she who has harmed the baby.*

The enormity of their unspoken accusation galvanises her half-dead mind and body into violent life. But before she can move or speak, Jack is at her side. It is four in the afternoon and school is out. She wonders how long he has stood there, listening behind the partially open door. His features are contorted with such fury that she hardly knows him. Four long strides bring him to the table where the visitors sit like judge and jury in a courtroom.

'So,' he says quietly, 'you finally found your way up here.' In the same low tone he speaks exclusively to his father. 'Let's have this whole thing out in the open, Dad. My God! It must be pretty bad to bring the four of you away from the farm, all at the same time. I believed when I first heard your voices that you had come to offer help, to support us. A bit late, of course, but better late than never, I thought.' His voice grows rough with an undertone of hatred which alarms her. He stares in turn at each closed face. 'Well — come on, then! Which one of you is going to cast the first stone? I've waited all my life for something like this to happen. Somehow, I've known that given the opportunity, you would all turn against me. It's always been there, that ill-feeling, just under the surface. The disappearance of our baby has given you just the chance you've always wanted. A reason to blame, to accuse, to point the finger. But you couldn't attack me directly, could you? You had to wait until Nina was here alone, a soft target, a distraught girl.'

In a family where grievances are never aired, hard words are always swallowed and only their bitter silences speak volumes, this outburst from Jack is so shocking in its frankness that his father and brothers are visibly shaken. They are unprepared for this open challenge from the son and brother who is the target of gossip up and down Ashkeepers.

It is Alan who finally grasps the nettle. Nervously, he clears his throat. 'We thought you ought to know what's being said. It's all over the village, in all the newspapers. Rumour has it that your child was never stolen by a stranger. The police have stopped searching, haven't they? So why do you think that is?'

'I don't know why that is, Alan. Why don't you tell me?'

'Oh, for Christ's sake! You're supposed to be the clever one, the schoolmaster; smarter than all of us clodhopping farmboys put together. *It's your misses they're watching, Jack. They believe that she did away with her own child.*'

Alan's heavy shoulders twitch uneasily, he stares down at his clenched fists. 'Well, somebody had to tell you. Somebody had to warn you.'

Jack moves to the door and opens it, all his anger gone. His voice resumes its normal quiet tone. 'I'd like you to leave now. I never want to see any one of you, ever again. From this day forward I have no father, no brothers.'

They shuffle from the room, one behind the other. Farmer Franklin is the last to leave. He holds out a conciliatory hand towards his son, which Jack ignores. Some sins are beyond forgiveness.

When Grandma Franklin walks in, two

hours later, she finds Nina and Jack, slumped in darkness in their separate arm-chairs, all their tears shed, all their anguish spent. Nina cuddles the pink blanket, re-turned to her that day by the detectives.

Grandma lights the oil-lamps, rekindles the fire to a high blaze, fills the kettle and sets it on the hob. The pie she has brought is put to reheat in the oven. She rattles cutlery and china, which is her way of ex-pressing strong emotion. She brings them mugs of steaming cocoa and plates piled high with shepherd's pie. She uses the af-fectionate, reproving voice they remember from childhood. 'Not a single word,' she says, 'until you've eaten every last scrap.'

Under her sharp gaze they behave like children, obediently eating the hot food, scraping their plates clean, draining their mugs of cocoa.

She is the only one of either family who has come to them daily since their child was stolen; who has offered them the strength and hope they can no longer summon for themselves.

When the dishes are cleared away she sits down in a facing armchair. 'So,' she says, 'two things! First of all, my son is a stupid blundering fool, and his three oldest sons follow his example like the sheep they are!

And secondly, the two of you must get away from Ashkeepers as soon as you can arrange it.'

Jack says, 'It's true then? What Alan said about the gossip?'

'Yes,' she says, 'it's true'. The angry red floods her face. 'It's my belief that Alan is encouraging these rumours.' She sighs. 'I'm not trying to excuse him; but there are reasons for the way he is. His father has always given him a hard time. And then there's his worry about Dinah. That baby is seriously overdue. I met Alan down in the village yesterday. Even he looks ill and exhausted. Get your wife over to the hospital, I told him. But he told me to mind my own business and keep out of their lives. Ah well! There's no helping some folk. I shall do as Alan says and let them hoe their own row. Time and enough I've been rebuffed by those two.' The tremor in her voice is an indication of her hurt. She pauses, composes herself, and speaks to Nina. Her voice is gentle now, her face compassionate.

'I've known you since you were a little girl. I know how much you loved your baby. I saw the way you were with her — Jack too! Anybody would have thought you were the first couple in the world to ever have a daughter!' She reaches out her hand and strokes the satin binding of the blanket. 'I loved her too. My first great-grandchild; and with us for such a short time. But we must have faith. We must believe that the police will find her. Somebody, somewhere, is taking good care of her, why else would they have stolen her? Sometimes, when a woman is unable to have a child of her own she will steal another couple's baby. We have to be patient. We have to wait, until that woman sees the error of her ways. Meanwhile, it might be a good thing if you were to leave Ashkeepers. Just for a while. Just until the police have found the baby.'

Jack says, 'If we go now it will look as though we are running away.'

'Never mind how it looks! You must do what is best for the two of you. You're not sleeping, hardly eating. How long do you think you can go on like this? You're both heading for a breakdown, and what use is that to anybody?'

She is right of course. Nina and Jack have made their own desperate searches of the woods, the hedges and ditches, the derelict barns and cattle shelters which stand in distant fields. They have discussed, rehashed, resurrected every second of that dreadful evening. They have investigated every possibility, no matter how improbable or bizarre.

Jacks walks his grandmother back to Sunshine Farm. He stands at the gate and takes a long look at the house where he was born, and where his mother died. He will never enter that house again; he will never see or speak to his father and brothers. Nina is his only family now. Three months later Jack and Nina leave Ashkeepers.

Jack is to train as a probation officer. He will work in the city gaol. In his way he will be as much a prisoner as the criminals he is employed to help and counsel. He has actually bought a house which stands in the shadow of the prison wall.

Time passes; three years in which a raw wound scarcely heals. And then the birth of their second daughter brings a happiness that Jack and Nina feel is undeserved. They are over-protective of her. But is it any wonder? Their marriage is saved by the deep love they have for one another.

But it is not easy, this new life of theirs. Oh no. It is not easy.

# BARNACLE'S BOOK

## Chapter 5

The gypsies had caught the smoky, sweetish reek of snow on the east wind, and that smell had given an extra urgency to their hurried dismantling of the bender tents and the packing of the flat-carts. When Georgie Barnacle strode into Burdens' Wood on that November morning he learned that the Lees and Lovells had been the first in the district to be visited by the militia. The benders had been overturned, the blankets trampled by the horses' hooves, the flat-carts searched and every infant examined closely for the small brown birthmark which would mark it out as being Roehampton's son. Every Romany man and boy bore the stamp of the soldiers' fists about his face and body, while the mothers, who had sought to resist the rough treatment shown to their babies, had been slapped about the mouth until their lips were split and their teeth loosened.

The assumption, as always, was that all of them were lying and only a beating would elicit truth. Rowan Lee, the most vociferous of the menfolk, had suffered a broken jaw for his brave stance. If, said the captain of the militia, the man who had stolen his lordship's heir and murdered the nursemaid was not apprehended by nightfall and the child recovered, then a scapegoat would need to be found. The gypsies had been present at the castle at the very hour when the crimes were committed, so what further proof was needed of their guilt?

On hearing these words, Silence Lee knew better than to allow his people to linger in Burdens' Wood.

They moved swiftly on that first day and night, never halting for food or rest, but maintaining the long and loping stride which was common to both men and women. Infants were carried in blankets slung about their mothers' hips. Young children were put aboard the flat-carts and ordered to stay quiet. Considering their numbers, the company moved with extraordinary stealth and in almost total silence. Except for the one named Georgie Barnacle, who refused to go barefoot as did his companions, but stumbled noisily in the rear ranks in his heavy leather boots. It was not until they were many miles clear of Roehampton country that the order to halt was given, and then the stop was a short one, just long enough to light a fire and prepare hot food and drink.

George sat together with Silva and Coralina. They drank the thin hot broth and chewed on the small portion of hard mouldy bread which was the last of the provisions brought with them in their precipitate flight. He began to question Silva about their destination.

' 'Tis a place us goes to only in great trouble. 'Tis called ancient forest and the king's men never set foot there because of the *mullo*.'

Georgie turned to Coralina, the question in his eyes.

'The spirits,' she explained. ' 'Tis the place where the just-lately dead ones gather before they sets out on their last long journey. That is a terrible bad *atchin-tan*, but when a hard thing happens to us 'tis the only spot where the militia men won't dare to follow. Why, even the gentry gives it a wide berth.' She turned her full dark gaze on Georgie. 'There's some,' she murmured, 'that knows the truth about what happened to Roehampton's babe. But that someone is keeping a still tongue. Remember this, Manju! 'Twas thy own people took a beating for that bad deed.'

He ceased to differentiate between night and day as they moved ever deeper into the green gloom. The fear in his head and heart trickled down into his loins and the muscles of his thighs and calves until he could scarcely set one raw and aching foot before the other. He knew his weakness for a shameful thing, especially when set against the hardiness and resilience of these ill-clad and poorly nurtured gypsies. When it came to a question of survival, Georgie thought it was he who would not see out the coming winter. He, with his good boots and woollen coat, his great height and broad shoulders, was nothing better than a liability and a hindrance in the flight from Ashkeepers.

Unused to travel, to the bewilderment of perpetual movement, he lost all comprehension of time and place. His mind now lapsed many miles behind his suffering body, his memory caught fast by the dramas of the Toll House, the perfidy of Pennina Lambton, and his ambivalent feelings about her wicked actions. On that last push towards the forest *tan* it was only Coralina's hand in his hand, the rhythmic slap of her bare feet on the frozen path, which kept him moving ever forward.

No songbirds sang in the ancient forest.

The great stands of oak and beech, chestnut and birch marched through mile upon mile of dim glades until, according to Silva, they reached the open sea, which was the place where the world ended.

The absence of birdsong brought an eerie kind of silence. But there were other sounds, rustlings and tappings, unidentifiable shrieks, and the awful near-human scream of a rabbit, its throat ripped by a stoat's teeth.

They came into the chosen place on an afternoon of aching cold, with a fine snow sifting down, and the clouds glimpsed between the bare boughs of the trees showing the purple backs and saffron underbellies which meant blizzard.

Georgie Barnacle did not appreciate on that first evening in the *tan* the wisdom shown by the Lees and Lovells in their choice of winter quarters. In the months to come he would be thankful for the shelter of great trees, the copse-growths of alder and hazel; for the pure spring water which gushed from a nearby rocky outcrop, and the abundant wildlife which would assist their precarious survival in a severe winter.

But when the final halt was ordered by Silence Lee, the assistant toll house keeper did not even realise his own good fortune in having outrun the coming blizzard.

Counting children and babies, the company who settled into the ancient forest numbered twenty-two. Left to himself, Georgie would have lain his body straightway down on their arrival, on the snow-powdered ground among the tree roots, but Coralina the scold would have none of it. Pushing and prodding, berating him in words he did not understand, but whose meaning could not be mistaken, she urged him to cut hazel wands, to dig post-holes, for the bender tent which would be hers.

While she gathered firewood, and pine boughs and bracken for her bedding, and carried water from the spring, he bent his back unwillingly to unfamiliar tasks, and craved for sleep.

It was when the benders stood in a wide circle around the fire, when the fresh meat caught by the young boys simmered in the cauldron, and bread dough sizzled on a griddle, that Silence Lee called Coralina and Georgie to his side.

He gazed long and hard into their young faces. He said, 'It will not do for us to bide the winter in this place with the two of thee promised and as yet unwed.' He called out to Jai and Jared. 'Stand by me here, brothers. I need thee for witness.' To Georgie he said, 'I must ask thee to bare thy left arm, Manju, and to kneel before me.'

Coralina, knowing what was to come, had already pushed back her shawl, knelt down and bared her left arm. Georgie, not dreaming what was about to befall him, stood doltish and unsuspecting at her side. Puzzled but obedient, he knelt, rolled up the sleeve of his good wool jacket and at once his arm was gripped by Silence. He felt the sting of a keen blade and saw the blood well up thick and dark across his left wrist.

In his stupid and exhausted state he wondered what crime he had unwittingly committed to merit such violent retribution. And then he saw the same outrage being performed upon Silence's daughter, who seemed actually to welcome the knife's kiss.

The witnesses moved closer and a hush fell across the watching group who were gathered in the firelight. A great sigh passed among them as the bleeding wrist of Georgie Barnacle was clamped hard to the bleeding wrist of Coralina Lee, so that their mingled blood dripped warm and dark upon the forest floor. Almost at once two women stepped forward and bound wedges of fresh moss very tightly to the opened veins.

Silence said, 'The feasting and celebration will come later, when we are recovered from the long trek. But for now the Law of our Elders has been kept.' He touched the heads of the kneeling couple. 'God's blessing on thee,' he said. 'Mayest thou live long and content together, and be blessed by many strong sons.'

It was only when the couple walked back hand in hand to their tent that George saw how the spot indicated by Coralina for the placing of her bender was in the most sheltered and secluded of positions; which meant that he alone of all the group had been unaware of his impending wedding. He wondered what would have transpired had he refused to wed her. It was a thought which would often return to disturb him in the months to come.

Coralina had prepared the bed-of-glory she would share with her husband, according to the old ways of her people. She had laid bracken and sweet-smelling pine boughs in the bender, and covered them with the thick woollen blankets which were her family's gift. In spite of the bitter cold, when the bender was built she had gone with her sisters to the spring and washed her hair and body, and put on her one good gown and finest shawl. When she had indicated earlier the spot behind the alder bushes where the bender was to be set, she had thought that Georgie would have guessed the reason for its isolation. After all, they were promised to each other, and there had been no time for rest or contact between them on the flight from Ashkeepers. He surely must have known that it would not be allowed for them to live in the close proximity of the *tan* as betrothed but still unmarried people. But even when he knelt beside her and obeyed her father's order to bare his left arm, he still wore the expression of a stunned ox; a look which had changed to one of horror as he watched his blood spill out upon the ground. When her father clamped her wrist to Georgie's, in the most beautiful and significant part of the ritual marriage, she had felt deep in her bones the awful shudder which racked his body.

Now she walked with him in silence from the fireside to the bender. It was she who entered last, she who turned to drop the covering across the entrance and secure it with large stones. When she turned towards him in the darkness expecting his touch, his tender words, it was to find him prone upon the bed-of-glory, his snores sounding loud enough to be heard by the whole camp.

The Lees and Lovells, out of reach of the militia and within sound of the ocean, were to experience that night the sleep of utter exhaustion, oblivious of the blizzard which raged above them. Families lay curled together, rolled into blankets, trusting to the canvas-covered benders to protect them from the storm. Still wearing his boots and long, broadcloth coat, George Barnacle went down into a sleep so deep that it was like a sickness from which he might never stir. Coralina's hands sought and found the blankets; she spread them over her husband and then lay down beside him. She lay for several minutes hoping he might waken. When he did not she unbuttoned his greatcoat and crept into its folds. The warmth of his body was all she would win that night from this man known to her people as Manju, son of Estralita.

On the headlong flight from Ashkeepers she had dreamed about this moment, had wondered how his hands would feel upon her body; if he would cause her pain. Her married sisters had warned her there would have to be pain before there could be pleasure. She had also watched him as they travelled. She knew that in his mind he was still in the Toll House, with the witch-woman, Pennina. The abrupt introduction to her people's way of life was bound to be hard on him. There was no denying that in his heart, her husband was more *gorgio* than gypsy.

George slept like a man who had looked upon death and wakened reluctantly, coming up from a dark place, resentful of his resurrection. He woke to the smell of woodsmoke, and the glare of reflected light from snow, which was painful to his eyes. He hurt in every corner of his body. There was a stiffness in his back and legs which made it difficult to stand. Each tentative attempt at movement made him cry out; he lay back on the pine boughs and pulled the blankets around him. The fiercest agony of all was centred in his booted feet.

The bender tent lay open to the winter's morning, the canvas flap which had covered the entrance overnight was thrown back now to reveal the fires, the tripods from which hung kettles and cauldrons, and a glimpse of blue sky between the branches of trees glistening with hoar frost. He closed his eyes against the light. At some time in the night he had wakened briefly to find Coralina laid across his chest, her arms tight about his body. He had smelled the fragrance of the sweet almond oil she used to dress her hair, and felt the softness of her. He remembered then that this was his wedding night, that he lay with his new wife on what the gypsies called the bed-of-honour. But even as his own arms tightened about her he went down again into deep sleep.

It was mid-afternoon when he came properly back into himself. He woke to find Coralina standing over him, a bowl of steaming broth in her hand. He pulled himself up into a sitting position, and she knelt at his side and began to feed him the hot food from a silver spoon. As he ate, she crooned softly in her sing-song voice. 'There now, my love! Well, thou hast slept good. Now eat and get thy strength back. We shall not move from this place till the vi'lets peep out and the hares leap. Time and enough for thee to mend in body and to learn our ways.'

When the bowl was empty she pulled up the blankets and pointed a finger at his booted feet. Her voice was no longer soft and crooning. 'There lies thy trouble, Manju. We all tried to tell thee that going leather-shod was folly.' She seized a boot and began to pull gently at it. Georgie's roar of anguish brought several Lees and Lovells running to the bender.

' 'Tis the boots,' cried Coralina. 'His feet is all swelled up inside 'em. They got to be took off for sure, lest he lose his toes.'

'No,' Georgie shouted. 'Leave me be. All I need is a day's rest.'

'Thou had thy day's rest already, brother.' It was Silva who spoke up. 'While the women and *chavvies* fetched wood and water, milked the goats and made the fires, thou has laid inside here all snug and easy. Who dost thou think killed the meat for the broth thou just ate? Thou art one of us now, Manju. The boots must come off before thy feet turn black and rot away, and what use is a crippled man to Coralina?'

He pulled the hunting knife from his belt and stood over Georgie. There was a certain satisfaction in Silva's look as he seized upon the first boot.

It needed four men to hold Georgie down while Silva slit the soft brown leather from knee to toes. Inch by careful inch the boots were pared away to reveal the swollen dis-coloured flesh, the toes already turned blue-black with frostbite. As the final strips were lifted from his skin, to his shame Georgie fainted clean away.

When he came to himself only he and Coralina remained in the bender. She was spreading a thick layer of ointment on his raw skin, and binding the lesions with strips of cotton torn from an already frayed skirt. His boots, his most prized possessions, lay in tatters on the bender floor.

'What now?' he howled. 'How shall I walk without boots in this wild place, in this bitter weather?'

Coralina bent her head to the task of binding and tying. 'Thou must go barefoot, dear husband,' she murmured around a smile. 'And when thy feet are healed over, believe me, they will grow a skin as tough as cowhide.' She looked up, and her keen gaze caught his full attention. 'Until now,' she said, 'thou hast found life soft in the Toll House, with the whore Pennina. But those days are over, Manju. It was thy own free will that brought thee to me. I know the secrets of thy heart. Because of thy warm feelings for Roehampton's daughter, thou hast brought trouble on thy ownself, and upon my people.' She tied the final bandage, sat back on her heels and viewed her work with satisfaction. 'Fear not, Manju, I shall not tell my father and the rest of them the true reason why thou art come to live among us. We are man and wife now. Thy secret is my secret.'

She rose, stood above him, and gazed

down into his startled face. 'I will care for thee until thy feet mend, but I warn thee now, do not shame me further, husband! The elders already wonder how one who has the looks and body of a strong man can so easy play the weakling. Heed my words now! Do not lie idle for too long, lest thy own people cast thee out.'

# Nina

I love the time of very early morning. I like to sit beside the kitchen window, sipping my first cup of scalding coffee and watching the light come up across the rim of the world.

I find an especial satisfaction at the end of October in turning the hands of the clock back by one hour; it pleases me to advance the dawn by sixty minutes, and never mind that by doing so the November afternoons are made shorter, the evenings begin at four p.m. This is, after all, winter, and to be expected. A time to build up the fire, draw the curtains across the window, and dream away the hours until bedtime in a comfortable chair.

I do a lot of that lately. Dreaming. Mulling over the past. I blame much of this habit on Barnacle's book, the rest I attribute to the influence of Primrose. That woman has one foot permanently planted in memory lane. I have had blow-by-blow accounts of her difficult birth (which almost killed her mother). Her unsettled childhood, and torrid teenage years. Her tumultuous marriage (which had almost killed Primrose), and her improbably perfect relationship with Ashley, her grandson. She does not appear to be aware of the unexplained gaps in her memoir. I long to say, 'But what about your son? Your daughter-in-law, the birth of Ashley?' And then I remember her brief mention of the accident in which two of them died, and Ashley was left orphaned. She is quite right not to talk about it.

Some memories are best left lying undisturbed; to put them into words could be to press the button of self-destruction. And who am I to criticise Primrose over what she tells and does not tell? There are some past events I never dare to speak aloud.

Primrose had made a habit of casual calling; for morning coffee, afternoon tea, or a before-supper drink. As I was not myself a dropper-in I found this practice disconcerting. As I have said, I preferred to be forewarned of callers. She sensed my reservations and tried to convince me that her visits were not premeditated. 'Just passing,' she would cry, already two strides inside the front door. But since my house was the last one standing before Witches' Hollow, her appearance was not the result of impulse she would have me believe it to be.

Curiously enough, when more than two days elapsed without one or more of her breathless eruptions into my life, I found myself growing uneasy and watching for her approach. On this occasion almost a week had passed without sight or sound of her, and so I decided to walk to the village postbox by way of Ding-Dong Valley.

The first thing I noticed was the Simpsons' car parked neatly in their driveway; the second surprise was the shuttered look of Primrose's house, every window curtain close-drawn. I pressed the door bell but 'Una Paloma Blanca' failed to flush her out. I persisted. When she finally opened up I was shocked at her pallor, the puffy eyes and uncombed hair. She made no move to invite me in, so I edged around her. 'Just passing!' I cried, and walked ahead into the darkened lounge.

From facing armchairs we viewed each other.

I said, 'You look terrible. What has happened?' My concerned tone was a mistake. It was the signal for her complete collapse. There was also a powerful smell of gin emanating from her. Her shoulders heaved, her tears flowed.

'Tea or coffee?' I enquired.

'Coffee,' she moaned, 'and two or three Disprin.'

If the condition of her kitchen was any indication of her state of mind then Primrose was in a bad way. I found a cafetière and two clean mugs. In her bathroom cabinet I discovered a stock of hangover remedies sufficient to treat a drunken rugby team.

I plied her with coffee and tablets, and put a fresh box of pale pink tissues on her lap. I was intensely curious as to the reason for her distress. After ten minutes of significant silence in which she regained a measure of control, I again asked, 'What happened, Primrose?'

I braced myself to hear that Sergeant Drew had found a younger more attractive ladyfriend, or that April Simpson was threatening her with prosecution. Or, worst of all, that something bad had happened to Gorbachev.

I was unprepared for the tirade which began with the name of Ashley, beloved grandson. 'He's become involved with one of those trollops from the Simpsons' squat. She's actually moved in with him. Her name is Angelique — they call her Angel!'

She began to laugh, normally at first and then with mounting hysteria. She rocked back and forth in a paroxysm of tears and mirth, waving her mug and spilling coffee all over her beige moquette.

I was tempted to slap her; instead I grabbed the coffee mug and shouted at her. 'Get a grip on yourself, you silly woman.' To my surprise and relief she was shocked into silence. Ashamed at my lack of sympathy I sat down, and for several minutes we avoided looking at each other. When she spoke her tone was that of a chastised child.

'Sorry,' she said, 'It's all been too much for me.'

I picked up the almost-empty gin bottle which stood on the low table. 'Too much of this stuff is your greatest problem. Now tell me properly. What has happened with Ashley?'

The story came out disjointedly and out of sequence. Summarised, it was very simple. Ashley Martindale, formerly footloose and fancy-free, had allowed himself to be seduced by a Soul of God and taken her into his home and bed. He had become infatuated while negotiating with the squatters. He had been persuaded, simpleton that he was, that Angelique was more sinned against than sinful, and that the prime mover in the squatting venture was her friend, the chunky one called Maisie who wore chiffon and Dr Marten boots.

I said, 'So this Angelique must be the attractive one, the slim girl, hair in a French pleat, nice manners, lovely smile?'

Primrose sniffed. 'Well — I suppose that's one way of describing her. But she didn't find out that *she* cared for *Ashley* until the Simpsons turned up at the weekend, and threw the whole bunch of them out into the street. And then it was, "Oh, Ashley darling, I can't bear the thought of losing you. If I go off with the 'Souls' we shall never meet again." He fell for it of course. He's so naive, so innocent and simple.'

Primrose spoke like a true grandmother. Who says that love is not blind! Privately, I thought, good on you, Ashley! I would never have thought the lad had it in him. I recalled the alternative and exciting lifestyles I had envisioned for him when we met in his office. His shacking-up with a Soul of God named Angel had never even crossed my mind.

I said, placatingly, 'Well, she is the most presentable one of that scruffy bunch. And she is really rather beautiful, you know. Without the black clothes and the dead-white make-up, and the purple eyeshadow and lipstick, I'll bet she's pretty stunning.' I leaned forward to emphasise my words. 'What is more important,' and now I used words that would comfort Primrose, 'she is *ladylike*, refined. When I was selling my house in the city, she and her chum came to look it over. She was really charming and most polite. Quite unlike her awful friend.'

There was a tremor in Primrose's voice, a plea in her eyes that more than justified my over-optimistic picture of Ashley's new inamorata. 'Oh, Nina,' she murmured, 'do you really think she is suitable for Ashley?' She looked thoughtful. 'Ladylike. charming. Refined.' She repeated my words as if they were a mantra. 'I do respect your judgement, dear, you know that, don't you. You must think me a very silly woman, the way I fall to pieces. But he's all I have in the world. I couldn't bear to see him make a really big mistake.'

'Look,' I said. 'You and I made mistakes when we were young. But they were *our* mistakes. We learned to live with the consequences — we had to. It's a learning process, don't you see? Nobody goes through life without making one or two blunders. Supposing this Angel isn't right for Ashley — he'll put it down to experience and find some other girl. Men recover quickly from a broken romance.'

Primrose looked doubtful. 'You wouldn't say that if it was Fran.'

She was so absolutely right that I was momentarily robbed of speech and breath. 'Oh Lord,' I said. 'I do pontificate, don't I. How could I be so bloody self-righteous when I know very well that if any man hurt Fran or Imogen, I would strike him dead!'

She brightened. 'Would you? Would you really? How would you do it?'

Improvising wildly, and not wishing to dampen her improved spirits, I said, 'Well, in view of my advancing years, and my slight, very slight infirmities, I should have to box clever.' I hesitated. Never having contemplated murder I was somewhat at a loss.

'Poison would be easiest,' she offered brightly. 'Or a string stretched across the staircase. Or you could tamper with his brakes.'

The plots tripped so readily from her lips that I began to suspect that she maybe did watch *Colombo* on a Sunday afternoon. I began to laugh. Hesitantly she joined in, until we were both convulsed and tearful. I mopped my eyes and pulled myself together.

'It'll be all right,' I said. 'Your boy is nobody's fool. He's just having a little fling, testing the water. Trust him, Primmie. If she's not the right one for him, well, he'll boot her out, and no harm done.'

'You're right. You're absolutely right. I know it really — I always seem to need somebody to tell me. It's just that he's never done anything like this before.'

I said, offhandedly, 'Have you seen Sergeant Drew lately?'

Her hand clapped across her mouth. 'What day is it?' she asked.

'It's Friday.'

'Oh no! I invited him for supper. Look at me! Look at the state of the house! And I'm still a little — a little inebriated.' She was in fact more than three parts drunk and incapable of serious action.

'Get upstairs,' I told her, 'and sort yourself out.'

I walked to the window and pulled back the heavy curtains. I began to gather glasses and plates, and cushions which had been presumably hurled in anger into far corners of the room. Ashley's studio portrait had been slammed face downwards; I set it to rights and studied the young face. There was something disturbing about him that I seemed to remember from long ago in another time, another place.

I dragged the vacuum cleaner from a hall cupboard and ran it quickly over the acres of beige Wilton; a flick here and there with a yellow duster and order was more or less restored. The kitchen was a greater challenge. Primmie had at least made some attempt at eating in the past week. Slices of charred toast lay about the counters; saucepans holding dried-up baked beans and sad-looking poached eggs stood on the hob. I filled the sink with scalding water and did a mammoth washing-up. I wiped the counters and mopped the tiled floor. Exhausted, I sat down on a kitchen chair. I wondered briefly about the state of Primmie's bedroom, and the white-lace draped four-poster bed. I had no idea of how far her friendship with Drew had progressed. I shied away from the route my imagination was taking. If her bedroom needed squaring up for any reason, she could damn well see to it herself.

I walked slowly home through the early dusk and thought about my own life. There were so many things I had meant to do and had not done in the past months. I had resolved to keep in touch with Sorsha, but each time my footsteps turned towards Witches' Hollow, I remembered that Estralita Lee also lived there. Estralita, whose family had been questioned closely when my baby was stolen, and who had almost certainly by now repeated that old story to her granddaughter, Sorsha.

I had meant to give the lawn its final tidying cut before winter started, to plant daffodils and crocus, to clip the privet hedge.

I had meant to clear the garden shed of Monty Barnacle's mouldering books; to investigate the wraith who looked out from my bedroom window; and to discover the reason why a mutilated crow had been left on my doorstep.

My woolly-mindedness had commenced with my involvement with Primrose. I had allowed myself to be side-tracked by April Simpson's squatters. I wasted precious hours chattering with Primmie across the coffee and teacups. Now I faced involvement in the drama of Ashley Martindale's love life.

It was becoming all too much for one who was well into the upper reaches of advanced middle age. What I really needed was some means of delegating the responsibility for Primrose and her gin habit when distressed. And she was so frequently upset about one thing and another!

To shuffle her off onto Ashley was impossible now for obvious reasons.

My sneaky thoughts turned shamelessly towards Imogen and Niall. Well, my daughter was always offering aid and support in quarters where they were not needed.

It could be seen as a kindness to allow her at last to come into her own.

I telephoned my daughter that evening, explained the situation in which I found myself, and begged her advice. It was the sort of dilemma that brings out the very best in Imogen. She and Primrose had found an instant rapport at their first meeting, and now Ashley's unexpected liaison with a member of a weird cult, the distress of his grandmother, and my own involvement in their problems, touched my daughter's tender heart to a degree that made me ashamed of my own cynical thoughts before dialling her number.

The difficulty facing us, as Imogen pointed out, was the fact that she and Niall had never met Ashley Martindale and his Angelique; and that I myself had known them only in less than friendly circumstances. What was needed, she said, was a good and valid reason for a meeting, a social gathering which would rouse no suspicion in Ashley's mind that his girlfriend was being vetted as to suitability by his devoted grandmother.

There was silence at her end of the line; I could hear the tap of a pencil against her front teeth, and then her voice came back confident and strong. 'I've got it, Mum! The perfect answer. Fran and Mitch are househunting. Now that John is walking, the cottage is much too small for them. Suppose I give a little dinner party and invite the Martindale family. Something quite informal which will ostensibly give Fran and Mitch a chance to consult Ashley about properties and so forth?'

'A wonderful idea,' I said, 'but a little bit obvious, don't you think? After all, Ashley could be visited at any time in his office, if they really want to see him.'

'Ye — es. You could be right, and it would make matters worse if he suspected we were spying. On the other hand, Primrose really needs to meet this girl, and it's so much easier on neutral ground. How about I invite them to our bonfire party? Mitch's parents will be coming, and Fran and Mitch of course, and some of their young friends; and a few of our neighbours.'

'But you never have a bonfire party.

You've always hated fireworks.'

'Not any more,' she said smugly. 'John will love it!'

'Yes,' I said. 'Well, that sounds perfect. Sausages and sticky toffee around the bonfire. Niall letting off the fireworks. Meanwhile, you and I and Primmie can skulk among the rhododendrons sizing up this Angelique.' I paused. 'There's just one point we seem to have overlooked. I hadn't planned on dragging Fran and Mitch into all this.'

Imogen laughed. 'Don't be silly, Mother. They really need advice about moving house, we shall be doing them a favour by introducing them to Ashley. If we don't tell them what we're up to, well, I'm sure they'll never guess.'

There are times when my daughter outstrips even me in deception and guile. It is a rarely seen side of Imogen's otherwise flawless character, and one which affords me the greatest possible satisfaction.

The bonfire burned and crackled, Catherine wheels, pinned to the trunk of the apple tree, whizzed around in a blaze of colour; Roman candles fizzed and glowed. Held high and secure in his father's arms, John gazed wide-eyed at the spectacle. I found myself watching the baby's face. He was too young to remember later in his life a single moment of this evening, and yet perhaps some sense of wonderment would stay with him. How much does a child remember of its earliest experiences?

I found some consolation in the thought that my baby would not have remembered, later in her life, that night when she was snatched from her pram and stolen by a stranger. The only thought that had made life possible for Jack and me was a belief that she had been taken from us to ease another woman's desperate need. If true, this could mean that our daughter still lived, was loved, cherished. That she had experienced all the childish delights, like Guy Fawkes, funfairs, Christmas, birthdays, although not with us. I stood in the shadows and saw the delight of Imogen and Niall, of Fran and Mitch, as they organised this show which had been put on exclusively for John's sake. Somewhere in the world, I had another daughter, probably herself a grandmother, who might, at this very moment, be lifting up a wondering baby to see the bonfire's blaze.

Primrose stood at my elbow. She wore a bright green, rhinestone-encrusted outfit, which I would describe as being an upmarket tracksuit, the trousers of which were tucked into natty green leather boots. She seemed to have an eye-catching outfit for every possible occasion. On this mild damp evening, Imogen and Fran wore jeans and heavy-knit sweaters. Conscious of the fact that I would be scrutinised closely by my daughter, I had fished out my decent brown slacks and orange jacket. I was not normally so keenly aware of these boring sartorial details, but the girl from the squat was very much on my mind. I expected to see her, white-faced and purple-lipped, clad in the usual all-enveloping black. Now that the moment was almost upon us, I grew nervous at the thought of meeting her again. Primrose and Imogen would judge her mainly by her style, or lack of it. I resolved to be broad-minded. I had suffered myself on that very score.

As it turned out they were late arriving, and since it was her garden, her bonfire, it was Imogen who greeted them, fixed them up with hot dogs and paper napkins, and coffee in Styrofoam cups. Fran and Mitch were introduced. There was handshaking and laughter.

Primrose and I stood on the far side of the bonfire; I heard the sharp intake of her breath and amazed sigh. It is not often she

522

is rendered speechless; but at the sight of Angelique, Primrose was stunned into silence. I followed her gaze and was similarly overwhelmed. Ashley's new love was clothed from neck to ankle in an all-in-one outfit of skin-hugging scarlet leather.

Primrose found her voice. 'How do you suppose,' she whispered, 'she manages to insert herself into that lot? Or get out of it again?'

'Only with Ashley's assistance, I should imagine,' I said. 'She could never manage single-handed. Of course there are all those zips, but even so — ?' We peered at each other through the smoky gloom, and began to giggle. Primrose looked down at her own ample curves.

I read her thoughts. 'You wouldn't dare — would you?'

She said, 'It would certainly pose a challenge for Sergeant Drew. In a suit like that I could be the one case he never manages to crack!'

We began to laugh, leaning weakly against each other, convulsed at the images her words created.

'Stop it!' I said. 'We are here to sort out Ashley's love life, not yours.' We began to edge our way slowly around the bonfire, and towards Angelique, former Soul of

God, experienced squatter, and one-time spurious viewer of my city home.

She was every bit as charming as I remembered, except that away from the restricting presence of her Rasta-haired chum she positively glowed. As we approached the group which stood beneath the apple tree, I slowed my step. I stayed in shadow while Ashley introduced to each other the two most important women in his life. And it was a significant moment. I needed only a glance at Ashley Martindale's face to know that this girl was to be *the one*. The partner with whom he wanted to spend the rest of his life. I could only hope that Primrose also recognised the seriousness of the occasion. The whole of her future relationship with her grandson might well depend on her initial attitude and behaviour towards Angelique. I edged closer into earshot.

Primrose was playing it safe, admiring the skin-tight red leather, looking envious and wistful; saying that only someone who had Angelique's slim figure and beautiful colouring could successfully wear such a fantastic outfit.

Angelique returned the compliment. She praised effusively the rhinestone-spattered green which, she said, set off so well Primrose's blonde hair. I could feel my stomach muscles tighten with the effort of suppressing laughter. Who would have guessed that these two women had spent the spring and summer in deadly conflict with each other? Tedious as I found their talk of clothes and fashion, I was filled with admiration at their ability to dissemble. Words like eviction and persecution might never have been used by either of them. I saw the tension draining out of Ashley, and only then did I appreciate how apprehensive he had actually been.

I was next in the receiving line. Imogen beckoned me forward. Unlike Primmie I did not need to look up into Angelique's face; in fact my extra inches required that she gaze up at me. 'And this is my mother, Nina Franklin,' Imogen was saying.

It is difficult to gauge exactly by firelight the expression on another person's face. I thought I saw a flash of fear in the dark eyes, a spasm of anxiety tighten those classical features. Her discomfiture pleased me in as much as it showed a degree of vulnerability, an awareness of her own ambivalent position among us. But even as I shook her hand and uttered the usual banalities, it was on Ashley Martindale that all my anxiety and guilt was concentrated.

I had the strangest feeling that having

once awarded him in my thoughts a series of alternative lifestyles, I had in some unfair and uncanny fashion made myself responsible for the continued happiness of his existence. For the preservation of his soul. If it is possible to ill-wish a person, then surely it is also possible to well-wish him? I wished Ashley well with all my heart. It seemed to me that, however indirectly, I had been the cause, or the catalyst, which had brought these two together. Now I owed it to Ashley to do — to do what?

I relinquished my grasp of her smooth cool hand, and turned away from Angelique and back to Primrose. I pointed at the bonfire.

'Oh look,' I cried, 'the guy has caught at last! Let's go back to the fire and watch him burn.'

The debriefing was held on the following morning. It had been arranged that Primmie and I would meet Imogen for coffee in a city restaurant. The excitements and emotions of the previous evening meant that Primrose and I had hardly slept. I am, at the best of times, an unwilling and nervous passenger when riding in my friend's car. She would say that she drives with a certain *panache,* with an individual style. I have long suspected that it was Primrose who was the original instigator of the recent phenomenon known as road rage.

I fastened my seat belt in a mood of resignation and braced myself to suffer the usual series of what I hoped would be near-misses; and the infuriated honking from swerving cars which would grow more frequent as we came into city traffic. I try not to enter into conversation with her at such times, hoping that silence will concentrate her mind. I also try to avoid guessing how many nips of gin she has taken before switching on the ignition.

But Primmie, convinced as always that she can successfully do at least three things at once, had that morning lit a cigarette, gripped the wheel until her knuckles whitened and, while rehashing the events of the previous evening, attempted to check her make-up in the overhead mirror.

By the time we arrived in the multi-storey car park, my trembling legs would hardly support me. Primrose looked into my ashen face and remarked that late nights clearly did not suit me. She opened her oversized gold-coloured handbag and drew out a ladylike version of a gentleman's hip flask. Since it would not do, she said, to fortify our coffee in Imogen's presence, we had better take a little snifter in the privacy of the car.

Imogen was also rather the worse for wear. I thought her rare dishevelled look quite becoming but did not dare to say so. We slumped onto cushioned seats in a secluded corner of the café, while my daughter explained how the bonfire party had gone on until the small hours. Fran and Mitch and John had stayed over, since the baby had fallen asleep and it had seemed a shame to move him. Ashley, deep in discussion with Mitch about properties and mortgage matters, had shown no inclination to depart; which suited Imogen very well since she was able to concentration on Angelique.

'So,' asked Primrose, 'what did you find out?' There was a tremor in her voice, a crumpled look to her normally bright face. The feelings of shame and guilt over this investigation she had initiated into Ashley's love life, were aging her visibly even as she spoke.

Imogen, sensitive to the seriousness of the moment, paused to take a long drink of her coffee and marshal her thoughts. Speaking slowly, spacing her words for maximum effect, she leaned across the table and looked directly into Primmie's eyes.

'You have nothing to worry about. Absolutely nothing.'

'You talked to her?'

'She talked to me.' Imogen smiled. 'Oh, don't worry. I didn't question her, didn't need to. While Ashley was busy in the living room advising Fran and Mitch about mortgages and so forth, and Niall was in the garden damping down the bonfire, I manoeuvred Angelique into the kitchen. It turned out to be a wise move. There is something about kitchens which sometimes disarms the most sophisticated young woman. Seeing her looking so glamorous in that scarlet leather had been a bit daunting, but when she started to scrape half-eaten, congealed hot dogs into the bin, and pick at the bits of leftover bonfire toffee, I began to warm towards her. By the time we had straightened up the kitchen, and sat down at the table with mugs of hot chocolate, I could see she was anxious to talk. She thanked me for inviting her. It had made her first meeting with Ashley's grandmother less of an ordeal, she said, since in the circumstances Mrs Martindale would have been perfectly justified if she had refused to even speak to Ashley's disreputable friend.' Imogen looked swiftly at Primmie, and then away. She said, 'So I made sympathetic noises. I told Angelique that Primrose would never hold a grudge. That she respected Ashley's judgement in such matters, and that all she wanted was for Ashley to be happy.

'Angel's relief was so great she became quite tearful. I sat,' said my daughter, 'with my fingers crossed underneath the table, and hoped that what I had just told her was somewhere near the truth. There was no need for further prompting; within half an hour she had told me her entire life history.'

Imogen was looking grave. She said, 'Are you ready for this, Primrose?'

Primmie nodded. I hardly dared to draw my next breath. My daughter's childish delight in the shock she was about to give us was so obvious she all but danced and clapped her hands together.

'You may remember,' she said, 'about eighteen months ago there was a massive hunt for Earl Thingummie's daughter? It was on TV and in all the papers. "Beautiful but wilful heiress goes missing after row with famous father; controversial member of the House of Lords, and master of foxhounds. Family distraught. Come home, Angelique, all is forgiven!" ' Imogen smote her forehead with a clenched fist. 'I should have remembered,' she said, 'it's an uncommon name, and that story of her disappearance fascinated me at the time. But who would have imagined an Honourable to be shacked up with a bunch of religious freaks, and in April Simpson's house of all unlikely places?'

Primrose, too stunned to utter, but with a gleam of resurrection in her eyes, turned imploringly to me.

'So why did Angelique do what she did?' I asked Imogen, right on cue.

'Well, it seems,' said my daughter, 'that Angelique was bored and lonely. Her words, not mine. Spoiled rotten and ungrateful sounds nearer to the mark, but who am I to judge? Winters in Jamaica, more designer outfits than she could ever wear, a generous allowance from Daddy, a new car every birthday — would you be bored? I don't think I would. But our Angel wanted to find out how the "real people" lived. At that point she actually saw herself as being experienced and worldly, not to say streetwise. How a few visits into sleazy Soho, and a stolen weekend or two in Brighton with a chinless wonder qualified her to believe this, I can't imagine. She was, of course, as naive and innocent as a convent nun. When she met the proselytising Souls of God at a "rave" held in a barn she was completely bowled over by them. She did a lot of things that night for the very first time, and I don't mean praying. When the group drove away the next day in a converted double-decker bus, Angel, stoned out of her mind, felt privileged to be allowed to go with them.'

Imogen sat back in her seat and sighed. I signalled the waitress to bring a second round of coffees.

'Everything about the Souls impressed her,' said Imogen. 'They were an assortment of university dropouts and runaways who were looking for a place to hide. There was one who was an escapee from an open prison. Their leader, a young man who called himself Elijah, told her about their simple faith that the Lord would always provide for those who truly believed. The Souls, he said, pooled their resources, everything was shared. It was at this point she handed him her car keys, credit cards and cheque book.'

I said, 'How could she have been so stupid?'

'I asked her that myself,' said Imogen. 'It seems that this Elijah was good-looking and persuasive. I think the word is charismatic. She was also bowled over by the way she was instantly accepted in the group. Their attitudes towards authority and the law intrigued her. When the converted bus in which they lived and travelled broke down and was obviously beyond repair, she was only too happy to prove her commitment to the group by helping them to find a convenient squat, until another vehicle could be found. They were camping out in Glastoubury, investigating ley lines, when they met Felicity Simpson, who was already a so-far uncommitted, but a likely, victim of their teachings. It was on that night that Elijah learned of the Simpsons' plan to sell their house and their proposed world trip. Before Felicity left Elijah's tent that night, her front door key had found its way into Elijah's pocket.'

'So that was how they did it,' whispered Primrose.

Imogen nodded, 'And according to Elijah, Felicity showed her belief and trust in him by inviting the Souls "to come to her house and stay anytime they were in the district".'

'So,' I said, 'Angelique actually believed that they were in the Simpsons' house by invitation?'

'Well, Elijah had a front door key, but his explanation that they were house-minding for the owners did not really ring true, and in view of the fact that the Souls had been looking for a suitable squat without success, it was at this point that Angel first began to feel uneasy. Rather unwisely she asked some awkward questions and received some pretty sharp answers. She suspected that the group, which had been so welcoming and sympathetic to begin with, were interested only in her monthly allowance and the use of her car. After Ashley's first visit to the Simpson house, the girl Maisie was appointed to be Angel's "minder". Nothing overt was ever said or done, but from that moment she was watched all the time.'

'She could have just walked out,' said Primrose.

'That's what I said.' My daughter paused. 'But it was not that simple. They had her car keys, her credit cards and cheque book. She had no cash, and there would certainly have been little goodwill shown to her in Ashkeepers if she had asked the villagers for help. By this time she was desperate to go home to her family, but the thought of the debts run up in her name by the Souls was a strong deterrent. Her only hope of rescue lay in Ashley. Eventually she managed to pass a note to him, explaining her situation.'

'And he never said a word to me,' muttered Primrose. 'Time was when my Ashley told me everything.'

'Just as well he didn't,' I said tartly. 'You

were hitting the gin quite hard enough as it was.'

Primrose shot me a sideways glance of pure poison, but I didn't care. 'Go on,' I told Imogen. 'What happened next?'

She sipped at her fresh cup of coffee. 'You can imagine Ashley's state of mind. For the sake of the girl's safety he was obliged to keep the whole thing to himself. He knew the Simpsons would return, and only then could a move be made against the squatters. Meanwhile he could only watch and wait.'

Primrose, by no means quelled, sat bolt upright in her corner. 'I should have been informed,' she spluttered. Two bright spots of red flamed in her pale cheeks. She turned on me. 'We could have staged a rescue if we had known the true situation, instead of just peering at April's house from behind my curtains.'

'Oh yes,' I snarled, 'and how do you suppose we could have done that? Really, Primmie, you are a very silly woman sometimes!'

'Mother! Primrose! This is no time for you two to start squabbling. Do you want to hear the rest of the tale, or shall we continue on another day?'

The threat in Imogen's voice brought us both to order. Primrose forced a smile, inclined her head in the style of the Queen

Mother, and in her very poshest voice said, 'Do please continue.'

'Well — as you know,' said my daughter, 'the Simpsons eventually returned.' She paused, looked shifty, and took a long drink of her cooling coffee. An uneasy silence contrasted oddly with her previous enthusiasm for her story.

'So what happened next?' demanded Primrose. 'As I understood it, the Simpsons threw the squatters out?'

'Not exactly,' said Imogen. 'By law, a house-owner is not allowed to do that.'

'Oh, for Heaven's sake,' I growled. 'Damn the law. I'd kick out anyone who camped in my house.'

Imogen turned to Primmie. 'If I tell you, you must promise never to tell your policeman friend Sergeant Drew.'

'I promise! I promise!'

'April Simpson paid those squatters five hundred pounds to leave the house.'

'Never,' cried Primmie. 'Not April! She'd walk ten miles to save a penny.'

I said, 'But surely — that's blackmail?'

Imogen nodded. 'Of course it is, but the Souls call it payment for services rendered. House-sitting, they call it, all that mowing and weeding and window cleaning. They did no damage, you see. They left everything in good order. So the law would in any case have had no charge to bring against them.'

There was a silence. I watched as Primrose scooped the froth from her untouched cappuccino and deposited it absentmindedly in the saucer. 'And Ashley?' she asked quietly. 'What part did he play in these shenanigans?'

Imogen spoke carefully. 'He agreed to negotiate the Simpsons' payment to the squatters on condition that Angel's car and keys and credit cards and cheque book were returned, and that they made no move to contact her in future.'

'I can't believe he'd do that,' wailed Primrose.

'Ashley is very much in love,' said my daughter. 'He intends to marry Angelique — if she'll have him.'

And that seemed to be the final word in the story. Primrose thanked Imogen for her time and trouble, and then drove home, cold sober and in silence. I worry when she is garrulous and her driving slapdash. I am seriously disturbed when her behaviour is exemplary. I invited her in and she followed me into the kitchen. She made for the rocking chair in the warm corner by the stove. I rummaged through the fridge and found the depressing bits and pieces that are the usual hoard of the lone woman who is no longer interested in food. There was some grated cheese, a few slices of salami, a tomato and half a can of baked beans. I toasted thick slices of wholemeal bread, spread them with tomato, baked beans and salami, topped it off with grated cheese, and thrust the whole lot underneath the grill.

Primrose, who is able to produce delicious little snack meals without effort on any cold wet Monday lunchtime, consumed my potlack in the appalled silence it deserved. But as she ate her face lost its pale withdrawn look. By the time we had moved to the sitting room with a tray of tea and a plate of Lady's Fingers, she was almost recovered.

I said, in what I hoped was a nonchalant tone, 'Good news, on the whole, about Angelique, don't you think?'

No answer.

'At least,' I persisted, 'she's not some penniless runaway.'

'I'd feel easier in my mind if she was.'

'You don't really mean that. Just think of the fun you'll have telling April and the rest of the girls that your grandson's intended is an Honourable.'

'She's just not the type I wanted for my Ashley.'

It was then I exploded. I thumped the table top so hard that the tea-cups leapt from their saucers.

'Point one,' I shouted, 'he is *not* your Ashley. He's a grown man capable of making his own choices. Point two. What type of girl is it who will ever meet with your very critical approval?' I lowered my tone to a more civilised level. 'Look,' I said, 'these grandchildren of ours, they're not just a different generation. Unlike us, they have refused to become carbon copies of their parents. Especially the young women. And why the hell should they? Just take a good look at yourself, Primmie, take another look at me. What have we ever done in our lives to justify our existence? Dull! dull! dull! That's us summed up in three words. Now today's young woman expects equality in all things. The days of the little wifey who sits at home and warms hubby's slippers are long gone. They have their independent lives, careers, own bank accounts. Okay — so they read these peculiar magazines which tell them they have a right to multiple orgasms, and that it's perfectly normal to hate their parents, but at the same time there is no pressure on them to marry young, as we did. A large proportion of couples simply live together as loving partners. And that is also, in my opinion, *a good thing*. That way, there is no feeling of entrapment on either side. A true commitment needs much more than a scrap of paper to endorse it.' I paused for a much-needed breath. 'You may find,' I continued, 'that it is Angelique who rejects Ashley.'

Primmie's pale withdrawn look had returned, and I felt almost guilty. 'I know you're right,' she murmured. 'I shall simply have to get a grip on my feelings. But, oh, it's so hard, Nina. Very hard.' She struggled to express the feelings she had never before put into words.

'You see,' she floundered, 'he's more to me than just a grandson. It's all very fine for you to talk — you have Imogen, and Niall, Fran and Mitch, and baby John. I lost a whole generation of my family when Tim and Lucy died.'

'Yes,' I said. 'I can appreciate that.'

It was her turn now to explode. She turned upon me with a fury I perhaps had asked for.

'How dare you! What can you possibly know about the heartbreak of losing a longed-for and loved child? You with your cosy little life, your long and happy marriage, your devoted daughter, who, by the way, you don't deserve or in the least appreciate or value. You have so much, Nina. I have only Ashley.'

She was right. There was nothing I could say by way of reparation, although she was wrong about my not knowing what it means to lose a longed-for child. I am not by nature a comforter of the distressed, or a shoulder-patter, but now I found myself kneading Primmie's plump upper arm with a desperation which raised bruises. Guilt makes me incoherent. 'I'm sorry,' I muttered. 'I was being insensitive, to say the least. I wouldn't blame you if you never spoke to me again.'

And then she said the words that left me speechless. 'But you're the only friend I have. I need you, Nina.'

# BARNACLE'S BOOK

## Chapter 6

Long before the lesions to his feet had healed, before his health and vigour had returned, George Barnacle realised once again, and this time with a terrible finality, that he was not, nor ever would be, fitted to the travelling way of life. Lying helpless in the flimsy bender tent, with only a strip or two of canvas between himself and the never-ending blizzards, he longed more than ever for the protection of the stout Toll House walls and sound roof, for the comfort of his quilt at night beside the kitchen fire, and the regular hot meals provided by Pennina.

He knew now that it was not in his nature to adapt to changed circumstances. He had made the transition once from poorhouse orphan to Toll House apprentice; and that, it seemed, was as far as he could go. But despite his melancholy spirits, and almost against his will, his young body mended itself, the swelling in his legs diminished, new skin grew back upon his raw feet. There came a day when he could no longer hide inside the bender and dream of Ashkeepers village. He chose the hour of his emergence with some care, stepping forth on a windless afternoon when the men and the younger women of the *tan* were absent, and only grandparents and children remained to tend the fire. His presence among them was noted by the elders of the tribe without comment. The children, who had all but forgotten his existence, gathered around him to inspect the strange coverings he wore upon his feet.

He would need, Coralina had said, to learn to go barefoot — but this was not the time for his first lesson. The new skin of his feet was still thin and tender and would have to be protected. Come the spring, she warned him, and the wrappings would no longer be necessary, but while the frost continued and the snow lay deep, no risk should be taken. She and Silva argued long and hard about the best means of lapping Georgie's feet. In the end, Silva brought her the pelts of several freshly-killed rabbits, Coralina begged lengths of twine from her father, and between them they fashioned two rough-and-ready moccasins for George. With the fur next to his skin, and the twine laced securely up around his ankles he knew that he looked comic, but cared nothing for the children's laughter. Come the warm days, the small boys told him, and his fancy footwear would stink to Heaven; even skunks would run at his approach. George smiled and said nothing. Come the warm days, and his secret intention was to be back in Ashkeepers, going properly shod and with good food in his stomach. As for Coralina — ? It was always at this point in his forward-looking that the picture blurred.

Nothing was as he dreamed it would be.

Everything that could go wrong had gone wrong.

They were wed but still there had been no true marriage. The bed, so lovingly prepared on their wedding night by Coralina, remained as yet unhonoured.

And there was always Silva, who had shared her childhood, who was her dancing partner; and whose hot gaze followed Coralina all the more keenly since it was known among their people that the recent wedding had not yet been consummated.

There were no secrets between these people who lived so closely together; who depended so strongly upon one another. It sat ill with Georgie, the lack of privacy, the growing suspicion that in this Romany community he was destined never to be respected or allowed to be his own man. His one spot of vulnerability was the woman Estralita who said she was his mother. In moments of weakness he longed to believe that her claim upon him was the truth. He would imagine that day in the House of Correction, the newborn baby torn from its mother's arms and pronounced dead; and later on that same child, for some reason known only to the prison officers, delivered alive to the poorhouse by the village parson. His physical likeness to Estralita could not be denied, and such redness of hair and pallor of skin was a rare sight among the Rom. It was always at this point that his thoughts turned to the man who had fathered him, but whose existence was never acknowledged. He had asked only once and was told that the man was dead, and good riddance to him.

George suspected that his father had been *gorgio*. It would explain his own instinctive lack of love for the wandering life. But his reasoning always brought him back to the unarguable fact that he loved Coralina Lee, and would sacrifice much to remain with her.

The gypsy men were not true hunters. They preferred to eat only the meat from those creatures whose death had occurred from natural causes, or was accidental. They would cheerfully put out of its misery and eat a stag or a horse which was dying of old age, or had broken its leg. But to track down and deliberately slaughter was not a part of their tradition. Only in the severe conditions of this enforced winter in the ancient forest were they obliged to either kill or perish.

There was no shortage of meat in this remote area of forest. Because of its haunted reputation, herds of deer, colonies of wild boar, and many species of smaller creatures, had always bred and roamed freely among the great stands of trees and coppiced woodland. Trapping was the favoured method used among the Lees and Lovells, and here it was that the height and strength of Georgie Barnacle was finally appreciated. The traps he dug were deeper and wider than those made by the small men of the Rom. The frost had not yet sealed the forest floor to any great depth; a fire lit for an hour or two above the selected spot was sufficient for their purpose. When the trap was sprung, when some unwary creature had fallen through the concealing branches and bracken into the pit below, it was time again for George to prove to them that he was not altogether useless.

On those successful days it was he who marched back in triumph to the little circle of brown benders, a dead stag or boar slung across his shoulders, almost as if it was he alone who had made the kill. It was at such moments that Coralina smiled at him. He began to hope that the night might come when she no longer flinched and turned away from his outstretched arms.

The fever struck and the temperature fell on the same February day.

The usual signs of increasing cold had gone unnoticed by the tribe. With the first heat of the fever already upon them, the warning signals of a great freeze from the blue flames of the fire, the smoke which rose to the heavens in a straight white plume, had been ignored. Stocks of firewood and fresh meat which would otherwise have been replenished were allowed to dwindle. As the iron fist of an unprecedented freeze gripped the land, the Lees and Lovells crept into their benders to huddle together under blankets, to burn and shiver, to cry out in their delirium and then, for some of them, to fall silent in a final sleep.

Coralina, George and Silva were the last

to succumb to the winter sickness. In the first days of the great cold they alone kept the fire burning and fed broth to their stricken people. But first Silva, then Coralina, fell victim to the illness. The day came when Georgie too crawled on hands and knees into his bender, and lay down beside his young bride, expecting never to awaken.

It was Silva who recovered first. Weak and dizzy, mewling like an infant, he sought the tinder-box and a handful of dry sticks and coaxed a fire into life. A damaged flat-cart lay close by and he upended it above the flames to make a great blaze. He lay down, exhausted, and let the warmth seep into his blood and bones. His only thought was for Coralina, and when he judged his legs were strong enough to hold him, he made first for the bender where she and Georgie lay. In that moment when he dragged their bodies to the fire he believed them both dead, and when the agony of returning circulation stirred them into moaning life, he laughed aloud. The sound of his laughter brought the ponies and goats from a nearby thicket. Thin as rails, their coats white with hoarfrost, the animals limped into the clearing, bringing with them two newborn kids which had, miraculously, survived. In spite of the shortage of fodder, the birth of the kids would ensure a supply of milk sufficient to lie easy on human stomachs shrivelled from a long starvation. He looked to the two who, wrapped in their blankets, now sat upright, the colour returning to their faces, the painful sensation to their limbs.

Silva clapped his hands for joy above his head, as he did when dancing. He nodded to George. 'Time to wake the rest of 'em, brother! What say you go first to rouse 'em, while I bring in the doe we trapped before we fell sick, and Coralina goes for firewood and water?'

George said, 'But you've taken the heaviest jobs for yourselves. Why don't I fetch in the doe — ?' and then he saw the dread in the faces of his wife and her cousin, and he recalled the reputation of this place, and the reluctance of the gypsies to approach, never mind to touch, the newly dead. And so it was George who ventured where others were afraid to go. He who brought out his mother and her children, emaciated but still breathing, and laid them close to the fire. Next came Coralina's three sisters and their husbands and babies, and a few more distant relatives whose hold on life was still frail. He committed the unpardonable sin of burning yet another flat-cart, and watched the stirring of those frozen limbs, the eyes flicker open, the faces turn towards the flames, their gaze focused onto life. He found the dead lying side by side in a single bender. Each bony body was wrapped in its own blanket.

The grandparents of Silva and Coralina, and her parents, Silence and Lura, had perished together.

It was Georgie's first experience of death, but he recognised its truth by the special silence of those gray-wrapped bundles. He had no fear of the unburied dead, he felt only the aching void inside him which, he thought vaguely, must be sorrow. He hunkered down beside them and muttered an incoherent prayer.

When Silva and Coralina came back into the *tan* he saw how they looked uneasily from one bender to another, and then to the survivors who sat huddled at the fire. There was no need to tell them who had died.

And now began a time George rarely spoke of.

They were a people who could not function without a leader. Fever and starvation, combined with unprecedented cold, had sapped their collective wills. Together with their superstitious terror, their belief that the spirits of the dead sat with them in the clearing, it was small wonder that the goat's milk curdled on their tongues, the roasted doe-meat would not pass their throats; that they sat unmoving and silent through the days and nights.

Georgie, unhampered by such fears, ate and drank and felt his blood run warm and strong again, his strength returned. He dared not sacrifice another flat-cart. He bullied and chivvied his brothers-in-law and Silva into bringing logs and woodchips, anything that would burn and keep life in the remaining Lees and Lovells. But the fire once stoked, Silva and the men would return to their motionless vigil, still weak and listening for the voices of their dead who called to them from some uncharted road.

Meanwhile, the bodies needed to be decently disposed of, the rites of passing must be observed. George looked from one mute male face to another, and settled finally on his mother Estralita as his only hope. He went to her, took her hands in his and called her 'mother' for the first time. He begged her to help him; asked her to come up from the dark place into which she had fallen and consider her small children. He held the cup of warmed goat's milk to her lips, persuaded her to take some meat broth. Only when he saw recognition in her eyes did he dare to speak about Silence and Lura, Elias and Sara, and the burial which could no longer be delayed.

It is said that 'the hour will provide the man'.

George Barnacle, hitherto considered by the Rom to be an inept and blundering fool, now seized the moment and redeemed himself in all eyes. Especially those of Coralina.

With the elders dead, and without a leader, they would surely by now have succumbed to that sickness of the mind and soul which kills as certainly as any fever.

It was George who stood up among them, who shouted and harangued. There could be no burial before the melt, Silva told him. The ground was iron-hard, and would be for a long time.

But pits had already been dug, George reminded him, and one was a particularly large trap, which would easily take four bodies; and such a burial would mean that their loved ones could remain together.

It was this final sentiment which won the day.

Slowly, reluctantly, the men allowed themselves to be lured away from the fire, and to lay decently to rest the most loved and respected of their people.

In the spring of that year an east wind howled up from the ocean, twisting the trees which edged the shoreline into deformities never intended by nature. Perhaps the shock of the tortured trees should have prepared Georgie Barnacle for the greater alarm he was to feel at the sight of the great waters, just visible beyond the little cove. But nothing he had seen or heard since leaving his home village could equal the shock he felt on witnessing for the first time those vast wastes of heaving grayness.

He stood next to Silva, unable to move or speak.

Silva raised his hand and pointed. 'Well then,' he whispered, 'there 'tis, just like I always told thee. That's the end of the world, Manju. A body can't go no further than this without falling off the edge.'

George at once moved several paces back from the incoming tide. Not wishing to show fear, he put a growl into his voice. 'I don't see no edge,' he muttered.

'Course you don't! But 'tis out there all the same, just beyond the sandbar. I heard sailors tell about it. There's a great big dip underneath the water. A man comes upon

553

it sudden-like. He is sailing along all happy in his little boat, and then, *dordi!* He reaches a deep, deep place what goes down and down, and has no bottom to it. Sunk ships is never found again, out there. Nor sailors neither.'

'Why for have you brought me to this place?' George asked.

Silva laughed. ' 'Twill make a good tale for thee to tell thy grandchildren. That thou hast stood at the world's edge.'

George looked away from the water and back towards the mist of tender green that trembled on the forest trees. 'To get grand-children,' he said bitterly, 'a man must first have children.'

'Thou hast a young wife,' Silva said softly, 'and 'tis the springtime of the year.'

'She will not have me.'

'Not now, she won't. Not in this *tan* where the spirits of our lost ones still sit with us around the fire each night. But away from here it will all be different.'

'You mean that I should leave and take her with me?'

There was desperation now in Silva's face and voice. 'Go quickly, Manju! If thou wilt keep Coralina safe from the militia, then move out from the *tan* and go back to Ashkeepers. Let the people of that place bear witness that the stealing of Roehampton's child had naught to do with thee and thy wife.'

'But they already know that Coralina had naught to do with it. Your camp was searched, your people were beaten and the child not found.'

Silva paced some steps away from George, and even as he walked the encroaching tide wiped out his footfalls. He turned back, and the agony in his face could no longer be ignored. 'Roehampton's son has been with our company since a few hours after we pulled out of Ashkeepers.'

George stared at him bemused, and then the full meaning of Silva's words seemed to burst behind his eyes. 'You lie,' he shouted. 'You are all stories and tall tales. Silence Lee would never have took such a great risk.'

Silva said, 'The man had no choice in the matter. Our only safe place at the time was to over-winter in the deepest forest, and where would we have found fodder for our beasts, meal and flour for our bread and porridge? Hast thou never wondered, Manju, in these past months, where the full food sacks come from? We left Ashkeepers all unexpected and without provisions, and Silence's only care was for his own.'

'I saw no child delivered to you, no sacks of vittals.'

Silva smiled. 'Cast your mind back to that journey. Remember the flat-cart that cast its wheel? How Silence was obliged to lag behind the rest of us while it was mended? It was then that delivery was made.'

George turned his face into the wind. He gazed out across the terrible waters, and believed at last that this was indeed the world's end. Fearful of the answer he asked, 'Who brought this delivery to Silence?'

'A cousin of thy patron, the Lady Pennina.'

'And how long do you think you can hide the boy?'

'Forever if needs be. He is as dark as any of our own *chavvies*. He will learn our ways, our style of speaking. Estralita will see to all of that, and Pennina Roehampton will pay well to keep him hidden.'

'He is in my mother's care?'

'Of course. From the very beginning her ladyship asked special that the *chavvie* should be kept with Estralita.'

George felt the wet sands shift beneath his feet. So many mysteries and secrets, and he not considered worthy to be privy to any of it, even though he had wed Coralina, and Estralita Lovell claimed him as her own. His thoughts darted back and forth until his head ached. He remembered the dead ones who had perished in the great frost; those old and wise ones he had been obliged to bury single-handed because their closest kin feared to touch them. He thought about the places, left empty each evening at the fireside, so that the spirits of the newly-dead might join their kin.

He looked at the shoreline trees, their bent trunks and twisted branches, and knew that he would never understand the Rom. For the sake of his sanity he must leave this place, and soon.

With his back turned on Silva he muttered, 'And Coralina? Will she come with me when I go?'

There was a stillness and a silence, and then the reluctant answer. 'Ask her.'

A soft warm rain fell on that morning when they left the *tan*. It washed away the last stubborn patches of snow and ice, and brought colour back into the forest. Coralina walked beside the donkey, George led the pony which pulled the flat-cart. They had journeyed for some miles, heads bent and silent, when he called a halt so that they might eat and drink. He found it painful to look directly at her. He was not sure if the wetness of her face was due to rain or tears. As they sat beneath a beech tree the gray clouds parted. A sudden shaft of sunlight fell across them; its heat was so strong that the wet clothes steamed upon their bodies.

George said, 'You don't have to come further with me, if you can't bear it. I know it is hard for you to leave your family.'

She spoke, her head averted, her voice so quiet that he strained to hear. 'My close family are all dead, save my sisters, and they have their husbands and babies. My place is with thee. We are man and wife, Manju.'

They were still travelling in deep forest where no birds sang. The silence had its own sound, like a great shout in his heart.

He turned to face her then where she sat in pale spring sunlight. The soaked blouse and skirt had moulded to the sweet curves of her body as if they were a second skin. He had never seen her so revealed, not even on the night at Roehampton's, when she danced with Silva. There was an artlessness about her now, an innocence which fired his senses. His gaze moved slowly over the downcast almond eyes, her delicate mouth and nervous fingers, the faint sheen on her coppery skin. His breath caught at the proud tilt of her small sleek head, the black and glossy braids looped beneath her ear lobes, from which hung thick copper rings. The shaft of sunlight broadened, the air grew warmer. Now that he was about to leave the forest, George became aware of the beauty of it. The sadness of autumn, the white cruelty of winter was hard to remember on this sweet mild day; drifts of many-coloured flowers bloomed where lately snow and ice had lain.

Clumsily, because this was his first time and he had never done anything so daring, he began to strip away the damp garments, first from her body and then his own.

He had imagined in the dark nights of winter that her skin would be an all-over tawny colour, the same dark hue as that of her face and her bare arms and legs. Now he saw that beginning at her shoulders and down to her smooth knees, she was the same shade of soft cream as a young doe. He turned towards her, and the contrast between the startling whiteness of his body and the coppery tints of hers was a matter of wonder to them both. He pulled the pins from her coiled braids and she moved her head so that the curtain of hair fell about her shoulders.

She pulled him close and he felt the nervous tremor of her body as his skin touched hers.

'I should have made time,' she whispered, 'to fix up the bed-of-honour. I waited all winter for you, Manju, but you never took me.'

The light greens of new leaves trembled down the groves of trees; the blue of clearing skies hung above them. He patted the springy green moss on which they lay. 'This'll do for us,' he told her. Now that the time had come they were uncertain, still shy and fearful of each other.

'Silva?' he asked her.

'No,' she said. 'Never. Thou art my one and only love.'

George felt as though the weight of the world had rolled from his shoulders, and with it went all his hesitation.

# Nina

Imogen phoned. 'Now I know,' she began, 'that you don't much care for the pictures — ?'

I braced myself for the invitation to watch *One Hundred and One Dalmatians* or *James and the Giant Peach*.

My daughter is an uncritical cinema-goer. 'It's *Evita*,' she wheedled down the phone. 'Lloyd Webber's music and starring Madonna and Jimmy Nail. I'm sure you'll like it.'

Well, even I had heard of Madonna, who hasn't? The name of Jimmy Nail meant nothing to me, but in view of my limited knowledge of the pop scene this was no reflection on his fame.

'I'll treat you to tea afterwards,' she promised. 'I think it's time we had a serious chat.'

I held firm to my memory of Primrose and her accusation that I did not appreciate my daughter. 'That will be very nice, dear,' I said. 'When are you planning to go.'

'Tomorrow,' she said.

The mention of a serious chat sounded threatening. I could feel a mood of truculence coming on. I resigned myself to a wasted afternoon of gazing at the antics of a sex-goddess.

As it turned out, I loved every minute of *Evita*!

I was entranced by the music, the trite but oh-so-true lyrics of Tim Rice. 'Don't cry for me,' sang the unexpectedly sweet voice, 'the truth is I never left you.'

And we don't, do we? We never really go away from the people and the places where we found our first impressions of the world.

The cinema café had red plush armchairs and little dark oak tables. The lighting was so muted that it was difficult to read my daughter's face. She ordered tea. I waited for her comment on the film. She fidgeted with her purse, and gazed at the far wall.

I said at last, and irritably, for *Evita* had been her choice, not mine, 'Well — did you enjoy it?'

She poured tea and pushed a plate of rainbow-coloured cakes in my direction. 'You certainly did,' she said. 'I've never known you so riveted. I spoke to you twice and you didn't hear me.' She bit into a lurid yellow jam tart, chewed and swallowed, then drank her tea very slowly as if marking time. Involuntarily I felt my spine brace, my stomach muscles tighten.

So what was it to be? My hand went to my hair which had grown a little shaggy. I looked downwards and saw to my horror that I was wearing brown shoes with a black suit.

But Imogen had quite other matters on her mind.

Apropos of absolutely nothing she said, 'You never talk about your childhood, do you, Mother?'

I stirred my tea and took a burning mouthful. I could shrug quite as eloquently as Madonna. 'Nothing to tell,' I said. But I knew from the tense set of her shoulders that this was no idle enquiry.

'You must have had a childhood,' she persisted. 'Everybody does. Most people's mothers I know have the odd baby photo, anecdotes from schooldays, memories of their own parents.'

The scalding tea lodged in my throat, almost causing me to choke. I swallowed painfully. I said firmly, 'Well, I don't.'

She snatched a second jam tart from the plate and began to mash it with her fingers.

Amazed, I watched her lick the bright green jam from the palm of her hand.

'Is it,' she asked, 'because you didn't have a mother that you've always refused to talk about the past?'

In moments of stress I tend to be unsuitably facetious. 'Don't be silly,' I laughed. 'Everybody has to have a mother. It's a pity that some easier method of reproduction has not yet been invented, but until the scientists come up with a simpler process — ?'

She thumped the table top with her clenched fist, in a rare display of temper. She said aggressively, 'You know damn well what I mean.'

Of course I knew exactly what she meant, what she wanted of me. But I turned the question back upon her. 'Who told you I didn't have a mother?'

'My father told me.'

Her mention of Jack sent a pang of anguish through me, made me take evasive action. I began to look around; it was to this cinema I had come on those blissful afternoons when one shilling and ninepence saved from the housekeeping allowance had bought me a few hours of magic. In those wartime days the café had boasted an American-style soda fountain. I remembered sitting in a wicker chair beside a glass-topped table and drinking banana milk-shake, feeling sophisticated and grown-up. The Art Deco style of the cinema was still to be seen in the yellow and green stained glass of the long windows.

'Are you listening to me?'

Her voice became shrill; it rose on a note of near-hysteria. People were staring at us. I felt a coldness settle on me. This was the moment I had always dreaded.

I turned towards her intending to tell her to be quiet, but the words stuck in my throat. Her features were contorted so that I hardly recognised her. And now I saw my daughter as if for the first time, not as I had always viewed her, as an extension of myself, a person I took as much for granted as the air I breathed, but as a woman in her own right, one who merited respect, considera-tion. One who deserved answers.

We drove back to the Toll House in what can only be described as an explosive si-lence. In order to calm her I had pointed out that the cinema café was hardly the place for painful revelations of a family na-ture. On a promise that I would talk to her on reaching my house, she consented to go to the ladies' room and wash her jammy fingers, and behave like the calm and controlled daughter I had brought her up to be.

As for my own calm and control, I could feel it slipping away as I poured a stiff brandy for myself and a glass of that revolting Coca-Cola that Imogen insists on drinking when she is driving. My thoughts twisted and scampered and sought escape routes, but there was nowhere left to hide. I thought about all the years of deliberate evasion; of my insistence that life for this branch of the Franklin family had began with Imogen's conception, and all that went before was of no consequence; not worth talking about.

But Jack had talked about it. Not knowing what, or how much he had told her, now put me at a disadvantage. Seated face to face, across the coffee table which held Barnacle's book and my reading glasses, I saw her waiting stillness. I took a sip of my unwatered brandy. I said, 'So what did your father — ?'

'Not much,' she interrupted swiftly. 'Hardly anything at all.' Her voice was still pitched on that high note of incipient hysteria. I had never seen Imogen in this state, had not guessed her capable of so much anger. Each waited for the other to speak. The silence was unnerving. And then she reached for her handbag, that capacious, unfashionable bag I had given her at Christmas, and which she had said she liked even though she didn't.

She pulled from it a single sheet of cheap lined paper, and laid it between us on top of Barnacle's book.

'I think,' she said quietly, control regained, 'you owe me some sort of explanation, Mother.'

For one stupid, heart-stopping moment I thought the note might be some sort of threat concerning John. I actually said, 'If this is a ransom demand, why have I not been told about it, and why are you wasting time asking me about my family history?'

'It's not a ransom demand. It doesn't concern John.' She paused. 'You're really hung up, aren't you mother, on this business of stolen and murdered babies. You had poor Fran in a state of panic when he was first born, with all your warnings, and obsessions.'

She laid a hand on the note and pushed it closer to me. 'Perhaps you would like to explain to me now what this is all about.'

If sensations can really be felt through contact with inanimate objects, then that bit of paper scorched my fingers. The single sentence, printed large in uneven letters, burned into my brain.

YOUR SISTER WAS MURDERED AND
YOUR MOTHER DID IT.

I felt the blood drain from my face. The
room seemed to sway and shimmer and then
disappear from view. I heard myself protesting that I was perfectly all right while Imogen poured brandy down my throat and
slapped a cold wet dishcloth across my forehead. When the drama had subsided, and
with mugs of hot coffee in our hands, we
were both apologetic.

I was even able to reassure her that the
shock she had given me was beneficial, just
what was needed to uncork the bottle and
let the genie out.

'But where do I begin?' I asked her. 'It's
a very long story.'

She was gentler now, but still determined.
'Tell me first about your parents.'

'What do you already know?' Even now
I could not help prevaricating.

'Dad said that you and he both lost your
mothers on the same night?'

'His mother died. Mine ran off with an
encyclopaedia salesman.' And so, on that
winter's evening, I began to tell my daughter
all those things I had taken so much care

to keep from her. Jack, it seems, had parried Imogen's childhood questions with the explanation that the loss of my mother in childhood had so devastated me that just to talk about the past would make me very ill. He had told her that his father had been a farmer, mine a doctor. He had been careful never to let slip the name and location of Ashkeepers.

She had been close to Jack, trusted him, had asked him no more awkward questions. But her view of me had changed. She no longer saw me as her natural protector but rather as someone to be feared, to be propitiated and indulged. She began at the age of eight to watch for signs of the depression which Jack had said would settle on me if I was reminded of the past.

A burden had been laid upon my child which she so obviously still carried. I cursed myself, silently, for the self-centred insensitive fool that I had been.

I tapped the scrap of paper which lay between us. I said, 'There is no truth in this. You know that, don't you?'

'Are you telling me I never had a sister?'

'Not in your lifetime. She was our first-born child.'

'Her name?'

'She didn't have one. She was stolen from

us before we had decided —'

I had never wept in my daughter's presence, but now the tears poured from me and there was nothing I could do to halt them. She knelt beside me, put her arms around me, and gradually, with many pauses, I told Imogen those things I should have told her long ago.

There were times in the telling when I faltered and could not continue; long silences during which she watched me steadily but asked no questions. From time to time she went to the kitchen and brewed strong tea which we drank hot and sweet from old chipped mugs which I had meant to throw away. She had shown Niall the unsigned note; he knew that she planned to confront me with it. He was not surprised when she phoned to say that she was at the Toll House and stopping over.

I talked until the first grey light edged around the curtains. When I told her about her own birth, I was able to explain at last the confusion of my feelings, how I had felt that she was a miracle I did not deserve, but at the same time feared to love too fiercely, lest she also should in some way be stolen from me.

It was only then that I dared to look up

into her face and found understanding and compassion.

'Why didn't you tell me all this long ago?' she whispered.

'Jack wanted to. We argued about it. But it's not the sort of tale you tell to a child, and later on — well, it no longer seemed important.'

'Ah, come on,' she said gently. 'It's always been the most important thing in your whole life. Time stopped for you on that night she — she was taken from this room. Even though you had another child, then a grand-child, and now a great-grandchild, still you came back to Ashkeepers, to the very house where it all happened. It's still a great dark shadow that looms over every-thing you do and think. It's robbed you of your life, Mum, and in a way it's robbed me too. I lost a sister on that night — but I was also deprived of a mother.' Her voice became abrupt with old hurts. 'I believed all my life that you didn't love me; even worse I believed that you actually disliked me.'

'You know now that isn't true.'

'Yes. I know it now. But it's not enough. In your heart you are still the same person, rooted so deeply in the past that you can't enjoy the present.'

'I can't change that, Imogen.'

'But you can. You can try to find out who took your child. What was the point of coming back here, if all you do is walk the dog and read old Barnacle's damned book?' She leaned forward in her chair. 'That dead crow on your doorstep, the note accusing you of murder, both of them spiteful and nasty, and bordering on hatred. Has it never crossed your mind that you could be in danger? Somebody doesn't want you living back here in this house, in Ashkeepers village. Somebody out there still sees you as a threat.'

I said, 'But it was all so long ago, and the people who knew me then are my contemporaries, in their seventies and eighties. Old codgers.'

'Supposing,' said Imogen, 'just supposing the person who stole her — my sister — is still living in the village? Supposing your baby survived and was brought up as their own daughter, that she now has children of her own? Wouldn't that be reason enough for the kidnapper to fear you? Have you never thought that when you walk or shop in the village you might be looking at the faces of your daughter and grandchildren? Supposing you recognised a face and began to ask questions?'

I said, 'I've studied young faces sometimes, on city streets —'

'No, Mum, she wasn't taken by city people.' Her tone was soft now, persuasive. 'It had to be someone with local knowledge. Don't you see? This was no opportunist kidnap. Remember how it was when you and Dad were young here? Homesteaders' Valley had not been built then. This house stood alone among fields at the end of a narrow lane. What passing motorist ever drove down it? How many casual callers ever stopped here? What stranger would have known that Dad was working late that night, that the door was always on the latch, that a very young baby lay sleeping in her pram just handy for the taking?'

'What are you saying?'

She paused, hesitated. 'The city police had decided from the outset that you had killed your child and hidden the body?'

I nodded.

'No one else was ever suspected?'

'I don't know. The state I was in, I would hardly have noticed. Jack was ruled out almost at once. I imagine other people would have been asked if they had seen anything suspicious. I doubt that many people knew that Jack and I had moved in here. The Franklins never discussed their affairs with village people.'

'So tell me,' she asked, 'exactly who had visited you and Dad before the baby was taken?'

'Only family,' I said. I reached for the anonymous note. I said, 'Did it come by post?'

'No,' she said. 'It was pushed through Fran's letter-box. There was no name on the envelope, just printed words — FRANCESCA GIVE THIS TO YOUR MOTHER.

She took the note from me and put it in her handbag. 'This was written by someone who knows you,' she said. 'Somebody who knows me, and every member of our family.'

I stood at the garden gate, shivering a little in the damp of the February morning. I listened to the sound of Imogen's car as she drove away towards Nether Ash. I had offered her breakfast, but neither of us had the energy to cook or the appetite to eat it. I turned back into the house, and Roscoe gazed reproachfully at me from his bed by the kitchen stove. I stood at the sink, splashed cold water on my face and dried it on a kitchen towel. I had promised Imogen that I would sleep, knowing as I said the words that I would not. I reached for Roscoe's lead and my boots and quilted raincoat. I left the house and began to walk very slowly towards the lane which led up to Sunshine Farm.

Little had changed in this part of Ashkeepers. Franklins held fast to what was theirs. Roscoe, in a state of delirious excitement, snuffled and rooted in hedgebottoms, investigated tree trunks. I leaned on a five-barred gate and willed the tightness of my mind to ease. I thought of all the repercussions that would come from my night-time confessions. Had I chosen the right words to tell my daughter all the things I wanted her to hear? And what would be our relationship in future?

There was Fran, who would also need to know the whole story; and who would tell her? It would have to be Imogen, for I could not.

The problems were endless.

I tried to push away the questions Imogen had asked. What could she know about such things; she had not been there on that night. But a voice in my head was saying that hers was a fresh mind, a keen intelligence, a unique view of an old mystery, and that I should listen to her. Family, I had told her. Only family had known the habits and details of Jack's life and mine.

I called to Roscoe and reluctantly walked on. When the farmhouse came in view I saw that it too had remained unchanged. Alan Franklin must long since have come into his inheritance. I remembered his resentment and jealousy of Jack, the bitter hostility of Dinah his wife. It was a part of the family saga I had seen fit to conceal from Imogen. Even now, after all these years, I still felt a pang of sorrow when I recalled their inexplicable attitude towards us.

I had told Imogen about her great-grandmother Franklin who loved Jack and me, and believed in and supported us through all our troubles. In a family where negative emotions were considered normal, my daughter needed only to learn about the loving members.

After one long look at Sunshine Farm I turned back into the lane, before my presence could be challenged by the present owner. I was tired, but it was an exhaustion which had gone far beyond sleep. One foot placed carefully in front of the other and I came slowly down into the village. Once level with the church I veered without thinking towards the lych-gate.

The Franklin family burial plot lay in a distant yew-shaded corner of the churchyard. I made my way along the sloping mossy path, towards the ornate Victorian marble headstones with their weeping angels and obese cherubs. A little to one side were the more recent and less flamboyant black and grey marble markers, and a single head-stone, rough-hewn from a block of granite.

'Made to last, that one,' said a voice, and I had a sudden uneasy prickling sensation at the back of my neck. He must have fol-lowed me down the path. I turned and there he was, Jimmy Luxton, sexton. He nodded towards the granite slab. 'Made to last,' he repeated, 'which is more than you can say for the chap who lies underneath it.'

I focused my gaze on the gold lettering.

ALAN FRANKLIN. AGED 51.
BELOVED HUSBAND OF DINAH.
DEAR FATHER OF LUCY.
REMEMBERED ALWAYS.

'She's always down here, you know, that Dinah! Every day, no matter what the weather. Sent her right out of her mind it did, losing the both of them inside the same year.'

I made a swift about-turn and tried to conceal from Luxton my sense of profound shock. I walked quickly back towards the lych-gate, but he was right behind me, his face bobbing at my shoulder, his penetrating whisper causing me to tremble.

'Funny old business that was. Some called it kidnap, some called it murder; but I expect you remember it better than I do. Well, you would, wouldn't you, it being your baby that got mislaid.' He made a sound that might have been a chuckle. 'I heard that you and Jack moved up to the city. Biggest mistake you ever made, Nina. You should have come to me, there's a lot I could have told you. But perhaps you forgot that Jimmy Luxton misses nothing that goes on in Ashkeepers. Remember school, Nina? How the boys used to pay me a halfpenny if I'd tell 'em the colour of the big girls' knickers?'

I rounded on him then. 'Oh, I remember you, and you haven't changed. You're just as loathsome now as you were then. If you continue to pester me, I'll report you to the constable.'

He laughed. 'Still the hoity-toity lady, eh? Well, being the doctor's daughter didn't help you back then, did it? As for going to the constable, I wouldn't do that if I were you. Oh no, I wouldn't do that, Nina!'

Giddy from exhaustion I lay on my bed that afternoon meaning only to sleep for an hour or two. But when I awoke it was to a new day; the rain had ceased and a sharp frost sparkled on the fields and hedges. I went down to the kitchen, opened the door and released a desperate Roscoe into the garden. I made a cafetière of coffee and carried it into the sitting room. I felt weak and strange, as if I had suffered a long debilitating illness, and this was my first day up, on my feet again and moving.

I sipped the strong hot coffee and the mists in my mind began to clear. I found myself snatching at random thoughts but failing to grasp them. Jimmy Luxton. As a boy there had been nothing he would not do to attract attention to himself. Yesterday's performance in the churchyard could just have been the old Jimmy, still playing his stupid games. Alan Franklin, who was not, as I had imagined him to be, the master of Sunshine Farm come at last into his inheritance, but a name on a gravestone, visited daily by his widow. And Dinah herself, who according to Luxton had lost her husband and daughter in the same year. What was the girl's name, Lucy? There should, I thought vaguely, have been another headstone in the Franklin plot, since father and daughter had not been buried together. Perhaps the other stone had been there, and the arrival of Luxton had distracted me? And then there was Imogen who believed that the kidnapper had been a local person.

There was a serious flaw in her reasoning, but in my present state I could not quite grasp exactly what it was.

I lay back in my chair and the musty acrid smell from Barnacle's book seemed especially strong this morning. I lifted it from the table, placed the book across my knees and began to read.

Georgie Barnacle talked often and optimistically about the future, he made plans and dreamed dreams which bewildered Coralina. She wished with all her heart that he was less determined, more easy-going, more like the men of her own family. She had watched him secretly through all the long and bitter winter, had come to know his heart and mind. She accepted now his need to live within walls and under the thatch of a house roof. She had also witnessed him in the great freeze, when the Lees and Lovells had feared to so much as look upon the faces of their departed loved ones, and she had seen how fearlessly George prepared their dead for burial, carried the bodies to their grave, and said a prayer across them. Even Silva had been bound to allow that George was a brave man in some departments.

It was evening when they came into Somerset. Coralina would have lingered in the forest in these mild sweet days of early April, but George was impatient to reach Taunton Town. It was Coralina who chose a safe pitch in a copse beside a river, she who cut fresh hazel wands to build the bender tent. George fetched dry wood for the fire, and filled the water cans, but he would never master the skills required to survive the roaming way of life. It was lucky for them that the dog had caught a fine fat rabbit that morning. While she cleaned and skinned it and set it to roast upon the spit, George sat beside her and told her again about his great plans.

The future for Coralina encompassed no more than the next hour, the next meal. For a people whose lives were dependent on the changing seasons and the weather, the good-will of farmers and the temper of militia sergeants, it made no sense to look any further forward. When George talked about tomorrow and the day beyond that one, her mind had a tendency to wander. It was only when he pulled a length of twine from his breeches' pocket, and she saw the attached gold ring glinting in the firelight, that she began properly to listen to his words.

'Where you get that from?' she asked him.

He smiled, gratified by her full attention.

'I once done a favour for a gentleman. I tended his wounds when he was hurt. He said if I should ever need his help I could find him at the spring assizes in Taunton.' He loosened the knotted twine, released the ring and slipped it onto his longest finger. 'I shall need to sell this first,' he said. He looked down at his ragged clothes, his bare feet. 'Can't go looking for Sir Roehampton looking like a —' He paused, needing to choose the next word with some caution. 'Looking like a poacher.'

'And where 'ull you sell it?'

'I might go to an inn, or a shop that buys such trinkets.'

Coralina laughed. 'You don't know much, George, do you, when it comes to bartering? You go into the town barefoot and wearing that much gold and you'll be took for a thief, or else robbed and murdered.'

'So what shall I do?'

'I got some family, cousins and uncles, pitched not too far from this place. They'll give us a fair price for the ring when I tell them you're my husband.'

Later that day Coralina sold the ring at a good price; and in a shop in a nearby village George bought for himself a pair of good broadcloth breeches and a jacket, two linen shirts and a fine pair of leather boots. For

Coralina he chose a simple gown of grey and white sprigged cotton, and a white cambric bonnet which concealed completely her dark braids and distinctive copper earrings. When she refused absolutely to put boots on her feet, he persuaded her into a pair of soft leather slippers.

'Just while we show ourselves around the town,' he wheedled. 'You can't go into the courthouse looking like a —'

'A dirty gyppo? A vagrant — a rogue — a vagabond?' For the first time ever he heard a sharp note in her voice. 'Don't fret yourself, husband, it was I chose to come with you. I won't never bring shame on you.' Sadly she tweaked at the gown and bonnet. 'Look at me now, all done up like a milksop *gorgio* maiden! Ah, *dordi*, how glad I am my dear ones are so far away, and never likely to see what a sorry pass Coralina have come to.' It was to be the only time in their lives together that she would reveal to him her mixed emotions. And because she was not a scold or shrewish, George took heed of her words, did not forget them, and from that day forward he was more mindful of her feelings.

The Taunton assizes were held in April. The people of the town regarded this yearly assembling of judiciary and prisoners as being a rare brand of entertainment which would in the fullness of time be bound to culminate in several public hangings and, if they were lucky, that most thrilling show of all, the burning of a wicked woman at the stake. Shop fronts and signboards were repainted. Hotels and lodging houses were refurbished to house the visiting judges, counsellors and attorneys.

George and Coralina, having bathed in the river and arrayed themselves in their new fine clothing, set out on the flint road which led down to Taunton. As they came into the town many eyes turned to gaze upon them, for they made a handsome couple. George, with his great physique and shock of red curling hair, made the perfect foil for Coralina's slender darkness. As they walked under Castle Gate and paused on Castle Green, Coralina said, 'Leave me here, George. Let me sit on the grass and wait for you. I will surely die of fright if I must go into that great house of cold stone.'

'I cannot leave you here. We must stay together. I need to show milord that I am wed and settled in my life.' He took her hand and led her up the steps of the assizes; they came into a vast press of jostling people; he could feel the tremors that ran through her body. They came into the public galleries where the crowd of spectators was already great. By the use of his shoulders and elbows George made a way for both of them towards the front, where the view of the courtroom was uninterrupted. Coralina, eyes downcast, did not dare to look about her, but George, confident of Roehampton's goodwill, gazed boldly around him, familiarising himself with the already seated judiciary and the court officials.

Silence was called for, and the rabble in the public gallery came gradually to order. The first prisoner was brought in, a boy of fourteen years, a skinny ragged urchin who wept without cease, and was accused of stealing the Mayor's silver cup.

'Are you guilty of this crime?' George recognised the voice of Pennina's uncle.

'No, your honour,' sobbed the youth.

'If it please your lordship, he was found with the said cup underneath his jacket,' said a turnkey.

Roehampton passed sentence without hesitation. 'Seven years transportation to the Americas. No appeal.'

The next prisoner to appear was a man of eighteen years, who stood accused of the rape of an eight-year-old girl. An account of the crime was given by the mother of the girl, and confirmed by the child. The rapist admitted to his sin, and was sentenced to be hanged; again without hope of appeal, and within the week.

There followed in quick succession two further sentences of hanging. One for the theft of a horse, and the other for highway robbery.

The next case to be heard was that of a young woman who, when accused of poisoning her husband, protested her innocence while tearing at her hair and clothing, and weeping loudly. The only evidence against her rested with her brother-in-law, who clearly disliked her. She was ordered to be burned at the stake, the sentence to be carried out within the month on the Green of her home village.

But in her case at least it seemed that the judiciary were prepared to show some mercy. Her plea to be allowed to appeal against sentence was granted.

The morning's business had so far been conducted at a fast clip. Now there was a lull; a hushed excitement rippled through the spectators in the public gallery. By the remarks of those who stood nearest to him, George concluded that this last case of the day was to be one of vast importance.

A door slammed, there was a rattling of chains; a murmur which became a roar erupted through the building as two prisoners, a man and a woman, hands bound, legs shackled, were brought in to stand before Sir Jeffery Roehampton.

George felt the blood drain from his head and face. Coralina moved closer to him and held on tightly to his hand. ' 'Tis the Lady Pennina,' she whispered, 'and her lover.'

'Yes,' said George, 'and the judge is Pennina's uncle, and no friend of hers.'

The charges against the couple were many, and announced by the clerk in ringing tones.

'Here stand accused on this fifth day of April the Honourable Hugo Fitzgibbon, gentleman, of Exeter in Devon, and his partner in evil, the former Lady Pennina Roehampton, known latterly as Mrs Lambton, wife of the toll-keeper Ezra Lambton of the village of Ashkeepers. The crimes of this pair are all the more reprehensible in view of their gentle birth and high position in society. The least of those crimes being robbery of stagecoach passengers travelling on the King's highway, and of trespass and sundry other thefts and deceptions. But we are not concerned this day with minor matters.' The clerk drew breath, raised his head and stared directly into the faces of the two accused.

'Pennina Lambton — Hugo Fitzgibbon. You stand before this court to answer charges of the unlawfull taking away and likely murder of a male infant, name of Neville Roehampton. The said child being torn from the arms of his nursemaid and removed from his home by Hugo Fitzgibbon, aided and abetted by Pennina Lambton. The same Hugo Fitzgibbon having also, in order to ensure her silence, wickedly stabbed to death Emily Green, the infant's nursemaid, since Fitzgibbon's face was known to her, he being a family member and frequent visitor to the castle.'

George looked down on the pale drawn faces of Pennina and Hugo. His body felt numb, as if turned to stone, but his mind raced feverishly, foreseeing the possibilities of danger to Coralina and her family should Pennina seek to save herself by implicating the Lees and Lovells in her crime. But surely she would never do that. He bent his head to Coralina's urgent whisper. 'This will be a bad day for us, husband, if that woman should confess to the judge — where she left the boy last autumn. Mayhap she will say that 'twas my people what took him in the first place?'

George said, 'She would not be so wicked! Whatever else she might have done, she is still a highborn lady and truthful.'

They stood together in a little wooden box which concealed their leg-fetters, but afforded a clear view of their upper bodies, hands and faces. Hugo had lost his high-and-mighty airs, his ruddy complexion. Pennina was thin and sickly looking. Both had the look of animals caught in the jaws of an iron trap; it was almost possible, George thought, to smell their fear. He remembered Pennina's kindness to him and felt a stab of pity for her.

The importance of the case was heightened by the blood relationship between accused and judge. There were other differences. Pennina and Hugo, unlike their needy fellow felons, were not called upon to state their own version of events, but relied upon a number of hired attorneys and counsellors to give evidence on their behalf. Protestations were made by lawyers of mistaken identity; and malice aforethought shown towards the accused by certain members of the Roehampton family. The judge grew ever more restive while listening to those long-winded statements, until at last, his patience exhausted, he called a halt to the proceedings.

'Bring Mrs Lambton to stand before me,' he roared. 'She shall speak for herself. As for that lampoon beside her, I have no wish to hear him.'

Pennina, escorted by a turnkey, came slowly forward. Her uncle spoke at first in a conversational, almost pleasant manner, leaning towards her across the bench, smiling at her.

'You may recall, madam, a certain morning last year when I came to see you at the Ashkeepers Toll House. I warned you then about your irregular way of life, and the dangers attendant upon it. You would have done well to heed my words.' He paused. 'I am giving you this chance to explain your part in the crimes of which you stand accused. But I warn you now, be truthful in what you tell me, madam. If you lie I will show you no mercy.'

Pennina looked out across the packed courtroom and then upwards to the public gallery. Her surprised gaze locked into that of Georgie Barnacle, and then took in the presence of Coralina at his side.

She lifted her right hand and pointed. She said in loud and ringing tones. 'You need look no further, my lord, for the guilty parties in this awful business. They stand together up there — the red-haired man and his gypsy trollop.'

There was a silence, and then a stamping of feet and a pandemonium of shouting. By the time order was restored in the courtroom, George and Coralina had already bean hustled below and stood arraigned before the judge.

'So,' said Roehampton to Pennina, in the same pleasant tone of voice, 'perhaps you will be good enough to tell us, Mrs Lambton, just how this young man, your former servant, comes to be guilty of the crimes of which you and Fitzgibbon stand accused.'

Pennina spoke up in a sincere voice. 'He was up at the castle on the night my half-brother was stolen, and so was his woman, the dancer Coralina. Between them they killed the nursemaid Emily Green and stole the child. On the following morning, George Barnacle, alarmed by the visit of the militia, confessed all to me and showed me the child hidden in my barn. At some time in the night the Lees came to the Toll House and took possession of the babe. I was very much afraid, a defenceless woman. There was nothing I could do to stop them. I asked the purpose of the abduction and was told that my father would soon be asked to pay a ransom for his son's safe return. That is the truth, my lord, although it pains me greatly to say it.'

Judge Roehampton feigned astonishment. 'A truly dramatic tale, lady! But I do not understand why, since you have known all this time of your half-brother's whereabouts, you chose to keep silent on the matter?'

'But these gypsies are dangerous people, sir! I dared not speak up lest I risk the child's safety.'

Roehampton smiled. 'You have a persuasive tongue, niece. But then you always had. How thoughtful of you to continue to consider the child's safety when your own neck is so close to the noose.'

The mockery in her uncle's voice enraged Pennina. She pointed a shaking finger towards the place where George and Coralina stood. 'Look at them!' she shouted. 'See how the guilt is writ plain on both their faces. Ask them where my half-brother is, and how he fares!'

The judge turned towards George. He asked in a level tone, 'Do you have knowledge of the whereabouts of Neville Roehampton?'

George, overawed by the grandness at close quarters of the curled wigs and the fine apparel of the court officials; and aghast at the treachery of Pennina, could not find his voice.

It was left to Coralina to speak up. She said in her husky tones, 'The babe is safe. It is true he is with my people, in the charge of my aunt Estralita, who loves him as if he were her own. But he was never in danger from us.'

'And how came the child into your aunt's care?'

'He was brought to us in the forest by Lady Pennina. She told us she feared for the little lordship's life, that he was in mortal danger, that there were those at the castle who would have him dead.'

'And did she say from whom the child was in this danger, and why?'

'Why, from your own self, my lord, since the late birth of a son to your older brother meant that you yourself could not now inherit the castle should your brother die.'

'Ah — !' The word was spoken on a long sigh. 'So now we have it all, the whole wicked tarradiddle.'

Pennina cried out. 'Do not listen to her, uncle! Can you not see? Under the modest calico and petticoats lurks a loose and evil woman; you are exchanging words with a gypsy trollop. They are all a pack of mongrels known for their fluency in lying! And

George Barnacle, my once faithful servant, has chosen to live with them and adopt their ways.'

'And you, dear niece, are noted for your adherence to the truth, are you? You have lied before. It is your habit to accuse others of theft and murder.' Roehampton slapped the flat of his hand upon the bench-top. 'Enough,' he roared, 'of this charade! Bring Ezra Lambton before us.'

Ezra came shuffling his way into the well of the courtroom. He looked old and broken and totally bereft, but he spoke in a strong voice and with conviction.

He told of the ever increasing lawlessness of Pennina and her cousins. He spoke of the night of celebration at the castle, when Hugo Fitzgibbon brought an infant back to the Toll House, concealed underneath his bloodstained cape; and the concealment of that same child in the hours that followed, and the token search of the house by the militia. He revealed how a young nursing mother and her babe had been brought to the Toll House for the express purpose of misleading the militiamen, and to provide a temporary wet nurse for the stolen infant Neville Roehampton.

In a voice which trembled, Ezra confessed to driving a cart into the forest later on that same day; a cart on which rode Pennina his wife, with the Roehampton child and many sacks of vittals.

He had heard his wife tell Silence Lee that the babe's life was in danger from certain relatives, and that she would return and reclaim him when the peril was past. Meanwhile, the Lees and Lovells should remain in the deep forest until such time as she judged it was safe for them to leave.

The judge gazed compassionately on Ezra ton. He said, 'So what think you now to your wife's accusation against George Barnacle? What say you, man, in the matter of these crimes?'

Ezra raised his head and spoke up, again in a strong voice. 'The woman Pennina lies, your lordship. The woman has lied since that accursed day when I first met her. She is at her most dangerous when she is sweetest. As for Barnacle and his wife, they are innocent of all crimes.'

No charges were brought against Ezra Lambton. Coralina and Georgie Barnacle were likewise free to go upon their way, although all three were instructed to wait upon the judge in his private room in the rear of the assize court, where he would later have matters to discuss with them which would be to their advantage.

Hugo Fitzgibbon was sentenced to be hanged by the neck until dead, for the murder of Emily Green and the theft from its parents of an infant child.

Pennina Lambton, for her complicity in these comes, was ordered to be burned alive, at the stake, on the Green of Ashkeepers village, at a time and date to be decided by her uncle, Sir Jeffery Roehampton.

# Nina

It was the morning when mothers collected their child benefit payments. I sidestepped prams and pushchairs on the narrow pavement beside the village post office. Groups of young mums stood laughing and chatting in the sunshine of that day in early May. Unintentionally they gave the impression of being a small select club, the membership of which was open only to those who possessed the necessary child.

The same exclusivity had operated in this village in the nineteen forties and fifties. I recalled how, fifty years ago, my pregnancy had gained me instant recognition among those of my generation in a similar condition. Even Dinah and I, who had not been bosom friends or even mere acquaintances, had instantly recognised each other, and discussed our swollen ankles and indigestion sitting on a bench on Ashkeepers Green. I thought about Imogen's conviction that the taking of her sister had been done by somebody with local knowledge. No opportunist kidnap that, she had said. What stranger would have known that Jack was working late that night, she had asked; or the front door on the latch? As she spoke I had sensed, but not pinned down, the flaw in Imogen's reasoning. Standing now among the village mothers and their babies, I knew exactly what that flaw was.

It would have been as impossible then as it was now to appear in public in this close-knit community with a newly acquired infant for which the requisite nine months of discomfort had not been duly observed and suffered.

Instant parenthood might of course have been claimed with adoption as the reason. But there would have been legal procedures beforehand, and the district nurse calling in on a regular basis to monitor a very young baby. I could not see how, if Imogen's theory was correct, and the taking of my child had been a local matter, an infant had suddenly been introduced into a gossipy, ever-watchful community, by a person or persons who had shown no previous signs of expecting such an addition to their household.

For no obvious reason, I began to think about Sorsha and her grandmother Estralita. I walked slowly across the Green to the benches where the very old men sat waiting for the pub to open. As I approached the benches, the doors of the Bird in Hand creaked back, and the wooden seats were swiftly vacated. I sat down, and the weariness of incipient depression settled on me. Perhaps I too should have galloped over to the pub with the octogenarians who displayed a turn of speed which shamed me. The group of young mothers and their prams and buggies slowly dispersed. The final pushchair to emerge from the post office door was wheeled by Sorsha. I half rose to intercept her and then thought better of it. What would I say? I had promised long ago to visit and had not kept that promise. She might well see my failure as a deliberate slight. I half hoped she had not seen me, that she would go straight back to Witches' Hollow, but there she was coming fast towards the benches where I sat.

She sat down beside me.

I said, 'I was just thinking about you.' I smiled to prove to her my thoughts were well intentioned.

'I know you was,' she said, not smiling. 'You were thinking about my granny, too.

We was talking about you only yesterday. Granny said it was time you come to see her.' Sorsha paused. She fixed her gaze on the pushchair where Elvira slept, her head on a lacy pillow, her small form cosy beneath a satin-bound pink blanket. Sorsha's next words came out with the force of an explosion. 'My gran told me what happened to your baby! I only wish she hadda told me sooner!' Sorsha briefly laid a hand on mine. 'I'm that sorry for your trouble, Mrs Franklin.'

Tears pricked behind my eyelids. Sorsha's blend of gruff hostility and sudden kindness would never fail to amaze and touch me. 'Thank you,' I said. 'It was a long time ago —'

'But you never did find her, did you?' We both looked down on the sleeping Elvira, her round and rosy face, the black curls tumbled round her ears and forehead. She was no longer a baby, but a toddler like John.

'No,' I said. 'I never found her.'

Sorsha lifted a corner of the pink blanket and started to pick at the satin binding, and I began to realise that she was actually more nervous of me than I was of her.

'I been looking out for you these recent days, Mrs Franklin. I got a message for you from my Gran. She wants to see you, pretty urgent!'

Later that afternoon I walked down to Witches' Hollow; I remained for a long time outside the high fence which separated Estralita and her people from the settled inhabitants of Ashkeepers. I found myself pacing back and forth, taking deep breaths and clenching my fists inside my jacket pockets. I was deeply afraid of meeting Estralita, and I thought that my fears might have been triggered by what I had read in Barnacle's book. In the end, when I could prevaricate no longer, I pushed open the tall gate and stepped inside.

It was all as it had been on my last visit, except for the old-fashioned bow-top wagon which stood in a far corner. A flight of metal steps led up to the neat veranda which fronted Estralita's custom-built trailer. I knew from the small gold crown emblazoned on her door that this was the home of the matriarch, the head of the family. The door stood open and she was waiting for me. She took both my hands in hers and drew me in.

'Nina Lambton,' she said, taking in my white hair and lined face. 'Ah! I can see that you have had your sorrows, woman!

Come you inside and let us talk awhile.'

She had been the most beautiful young girl I ever knew.

In old age she was still slim and upright, her hair as black, her gaze as piercing. The lines in her face had been made by laughter and exposure to the wind and sun, and the old intelligence, the uncanny perception was still there, just as keen, but tempered now by wisdom. Estralita had become, without benefit of regular education, quite a formidable woman.

I kicked off my muddy shoes and entered through the kitchen which was, like my own, all-white and full of modern gadgets, but smaller, more compact. The sitting room was all tints of blue with pink-shaded lamps and fluffy white rugs on a dark blue carpet. The cabinets, fixed to every wall and stacked with Crown Derby china, simply took my breath away. I sat on a pale blue brocaded sofa and curled my toes into a sheepskin rug.

I said, 'I have a great-grandson who is the same age as Elvira.' I waved a hand at the elegant room. 'Whatever do you do when Elvira comes to visit?'

Estralita laughed. 'Hide the white rugs in the bedroom, and cover the sofa with an old blanket.' She saw my glance towards the priceless china. 'The cabinets stay locked,' she said.

The small domestic exchange had almost relaxed us, but not quite. We were each nervous of the other.

I said, 'Sorsha tells me you want to see me.'

She put her hands together, arranging her thumb and fingers in the old horned sign which is believed by travellers to ward off evil. As she spoke, her carefully angled fingers pointed east towards Ashkeepers.

She said, 'Why for did you come back here?'

I thought of all the euphemisms, all the lame excuses I had used to other people. I felt her gaze pierce my skull and knew that with Estralita, lying would be a waste of breath and time.

I said, 'You know what happened years ago?'

'I know.' She paused. 'We all knew down here, couldn't help but know it, could we? The *gavvers* came in here, turned us all over, searched every inch, questioned us for days on end. Even poor Priscilla who had ten *chavvies* already and another expected any minute. "What would I want with pinching a little 'un?" she asked the detective. But he took no notice. "The babbies come to

603

me," she told him. "I don't need to go out looking for an extra one. Try feeding and clothing this lot if you don't believe me." '

Estralita shook her head. 'That was a bad time. But you should never have run away like you did. I wanted to come and see you, but one day you was there — the next day gone. I asked around but nobody could say where you had flitted to. Why didn't you stay, Nina?'

I said, 'Because I had no courage, no faith. I should have listened to my husband.'

I took a moment to remember Jack, how at that time he had tried to reason with me. 'He was convinced,' I told Estralita, 'that the baby was still here in the village. He was sure she had been taken by someone who knew us, knew the layout of the house. But I was so sure there must have been a car involved — she was taken without so much as a shawl or blanket round her. And to be honest, I panicked to get away. There were letters — "hate mail" I believe they call it these days. And nobody came forward with information. There was never a hint, a single clue — the police kept a watch on me long after I had left Ashkeepers.'

'You had another daughter, Sorsha tells me.'

'Yes,' I said.

'So that made it easier for you, another little one to love.'

'No, no, it didn't.' Now I found myself telling Estralita all those things I had never told anybody. How, because of the lost one, who I had held in my arms for such a short time, I could not bear to hold my second daughter; even to touch her was a physical pain.

'Poor little second daughter.'

'Yes,' I said. 'But her father more than made up for my lack of mothering.'

'Not the same, Nina!'

'No. I can see that now.'

'So what does your daughter think about all that happened?'

'We didn't tell her. Thought it better not to. But recently — well, somebody sent her a letter, and she began to ask me questions.'

'That must have been a terrible shock for her, to know the truth after all this time.'

'Yes,' I said thoughtfully. 'Yes, I suppose it was.'

'I have tried to find you, Nina, but you had covered your tracks too well. I even went to see your father, asked him where you were living, but he wouldn't ever talk about it.' She looked long and hard into my face. 'Folk think that because we live down here in the Hollow, because we comes and goes in the season, that we don't know what happens up in yonder village. Well, the most of times we don't. But what happened to your *chavvie* was a good bit different, and we stood accused ourselves by the *gavvers* in a manner of speaking. Something like that — it makes you sit up and taken extra notice. Sometimes,' she said slowly, 'we see things the *gorgio* don't see. Trouble is,' she looked at her folded hands, 'trouble is, when we do speak up nobody believes us.'

I could see her distress, her hesitation, and then she seemed to come to a decision. 'If I was to tell you something very strange would you listen to it?'

'Well — yes,' I said, 'of course I'd listen.'

'I've spent many a sleepless night turning it all over in my head. More especially since you came back to live here. If I was to tell you now that a young woman once growed up and lived in Ashkeepers who was your very image — would you believe that?'

My mouth went dry, my tongue cleaving hard to the roof of my mouth.

Estralita leaned towards me, she tapped me on the knee.

'What is more,' she continued, 'that young woman could have been the twin sister to the daughter that comes to see you in her dinky little red car. If you had only stayed put in Ashkeepers, if your second girl had growed up here — why then, woman dear, you would have spotted the likeness for yourself.'

Something loose moved inside my head. It was a curious sensation, as if jigsaw pieces were slotting slowly into place. I leaned back against the satin cushions; if I had tried to stand I know I should have fainted. I waited for the buzzing in my ears to cease.

'Take your time, Nina. I'll brew a pot of tea. I've given you a bad shock, but you had to know.'

I said, 'This girl — the one who looks like me and like my daughter, who is she — whose child?'

'Alan Franklin's. Him up to Sunshine Farm. Wife knowed as Dinah.'

'But Alan and Dinah had their own child. The baby was due about the same time as mine.'

Estralita nodded. 'That's what they told folks, and Dinah surely did give birth. But think, Nina! How could a child of Alan and Dinah Franklin come to be born with your own exact looks? I was sure in my own mind all them many years ago. When Sorsha pointed out your Imogen to me — well, I was certain sure that the girl the Franklins called Lucy was your stolen one.'

I felt a coldness settle round my heart. I found the next words difficult to utter. 'Alan Franklin is dead, and so is Lucy his daughter.'

Estralita nodded, 'So they are, so they are. But Lucy had a child. I used to see her with him in the village. That child was saved in the accident that killed her and her husband. Somewhere or other, you have a grandson, Nina.'

I leaned back in my chair and deliberately forced my thoughts away from Estralita's final words. There was a special kind of quiet down here in the Hollow; no sound of traffic could be heard beyond the high fence. I was conscious of the cushion's softness behind my head, the immaculate cleanliness and order of Estralita's trailer, the muted blues and soft pinks. I recalled the truculent child she had been, and the beautiful girl who was once described as 'university material' by the headmaster of the village school. Perhaps her father had been right after all to insist on early marriage for her. This secluded grouping of trailers, the fierce independence of the travellers, their determination to maintain their way of life; the importance they gave to preserving family ties; seemed to me at that moment to be infinitely more desirable than the detachment and coldness shown by the Franklins and the Lambtons. I wanted to believe that Estralita was mistaken in her judgement of Alan and Dinah, but I knew that she was not. I remembered Jack's brothers, their veiled hostility towards each other, and especially to Jack, the youngest.

Estralita poured tea and set the cup and saucer down on the low table. The glance she gave me was nervous, almost frightened. 'I shouldn't have sprung it on you all unawares. I should have led up to it slowly so as not to shock you too much.'

'No,' I said, 'that kind of news can't possibly be broken kindly. If what you say is right, our child was growing up, getting married, having her own child, all without our knowledge, and only twenty miles or so from the city where Jack and I lived.'

'I held back a long time before telling you, Nina. I had to be very sure before I spoke up.'

'So what happened lately to convince you?'

She stirred her tea and sipped it. She studied me across the cup's rim. 'Several things. That Dinah Franklin — she always was a bit dippy — but since you came back here she's in the churchyard every day, and Sorsha and Kingdom have spied her hanging around your house late at night and early morning. Our Sorsha, she feels things, senses trouble coming. She reckons you're in some danger, Nina. That woman watches you and your family, she checks up on your comings and goings. I reckon her bad conscience is making her crazier than she was already. And then there's your daughter. Oh, I had a shock I can tell you, first time I saw her. Like I said, it was as if Lucy Franklin had come back to life.' Estralita set her cup back in the saucer. 'There's yourself too. It seemed queer to me that you should all at once come back here and buy that tumbledown old house where all your troubles happened. You must have had something in the back of your mind when you decided to do that?'

'I suppose I did. I never quite gave up hope that one day I would find out what happened to my baby; but I've been frightened too. Sometimes the truth can be unbearable to live with.'

I began to worry about Imogen, which in the circumstances was quite a role-reversal, since I had always assumed it was her duty in life to worry about me.

'That must have been a terrible shock for her, to know the truth after all this time,'

Estralita had said. I hadn't really considered Imogen's present state of mind, but I began to think about it now. I waited a day and a night for her to visit or ring me. When she did neither I became anxious to the point of frenzy. There was still so much that needed to be put right between us, and I would have to tell her about my visit to Estralita. There had been too many damaging secrets already.

I phoned her office at a time when I could be sure she would be busy, and could be depended upon to keep the conversation short. I said, 'Something's come up, something new; I need to talk to you about it.'

She did not ask what kind of 'something'. We both knew there was only one subject in the forefront of our minds.

She came in late afternoon, straight from her office. She looked tired and anxious. Before she had taken off her coat she was demanding to know what the trouble was. Feeling guilty, I sat her down at the kitchen table while I made hot chocolate and toasted cheese sandwiches, her childhood favourites. I suppose I hoped that what I had to say would seem less dramatic and more believable when told in a kitchen which smelled of toasted cheese and Branston Pickle.

I began, 'Now, you remember Sorsha, the traveller girl who shared a room with Fran in the maternity ward? Well, Estralita is her grandmother, we were at the village school together. I went down to the Hollow a few days ago and talked to —'

'Mum!' she said irritably, 'do stop waffling! Just tell me quickly what you found out that's new!'

I said, 'Estralita believes that your baby sister was stolen by your father's brother Alan Franklin, and brought up here in Ashkeepers by Alan and his wife Dinah as their own daughter.'

I saw the colour drain from Imogen's face. 'Has this Estralita any proof?'

'Only the evidence of her own eyes. It seems that the — the child who lived with Alan and Dinah was called Lucy. According to Estralita that girl was your double, could have been taken for your identical twin.' I paused. 'Think about it, Imogen. You have my looks. People have always remarked on the likeness; you are a Lambton, not a Franklin.'

She struck the table top softly with her bunched fist. 'I knew it,' she murmured. 'I knew it had to be something of that sort. Now we're really getting somewhere.' Her voice rose with excitement. 'So,' she said briskly, 'our next move is to visit this sister-in-law of yours, my aunt in fact. Where exactly do we find them? Alan and Dinah and Lucy?'

At the thought of confronting Dinah I began to breathe very fast. My chest became painful, and I thought that I might suffocate. I was looking at Imogen, but at the same time I saw Lucy.

Lucy, whom I had held in my arms for such a brief time, and after that had never known; and about whose death I must now tell my surviving daughter.

Imogen was bending over me. 'What is it? What's wrong?'

My breathing eased a little, the tight band loosened in my chest. 'There's something else that I haven't told you,' I said. 'Lucy Franklin is dead. She is buried in the Franklin plot, in the village churchyard. She and Alan both died in the same year.'

Imogen sat down. She tried to speak but no sound came.

I held her hand very tightly, I could think of nothing else to do. I at least had known for some time that Lucy Franklin had died in her late twenties. For Imogen the shock was doubly devastating, coming as it did before she had properly assimilated the fact that Lucy her sister had even existed.

'We have to be sure about all this,' she said.

'I don't see how we can be.'

'But you or Dad must have registered the baby's birth!'

'No. We couldn't decide on a name for her, and there was still plenty of time. But even if we had, it would prove nothing.'

'So Alan could quite easily have registered her as his child, in his name?' Imogen stood up. She began to pace about the kitchen. She said, 'We have to find Dinah Franklin and refuse to leave her house until she tells us the whole truth.'

That walk through the woods was a curious experience, partly because I was in the company of Imogen, who was neither a walker nor a country person, but mainly because of the purpose of our mission. I had loaned her a pair of my low-heeled brogues, which looked as out of place as she had said they would when worn with her smart black business suit and white tailored shirt.

Before setting out I had asked the postmistress where Mrs Dinah Franklin was living these days. 'In the gamekeeper's cottage, up in the woods,' I was told, 'but if you're thinking of visiting, don't bother. She never speaks to anybody.'

The woods were no longer managed and cared for as they had been in Grandma Franklin's time. The paths were overgrown with brambles, exposed tree roots lay hidden beneath last year's fallen leaves to send the unwary walker sprawling. I showed my daughter the exact spot where, at the age of seventeen or so, I had manoeuvred Jack into kissing me for the first time. I could tell by the shocked look on her face that she had never associated Jack and me with anything so light-hearted as teenage passion.

I sensed her unease as we moved deeper in among the overcrowded groves. I thought about Georgie Barnacle and Coralina, and the stolen baby who was hidden in this forest by the gypsies through a long and bitter winter.

Imogen shuddered. 'I can't understand how anyone could bear to live in this place. Oh, it's beautiful, I know, but so lonely, so isolated.'

'Yes,' I said, 'and Dinah was a city girl.'

'Just as I am.'

'Exactly as you are.'

We walked in silence for a while, and then Imogen stopped on the path and turned to face me. She was becoming more troubled with every step we took. I had never seen her so agitated. 'All this,' she said, waving a hand at the dense green foliage, 'it could drive a young woman crazy, especially someone who was used to pavements and window-shopping. Dinah must have been very young when she first came here.'

'Young and friendless — and pregnant.'

'Pregnant?' Imogen halted again, gripped my upper arm and gently shook me. 'You didn't tell me that little detail!'

'What difference does it make?'

'Why, it means that Lucy must have been their own child after all!'

'In that case,' I said, 'how did she come to look like you and me?'

Imogen said, 'Then there must have been *two* babies, both born around the same time.' She paused, an expression of horror on her face. 'So, if what Estralita says is true, what happened to the other one, the child Dinah Franklin was expecting?'

The clearing in which the gamekeeper's cottage stood had become engulfed by the encroaching forest. But for a curl of blue smoke wreathing up from a chimney, I would have missed the house altogether.

We stood for a moment, uncertain now that the time had come as to how we should proceed. What could we say to her? What would she say to us? If I had been alone, it was at this point that I would have turned and stumbled back to Ashkeepers. But Imogen was moving forward now, fast by-passing the peeling paint on a front door which was clearly never opened, and going around to the rear of the house, and out of my view.

I caught up with her as she was introducing herself to Dinah. 'I am Imogen Donovan,' I heard her say, 'and this is my mother Nina Franklin.'

I tried not to stare at the emaciated figure and ravaged face of the woman who was my sister-in-law. Her gray hair hung in lank strands to her shoulders; her eyes had such a blank unfocused gaze that I was convinced she did not recognise my name. I was about to persuade Imogen away from the kitchen door when Dinah said, 'You had better come in, Nina; I've been expecting you for a long time.' Her voice had the rasping croak of one who rarely speaks. She led us straight to the room which lay beyond the cluttered old-fashioned kitchen. It took a few moments for our eyes to adjust from the bright May sunshine to the deep gloom caused by the close-drawn curtains of heavy velvet. I heard Imogen gasp and then, as my own vision focused, I was seeing what she was seeing.

Dinah had made this room into a shrine. A shrine to a dead daughter. Slowly I took in the many bizarre arrangements on shelves and tables of lit candles, and vases filled with woodland leaves and flowers, all of which stood before framed photographs of Lucy. Lucy at three months old, six months. Lucy a laughing toddler; a five-year-old looking solemn in her first school uniform. Followed closely by Imogen, I moved from one shrine to the next. Lucy at sixteen, at twenty. I did not need to ask the ages. When I looked at the photos I was also seeing Imogen, and then myself.

A large, glass-fronted cabinet stood in a corner; as we approached, Dinah pressed a switch and the interior was flooded with brilliant light. I felt Imogen's arm go around me in support; we were looking at the kind of arrangement usually seen in museums of historic costume. The shop-display dummy wore a wig of long dark waving hair. Her wedding gown, narrow-waisted and full-skirted, was of heavy white lace over satin. She carried a bouquet of artificial pink roses, and a coronet of the same roses held her veil in position. On her feet she wore white satin shoes, and a heavy silver cross hung around her neck. There was a framed, embossed wedding invitation prominently displayed, but without my glasses I was unable to read it.

'She's beautiful, isn't she?' said Dinah, in her cracked bright voice. 'That's her wedding gown and veil, you know. The same shoes and silver cross.'

When I turned to confront her she was smiling, a fevered overstrung expression on her face as if she might at any moment shatter into a million pieces.

'I clean the cabinet glass every day,' she said. 'The smoke from the fire makes it cloudy.'

'Yes,' I said helplessly. 'You must work very hard. Everything is so well cared for, all these fresh flowers and candles, and not a speck of dust anywhere.' These were not the words I had planned to say to Dinah, but my fulsome praise seemed to relax her. This time her smile was almost normal. 'I'm so glad you like it all, Nina. I did my best for her, you know. I always did my very best. You would have been pleased if you'd seen how well I cared for her. She was like my own. Well — after the first few days she *was* my own.' Dinah's calmness was to be short-lived; she began to twist her hands together, her mouth trembled. Imogen was nodding her head in the direction of the kitchen. We needed to talk to Dinah away from these images of Lucy, if we were to learn more of what had happened all those years ago.

'A cup of tea would be nice, don't you think?' Imogen spoke quietly; at the same time she took Dinah's arm and led her towards the kitchen. 'Why don't you let me make one for you, Aunty.'

'Aunty Dinah? Why yes, I suppose that's what I am. Your father and my husband were brothers, you know.' Dinah twisted suddenly around to face me. 'He wasn't a bad man — my Alan. He didn't mean you any harm.'

'No,' I said soothingly. 'I'm sure he didn't. But why don't we sit here in the kitchen, and Imogen will put the kettle on, and you can tell us all about it.'

I could hardly believe we were talking to her like this, humouring her as if she was a difficult child, or someone who was suffering a terminal illness. And perhaps she was both of those things. Even Imogen, who had come here with confrontation in view, was being forced into cajolement.

I tried to wipe from my mind the burning candles, the wedding gown, the photographs. Three mugs of tea stood cooling on

620

the table when Dinah said in a sane voice, 'You want to know what happened, don't you, Nina?'

'Yes,' I said, trying to keep my own voice steady. 'I think you owe me that much. The last time we spoke was on Ashkeepers green. We were both within days, even hours, of giving birth. You looked very ill. I said you should see a doctor right away.'

'I remember. When I got home I told Alan what you had said. He was angry. He said you should mind your own damned business; that you were not the doctor but only the doctor's daughter. Anyway, he had no faith in doctors. He blamed your father for his mother's death. He said if Dr Lambton had been home that night instead of scouring the countryside searching for his whoring wife and her fancyman, then *his* mother's life would have been saved.'

She sighed. 'He was a strange one — Alan. Wouldn't have people here in the house. When he knew I was pregnant he said we could manage it all by ourselves. No need to bring in a midwife or doctor. And I was a nurse; worked two years on the maternity ward before I met Alan. I thought I would know exactly what to do when my time came. But towards the end I began to suspect that something was not quite right with me and the baby. I tried to tell Alan, but he said that he'd take care of me. He was so — so agitated, so upset every time I mentioned the subject, that I — well, I sort of let it go.'

'You mean,' said Imogen, 'you mean that you deliberately gave birth in this place without any skilled help?'

'I had Alan.' Once again her gaze became unfocused and I knew we had lost her. I heard myself saying, 'What happened, Dinah?'

'I was late, gone well beyond my time. It was a bad birth, I thought we both should die. I screamed at Alan then to bring the doctor but he wouldn't leave me. When the baby was finally born the poor little mite was in a bad way. The long labour had done him damage. He had breathing problems, he couldn't feed properly, hardly had the strength to cry.'

Imogen said, 'Do you mean that Alan still didn't fetch help, not even for your child?'

This time the horror in my daughter's voice and face stung Dinah to retaliate. 'What would you have done in my state? I had lost a lot of blood — I already knew that I should never bear another child. I was too weak to help myself or my baby, and gone well beyond arguing with Alan.'

She put her hands up to her face and began to rock back and forth in her chair. I went to her and put an arm about her shoulders.

'It's all right,' I said stupidly, because it was clearly not all right, and never would be. 'Don't say any more if you can't bear it.'

Imogen, who is made of sterner stuff, shot me a warning glance over Dinah's head.

'It sometimes helps to talk about these things,' said my devious daughter.

'Oh, I want to!' Dinah's hands came back into her lap; she ceased her rocking. 'I've got to get it all off my conscience.' In the same almost normal tone she said, 'He died, of course, my baby. After two weeks of struggling he simply gave up.'

We waited, not daring to move or even breathe. After a long, heart-stopping pause Dinah said, 'I blamed Alan, of course. I called him a murderer that night. I said his pride had just cost my son his life. I screamed and shouted until he ran out of the house. He was gone a long time. When he came back he had a baby zipped inside his windcheater. He said I must never ask him where it came from — even if I guessed. He said the child was being neglected by its mother, left alone in the house — he heard it crying and so he took it from its pram. He said he had not planned to steal it, but once it was in his arms he couldn't bear to put it down.'

Dinah's unfocused gaze drifted from Imogen to me and back again. She said, 'I had a lot of milk. My own baby hadn't fed properly for several days. Without even thinking about it, when the gift child cried I put it to my breast, and that was when it happened. I knew at once, that no matter where she had come from I could never give her back.'

I found it difficult to speak. 'When — when did you realise that she was mine?'

'As soon as the policemen came here, asking if we had seen or heard anything suspicious. I was actually feeding Lucy when they walked in.' Dinah's smile was sly, secretive. 'They were never in any doubt that she was my own child.'

Imogen said, 'Didn't it worry you, concern you, that you had stolen another woman's baby? Did you never wonder how that mother and father were feeling?'

Again Dinah flared at Imogen. 'They didn't wonder, did they, how Alan and I were feeling about our dead son? Nobody cared about us — ever.'

'How could they guess how you were feeling about anything? They didn't even know you had given birth.' Imogen was very angry. 'And your baby's death was your own fault, yours and Alan's. Wilful neglect is what it was, and it certainly didn't justify you in stealing another couple's child.'

I shot a warning look at her. I said to Dinah, 'You must have had a lot on your mind at that awful time.'

She turned almost thankfully towards me. 'Oh, we did, Nina! Our son had not been baptised or registered, and we knew there couldn't be a proper funeral, in the circumstances. There was such a lot to do. Alan made a little wooden casket. I dressed the baby in what would have been his christening robe, and I wrapped him in the shawl I had crocheted. Then I sprinkled water on his forehead and named him Alan. We had our own private funeral in the garden. We buried him under the buddleia bush. He's never lonely there, you see. The butterflies come to him all summer long, and we put flowers on his grave in the winter.'

There was pride in her voice when she said, 'We like to do things properly, Alan and me; for both our children.'

Imogen and I exchanged a long look. Dinah had spoken of Alan in the present tense.

Imogen said, 'You must get lonely here, Aunty Dinah, all by yourself.'

'Oh no! Alan will be back soon. He's out looking for another poor neglected baby.' She smiled a normal, happy smile. 'We both have such a lot of love to give.' She turned to Imogen. 'But you know that better than anyone, don't you, Lucy dear.'

I guessed then, without needing to look to Imogen for confirmation, that to question Dinah further would not only be pointless but very cruel.

Imogen said, 'I'd like to ask a great favour of you.'

Dinah said, 'Why of course, Lucy, anything you want.'

'I noticed you have a photograph — I think it must be,' Imogen coloured and faltered, 'I think it must be one of my husband and me, and our little boy. Do you feel able to part with it? I shall quite understand if you can't. But I don't seem to have a copy of that particular photo.'

Dinah rose at once. She patted Imogen's hand. There were tears in her eyes. 'Of course you shall have it, Lucy dear. I have lots of copies of all your photos. I'm so glad you came today. Alan will be sorry to have missed you.'

On her way into the shrine Dinah paused beside my chair. Suddenly she gripped my shoulders with a strength that was to leave bruises. 'As for you,' she shouted, 'I know what you are up to. You came back to Ashkeepers to steal our daughter from us. I tried to warn you, but you were always a stuck-up madam. Alan is quite right. We shall have to get rid of you, one way or another.'

When she emerged from the shrine she carried the photograph wrapped in brown paper. 'There you are, my dear,' she said in her normal tone. 'Now don't stay away from us so long in future. Don't be a stranger, Lucy.'

The sun was warm on our backs as we walked away down the woodland track. Imogen held tightly to my cold hand. We did not speak, could not. As we came into the Toll House I thought I heard the faint sad wail of the abandoned baby. I almost said as much to Imogen, but then I remembered Dinah's precarious mental state, and thought it wiser to stay silent about my own imaginings.

Imogen switched on the electric fire and seated me beside it. She poured us both a stiff drink. She leaned back against the sofa cushions and I noticed her pallor, the new lines around her mouth. I said, as gently as I could, 'Dinah thought at the end there, that you were Lucy. I shouldn't have taken you with me, Imogen. I never dreamed it would be so awful for you.'

'Far worse for you, Mum.' Her voice was shaky with the tears she was suppressing. 'It would have been easier if we could have blamed her, got angry with her, shouted at her. God knows what goes on in her muddled mind!'

I said, 'There were so many things I wanted to ask her. I had all my questions ready. I need to know such a lot, Imogen. I thought she could tell me about Lucy's babyhood, her growing up, her marriage. But as soon as we entered that terrible shrine I could see how hopeless it all was. In her mind Dinah is no longer in this world.'

Imogen had placed the brown paper package on the coffee table. She began to unwrap it. 'You didn't spot this photo, did you?'

'No,' I said. 'There was probably a lot I didn't see in that room. I found it quite unbearable —'

Imogen rose and came to kneel beside my chair. She laid the photograph on my lap and handed me my reading glasses. I looked down and could not believe what I was seeing.

It was, as she had said, a little family group.

A young couple and their small son.

The girl was, without a doubt, Lucy.

The blond young man bore a faint resemblance to someone whose identity I could not place.

The child had freckles, and his neatly brushed hair was a fiery red.

The caption, printed in capitals beneath the group said:

LUCY AND TIM, AND ASHLEY ON HIS
FIFTH BIRTHDAY.

Be careful what you wish for, somebody once said.

Now at last I knew the how and why of my baby's abduction, but of the ensuing twenty-nine years I could only guess, and it was that blankness which would not let me rest. I could never bring myself to return to the house in the woods, never beg Dinah to compensate me for the missing years of my child's life. And there was no one else who would have those memories of Lucy that could ease my mind.

After Imogen left I turned the wing chair so that it faced towards the window and the evening sky. I sat for many hours with the photograph of Lucy, Tim and Ashley propped before me on the windowsill. I thought I knew a little of how Lottery winners must feel on learning they had scooped the jackpot. 'It won't change my life,' they chirruped through the champagne bubbles.

Not true.

Momentous events will overturn the most prosaic, the most entrenched ways of thinking and living.

I slept that night in the wing chair and awoke to the sound of knocking on the kitchen door. I opened up to find Primrose Martindale standing on the doorstep. She began to push by me with her usual greeting of 'I was just passing — !'

Then she took in my dishevelled appearance and switched to 'Oh, my God, Nina! Whatever happened to you?'

I plugged in the percolator and made a deliberate performance of setting out mugs and biscuits, so that Primmie would take the hint that today elevenses were to be taken in the kitchen. But time and again her glance went back to the closed door behind which lay the photograph of her own little family.

The time would come when I should have to talk to her about it, but I was not quite ready for that yet.

'You look,' she said, 'as if you've had a rough night.'

'Couldn't sleep,' I said shortly, as I thumped a coffee down before her.

'Any special reason?' When I did not answer she continued, 'I saw you yesterday with Imogen. You were on your way into Burdens' Wood. Nice walk, was it?'

I studied her across the table; every blonde hair in place, her make-up a work of art, but her attitude was kindly and concerned. I felt the bemusement which, since the visit to Dinah had muffled my senses, begin gradually to clear. This woman, this pleasant, slightly vacuous, very nice woman had been Lucy's mother-in-law, was Ashley's grandmother. Primmie's likeness to the young man in the photo was undeniable. Tentatively I allowed myself to acknowledge the connections already made by Imogen. She had said, before leaving, 'You see what all this means, don't you, Mum? We shall have to tell Primrose and Ashley what we have discovered. It concerns them as much as it concerns us.'

I said of course I saw what it meant, and of course I would speak to Primrose. But by that time of the evening I had reached a point of exhaustion where my head had that woolly, overstuffed feeling, as if it might soon burst.

All I wanted was the silence of my house,

the solitude which would allow me to follow my own thoughts.

And those thoughts were all concerned with Lucy.

Again and again, like a piece of film endlessly repeated, I saw myself on that autumn evening, picking up the wicker basket and taking it out to the log-pile. But now the film continued on into areas previously unguessed at; I saw Alan Franklin lift the latch and come into the cottage through the front door. I saw him lift the baby from her pram and zip her into his padded windcheater. Of course he had not needed a shawl or blanket, and for transport he had the bicycle on which he had arrived. Had he planned to steal her, or had Dinah's accusations pushed him to a crime he would not, in other circumstances, have committed?

Primrose reached out a hand across the table. 'Nina,' she said, 'there's something very wrong, isn't there?'

I swallowed inappropriate tears with a mouthful of coffee. I said, 'I have something to tell you. This will all come as a great shock, and I'm sorry, but I can't help that.' I began to hunt for a form of words that would explain the situation but still sound plausible.

All I came up with was, 'Your grandson

Ashley — he's my grandson too.'

I watched her mouth fall open and then close. She too took a long drink of coffee, while her troubled gaze never left my face.

She spoke as if I was seriously deranged, and who could blame her. 'That can't possibly be so, dear. Ashley's other grandma is Dinah Franklin. She lives up in the —'

'I know where Dinah lives,' I interrupted. 'Her husband Alan was my husband's brother. Dinah is my sister-in-law. It's a terrible story I have to tell you. I am still trying to come to terms with it myself. You see — you see, Lucy wasn't Alan Franklin's daughter. She was mine, mine and Jack's.'

I told Primrose every detail of the kidnapping and its aftermath. After I had finished she was silent for such a long time that I became alarmed. I had expected a flock of questions but when she spoke it was slowly and with a touch of wonder in her voice. 'It's funny, isn't it,' said Primmie, 'but somehow I am not as dumbstruck as I should be. When I first met you and Imogen I was intrigued by your physical likeness to Lucy. But since you never mentioned having relatives in Ashkeepers I told myself it was my imagination. And there was always something odd about the Franklins. Lucy

633

was so unlike them in every way. I suppose I should have realised you had the same surname, but Franklin is a common name in these parts.'

I said, 'How long and how well did you know Lucy?'

'Why, right from her schooldays. She and Tim were at the City Grammar together. She was often at our house. You could say they were childhood sweethearts.'

I said, 'Could you, would you talk to me about her?'

'I'll tell you everything I know, every detail I can remember.'

There were other things I needed to know. I walked down to the village and spoke to the postmistress about Grandma Franklin. 'Lived on till her nineties,' said the village historian, 'spite of all her troubles.' She gave me a hard look. 'You'll find her gravestone in the churchyard.'

There was truth in Dinah's accusation that Jack and I had been selfish. I could only hope that Grandma had understood and forgiven our absence from her life.

I thought about the dead crow. The donor might well have been Dinah, or James Luxton. It no longer mattered.

As for the ghostly happenings in the

Toll House and the strange business of my drawings of Sorsha, I had no explanation.

Lucy. It was not a name that Jack and I would have chosen for her. It evoked an image of a sweet old-fashioned girl, and perhaps that had been Dinah and Alan's original hope. But according to Primrose the gentle name had not suited the lively child, or the wilful and adventurous young woman.

'Oh, she was a handful,' said Primmie, 'and they indulged her every whim. She was intelligent and very pretty. She wound those two around her little finger. Although, in view of what you've told me, it's not too hard to see why they spoiled her so. She wasn't theirs, and since they were neither evil nor stupid people, they must have felt impelled by guilt to give her all they could.' Primrose smiled. 'What saved her from being absolutely ruined was the sweetness of her nature. You simply had to love her. You couldn't help it!'

'How old was she when they married, she and Tim?'

'Early twenties. My Tim was a quiet, studious young man. It was Lucy who decided they would spend their first two years of marriage back-packing round the world. They came home when Lucy discovered she was pregnant. Ashley was born and I thought she might settle down to be a housewife, but not a bit of it! She was always restless. During the week she helped Tim in his garden-centre business. But at weekends she was off rock climbing, swimming, canoeing, surfing in the summer. Always restless.'

'What happened to the baby while Lucy was absent?'

'He stayed with me when he was tiny. As he got older Lucy wanted him with her, on her weekend trips. But it wasn't really working out. You see, Ashley was like Tim. Even as a toddler he liked order and stability, and regular mealtimes.' Primrose sighed. 'Do you want to know what happened, Nina? The accident — ?'

I hesitated. 'No,' I said. 'She's just beginning to come alive for me. Let me hold on to those impressions of her. I need to know everything, Primmie, every detail you can remember.'

And so I learned about the child, the adolescent, the young mother who had occasionally exasperated, but had still been loved by all who knew her. A strong character, and not easy to live with, but adored to the point of foolishness by Alan and Dinah. Alan Franklin had lived for only six months after Lucy's death. As for Dinah, her life had effectively ended with those two bereavements.

Primrose said, 'We — you — will have to tell Ashley what you discovered from Dinah. She wouldn't have him near her, you know, after Lucy died.'

'I can't. Let Imogen tell him. She's his,' I worked out the relationship, 'his aunt. She's better than I am at explaining.'

Primrose said gently, 'You're his grandmother, Nina. A shock of that sort can only come from you. Just think of the adjustments he will need to make. There are things about the past that only you can tell him.'

I thought about Ashley. Of all the alternative lifestyles I had imagined for him, this was the strangest. 'You're right, of course.' My respect for Primmie's judgement was growing by the minute. 'And to think,' I smiled, 'that when I first saw him I thought he was too young to be the manager of an estate agent's office. Young enough to be my grandson.'

Once again the FOR SALE board stands in the Toll House garden. This has been the most unsettling summer I have ever known.

Imogen and Niall are moving down to Taunton. I am to move with them. We shall live, you understand, in separate houses; but less distant. We are already closer in every other way that counts. I shall still see Fran and Mitch and John, who is no longer a baby but a little person, utterly adorable with his large blue eyes and shock of white-blond hair; saying his first words, still doing his John Wayne walk, and occasionally having the most spectacular tantrums.

Primrose is firmly rooted here in Ding-Dong Valley. Whatever would the ladies' circle, the sketch club, the coffee mornings do without her? But she will visit me for weekends. We shall drive down to Watchet and Blue Anchor Bay and picnic beside the sea. Perhaps, from time to time, she will recall and tell me some anecdote of Lucy; we shall smile at one another, and just for a moment Lucy will be alive again and sitting there with us.

There is so much to do. Primmie and I are helping Angelique and Ashley with their wedding plans. It will be a family affair. John will be a page-boy, Imogen matron of honour. I shall contact George Barnacle before I leave the Toll House. It seems only polite to tell him I am leaving. I shall not offer to give him back his ancestor's book, even if he begs me to return it. I have already promised it to Imogen, my daughter.

We hope you have enjoyed this Large Print book. Other Thorndike Press or Chivers Press Large Print books are available at your library or directly from the publishers.

For more information about current and upcoming titles, please call or write, without obligation, to:

Thorndike Press
P.O. Box 159
Thorndike, Maine 04986 USA
Tel. (800) 257-5157

OR

Chivers Press Limited
Windsor Bridge Road
Bath BA2 3AX
England
Tel. (0225) 335336

All our Large Print titles are designed for easy reading, and all our books are made to last.